THE AUTHOR

John Alexander Stewart was born the son of a farmer in the 1930s at Killinchy, Co. Down, Ireland. He moved to London in the late 1950s, where his writing career began. He is the author of a number of plays, and four historical novels, of which *The Centurion* is the first.

THE
CENTURION

JOHN STEWART

a&b

This edition published in Great Britain in 1998 by
Allison & Busby Ltd
114 New Cavendish Street
London W1M 7FD
http://www.allisonandbusby.ltd.uk

First published in Great Britain in 1995 by
Arcturus Publishing

A catalogue record for this book is available from
the British Library.

ISBN 0 7490 0337 5

Designed and typeset by N-J Design Associates
Romsey, Hampshire
Printed and bound in Great Britain by
Redwood Books
Trowbridge, Wiltshire

MY GRATEFUL THANKS TO:

Sheila Rosenberg for her inspiration; to Mary Allen
for her patient and untiring work of typing; to Mira
Shapiro for her help with research; to Arthur Frandell for
proof-reading; to Ian McLellan; and to the many others
who have helped.

The general framework of this novel is historical, but
the character portrayals, including the name of
the Centurion, are fictional.

ROME
OSTIA
BENEVENTUM
CAPRI
VENUSIA
BRINDISIUM
TARENTUM
DYRRHACHIUM
NICOPOLIS
ATHENS
CORINTH

MARE

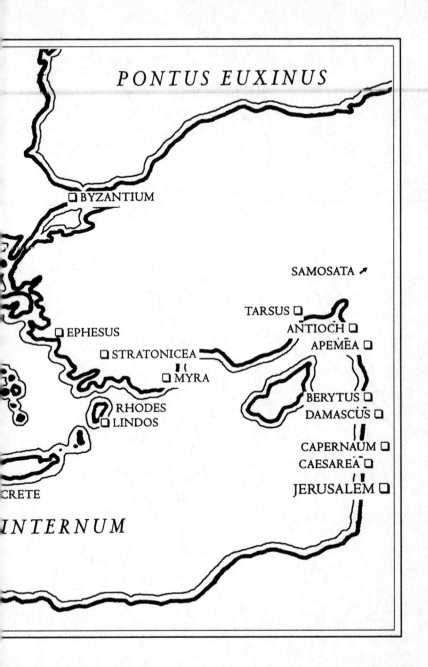

PONTUS EUXINUS

BYZANTIUM

SAMOSATA

TARSUS
ANTIOCH
APEMEA

EPHESUS
STRATONICEA
MYRA

BERYTUS
DAMASCUS

RHODES
LINDOS

CAPERNAUM
CAESAREA
JERUSALEM

CRETE

INTERNUM

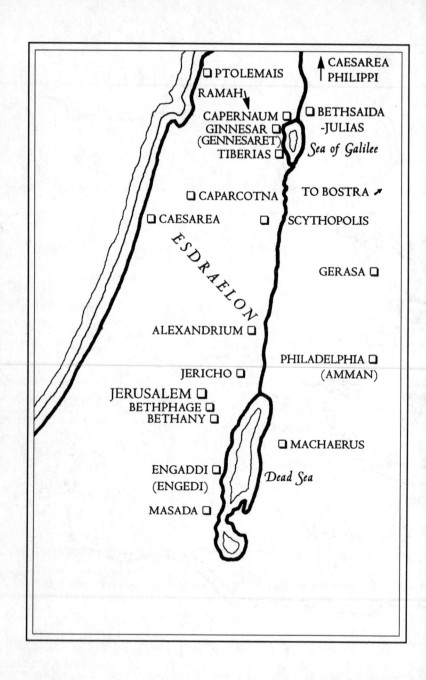

CHAPTER ONE

CAPRI

The tall twin doors swung open. The Tribune stood waiting, dwarfed by their height. Stepping forward, he bowed. In front of him, seated at an ornate table near the centre of the marble floor, was the Emperor.

Tiberius made to lift his heavy frame, failed, and sank wearily into his chair. Casually he indicated an adjacent couch, and in obedience the Tribune took his seat.

'You journeyed well, Tribune?' the Emperor enquired, breaking the silence.

'Yes, sir.'

Tiberius looked down at his desk pensively. The room was quiet.

'When we met five years ago,' he continued, 'you were about to join the Legions in Illyria, but then your illness confined you to Rome. Now you are bound for Syria – who knows the will of the gods?!' A smile slipped past the Emperor's guard.

'No plan is perfect, Tribune – not even Caesar's! Tell me,' Tiberius added, 'did the physicians ever discover the nature of your ailment?'

'No, sir, I remain a mystery to them.'

'A little mystery can be useful, Tribune!' A second smile escaped captivity.

The atmosphere grew soundless. Tiberius had retired within the empire of his thought, his head bowed in concentration, his shoulders hunched as if under the crushing weight of his office. The Tribune waited, watching with a mixture of awe and fascination, for before him was the master of the Roman world.

Tiberius breathed deeply but noiselessly. Then he began to speak, his voice deliberate.

'The Governor of Syria, Aelius Lamia, is one of the Senate's

1

most trusted servants. He is what I would call a true Roman – like my friend Nerva and your father.'

The Tribune's eyes sought the floor. To praise the father was to praise the son, and praise on the lips of Tiberius Claudius Nero Caesar was not lightly given.

'Lamia, as you know, is Governor-in-absentia, but his legate in Syria is well experienced, and has been there since the time of Germanicus.' Tiberius spoke quickly and dismissively, in the manner of one who assumed the details to be known. Then he fell silent.

Germanicus! The name still carried a strange magic. Ten years ago Germanicus, the idol of the young and heir to the principate, had suddenly died in Syria. Poison had been widely suspected, and suspicion still clung to the dull, unpopular Emperor. The Tribune had been twenty when it happened, but now, seated before Tiberius, it seemed as yesterday. His thoughts jolted into the present, but the Emperor was still pre-occupied. Then the old man raised his eyes and slowly scanned the ornate ceiling.

'Syria,' he began, his voice following his gaze, 'yes, there are four legions in Syria – a difficult border area – there are connections with Parthia, of course, and even as far away as India, but they usually trade with Egypt. The Empire is large, Tribune – too large!'

Tiberius spoke casually, in the habit of a powerful man anxious to keep his subordinate at ease.

'The Syrian legions,' he continued, 'also cover the territory that was ruled by old King Herod – a troublesome area,' he added forcefully, while looking pointedly at the Tribune. 'I'm told you speak Aramaic, a local language of the area.'

'Yes, sir,' the Tribune responded, 'two nurses in my father's household came from the district of Galilee, and I picked up words and sentences almost automatically. I was quite young – seven or eight, I suppose. My father encouraged me to learn the basis of the language, so it became a semi-formal practice – 'might come in useful one day,' he told me. I should say, sir, that my Aramaic remains basic with a strong Roman accent!'

'Your modesty becomes you, Tribune, but knowing the ability of your father, I suspect your average standard will be well above the average best,' Tiberius returned, humour flickering at the corner of his mouth.

Then once more the Emperor's eyes sought the ornate pattern on the ceiling, his brow furrowed in concentration.

'Galilee is a seed-bed of revolt!' he said, returning to the centre of his thought. 'The reports continually confirm this.'

He leaned forward confidentially. 'May I tell you a story? – When I was in command of the legions in Illyria during the Principate of the Divine Augustus we were confronted by a long and bitter rebellion. Eventually we captured the leader of the revolt, one Bato Dalmaticus. I asked him plainly why he had revolted, and he, with equal frankness, answered that the trouble was of our own making. To guard our flocks we Romans sent not shepherds, not even dogs, but wolves! I have always remembered that.'

Tiberius paused, his gaze fixed on the Tribune. 'Crushing a revolt is always costly,' he emphasised, 'so it's better to prevent the cause!'

Sighing, the Emperor sat back in his chair. Suddenly the struggle of his life seemed to surround him, just as an incoming tide swirls about an isolated rock on the seashore.

'The Bato story and your knowledge of Aramaic may give you some indication of your duties with the legion,' he continued, 'but we'll see, we'll see. We need to make contact with the people without losing our dignity. As I've already said, Galilee, Judaea, in fact the whole area of Herod's old kingdom, is one of the most troublesome corners of the Empire – it's the Jews, of course, and their precious religion. Nevertheless, we have to live with them, and there's that cunning barbarian Herod Antipas who has jurisdiction over Galilee. He tries to play the Roman, we despise him and the Jews hate him. They call him' The Fox'. However, there's a certain Centurion in Herod's Galilee who, it seems, the people trust, but that's all I've been told.

'You know, Tribune,' the Emperor's voice was full of intensity, 'the most difficult task your Princeps has is to find out what is actually happening, for if I ask a question I get vagueness. Even so, I've grown expert at reading between the lines.' A smile wavered briefly.

The Emperor had the Tribune's full attention. He was amazed at the old man's grasp of detail. The rumours of Rome simply did not fit. Was this the senile old fool the clever joked about, the grotesque and aged man who fanned his waning passions with excess?

'Instructions regarding your posting are already on the way to Syria. You will be responsible to Lamia, and, of course, finally to me.' Tiberius spoke briskly. 'You will report to the Legate at Antioch, and thence to Caesarea, where you will meet the Procurator of Judaea – a busy administrator who married well, named Pontius Pilate. He was recommended by my Praetorian friend Sejanus.'

Though the words were spoken casually, the Tribune could not help but notice the disparaging, if not cynical, edge in the old man's voice, for to slight the Procurator was to slight his powerful sponsor. That was startling, for in Rome Sejanus was all-powerful, the Emperor's great friend, Prefect of the Praetorian Guard and feared by all. Even to know the door-man at the house of Sejanus was considered a social advantage. In Capri, however, the perspective was clearly different.

Tiberius rose, moved towards the open portico and halted. He looked out beyond the crags of the cliff-top to the distant shimmering horizon of the sea. The world seemed poised, the Tribune thought, a Roman world waiting for its master. It was very quiet except for the faint murmur of the waves churning far below.

The Tribune stood to the side of his Emperor at a respectful distance. Already the few guards and attendants had shifted their position, as if connected to their master by invisible strings.

'I've enjoyed meeting you, Lucius, my boy,' Tiberius said, emerging from his thoughts. The main business was over. He had set the cares of state aside. 'Tell me, how is your father?'

'Very well, sir,' the Tribune answered. 'The estates and his studies keep him busy.'

'And your sisters?'

'Yes, both are well. My elder sister wants to come with me to Syria, and Father has reluctantly succumbed to her pleadings!'

4

'Most irregular, most irregular!' The Emperor's fatherly response was almost automatic.

'She's tired of Rome, sir, in fact it's a loathing. She needs a change, and I think that's why Father acquiesced.'

'Ah, well, a blunt sword cannot call a blunt sword sharp – after all, your Emperor is living in Capri!' Tiberius said with a chuckle.

To the devious or the fearful the old man's fatherly reaction might have seemed sinister, but in the heart of the straightforward Tribune there was no criticism of his Emperor, and no criticism was returned. All was well.

'How do you plan to travel to Syria?' Tiberius asked.

'Mostly by sea, sir. My sister has planned it all. I am but the witness!'

'A commendable strategy!'

The sad lines of the Emperor's face softened. There were no undercurrents of meaning for the practised ear of Tiberius to detect, for the Tribune was without guile, and he knew it.

'I suppose you'll go by way of Brindisium?' he questioned.

'Yes, sir, from Brindisium to Corinth, then to Athens and from there to Ephesus, Rhodes, and eventually to Antioch.'

'Ah, Rhodes! Your Emperor has many friends there. I must see that you're given proper introductions – Tribune! you ought to make your progress by war-galley like the mighty Cicero!' Tiberius added playfully.

'The measure of my grandeur, sir, is more likely to be a leaky grain ship!'

The Emperor did not respond. His mood had changed from ease to some inner contemplation. Absently he edged himself onto a nearby couch, but almost immediately he was on his feet again. He shifted a step towards the open portico, his eyes narrowing against the dancing brilliance of the sunlight.

'Syria is a border area, with four legions holding the peace,' he began slowly as his thought took shape. 'Ideally I should visit the legions myself, but that is not possible – too old, my boy!'

The aside was an acceptable pleasantry, as both men knew the danger of an Emperor absent in a distant province. Intrigue was ever bubbling in Rome.

'There is plenty of correspondence between Syria and

ourselves. Messengers are never off the road, but I need something personal, something to give a touch,' Tiberius appeared to search for words. 'Something to carry the magic of the Princeps, and you provide the answer,' he said emphatically. 'You will carry our message and proclaim it to the assembled cohorts. It has been done before, I know, but in the right hands it is very effective, and you are the right hands. Because of your illness you are older, more mature than the usual Tribune of your rank beginning his tour. Your family is beyond reproach. Your tall bearing, your voice – all, all is good.' Tiberius allowed himself a measure of enthusiasm. 'Even the war-galley seems right.' The sidelong glance of the Emperor toyed with the mischievous.

The Tribune stood as if hypnotised. He stumbled for words.

'I hope your – trust – sir. . .'

Tiberius raised his hand.

'I have perfect confidence in my personal legate. Now to the details. The proclamation to the legions, travel documents and all other items will be forwarded to your family villa near Rome.'

Tiberius turned to one of the waiting attendants with preliminary instructions. Already the beginnings of the Tribune's embassy were in preparation. The will of the Princeps knew no obstacle. Indeed there was a blinkered, if not brutal quality in its persistence.

'You should be married, Lucius,' he suddenly declared. Again the mood of the Emperor had changed. 'The law expects it. I know your illness intervened, but that excuse is wearing thin!'

He smiled, putting his hand on the Tribune's shoulder. 'We cannot let the Roman race die out!'

'No, sir,' the Tribune responded awkwardly, for he knew the friendly reminder was not spoken lightly.

Slowly they moved to the doors, the Emperor's hand still resting on the Tribune's shoulder. The audience was almost over.

'Nerva is waiting – problems at the Treasury. There are always problems at the Treasury,' Tiberius said, lifting his heavy shoulders with a tired shrug.

The Tribune and his Emperor parted warmly. Tiberius was clearly pleased, for another thread had been added to the pattern of his policy.

Accompanied by one of the Emperor's attendants, the Tribune Valerius walked down the long, pillared hall towards the centre of the villa in what seemed like a dream. It was not he who turned left and into the outer yard. It was not he who passed the bathhouse furnace and down the steps to where the two-horse chariot was waiting.

The sense of unreality persisted as the attendant took his leave, but when he saw the welcoming smile of Felix, his father's old servant, normality returned. At once he gave the grey haired servant an outline of his audience.

'I can't believe it, Felix! A year ago I was ill – yet again! The physicians were baffled, Father despaired, and most thought me an oddity, if not a laughing stock, and now this! – the Emperor's personal legate – why, Felix?'

'Tiberius may be many things, but he is not a fool. He has chosen well, Lucius, for your illnesses have kept you free of Roman politics, and you're the son of the Senator Marcus Gracchus Valerius – that alone is cause enough.'

The Tribune shook his head uncomprehendingly as they stepped onto the chariot, but his servant only smiled.

Felix, now sixty, had served the Valerii from boyhood, first as a slave and now as a freedman. Emancipation had made little difference, however, for in his master's household the yoke of the slave was light.

Meantime the chariot wound its way towards the harbour, passing the massive structure of the lighthouse and then descending slowly to the shore. Felix paid the driver more than he asked and received an appreciative grunt. Then he joined the Tribune standing by the waiting mules and all the paraphernalia connected with the Emperor's villa. Valerius's attention, however, was not on the busy waterfront. Instead his interest was focused on an approaching galley. Obviously it bore some dignitary; not for him the normal ferry-boat from the mainland.

First the oars were held firm as a brake, then they were

drawn in, and then the boat glided slowly towards the wooden pier. Suddenly the Tribune stiffened.

'The Praetorian!' he muttered with distaste.

Two guardsmen leapt onto the pier, quickly secured the boat, before the unmistakable form of Sejanus emerged, followed by three aides. Immediately they made for the waiting group of chariots.

Like a sea squall they swept onwards. They were too busy, too absorbed in their purpose, to notice the Tribune and Felix. Valerius scanned their faces. He recognised the aides – the up and coming brains of Rome – Gallo among them, brilliant in debate but base in conduct.

For a time they were close enough for their words to be heard.

'They have not raised one statue to your honour. . .' Gallo was saying.

'Statues,' Sejanus interrupted with impatience. 'We want eyes and ears, not stone!'

'Pilate?' Gallo suggested.

'Pilate is old and comfortable,' Sejanus returned dismissively. 'Someone has got to go. . .' he added, but the rest was drowned by screeching gulls, and soon they were out of earshot.

'What was that all about?' Felix questioned.

'Ambition!' The word escaped the Tribune's lips with unusual force. It fitted the receding figures well.

Already the Praetorian Guardsmen were ranging wide and growing inquisitive. Valerius was wary.

'Come, this is no place for us,' he said, turning quickly in the direction of their waiting boat. Soon they were under way.

As they approached the open sea the swell gradually embraced them in its rhythm. The sail fluttered as the sailors hoisted it into place. Suddenly it was taut, the oars were withdrawn and a new peace reigned.

Valerius looked back at the island fading slowly into the distance. The Emperor's villa was still just discernible. There, within a short time, the two most powerful men in the Empire would meet.

CHAPTER TWO

THE VILLA VALERIUS

The mature brick of the Tribune's family villa glowed in the evening sun, and the statues of the Gracchi, flanking the portico, shone warmly in the slanting rays. As had been his habit from boyhood, the Tribune paused before their polished stone, strangely lifelike in the soft evening light. They had been the subject of his first history lesson, when he had learned how Tiberius, and then his brother Gaius, had turned against the current of their time, and how the vested interest of the wealthy had savaged their reform. Later he learned how their lives had been forfeit to the crazed greed for property that had poisoned the heart of the Republican Senate. All this had happened more than a century before. Valerius looked hard at the silent sculptured features. What inner fire had held them to their lonely path?

His thoughts turned inward. Tomorrow his own path would begin to trace its way to Syria, and to what he did not know, but time would soon unfold its mysteries.

He walked through the garden, viewing its beauty without the commentary of thought. There was the trellis, renewed in parts, carrying the ancient vine, and there the row of cypress trees. They seemed part of him. How peaceful it was, how enticing, willing him to stay.

At the far corner of the garden he could see his elder sister, walking slowly, no doubt troubled over her departure. Poor, sensitive Drusilla, life had not been easy for her, not at all.

Drusilla was seven years older than her brother, mature, quick-witted and outwardly composed. However, her composure belied a basic unhappiness. She had been married at fifteen, three years above the legal minimum, but the marriage bed had shocked and frightened her. Too late her husband had revealed himself to be a boorish man, as irritated by her refinement as she was sickened by his lewdness. It was ten years since he had died, in what was little more than a drunken brawl. After that she had returned to the peace of her father's villa, but the whole bitter experience, and the premature loss of two children, had left its mark. She had no wish to remarry, even though she had many suitors, and even though the laws encouraged it. Indeed, from time to time her father had presented men of substance, but to no avail, and he never had the heart to press the matter as the law allowed.

The Tribune waited quietly as his sister approached, and did not speak until she was close.

'Have no fear, Drusilla, all will be well.'

She looked up, her thought interrupted, her brown eyes clear.

'You've been seeing the soothsayer again,' she exclaimed, humour masking her unease.

Drusilla was full of uncertainty, her eyes moving restlessly from her brother to scan the garden. 'We're off tomorrow, Lucius, but I don't want to go!'

'Yes, Drusilla,' the Tribune returned, sighing with feigned indifference.

'I'm serious!'

'Until tomorrow! Do have a little sense, sister. Of course you don't want to leave Father, and yet you want to go to Syria. It's getting close to our departure, and your love of Father is uppermost, but if I left without you you'd be miserable.'

'Why do you have to be so bluntly logical?' she reacted. Her brother was right, of course, but the state of gentle war that prevailed between them never permitted such an admission.

'I salute you, Lucius Gracchus Valerius, Tribune Laticlavius of the Senatorial Order and Envoy of the Emperor. Will you take a humble sister's arm? It's time for supper,' she said brightly, hiding her emotions.

The Tribune bowed with affected gravity, and they walked arm in arm into the villa. With their arrival the supper party was complete.

Drusilla took the couch to her father's right, with her young slave- companion Cornelia, whom she treated like a daughter, beside her. Junia, Drusilla's sister, came next. Almost seventeen, both Junia and Cornelia were very nearly past the age when young girls married. In Junia's case, the Senator had made approaches to worthy families, but their young men had not impressed him. His painful memories of Drusilla's anguish made him cautious, even though Junia's nature was much more robust than her sister's.

With Cornelia it was different. She was a slave, a property to handle as he wished. Indeed, he had deliberately kept her in bondage, for she was beautiful. Cornelia was special, and he was determined that her future husband would be worthy.

Felix, the old family servant, occupied the couch beside the Tribune, who sat opposite his father. Except for formal occasions, when he waited on the Senator, Felix always dined with the family. The custom had started after the death of the Senator's wife, and now it was taken for granted.

Arria, the Senator's favourite freedwoman, had positioned her couch slightly behind and between Felix and the Senator. It was she who controlled the servants and the kitchen, and at her signal the courses of the supper came and went. She was mother to slave and servant alike, and she lived for the Senator.

Despite the imminent parting, it was an animated evening, in which they drank more wine than usual. Father and son did most of the talking, discussing and anticipating the journey to come. There were jokes, of course, many of which centred on the voluminous baggage of Drusilla and her young slave Cornelia. The Tribune was teased at having done the impossible in charming Tiberius, for gossip said the old man had not smiled for years.

'If such cruel jests were true,' the Senator said, suddenly serious, 'he would have my sympathy, for the burden of his office is a crushing slavery.'

'And he suffered greatly in his early years,' Felix added. 'His family life was ruined by the needs of the State.'

'How, Felix?' Junia asked.

'He was compelled to marry Marcus Agrippa's widow Julia, the daughter of the Emperor – you know the story?'

Junia shook her head. 'Marrying the Emperor's daughter seems a good move to me!' she quipped.

11

'Not when you're forced to divorce your own much-loved wife, especially when she's with child!'

'That's awful!' Cornelia reacted. 'Who forced him?'

'Augustus. He wanted his daughter to marry someone he could trust.'

'Awful,' she repeated in a whisper.

The Senator rose from his couch. It was time to retire, and time for farewells, even though there would be partings in the morning. Drusilla embraced him tightly, and, on the edge of tears, fled to her room, followed quickly by Cornelia.

The elder Valerius stood quietly for a moment, allowing his emotions to subside. Then he turned to his son.

'Stand apart from faction, Tribune, and flatter none,' he said firmly. 'And, Lucius, look after your sister, she is in your care.'

After his son had gone to his rooms the Senator laid his hand gently on Felix's shoulder. 'I shall miss you, old friend, but Lucius will need you until he finds his feet.'

'He'll do that quickly, master – he's his father's son!' the old servant said with a smile.

It had been planned from the beginning that Felix should accompany the Tribune on what was clearly an exacting mission, for in the initial stages especially his wise and friendly counsel would be invaluable. Also there was the nagging worry about the Tribune's health.

'Pray the gods will give my son continued respite from his illness,' the Senator said quietly.

'He's been free of trouble for a year, master.'

'I know.'

Master and servant looked at each other, at one in their concern. 'Be careful of Sejanus and his allies – they're out for themselves,' the Senator said finally.

CHAPTER THREE

THE JOURNEY

They left at first light, their pace brisk, the horses relishing the morning air. The Villa Valerius was outside Rome to the south, and only a mile or more from the busy Appian Way, so there was little delay before the two covered carts joined the main road.

On the Appian Way the world was very much awake. Fast two-wheeled carriages with quick-stepping mules swept past slow, creaking farm carts drawn by oxen. Pedestrians there were in plenty, ever looking for a friendly carriage, or at worst a snail-fast cart. There were officials on government business, conspicuous in their important haste, and merchants astride slow-gaited cobs, their slaves trudging in their wake.

Through this shifting kaleidoscope of travellers the Tribune's party moved steadily forward. Both vehicles had the front portion of their canvas sides drawn back, but the canopies remained in place as a shield against the summer sun.

In the second cart Drusilla and Cornelia sat perched on cushions to ease the bumps and jolting. They whiled away the time practising their Greek, and Drusilla tried to teach Cornelia what she knew of Aramaic. They both wore broad-brimmed hats, a protection from the glare, and their fans were ever busy. It was hot.

In the leading cart the Tribune and Felix were seated on a wooden bench behind their driver. They rode in silence, except for occasional remarks about the countryside or the oddity of a passing traveller. The Tribune's rough travelling garb showed no indication of his rank, and few, if any, would have guessed at his identity. It had always been the family custom to travel modestly. Not for the Valerii the mincing pageboys, the minstrels and the busy slaves rushing ahead to clear the way. The Tribune's modesty, however, was not in any sense apologetic. He was a Senator's son, born to rule, with all the confidence of his powerful class.

The two carts, fitted for sleeping, were crammed with baggage: pots, pans, lamps, tents for the drivers and the cook, presents for the friends they hoped to visit, clothes and bedding in abundance, but the bedding and sleeping bunks were only for emergencies. Like many wealthy families of their rank the Valerii tended to use either their own estates or those of their senatorial friends as stopping places on the way, and that was how the journey had been planned. Certainly a busy and noisy inn, no matter how well appointed, was something Drusilla was anxious to avoid.

After four long days on the road they reached Beneventum just as the sun was setting, and proceeded at once to the villa of a family friend. The owner, a Senator, was not in residence, but the servants knew of their coming, and all was prepared.

Beneventum, high on a windy hill, was a busy junction, and being so it teemed with inns. Diversions for the traveller abounded, and with their duties completed, the two drivers, their helper and the cook soon joined the swirling excitement that spun about the centre of the town. They went with the Tribune's knowledge. Far better a little rough sport than sullen resentment.

The carts were parked safely within the courtyard of the villa. The walls were high and there was no easy entrance. Yet during the night someone ransacked the Tribune's baggage. However, there was nothing missing of importance other than a roll with details of the Syrian legions. Fortunately he kept the Emperor's documents always on his person.

It was dawn, and the drivers were already harnessing the horses. They were too heavy-eyed, he thought, their revels too well laced with wine, to have noticed anything. Maybe it had been one of them, but he doubted that.

'An enjoyable evening, men?' Valerius asked with studied briskness.

'Oh, your honour!' one of the drivers reacted, holding his head; the large man who drove the Tribune's cart.

The Tribune smiled knowingly. 'You were late, no doubt. Who let you in?'

'One of the servants, I suppose – grinning from ear to ear, he was!'

'He let us in, and then slipped out himself – must have been keen at that time of night,' the other driver joked.

'What time was that?' Valerius asked innocently.

'Long after the twelfth hour – but don't worry, your honour,' the big man added, 'we're ready for the road.'

The Tribune did not confide in Felix until they were under way.

'What do you think?' he asked.

'A servant in the villa delivering to a paymaster outside.'

'Could be.'

'Did you have more than one roll in your baggage?' Felix asked.

'Yes, but in the second cart.'

'The drivers probably disturbed him, so he took the only roll he found – who knows – can't be a robber, though, with all the other valuables untouched,' Felix added. 'Could be a spy, though.'

'A spy! Who would want to spy on me!'

'You're the Emperor's personal legate. Someone may be curious.'

'About what! – I've got no secrets!'

'Someone thinks you have, perhaps.'

The incident soon became secondary to the pressures of the journey. The carts were slow on the difficult terrain, making the planned stops impossible to achieve. So for two nights running they used the staging posts. However, by the end of the third day after leaving Beneventum they reached Venusia.

'This is where I was born!' the Tribune's driver boomed, 'both me and Horace!'

'So that's why they call you Venio.'

'Yes, your honour.'

Venio was a huge man, immensely strong, yet he treated his horses with uncommon gentleness. Valerius liked him, and was determined to employ him further when they reached Brindisium. He was trustworthy, and he could be useful, not least as a guard for his sister and Cornelia.

In Venusia the comfort of a villa awaited them, and what

was more, their host was resident. Drusilla was captivated by the place, the distant mountains, the wide ravine below and the clear evening air, everything pleased her, and the tight knot of tension that had gripped her for so long seemed to weaken.

Their hosts were old family friends, and, reflecting this, the conversation over supper began naturally and easily. It was not long, however, before the subject centred on the Tribune's posting.

'Lucius, you haven't told me about your assignment – am I allowed to ask?'

'Of course you may, but apart from a few hints I know nothing. The details apparently are awaiting me in Antioch.'

'Typical Tiberius,' the host responded. 'If his toga knew his plans he'd throw it in the flames!'

The Tribune's comments had been sparing in their detail, and his host, rightly sensing his reticence, changed the subject to the topic of Sejanus.

'Is he still as powerful as ever?' the host asked.

'Yes, the Emperor still heaps honours on his busy Prefect,' Valerius rejoined.

'Like a fatted calf for the sacrifice!' Drusilla interjected.

Instinctively Valerius scanned the room.

'It's all right, my friend, we're alone. The servants have gone to their quarters.'

'A thoughtless gesture, please take no offence,' the Tribune said dismissively.

'My brother,' Drusilla quipped, 'will make the perfect Senator – always looking over his shoulder!'

'And my sister the perfect diplomat!'

The host laughed loudly, and they all joined in.

'I can hear your father's wit in both of you. Seriously, though, the name Sejanus is on every lip, and many think the purple will be his. What a choice the Emperor must make – Sejanus, or the brood of Germanicus!'

Valerius shook his head and smiled. It was tactless of his host to bring the subject up again, for being the Emperor's legate he had no wish to be involved in such discussion.

'Marcus,' their hostess intervened, addressing her husband,

'did we not entertain someone about a year ago who was bound for Syria?'

The good lady had changed the subject knowingly, Valerius guessed.

'Yes, young Maximus. He was bound for Caesarea as aide to the Procurator – Pilate was the name, I think. Poor Maximus – Sejanus was his idol; he could talk of no one else.'

Sejanus again, but the conversation veered to family matters. Drusilla did most of the talking, and although Valerius showed polite interest his thoughts were elsewhere. Indeed, at the mention of Pilate's name his mind had flashed back to the waterfront at Capri. He could almost smell the sea. 'Too old and comfortable,' was how Sejanus had described the Procurator.

Reluctantly the Tribune was beginning to realise that his future role could meet with treacherous undercurrents. Certainly the incident at Beneventum was not a happy precedent.

Early dawn saw the Valerian carts moving again. The road sliced through difficult terrain, reflecting the vigour of those who had laid its foundations – the citizen army, hardy, practical, relentless in their determination.

It took three days before they descended into the oven heat of the plains before Tarentum. Weary of the slow, jolting carts, all Drusilla could think of was the sea, but it was two more dusty days before they reached Brindisium.

A noisy night in a highly recommended inn was followed by a busy morning of organisation, not least the disposal of the carts and horses, but a ship, by order of Tiberius, was already awaiting their arrival. Once more the Tribune was amazed at the Emperor's thoroughness.

A brisk breeze speeded their departure, and soon the Macedonian land-line was discernible in the blue haze. The first stop was at Dyrrhachium, where they tied up overnight, and after two long days, peaceful, carefree days, they reached Nicopolis.

For a time the Tribune and his sister watched the busy waterfront. Close by, cargo was being unloaded with deafening noise and drama. Then, in the midst of the seeming chaos, a tent party of eight legionaries marched past, a knot of Roman order. Further distant to the right there was the slave market. One male slave was standing on the wooden platform, the last sale of the evening, Valerius guessed. Cornelia, he saw, was watching too, aversion written on her face.

'Don't look, Cornelia!' he said gruffly.

'Sorry, Master Lucius,' she responded shyly, but being occupied with his thoughts he did not seem to hear.

His thoughts were busy with the evening's plans and his decision to go ashore. He knew it would cause fuss and delay, and a necessary acknowledgement of officialdom, but he could not let Drusilla spend another night on board, as the sleeping quarters on the stern were crude and basic.

In the event he was helped greatly by one of the sailors, a friendly Greek named Demos, who clearly knew Nicopolis well, for not only did he find a clean and quiet inn, he also conjured, as if from nowhere, a closed-in litter for the ladies. Demos was clearly a man of initiative and experience, and, like the big man Venio he had retained, he could prove useful.

On the third day after Nicopolis they sailed east into the Gulf of Patrae. Then, after two slow days, often with the oars out, they came to Corinth, with its Acropolis standing high and commanding to the south.

The transfer of baggage across the narrow neck of land to Cenchreae was speedily accomplished on the following morning, aided by the strength of Venio and the Greek crew hand Demos, whom the Tribune had finally employed.

At Cenchreae another ship awaited them, its destination Piraeus. The next day at the latest they would be in Athens.

CHAPTER FOUR

ATHENS

For the Tribune Athens was full of memories. The book and papyrus shops; the narrow alleyways of the market; the short cuts known only to the native; the favourite taverns. He wandered through the city like a lover. He found his old tutor in the same familiar house, bent in body, but sharp in mind.

'You're old for a Tribune with the Senate's broad stripe!' the old man reacted with a hint of censure. He was still the tutor.

Valerius smiled and explained about his illness.

'Never mind, you're my favourite Laticlavius, and the Emperor's Legate, too!' Tears were close.

Valerius could well have spent a day wandering about the city, but formal duties awaited him. It was necessary to visit the Governor, and without delay.

The Governor had already heard about the Tribune's coming from the Emperor's secretariat, so when Valerius arrived at the residence he was shown every honour. The interview was lengthy, with the Governor generally bemoaning the troubles of his province, before at last bringing up the question of the Tribune's posting.

'The message from Capri said you were passing through to the east,' he stated mildly, though clearly hoping for more detail.

Valerius smiled. The Emperor was sparing with his information.

'I'm bound for Syria,' he said bluntly.

'Well, what a coincidence, what a coincidence. Our guest tonight is Herod Antipas, a prince of Jewry from that general area. He went to Rome and was friendly with the young princes of the blood – you may have met him.'

The Tribune shook his head. His illness had freed him from many social obligations.

19

'I'll make one comment, Tribune – I wouldn't like to be his slave.'

It was a damning statement, though clearly indiscreet. The Tribune said nothing.

'You too will be our guest of honour,' the Governor continued. 'Lucius Gracchus Valerius – a Roman! – a real Roman,' he enthused. He loved the flow of words. 'It promises to be quite an evening, for the Tribune Gallo is in Athens. A brilliant orator. He's sure to keep us laughing through the night!'

Gallo, Herod Antipas – 'the Fox', Valerius repeated to himself. Whatever the precise nature of his mission was, it would begin tonight. He was sure of that.

It was the Tetrarch's eyes that caught the Tribune's attention. There was something fixed yet restless in his look, a kind of glaze. In response to the Governor's welcome his speech was bland, predictable. He was the friend of Rome, but taxation was heavy. Of course the Army needed revenue, but his country was small. Defence, he knew, was vital, nevertheless the burden of its cost had to be equitable. It was the typical speech of a client prince, Valerius thought. Herod had said nothing in particular.

Gallo spoke next, and brilliantly. Sparkling humour punctuated his speech with such deftness that the Tribune could only admire his artistry. All listened, for Gallo's words sprang from the thought of Sejanus. He was especially gracious to the Tetrarch, doubtless to counter the anti-Jewish reputation of his master, and then he launched into the main substance of his speech. 'What we need is a new social ideal, where Rome and her provinces are wedded together in one indestructible union. The army is the people's friend, the protectors of this union.' How did Gallo convert obvious platitudes into such compelling rhetoric, the Tribune wondered.

The impassioned flow of words continued. Gallo used gesture to maximum effect, his arms conducting the emphasis of his speech with perfect measure. 'Length of service in the army must be realistic, with firm guidelines acceptable to all.' He shook his head, his round, full face serious. 'In my view the term of service is much too extended.' A murmur of approval circulated the hall. Encouraged, he continued, 'We simply cannot say one thing and do another,' he boomed, to loud approval, for the arbitrary extension of service by a hard-pressed government was bitterly resented. Gallo searched the faces of his audience. No man was omitted. 'The morale of the army cannot be purchased cheaply, and the civil population must accept this.' Then, his speech concluded, Gallo took his seat, to loud applause.

Valerius, who earlier had been nervous at the thought of speaking, was angry. Gallo, he knew, cared little about the length of service, and his exploitation of a genuine complaint had been wholly cynical. He imagined the rumours that would circulate within the local garrison. Gallo, or rather Sejanus, would reduce the length of service. The thought made him furious, enough to alert Felix, who was in attendance.

'Don't let your anger show, Master Lucius,' he whispered, 'and remember the pleasantries.'

'The Tribune Lucius Gracchus Valerius,' the Governor announced, and the tall figure of Valerius rose to speak.

He thanked the Governor for his generous hospitality. He was pleased, he said, to have met the Tetrarch, and hoped he would have the pleasure of a further meeting in Galilee. Then he turned to Gallo, praising the brilliance of his oratory. 'Everyone,' he suggested, 'would welcome a reduction in the length of army service.'

The Tribune's style of oratory was plain. He paused too long, between sentences which were spoken quickly. There was a shyness in his bearing, yet his upright figure and forth-right quality carried an impression of honesty. It was the man himself who held the attention, and as he spoke the company grew silent.

'Who would pay for army reform?' he asked bluntly. 'Who would pay for even a small reduction in the length of legionary service? Think of the revenue needed to support both retirement settlements brought forward by reform and the fresh recruitment necessary to replace the resultant loss of manpower; it would be enormous. We must be careful in raising expectations that cannot be fulfilled, for I'm sure we can imagine the difficulty of raising further substantial revenue!'

21

The Tetrarch nodded obligingly, but Gallo seemed unconcerned, almost lifeless. He cared little about the assembled gathering, for he had addressed his words to an audience well beyond the ornate pillars that surrounded him. Valerius was a nuisance, though. He would have to stop him.

With the speeches over, the wine flowed generously.

'Tetrarch,' the Governor called, swinging his cup precariously, 'the news we hear from other parts of the Empire tends to be coloured – we exaggerate, we elaborate, and the word we hear from Galilee, I'm certain, suffers in a similar way.'

The Governor paused, seeking approval to continue. It was the habit of the diplomat.

'We hear of plots and prophets and little else, but, my friend, I find such rumours hard to credit. Tell us, what is the real state of affairs?'

Herod sighed deeply and drank from his wine cup. The smile that shimmered on his face retreated and returned.

'Have I an evening or a month?' he asked, but no one responded.

'If Galilee were in a state of total rebellion,' he began, 'I should be in exile. The truth is that the vast majority of Galileans go about their business like any other citizen of the Empire. It is the fanatics and the criminals that cause trouble disproportionate to their number. The Zealots, as we call them, seek a perfect but impractical state, and nothing will dissuade them from their course.'

'Not even the army!' Gallo interjected.

'The army would make everyone a Zealot,' Herod retorted quickly.

'Then the job would be easy!'

'Gallo, the desert is peaceful, but no one lives there.'

'My friend, forgive me,' Gallo said, putting his arm round Herod's shoulders. 'I'm just a simple soldier, with a soldier's answer.'

It was an obvious retreat, and with that the conversation slipped into pleasantries.

'You must come to my quarters afterwards, Tetrarch,' Gallo whispered confidentially. 'There you can enjoy delights quite missing from this gathering.'

22

'What delights?' Herod boomed.

'Careful!' the whispering continued, 'we don't want all to know about the sweets of Aphrodite – the most delicious damsels to be found in Athens.'

'My gracious Gallo, already this assembly wearies me!'

They were discreet, of course, and did not make to leave until the time was right. Then, after gracious words with the Governor, they slipped away.

Valerius watched them go. He had not heard their conversation, but he guessed at their intention. There was no criticism, for he knew his own failings well enough.

'Herod's not a fool,' the Governor stated.

'Indeed – he answered Gallo well.'

'Now, Valerius, we must think of tomorrow, and the arrangements for your journey.'

For a time the Tribune and Felix listened to the Governor's suggestions and advice. Then suddenly, as if his cup of energy were drained, their host grew weary. It was the hour to take their leave.

'You did well, Lucius,' Felix said, as they walked to their quarters.

'Not so well as Gallo! He charmed the Tetrarch!'

'That means little – Herod will be Gallo's friend while he thinks it suits him!'

Next morning the Tribune's party made a final visit to the Acropolis, where they honoured the Goddess Athena. On the way back to their villa, guest quarters provided by the Governor, Drusilla and her young slave companion stopped for a last fleeting look at the market's wares. The big man Venio and Demos the Greek remained in attendance while the Tribune and Felix went ahead to conclude arrangements for their departure.

The market, ablaze with eastern colour, was busy, and at once Drusilla and Cornelia were engulfed in the swirling activity. Venio and Demos, with scant interest in the traders' goods, waited listlessly. Suddenly they noticed that Cornelia was not beside her mistress.

'Where is Cornelia, my lady?' Venio asked gently, in his deep, rough voice.

23

'I don't know,' Drusilla said, looking about her. 'She was beside me a moment ago,' she added, her rising alarm under control.

They searched everywhere, but the many they asked had seen no one answering Cornelia's description.

'She'll be back at the villa, my lady,' Demos said optimistically. 'Got lost and decided to return on her own.'

But Cornelia was not at the villa.

'All we can do is wait for the ransom note!' Drusilla said bitterly. 'When I think of what could happen to her . . .'

There was no need to furnish details to her brother; Valerius knew too well.

Sadly Felix watched the anguish of both brother and sister. He recalled the day when their father had introduced Cornelia to the household, a frightened eight-year-old with blond hair and grey eyes. The master had bought her, or more accurately, rescued her, on one of his northern journeys. Educated in the best Valerian tradition, she had grown to be Drusilla's personal servant and companion – more like a daughter than a slave. Now she was almost seventeen, beautiful, almost regal in her way. Drusilla's distress and the Tribune's deep concern were well founded. Compelled to act, Felix drew the Tribune aside.

'You must not forget – you're on the Emperor's business,' he emphasised.

'I hadn't forgotten,' Valerius reacted irritably, but Felix was not deterred.

'Gallo's ship left this morning. Like yourself, he's bound for Syria.'

'I know! I know! Why tell me the obvious?'

'You must not delay, Master Lucius. The Governor is well equipped to initiate a search and deal with any ransom demand.'

'I cannot . . .'

'You must,' Felix cut in forcefully. 'We have already lost a day, and we could easily be delayed for a week or more if you allow it. Your delay suits Gallo well, for I do believe he aims to bind the legions to his master's will. He wants no interference, especially from you, the Emperor's personal legate, and the more you linger here the better he'll like it.'

'That's all a bit dubious, Felix. What can I do against a determined Gallo and his agents?'

'A lot – and Gallo knows it!'

'Felix, you're not trying to tell me that Gallo's behind Cornelia's disappearance. He wouldn't do a thing like that!'

'Gallo would think it a joke. I can imagine his comments – 'that fool Valerius is sure to get emotional about his slave girl."

'But, Felix, Gallo's too clever to get involved in such a thing!'

'Not personally, but a little gold in the right hands . . .' Felix left the sentence unfinished. 'It's speculation, I know, but it's possible.'

'She's so devoted to Drusilla.'

And you, Felix thought, but he held his peace.

The Tribune rose from his chair and stood silently. His head was bent in thought, his arms folded.

'We'll leave in two days' time,' he said.

For Valerius it was a restless and frustrating day, but another note had entered his discordant thought. He began to notice Cornelia's absence in little ways, the small things that he took for granted. Her face appeared before his mind. She was very beautiful, he thought. A sudden image of a man defiling her filled him with rage. He began to pace the room.

'Where's Demos?' he asked Felix impatiently. 'Have we lost him too?'

'I doubt it. Demos the Greek is very capable of looking after himself!'

'And Venio?'

'Moping in the courtyard with the cook. The big man is quite sensitive, believe it or not.'

Just as the sun was setting Felix announced that Demos had returned, but very drunk.

'Dismiss him, Felix!' Valerius was in no mood to be tolerant of fools.

'He wants to see you, and I recommend it. I know he's got something to say, but you'll have to be patient, Master Lucius.'

'All right, Felix, send him in,' Valerius said, sighing with resignation.

'Master Tribune, sir,' Demos said, swaying wildly.

'Yes, Demos,' Valerius said sharply.

'Master Tribune, I'm drunk!'

'Get on with it, man,' Valerius snapped.

'Master Tribune, I've been in several taverns.'

Demos lurched, but remained on his feet.

'That's hardly a secret, Demos!'

The Tribune relaxed. Even when drunk, Demos was like-able.

'Master Tribune, she's not in Athens.'

Valerius sat bolt upright. 'Where is she?' he asked urgently.

'She's on a . . .' Demos failed to finish. Instead he moved his hand in a wave-like motion.

'A boat!' the Tribune prompted.

'Yes, a boat,' the Greek returned, while struggling to keep upright. With some effort he pointed towards the east.

'The east,' Valerius interpreted. This confirmed his worse fears. Pain coursed through his chest.

'What brute beast has done this?'

'No one would tell me,' Demos answered, swallowing hard. 'Deaf and dumb they were – too afraid – must be some of the big fish.'

'Who?'

'Oh – the big ones of crime. Everybody's mouth is shut when they're involved.' Demos's words came thickly.

'A cohort will help their memory,' the Tribune exploded.

'No! No! Do nothing! nothing!' Demos almost pleaded. He looked ill. 'Tell the Governor, and he'll alert his agents. The sight of one uniform would spoil everything!'

Demos struggled for words.

'Master Tribune, beware going on that ship,' he managed to say. 'Appear as though you're going to take it . . . but take another one!'

'Get that man a chair!' Valerius shouted.

It was too late. Demos had crashed to the floor, blood seeping through his tunic. Felix tore it open. An ugly knife wound reddened his chest – praise to the gods, a cut rather than a stab, he thought.

'I'll get Drusilla,' Valerius called, going towards the door. 'That wound needs a woman's care.'

The tough and wiry Demos was soon recovering. His wounds were dressed, but the surgeon decreed that he was unfit to travel. At that Demos became frantic, pleading desperately to sail with the Tribune.

'If you leave me here they'll get me!' he finally blurted out.

Valerius looked long and thoughtfully at his Greek servant.

'Who are you, Demos?' he asked, but Demos smiled weakly and did not answer.

CHAPTER FIVE

RHODES

The Governor's astrologer warned against it, the sooth-sayer at the gate warned against it, but the Tribune was adamant. He would depart next morning.

'Make sure that screeching soothsayer thinks we're bound for Delos and Ephesus,' he said to Venio, 'and then we'll slip away to Rhodes.'

They sailed south-east, but the wind was light and their ship, hired at the last moment on Demos's advice, was slow, with few oars to help their progress.

Demos still lay on the litter on which he had been carried aboard, and, kneeling by his side, Drusilla was busy re-dressing his wounds.

'You're a goddess, my lady,' he murmured appreciatively.

'Master Demos, this is the least that I can do,' Drusilla said quietly. 'Now a little godlike tranquillity is what we require from you. The surgeon was emphatic.'

Demos watched Drusilla as she rose. What a woman, he thought. It takes generations to cultivate such grace. His eyes turned to the Tribune as his sister joined him. The dignity of the brother and the beauty of the sister touched him. Affection rose, and tears came to his eyes. What a fool, he thought, stemming his emotion. His gaze turned to the grey-haired Felix – more like a senator than a servant; and poor Cornelia, a princess but never a slave. What a family; it was obvious why he had risked so much in Athens. These Valerii had no need to ask for help, for things began to happen of themselves within their presence. He closed his eyes, and the dull throb in his side diffused. Soon he was asleep.

They tied up at a small island overnight, and on the second day, with a stiff breeze to help, they passed through a world of islands, a magical world to Valerius and his sister. One island in particular, a myriad of different hues, had suddenly appeared, it seemed, a fitting dwelling for the gods, Valerius thought, but the abundance of beauty only made Cornelia's bitter plight more sharp and brutal. Pity gnawed ceaselessly at his being.

It took another three full days' sailing before they rounded the southern tip of Rhodes. It was calm, and the scent of the island floated over the mirror surface of the sea as they glided slowly landwards. The oars were withdrawn, and the rock of Lindos grew closer. The ship had some cargo for the port, and on the following morning they hoped to complete the sea journey to the city of Rhodes, but when they docked all their plans were changed. The island's Governor was in residence, and, hearing of their coming, rushed to met them.

With all due respect the Tribune's party was escorted to the official villa. There Valerius presented the Emperor's roll of recommendation, only to be told that Tiberius had already written.

As they dined that evening, the Tribune learned that a war galley awaited him at the port of Rhodes.

'So the Emperor wasn't joking!' he said incredulously, recounting the casual way in which Tiberius had spoken.

The Governor chuckled. He knew the Emperor from the old days, he said, recalling the time Tiberius had been present in the island.

'A fair magistrate, and he liked his cup of wine!' he added knowingly.

The conversation continued, with the Governor giving a general outline of affairs in the east, and in particular the borders of the Empire.

'Never be enticed into war beyond the Euphrates. Who knows what it could unleash or provoke – an alliance between Parthia and Armenia, for instance. Tribune, we Romans are much too thinly spread!'

He paused and viewed the circle of his dinner guests. 'Now, I have been talking much too much,' he apologised.

'Not for me, sir,' the Tribune responded. 'Any advice or information you can offer is most welcome. For instance, what should be our attitude towards the Jews in Galilee and Judaea?'

29

The Governor laughed. 'That is a subject for a whole host of dinners, Tribune. What do you think, Quintus?' he added, turning to his young aide.

'I've lost patience with the Jews. We show a great deal of tolerance, and all we receive is hatred, implacable hatred. Their behaviour is an insult to the Empire. They should be taught a lesson.' The young man spoke with passion, his face flushed. 'I'm sorry, Governor,' he added in apology for his vehemence.

'Quintus had one or two unfortunate experiences in Judaea,' the older man said, glossing over the matter. 'But say we took his advice,' he continued, 'we would need another legion, or maybe two, for we cannot leave Syria unguarded, and of course there's the Parthian border. The cost would be enormous, and what would be the gain – a wilderness?'

Bato Dalmaticus again, the Tribune thought, recalling the Emperor's story.

'So what are we to do?' the Governor pressed. 'Are we to absorb punishment indefinitely?'

The Tribune looked at Felix, waiting and alert beside him, and the urge rose to ask the old servant his opinion, but the Governor anticipated him.

'Felix, the Tribune has told me how much he values your opinion. What is your view on this vexed question?'

'Well, sir, I've never been to Galilee or Judaea, but I've met many Jews, in Rome and other places.'

Felix paused, looking pensively at the floor.

'The one thing I found they had in common was a strong and passionate certainty about the rightness of their faith. My feeling is we need to understand this faith before we understand the Jew. It is one thing to tolerate their religion, but quite another to respect it. The trouble is, we tolerate their religion in the same way we tolerate our own!'

The Governor laughed heartily. 'Brilliant, my friend. I agree entirely, but how do you . . .' – he broke off, rubbing his forehead, 'how do you educate Rome, or the Army, for that matter? It's difficult for a lion to be passive when he's continually provoked.'

'One man of understanding, in the right position, could do a lot.'

'Such men often fall the victim of both sides!'

Felix nodded, and the gathering grew quiet.

The Governor was impressed. The upright quality of the Tribune and the wisdom of the servant spoke for themselves. The tradition of a great family was evident.

'Tribune, it would help greatly,' the Governor began briskly, 'if you would address our garrison before you leave for Antioch. A few encouraging words to raise the spirit of the men. I trust you'll have the time.'

Valerius readily agreed. It would be a preview, he thought, welcome practice for the greater task ahead.

The banquet drew naturally to a close, and as they were leaving, the Governor took Valerius aside.

'I'll certainly let you know immediately if we hear any news about the young girl – a bestial business. There isn't much hope of finding her, I fear, especially in this quarter of the Empire – more than likely she's far beyond our borders.' His voice was flat and practical in tone. A slave was a slave. He little guessed that each word burned into the Tribune's mind.

'We have many young girls here, if your sister needs another servant.'

'Thank you.' The Tribune's voice was clipped, precise. 'Drusilla refuses to think of someone else. You see, Cornelia has been in the family since she was eight. She and my younger sister were educated together.'

'I see, I see – I'm sorry.'

'We're a somewhat eccentric family, I'm afraid,' Valerius added quietly.

CHAPTER SIX

ANTIOCH

All the Tribune's business on Rhodes had gone well. The inspection of the garrison, his address, his despatch to Aelius Lamia in Rome, even his departure, all had been accomplished with efficient ease. Now, with Rhodes receding in the morning haze, another efficiency, the ordered efficiency of a war galley, was speeding the Tribune towards his destination.

The rhythm of the oars was relentless as the great ship cut through the water regardless of the contrary wind. Handling the mighty oars required skill and stamina, and a good captain guarded his oarsmen's strength. Most of the sailors were freedmen, expected to serve for twenty years or more, but the pay was steady, and they were often in port.

With its complement of sailors and marines the galley was crowded. There was little space for passengers, and after the initial interest in the warship, the Tribune and his sister found the journey tedious. In the case of Valerius it was taxing, for each evening on shore there were official receptions in honour of the Emperor's personal legate. Indeed, the Tribune's progress to Antioch was in a sense triumphal, and no doubt what the Emperor had intended.

Ten days after leaving Rhodes, two with strong favourable winds, they arrived at the naval port of Seleucia Pieria, close to Antioch. On disembarking, the sacrifice for a safe journey was observed in the presence of the Naval Squadron Commander, his deputy, and the town dignitaries.

The tall, grave Tribune was an impressive figure, and to the Squadron Commander the broad purple of the Senate, even the role of the Emperor's representative, were secondary. This was the noble son of the Senator he had heard speak in Rome, a talk he had never forgotten.

'I heard your father speak in Rome,' the Commander was quick to recount. 'The Latifundia . . .'

'And the later Republic,' the Tribune completed, smiling at the friendly officer.

'It's many years ago,' the Commander continued, 'but I still remember – the large estates worked by slaves; the ruin of the small farmer; the speculator buying up his land; the landless unemployed in Rome.'

'Yes, little hope of work in Rome, with slaves abounding,' the Tribune interjected. He laughed. 'I think I know that lecture by heart!'

As soon as the brief reception was over the Tribune and his party set out for Antioch, accompanied by the Squadron Commander and an escort of cavalry.

Valerius and the Commander continued in conversation, and for both the journey seemed short as they came to the bridge over the River Orontes. Before them was the city of Antioch, with Mount Silpius in the background.

They went straight to the villa of the Chief Legate, and when the Tribune gained access to the fortress residence the Commander and his escort took their leave.

The great doors of the fortress shut behind Valerius and his party with a deep, echoing rumble. Inside, the large cobbled courtyard was deserted. The Valerian carts and two-horse chariot, hired at the naval port, stood isolated in the wide, high-walled enclosure. The guards who had let them in remained unmoving at their post, apparently uninterested in the newcomers.

Slowly the Tribune alighted from his chariot and stood silent and observant. After the past days of endless ceremony this sudden absence of official deference was theatrical.

Demos, now almost fully recovered, was the first to speak.

'Is this the mausoleum?'

The Tribune smiled thinly, his anger simmering. Notice had been given of their arrival, yet even the normal courtesies were being ignored. This was no way to treat the Emperor's personal legate.

Suddenly a Tribune of Equestrian rank rushed from the residence.

'The head undertaker!' Demos muttered.

'Noble Tribune,' the newcomer exclaimed breathlessly, 'may I introduce myself. My name is Largus. I must apologise for the absence of the Legate. He was called away to the Tenth Legion at the Cyrrhus fortress. He left this morning.'

'This morning!' the Tribune repeated quietly, battling to control his rage.

'Urgent business, sir – he was accompanied by the Tribune Gallo.'

'Gallo's business!' Valerius snapped angrily.

'I don't know, sir,' Largus replied, answering what he thought to be a question.

'Never mind,' Valerius returned, looking hard at the smooth, almost boyish face of Largus. 'Pardon me if I'm lacking in the usual pleasantries,' he continued, his speech clipped and sharp. 'I need to act quickly. How long would it take me to reach Cyrrhus?'

'Two days, sir.'

'Too long.'

'To do the journey in a day, sir, you'll need three changes of horse at least, and a sturdy chariot.'

'Then I'll have one – this thing here wouldn't last a mile. And an escort of cavalry,' Valerius commanded.

'I'm sorry, sir, but I've strict instructions that the garrison is not to be reduced in any way.' Largus was apologetic.

'I bet you have,' the Tribune barked. 'Do you expect me to believe that my small request could possibly endanger the garrison?'

'I have orders . . .' Largus began.

'Orders! Well, I've given you new orders. I will expect a chariot and an escort first thing in the morning. And I want this note delivered immediately to the house of Demetrianus,' he added, handing a roll across. 'My sister is to be their guest.'

Valerius continued to look hard at the Equestrian Tribune.

'Sir, there are two despatches awaiting your arrival,' Largus began almost tentatively. 'One has been here for . . .'

'We'll see those in a moment,' Valerius interjected. 'Now, this is important, very important. I want a thorough search initiated into the case of a missing girl, kidnapped in Athens and believed to have been taken east.'

'Master Tribune, sir,' Demos cut in quickly. 'I would like to do a little personal research first, after which I could report to the Tribune Largus.'

'Are you well enough?'

'I'll do, but I'll need money!'

'Here, take this,' Valerius said, tossing a pouch to Demos. 'What about some refreshment first?' he called as Demos made for the courtyard doors.

'Where I'm going there'll be that in plenty.'

'Be careful!'

Demos saluted, smiled briefly and left.

'Now, Largus.' The Tribune's voice had lost its underlying rage. 'You said there were despatches.'

'Yes, sir.'

As the Tribune and Largus entered the residence, Drusilla, aided by Felix, alighted from her cart. Until then she had sat immobilised, fascinated by her brother's behaviour.

'Felix, what has become of my brother, my once little brother!'

'Your grandfather was just the same if roused – never anger a Valerius,' the old servant responded, looking knowingly at Drusilla, but she did not notice.

'Clever old Tiberius, he couldn't have chosen a better legate, no, not if he'd searched the Empire,' she continued brightly. Then she saw that Felix was close to laughter.

'You rogue, you're laughing at me,' she said, taking his arm as they followed the Tribune into the residence.

There were two despatches awaiting the Tribune's arrival, one from Tiberius, and waiting for some time, and the other from Rome, a recent delivery.

'Drusilla, this is from Father,' Valerius said, handing her the roll despatch from Rome, while he carefully studied the Emperor's instructions.

There was little new. He was to convey the Emperor's personal interest in the welfare of the legions. He was to praise their courage, loyalty and endurance. It was the personal touch that mattered. He was charged to make contact with the people. He would, of course, pay due respect to the Governor's legate, but his final responsibility was to the Governor himself, Aelius Lamia. Again, he was to pay proper deference to the Procurator Pilate, and also to investigate reports concerning the revival of the Messiah cult in Galilee. Finally, in all these matters he was to keep the Emperor informed. It was enough, he thought with some amusement, but the tear-stained face of his sister soon changed that. Silently she handed him their father's letter.

As was his wont, the Senator came straight to the point. He had been accused of crimes akin to treason by two fellow Senators. Both men were well practised in idiocy, and he felt sure the Emperor would dismiss their accusations out of hand. There was no need for concern, but he wanted to ensure that they received the news aright from him, and not from exaggerated rumour. He hoped they were both well, and that Felix and Cornelia were enjoying the strange and new impressions. The cruel irony of the last words jolted.

He passed the letter to Felix, and at once turned to comfort his sister.

'Father is right,' he said, catching her by the shoulders, 'the Emperor will laugh at this stupidity, and in fact the two Senators might well look to their own safety. Even in the crudest sense, it's not in the Emperor's interest to let the father of his personal legate suffer such dishonour!'

Drusilla said nothing, but tears continued to course down her cheeks. The Tribune held her more tightly.

'Don't worry, Drusilla. Father is in no danger, and neither are we.' His last words had been said advisedly, for treason law affected the whole family.

'How can I help worrying, Lucius? Think of all his lectures on reform – they're bound to find something!'

'They'd be hard put, Drusilla. The truth is never treasonable.'

'To the truthful!' she shot back.

'Drusilla, the men who've lodged this charge are of little reputation. Even their accusation is vague – 'crimes akin to treason'.'

'Father's only saying that to stop us worrying!'

'Felix,' Valerius said, turning to the grey-haired servant, 'make my sister see some sense!'

'Your father's not in danger, Drusilla,' Felix responded quietly.

'Are you sure?'

'Tiberius respects your father, he always has.' Felix shook his head. 'Your father's not in danger, but someone's trying to make things awkward for your brother. That is my conjecture.'

'That could be,' she responded, her voice calmer, 'but the worry is still there.'

They dined at the Villa Demetrianus, but none of the Valerian party could pretend enjoyment. However Demetrianus, their large, jovial host, was both understanding and fatherly, and Valerius was relieved to know Drusilla would be in his care.

Just before the twelfth hour, Demos returned. He had drunk his way round the taverns of the town, and he looked exhausted.

'The beautiful Cornelia, I'm almost certain, has passed through Antioch,' he said wearily.

'Sit down, Demos, sit down,' Demetrianus said casually

'But my clothes are filthy, sir.'

'Your report transcends your raiment,' the host replied briskly.

Gingerly Demos perched himself on the edge of a couch, looking at each in turn before he spoke.

'One glassy-eyed drunk described a girl like a princess, and the details fitted Cornelia perfectly, and someone else said the same. She was well guarded, apparently, and it seems that she passed through on the way to some other destination. So far I haven't found the owner or the hirer of the cart.'

Valerius stared grimly at the floor, his lips pressed tightly together as if to contain his anger.

'She's probably bound for the court of Artabanus, and if he were to do anything it would be a diplomatic incident, and such an incident with Parthia is not to be encouraged. Gods! Gods! I cannot stand the thought of it. The trouble is, everyone will think it a trivial matter. She's just a slave.' He spat the final words out bitterly.

'What would you say, sir, if we found she had been taken to Herod's palace?' Demos enquired mildly.

'Herod!' Valerius reacted in astonishment.

'I have no proof, but rumour has it that he's fond of his women,' Demos went on.

'If that sly, smiling fox has touched her, I'll hack him into pieces,' the Tribune burst out in frustration, but even as he spoke he knew his words were empty.

'Cornelia will be resolute,' Felix said quietly. 'She'll not break easily.'

'Yes, Felix, I know. It may give us time,' Valerius said sadly. He scanned the long, low-ceilinged room. His sister and their hostess had retired. 'There are drugs, of course,' he added, almost inaudibly. Then he turned to Demos.

'Without your help we have no hope. No doubt you'll continue the search – you know the desperate urgency. And, Felix, you'd best stay and be counsel to my sister. I'll take our quiet giant Venio with me to the Cyrrhus fortress.'

Leaning across from his couch he put his hand on his host's shoulder. 'We've kept you from your rest for long enough.'

'Think nothing of it. Anything I can do for the son of Marcus Valerius is an honour – if only we had some means of instant contact with Rome!' Demetrianus added, 'then we could confirm your father's safety.'

'What's this, sir?' Demos said, instantly alert.

'Of course, you haven't heard!' the Tribune replied, spelling out the details of the treason charge.

'So that's why there was no formal reception at the residence,' Demos reacted cynically. 'This won't hurt your father, but it will hurt you, Master Tribune, and that is what it's meant to do.'

'Yes, Demos,' Valerius answered flatly.

The two men looked long at each other. The Greek's secret identity seemed to hover in the air. One thing was certain, Valerius thought, he had not hired a simple sailor.

'Yes, Demos,' he repeated, 'I fear the Cyrrhus fortress may be friendless, but with the help of the gods, who knows?'

CHAPTER SEVEN

CYRRHUS

'Shall I take the reins, your honour?' Venio asked, as he stepped onto the sturdy chariot. The Tribune nodded. There was a sudden surge as the two horses pulled away. They were off, the cavalry escort alongside.

The pace was relentless, reflecting the Tribune's will. There were three changes of horses, but in general it was a hard, jolting ride. The road to Cyrrhus was not the Via Appia.

At last, in the early evening, the straight line of the fortress wall became visible, along with the lesser bulk of the town walls. As they approached, the details of the camp's wooden towers and upper walls were discernible. It was the standard legionary fortress.

Close to the fortress, like chickens about their mother, was an assortment of dwellings. These were the rude homes of the enterprising traders living on the Imperial presence.

Due to the lookout posts and the activity of scouts, the Tribune's coming was known long before he entered the gates. So when his chariot came to rest before the square headquarters building a guard of honour was in place. Waiting to greet him were three men. Gallo he recognised immediately, and the legate, obvious by his uniform, a white-haired, wiry figure. The third man, a senior centurion, stood slightly behind and to the legate's left.

Clearly Lamia's Syrian legate was showing full honours to the Emperor's personal aide; his reservations at associating with the son of a possible traitor – probable, with Gallo's promptings – had been laid aside. Valerius had little doubt that his reading of the legate's thought was true.

'Tribune, welcome to Cyrrhus and a soldier's life. We were sorry to be absent when you arrived at Antioch . . . but urgent business . . .' he said easily, with a gesture of the hand. 'You'll understand, I'm sure.'

The legate used a long-practised charm. A good administrator, Valerius suspected, but cautious.

'You know the Tribune Gallo, I believe,' the Legate continued.

Valerius bowed politely in confirmation, the blatant sham jarring with his nature.

'This is the acting Camp Prefect, the Chief Centurion Marcus Tullus.'

They exchanged greetings. Valerius was impressed; the salt of the army, he thought.

'The resident Prefect is absent just now, so we called on Tullus's experience,' the legate added in explanation.

The initial greetings over, the four men moved through to the inner courtyard. There the pleasantries continued, with the legate playing the cautious diplomat. Such circumspection, however, could not subdue Gallo's domineering confidence.

'Valerius, I was sorry to hear of your father's trouble,' he said, the studied sympathy of his tone perfect.

'Yes, a ridiculous business,' Valerius responded. 'I'm sure the Emperor will soon dismiss the matter.'

'Quite,' Gallo said lightly. 'I've heard your father's accusers were once friends of the late Germanicus,' he added with pretended innocence.

'Who wasn't!' the Tribune snapped. 'The great man was noted for his charm.'

He had countered well, but not well enough, for the name of Germanicus had been voiced, a name sacred to the legate's memory. That he had learned from Demetrianus the previous evening.

Gallo was clever, he had made his mark, and the look of triumph in his eyes was undisguised. Nevertheless, the game of deferential charm continued. No one dared offend the Emperor's personal aide too openly.

The initial commonplace exchanges were drawing to a natural close when the Centurion spoke. 'You've driven hard, Tribune,' he said, his deep, steady voice attracting attention. 'You need some wine to wash the dust away.'

'A welcome offer,' the Tribune responded, looking straight at the Centurion. The eyes that met his smiled, not a surface

40

smile, but one of quiet presence, as if the whole man smiled. Again the Tribune was impressed.

'As ever, Tullus is practical,' the legate said, gesturing to a waiting attendant.

Wine was quickly to hand, as were a circle of wooden chairs placed under the courtyard's awning.

'Be seated, Tribune,' the legate suggested. 'Our army chairs are like the army, hard and unrelenting.'

'Plain and practical,' the Tribune returned, 'the mark of a healthy legion.'

Both men smiled. The legate's reserve was easing.

The conversation continued on army and administrative affairs in general until Gallo introduced the question of the Tribune's mission.

'What are your plans, Valerius? Are the Emperor's instructions arduous?'

There was nothing to hide, and the Tribune spoke easily of his role. Gallo was suspicious, however, for the old man on Capri was wily. It was certain he had sent Valerius for more than making speeches. As Gallo had resolved in Athens, Valerius had to be stopped or ridiculed, and the sooner the better. He, of course, would keep himself well clear, as both he and Valerius served the ever-smiling union, the Emperor and his much praised friend Sejanus. Gallo felt like laughing. He played at deference well, he thought, as he listened to Valerius tell some dreary joke about his war-galley transport. It was all very pleasant and plausible, he mused cynically, but merely half the truth. Only an idiot would believe it otherwise. Gallo was right in one respect. The Tribune had not mentioned Galilee and his proposed investigation into the Messiah cult.

'Is your business in Syria private or official?' Gallo heard Valerius ask. At once he was alert.

'As I've explained to the good legate here,' he began, 'Ive been asked to make a general report on road conditions and post communications between Brindisium and the eastern provinces. The report will probably occupy a legion of scribes, and most likely will never be read!'

The legate laughed knowingly, and Valerius pretended

amusement. It was clever, he thought, the perfect scheme to visit every corner in the east.

'Have you much help?' the Centurion asked.

'Yes – six assistants. There are many roads, and I hate to drink alone!'

The Centurion smiled briefly. To him, Gallo's wit and charm were shallow.

'I've seen some of your aides talking to the men, but never would have guessed at their profession,' the Centurion returned, his voice strong, even challenging.

The cursed camp Prefect saw too much, he thought. Thankfully he did not have a higher rank.

'How many assistants have you, Valerius?' Gallo asked, deliberately diverting the conversation.

'Servants, yes, but no assistants as such. I don't need any. It only takes one to read the Emperor's message!'

'You'll address the cohorts tomorrow, of course,' the legate suggested.

'If that's convenient.'

'Well, Tullus?' the legate prompted.

'We'll make it convenient, sir. I suggest one half of the garrison in the morning and the other in the afternoon.'

As he climbed the steps to the temporary wooden podium, the Tribune gave no sign of his inner tension and misgivings. Before him was a sea of faces, the massed ranks of a border cohort. This was not the small and friendly garrison at Rhodes.

After he was introduced by the legate he stepped forward to the front of the podium. The legate had retired behind him to the left, and to his right was the Chief Centurion Tullus, the acting Camp Prefect.

He read the Emperor's proclamation straight, with no elaboration. The message was simple. The Emperor sent his greetings and good wishes. He appreciated their steadfastness and their sacrifice. He was concerned for their welfare and his ears were ever open to genuine complaints. He, the Emperor, was the Princeps to the lowliest recruit as well as to the high and mighty general. The proclamation complete, Valerius spoke of his meeting with the Emperor. He emphasised the

42

Princeps's prodigious workload, his concern for detail and his plea for tolerance. Harsh coercion was a last resort.

Valerius had a rich, impressive voice, the Centurion noted, but he was not a polished orator. That did not matter, though, indeed, if anything it helped, for the average sturdy legionary liked a plain man who spoke honestly.

The proceedings were almost over when shouting broke the corporate silence of the soldiers.

'What about your father, then?' one asked harshly.

'He's a traitor, isn't he?' another added.

Emboldened, others followed, complaining bitterly of conditions and the length of army service.

The Tribune stood erect and unmoving until the noise subsided. Then he dealt with each complaint, adding that he would be willing to receive individual petitions.

'My father is a Senator of Rome,' he said in conclusion. 'The accusations levelled at him are a slander – nothing else!'

'That's what you say,' a voice shouted.

Coarse laughter, a merciless enemy on such occasions, followed. He watched, seemingly helpless. No doubt the camp wits were active,busily feeding the chaos. He felt the rise of panic in his chest. Some-thing had to be done. He raised his hand, and suddenly there was stillness, but it was the deep, powerful voice of the Centurion that spoke.

'The name of Gracchus is not a traitor's name. The Tribune Lucius Gracchus Valerius is the personal legate of your Emperor – remember that and show him honour.'

Valerius turned to the Centurion, the gratitude in his eyes obvious. Then slowly and deliberately he re-read the last part of the Emperor's address. For a moment he stood motionless, the ranks of watching men silent. He bowed slightly, a kind of personal acknowledgement, before turning to move from the podium. Suddenly, like a dam released, cheering burst out around him.

'It went well, Valerius,' the legate said, allowing himself some mild enthusiasm.

'It was a smooth sail until we reached the harbour,' the Centurion observed.

'Indeed, but the gods blessed me with a steady harbour master!' Valerius responded.

'Who told the men about your father? That's what I would like to know,' Marcus Tullus said forcefully, his attention turning to Gallo, who had been waiting at the base of the podium.

'Rumour is hard to contain,' Gallo said casually.

'And easy to spread!' the Centurion returned, looking straight at him.

'Agreed,' Gallo responded with a shrug. Who did this Chief Centurion think he was, he thought angrily. He was much too sharp for comfort, and another one to stop.

The Tribune's address in the afternoon was without incident, and after dealing with individual complaints he entertained the Centurion privately in his quarters. Venio was in attendance, and the big man performed his duties with surprising refinement; so much so that the Tribune was prompted to ask where he had learned his skill.

'Master Felix,' Venio replied with a grin.

The Tribune smiled.

'You'll like Felix,' he said, turning to his guest.

'I think I'll enjoy meeting all the Valerian party,' the Centurion responded.

The conversation had already been long and intimate, and Valerius had been grateful to share his troubles with a man he trusted.

'Tell me, sir,' Tullus continued, 'what is the precise charge against your father?'

'Father didn't say. I can only assume it's something to do with his work on property reform. At least it could be the excuse!'

'A lame excuse, if that's the case. The Emperor will squash this nonsense.'

'I agree. It's still a worry, though, especially for my sister; but when I think of Cornelia, I despair.' Valerius stood up, reflecting his agitation.

'You mentioned Herod's court as a possibility,' the Centurion said quietly.

The Tribune nodded, his lips pressed tight.

'I've got friends there, and if you agree I'll send a messenger by first light.'

At once Tullus had the Tribune's full attention.

'We cannot approach Herod directly, of course,' the Centurion continued, 'for he could disclaim all knowledge of the girl, and what is worse, keep her hidden. He's not called The Fox for nothing, and he has many powerful friends in Rome. To make an issue of a slave girl would be seen as politically inept.'

'I know too well,' Valerius said, almost in a whisper.

'We will have to force his hand in some way, but carefully,' the Centurion followed on. 'First, of course, we will need confirmation that she is in Herod's keeping. It will not be easy, though.'

'You've given me hope, Marcus, the first real hope I've had. All I can say is, proceed as you think fit, but how are we to keep in touch? for I return to Antioch in two days' time.'

Tullus pondered for a moment.

'The Camp Prefect is due back at any time, then I'll be released to return to my 'retirement' at Capernaum.'

'Retirement!'

'A semi-administrative post,' Tullus explained, but with unusual vagueness.

'Where is Capernaum?'

'On the western shore of the Sea of Galilee.'

By all the gods, the Tribune thought, this was the very Centurion the Emperor had mentioned, the one the people trusted. It had to be. It fitted too well to be otherwise.

'Tullus, why not come to Antioch and join us at the Villa Demetrianus? There you can learn the latest from our Greek friend Demos, and then we can travel south together.'

This they arranged to do, but the Tribune did not mention his brief concerning the Messiah cult. That could wait, he thought.

CHAPTER EIGHT

THE VILLA DEMETRIANUS

The Villa Demetrianus was quiet. It was just after midday, and Drusilla, sitting in the deep shade of the garden trellis, was scribing a letter to her father. Lost in concentration, she did not hear the approaching footsteps until they were close. Then, turning in her seat, she saw before her a Centurion of the highest rank. The impression of power emanating from him arrested her attention, yet his eyes were gentle.

'You must be the honourable Centurion my brother keeps mentioning,' she said in greeting.

'And you must be the gracious sister he keeps mentioning,' he responded, smiling.

She laughed lightly, a rich, beautiful laugh. 'I'm afraid the villa is somewhat deserted. My brother and our noble host are out. Felix is buried in Plato somewhere, and here am I, the only agent of welcome!'

'A charming welcome for a humble soldier!'

He bowed, captured by her qualities. The beauty of her voice, the fineness of her features, her natural grace and her maturity. By all the gods, she was attractive, but too high-born for him, yet he watched emotions playing through him that he thought had died long since within the history of his fifty years.

'Tullus!'

The sound echoed round the walled garden. Valerius had returned.

After greeting his friend, the Tribune was quick to impart his latest news. There was no further word about his father, but Demos had confirmed that Cornelia was bound for Herod's desert fortress.

'Machaerus!' The Centurion spoke the word through clenched teeth. Consideration for Drusilla stopped him from

46

describing the savage reputation of the place. Instead his words brought hope.

'The friends I have at Herod's court are close. I will send another messenger at once. Be assured, my lady,' he added, turning to Drusilla, 'that everything possible will be done.'

'There really is hope?' Drusilla's voice sounded innocent.

'Considerable hope,' Tullus answered. Their eyes met, and in that moment no barrier lay between them. It was as if their souls had met.

'You must have refreshment after your journey,' Drusilla said, lowering her eyes. 'I'll go and call the servants.'

Tullus watched her graceful figure as she entered the villa.

'Are all the Valerian as striking as the brother and sister I have met!' he said, smiling at the Tribune.

'Yes, we're all equally impossible,' Valerius quipped. 'My sister likes you,' he added. 'In fact, it's the first time in years I've seen her actually acknowledge a man!'

'You're teasing me, Valerius!' Tullus answered, but he watched, amazed at the wave of embarrassment that engulfed him.

They stood silent for a moment before the Tribune raised the subject of Gallo.

'Was he at the Cyrrhus fortress when you left?'

'Yes, waiting for his surveying assistants to return, while being the bosom friend of all,' Tullus answered evenly.

'What do you make of Gallo?'

'Let's put it this way – I find it hard to understand why an orator of his reputation is reporting on roads and communications.'

Valerius contemplated his feet; he looked up, his lips pursed, poised on the brink of speech. Then the words came quickly.

'There seems every reason why we should be one in policy, and every reason against working separately – you seem to anticipate my thoughts anyway!' he said jokingly. 'I will speak plainly. Sejanus owes his power to the patronage of the Emperor and the fear of his Praetorian Guard. The Senate pay him all honour, but given the chance they would destroy him tomorrow. His position is both powerful and precarious.

Notwithstanding, his drive for power is relentless. Much depends on his long frustrated plan to marry the widow of the Emperor's late son. If he succeeds in this and his power base continues to grow, the Emperor may have no option but to make him his adopted son. The title would be empty, however, if the legions rebelled in favour of the heirs of Germanicus – that is, if they stay alive. So here in Syria we have Gallo dutifully about his master's business. All this I'm sure you know already.'

'Most of it,' Tullus responded. 'Thank you for your trust. This I consider an honour,' he added, looking straight at the Tribune. 'But may I ask two questions?'

Valerius nodded.

'How do you view your role as the Emperor's personal legate? and why is Gallo at such pains to stop you? That is, assuming that Cornelia's kidnap and the charge against your father are connected. Of course there's no proof to substantiate this, but even so, I feel your suspicions are well founded, especially after the trouble at Cyrrhus. I'm certain that was deliberate. However, the question remains, why employ such extreme methods? You are conveying the greetings and goodwill of the Emperor to the legions, while Gallo is building up support for the premier servant and hopeful heir of that same Emperor. You could be a nuisance, but you don't pose an intolerable threat or anything approaching it. We've missed something, I'm sure!'

'I can't fault your reasoning,' the Tribune answered pensively, 'but what have we forgotten?'

'Perhaps the wine I see approaching will help!'

Drusilla and the servants arrived with cups and brimming beakers, their contents well diluted to assuage the thirst of a hot afternoon.

'Food is waiting inside, but I thought you'd enjoy a drink in the garden first,' Drusilla said, bowing slightly towards the Centurion. He thanked her warmly, and again their eyes met.

The conversation soon centred on the imminent journey to the south. They would sail to Caesarea, the destination Galilee, necessary because of Cornelia, for Tullus's friends would report to him at Capernaum.

As the discussion of plans continued, it became obvious that Drusilla had grown agitated.

'Is anything the matter?' her brother asked.

'There is, Lucius – I know you want me to stay here with our friends the Demetriani, and I know a woman should not be the travelling baggage of a soldier, but, Lucius, Galilee's so far away. Can I not at least come with you to Caesarea?'

'My dear sister, where would you stay? We have no friends there, and an inn would be unthinkable.'

Drusilla nodded tersely, holding herself in check. The longing unlocked by the powerful soldier beside her had grown suddenly at the likely prospect of never seeing him again. Hastily she excused herself on the pretext of preparing food.

The Centurion watched her go, the impulse to follow and comfort her strong, but he remained unmoved beside the Tribune.

Valerius sighed.

'After Cornelia's kidnap I simply cannot gamble with the safety of my sister.' He paused. 'Do you know of anywhere she could stay?'

At last a thought that Tullus had been nurturing could take root.

'I could not say this in your sister's presence lest I upset some special plans you may have had. But yes, there is a small villa that I know overlooking the Sea of Galilee. It is owned by a Jewish friend of mine, and both he and his wife would be kindly hosts. It's quite close to our barracks at Capernaum, and we could provide a guard.'

'Good, that sounds ideal. Let's go inside and tell Drusilla.'

CHAPTER NINE

CAESAREA

The Valerian party left by first light for Seleucia Pieria. They were six in number – the Tribune, his sister, Felix and Venio, along with the Centurion and his aide. The cook had attached himself to the household of the Demetriani, and Demos, now fully recovered, had found work with a shipping company. He also joked about an 'accommodating widow'.

'Someone has to keep the Emperor's ports open and flowing,' he said lightly as he took his leave.

'Keep in contact!' the Tribune urged.

'Don't worry, Master Tribune. I'll be here when you need me.'

He stepped back a few paces and saluted.

'May the gods protect the fair Cornelia,' he called out, before disappearing into the alleyways of Antioch.

At midday three war galleys pulled out from the naval base at Seleucia Pieria and headed south. Characteristically, the Tribune had thought the number immoderate, but the Commander simply said it was a training exercise, and going to Caesarea was a good extended test.

The Commander husbanded his sailors' strength with care. Harshness, he said, was too often mistaken for discipline. It was a general curse. Even the brutality in the arena was supposed to stiffen indifference to pain, he added with derision. He knew, of course, that the Tribune was a ready audience, and when they dined on shore the conversation was full and vigorous.

Drusilla dined separately with two attendants, girls provided by the Commander and gratefully accepted, as the exclusively male world of the galley was, to her, oppressive; a lesson learned on the journey from Rhodes. Drusilla was happy, yet a voice within forswore enjoyment while Cornelia's and her father's plight persisted.

The first stop was at Laodicea, where, during the following day, the Tribune addressed the cohorts of the Legion VI Ferrata – 'the Ironclads' – at their nearby camp, something he dared not avoid, having been to Cyrrhus, the home of the X Fretenis.

There was trouble again, this time when the Camp Prefect was introducing him, but with the promise of punishment the massed ranks grew silent, if not sullen. Nevertheless, the Tribune managed to ease the situation by praising the Legion's famous history, and by joking that the 'Tenth' at Cyrrhus, unlike them, had only fried him on one side.

Glad that a difficult day was past, the Tribune left the next morning, and after three further overnight stops he arrived at Caesarea.

Soon they set out for the Procurator Pilate's residence. It was afternoon, and on the way, the Tribune's party passed close to the dockland slave market. There a young girl, her head bowed, stood helplessly, her all but naked body on general view. At once the nightmare of Cornelia's peril was before the Tribune's mind.

'By Jupiter, this cannot be!' he shouted, and Venio, hauling on the reins, abruptly drew the two-horse chariot to a stop.

'Buy her!' he shouted at Felix in the following cart, 'you need a daughter to comfort your declining years!'

The busy market place was suddenly silent, and a sea of faces watched the Tribune, frozen, as it were, with curiosity. The slave merchant was beside himself with fear. He could see the broad stripe of the Senate on the Tribune's tunic. Only the highest ranks could drive their carts within the walls before the sun had dipped.

While Felix completed the transaction, the Tribune watched, his eyes blazing. Then, grasping his sword, his knuckles white, he walked towards the silent line of bystanders. First in Greek, and then in Aramaic, he attacked their barbarism.

'Would you like to see your child like this?' Some turned away, but most looked blankly at the tall, ranting soldier. It was common practice. What had they done wrong?

The young slave girl was already clothed and seated beside

Felix before Valerius remounted his chariot. He had lost his temper, a foolishness, no doubt, but he was unrepentant. He grasped the chariot rail, Venio flicked the reins, and they were off again.

'The Gracchi still live,' the Centurion said with a smile, but what had astonished him was the Tribune's use of Aramaic.

'This was the way Cornelia joined the family nine years ago. I was with the Senator when it happened,' Felix said, confiding in Tullus.

'That explains his outburst.'

'Will it cause him trouble?' Felix asked.

'I doubt it.'

The huge doors of the Prefect's residence opened to admit the Tribune and his party, and, as at Antioch, they found themselves in a large, open courtyard. Here, however, officials were already waiting to greet the travellers.

Valerius, Drusilla, the Centurion and Felix were immediately escorted to the audience hall – the Squadron Commander was to come later. As they climbed the many steps to the chamber, Tullus noticed that Drusilla had been weeping.

'You've been crying, my lady,' he said with concern.

'Oh, it's . . .' she fumbled for words. 'It's my brother . . . when he rescued the little girl . . . it reminded me . . .' she could not finish the sentence, but briefly touched the Centurion's arm.

At the centre of the audience chamber Pontius Pilate waited, his wife beside him.

'I trust you travelled well, Tribune,' he said grandly.

'Yes, our good friend the Commander pampered us with every luxury,' Valerius replied.

The introductions completed, Drusilla and the Prefect's wife retired to an adjacent room. Drusilla went with resignation, assuming that the conversation would circle around the gossip of Rome. She was mistaken, for Pilate's wife was not eager for such news. Indeed, Drusilla had found a like mind, and they talked easily, if not avidly, while the time allowed.

In the main audience hall the conversation was still bound by caution. Pilate, although deferential to the Emperor's legate, was wary and revealed little. He had no wish to be the controversial subject matter of the Tribune's report to the Governor Lamia. Yet on the topic of Herod Antipas he was blunt to the point of aggression.

'Herod's more of a Jew than he pretends!' he said, his lips drawn tight. 'I once set up gilded shields in the old palace in Jerusalem to the honour of the Emperor and his divine predecessor – no images to offend the Jews, you understand, just a simple inscription – but even so, there was a tremendous uproar from the Zealot element, and as a matter of expediency the priestly hierarchy lent them their support.' Pilate's tone was derisory. 'In this case I was determined to stand firm. The Jews, however, sent a tendentious appeal to the Emperor with the full backing of Herod, and I was forced to withdraw.' He paused and looked about his circle of guests. 'As you can imagine, relations between Herod and myself are somewhat strained. Maximus here,' he added, turning to his aide, 'will confirm the endless pettiness we endure.'

The young aide nodded vigorously.

'Maximus, I believe we have mutual friends in Venusia?' the Tribune interjected.

The Procurator's assistant was obviously pleased to be singled out, and for a moment the conversation took a social note. It was not long, however, before Jewish affairs again grew dominant, with Maximus leading the discussion.

'I was told before coming to Judaea that Rome should never be nursemaid to militant Jewry, and I believe our noble Procurator has ably supported that policy.'

Pilate was clearly grateful for his aide's support, especially with his Emperor's legate present.

'We simply cannot tolerate intolerance. It's not Roman,' he said with a flourish, vaguely wondering if his words would reach Capri. 'Tullus!' he continued, 'I may not agree with your views, but I respect them. What is your opinion? How should Rome behave towards the Jews?'

The Centurion answered quietly, as if it were a personal exchange.

'The Jewish faith has many devotees throughout the Empire, especially in Rome, but here it has its heart, and this, sir, makes your job difficult. For instance, if a Prefect in Gaul or Hispania enacts a controversial policy it generally remains a local matter. However, with Judaea it is wholly different, as any policy affecting the Jewish faith at its root is felt throughout the Empire, and, of course, in Rome.'

The Tribune looked on in admiration. This man was head and shoulders above them all, he thought.

'I know you will agree with me, sir,' Tullus continued, careful of the Procurator's dignity. 'You will agree that the term Jew embraces many differing shades of practice and opinion.'

Pilate nodded.

'We all know there is a world of difference between the fanatical Zealot and the generous philosophy of the late Rabbi Hillel,' Tullus proceeded.

'Indeed, indeed.'

'Now, to answer your question, sir, that is in the broad sense, Rome should behave towards the Jewish people so as to encourage the tolerant views of Hillel rather than the mania of the Zealot.'

'I cannot fault you, Tullus. Your principle is right, I know, but what about the practice? What about the High Priest and his well-fed clan?' Pilate's tone was derisory. 'It seems to me their God is gold!'

'Well, sir, we don't discourage them,' the Centurion immediately responded.

This was strong stuff, the Tribune thought. Certainly Tullus was no sycophant.

'How can we discourage them? We need them!' Pilate reacted with some exasperation.

'That I don't deny, sir,' Tullus said respectfully. 'They are our allies, but I fear our only allies!'

Pilate nodded. 'There is much in what you say,' he said with resignation.

'What do you mean, Tullus?' the Tribune interjected.

Tullus paused a moment, gathering his thoughts. All eyes were upon him.

'The ancient revered Temple of the Jews in Jerusalem is run by the Sadducees, rich priestly families, and the High Priest is one of their number.' Again he paused. 'The Sadducees,' he continued, 'tend to collaborate with the ruling power. The reason is simple. They want to keep the Temple going, and for that they need the maintenance of civil order.'

'At our expense!' Pilate retorted, while nodding in agreement.

'So the High Priest looks to Rome as well as to his people,' the Tribune said.

'Exactly, and many think he only looks to Rome!' Tullus returned, 'which gives the Zealots food to feed upon.'

'It sounds familiar. So we need to seek a broader support. What about the Pharisees? They're a broad grouping, are they not?'

'The 'Separated Ones'!' an old aide of Pilate reacted. 'Never in a thousand years. You'd never stop them squabbling over points of law!'

'I know many moderate Pharisees – and lawyer scribes,' Tullus said firmly.

'Why the term 'separated'?' the Tribune inquired.

'They opposed the union of the Kingship and the High Priesthood in the one person at the time of the Maccabees. In other words, they advocated a separation of powers.'

'What do the Pharisees do now?'

'Study the scriptures, interpret the law, some teach . . .'

'So they have the ear of the people.'

'Yes, and an educated ear, for the Jew is well schooled.'

'Noble sir,' Valerius said, turning to Pilate with a smile, 'I'm glad I'm not the Procurator of Judaea!'

There was a general ripple of laughter, and the conversation moved to other topics, and inevitably, who was winning at the Circus, and did the Whites still have their hero charioteer. The exchanges were easy and relaxed, and Pilate felt content that the Tribune's first impressions had been favourable. At least the tall aristocrat appreciated the difficulties.

'You will address the garrison, I hope?' he eventually asked of his guest.

'Of course,' Valerius responded. 'Late morning, if it's possible. I have the Commander's sailors first thing.'

The reception was clearly drawing to a close, and the Tribune took his leave with the Centurion. They went straight to the Tribune's quarters, and for some time neither spoke.

Then, in a flow of quick, staccato speech, Valerius outlined his plans.

'Cornelia's rescue is our first priority, so the sooner you are in Galilee to follow up your contacts, the better. What I suggest is that you, my sister, Felix and the little slave-girl should leave at dawn. I'll ask the Prefect for an escort. Will you be able to reach Capernaum in a day?' The quick pace of the Tribune's speech rested for a moment.

Tullus shook his head. 'We can stay overnight at Scythopolis, where I have friends.'

'Good. I will, of course, address the Commander's sailors and the resident garrison in the morning. In the afternoon, with Venio driving a two-horse chariot, I should reach the camp at Caparcotna before sundown. In the morning another address, and then off again. Hopefully I'll arrive by late evening at your barracks at Capernaum.' The rapidity of the Tribune's delivery had not abated. 'Caesarea received us well,' he added pensively, his tone a total contrast to what had gone before. 'Not a word about my father's situation.'

'Gallo hasn't been to Caesarea!' the Centurion said bluntly.

'True, where he's been there's been trouble – that is, except Seleucia Pieria.'

'And we know the reason for that.'

'Yes, the Squadron Commander; a man to trust, but I find it odd that Pilate had not heard the slander, for rumour circles the Empire like chariots in the Circus.'

'There'll be some simple explanation, I'm sure – the post delayed or lost,' the Centurion ventured. 'But what still puzzles me is why Gallo has used such extreme measures to stop you. It defies all logical explanation other than that the time is short, and the issue urgent.'

'We have no firm evidence, of course.'

'Have you any doubt?'

Valerius shook his head. Suddenly he felt exhausted. He sat down.

'Marcus Tullus, I fear my mind is blocked with thought. It's time we soaked away our cares,' he said wearily, while pulling at an ornate silk rope close to the door. 'Let's see if this gets a response.'

'Yes, your honour.' The gruff but friendly voice of Venio spoke at the open door.

'The baths are growing in their appeal, Venio.'

'They're ready, your honour!'

'How old is Venio?' the Centurion asked, as the sound of the servant's footsteps receded down the corridor.

'In his late twenties. Felix has been training him, and he's taken over much of the day-to-day work, which is good, for I view Felix more as an uncle than a personal servant. Anyway, he's got a new daughter to look after,' he said with a smile. 'Well, I must to the baths,' he added, striding down the corridor.

The Centurion watched him go through the tall open doorway. Lucius Gracchus Valerius, he mused, the highest nobility of civilised Rome. And what was he? A Tuscan farmer's son.

As arranged, Marcus Tullus, his aide, Drusilla, Felix and the slave- girl – Sarah, she had told them – left for Galilee at the first sign of dawn. Then, an hour later, the Tribune, with an escort of the Commander's marines, made his way to the docks.

The purchase of Sarah the previous day had grown into myth overnight. The Emperor's legate was a friend of the oppressed, a true Tribune of the people, and everywhere he was greeted with enthusiasm. The Commander's sailors cheered him on the least pretext, and it seemed that he could do no wrong. Later the resident garrison gave him a similar reception, receiving his address almost with a sense of hunger.

Pilate wondered at the Tribune's popularity, and Valerius, seeing the danger of official resentment, ascribed the success to the Procurator's good management. Pilate was gratified and impressed. He could not help but admire the Tribune's natural dignity, which had remained constant throughout the emotions of the morning.

'Well, Valerius, you have captured Caesarea,' Pilate said, acknowledging his success, 'but I must caution you that Caesarea is not typical of Judaea or Galilee. Caesarea is a Roman town with a Greek language. I'm afraid you'll find Galilee a very different place.'

'I'll have the Centurion to guide my steps, of course,' the Tribune answered.

'Yes, Tullus is a tower of strength.' Pilate's voice became confidential. He nodded knowingly. 'He likes the Jews, of course.'

The Tribune ignored Pilate's insinuation and turned the conversation towards the subject he had avoided, or rather forgotten – the Messiah cult. Pilate's opinion could be useful.

'I would be interested to hear your views on the appearance of a Messiah figure in Galilee.'

Pilate pursed his lips as if indicating a tricky subject.

'Galilee is not within my jurisdiction, as you know, so my information could be fuller,' Pilate began. 'However, I'm sure the person you mean is listed on our files as 'the Nazarene'. We keep an eye on all such potential troublemakers, especially when they attend the religious festivals in Jerusalem. Then we must be extra careful, for the Jews are volatile and passionate. A small incident becomes a riot all too easily, and we always get the blame.' Pilate paused, letting his eyes scan the empty circus where only moments past the cheering garrison had saluted Valerius's address.

'The province is full of prophets, Tribune,' he continued with a broad, expansive gesture, 'but I must say this; they are by no means ignorant farmers merely troubled by visions. Far from it; the standard of education is high. In fact, if a Jew cannot read his holy books he is nothing.' He paused. 'Now, where was I? Yes, of course, the Nazarene. I'm told he has a reputation for miraculous healing. He's what I call the other-worldly sort, yet we must be careful. You see, Valerius, to the extremist the Messiah will come as a warrior prince to lead the cohorts of his God Jehovah against the barbarian invaders.' Pilate looked at the Tribune to emphasise his point. 'We are the barbarians!'

'I'm afraid we often deserve the title,' the Tribune retorted. 'Once the army start they never know when to stop; but the Nazarene is not a warrior Zealot!'

'Not yet!' Pilate returned sceptically. 'To the Jew the desire for national fulfilment is intense, so any Messianic candidate, other-worldly or not, cannot be ignored.'

'So the Nazarene could be dangerous?'

'Only if we let him. He's often in Capernaum, I'm told. Tullus will know all about him.'

'Yes, I keep forgetting to ask, but there have been other things,' Valerius said, his voice fading as he thought of his father and Cornelia.

'Well, Tullus is the man,' Pilate emphasised. 'It's strange, though; I never cease to wonder why he stays in that forsaken place.'

'Capernaum, you mean.'

'Yes – why I don't know. He's a Chief Centurion, he's served his year, and the Equestrian order is open to him. A man like Tullus could pick and choose; an island Prefecture, for instance; but no, he stays to swelter in the heat of Galilee. Anyway, that's another mystery you may solve.'

Valerius nodded pensively. 'He has many friends in that area, it seems, and that could be the simple reason why he stays – in his 'retirement' as he calls it.'

'I know, he likes the Jews – the only one of us who does!'

An exaggeration, no doubt, but the Procurator had drawn the general picture.

'Well, it's been a most interesting exchange. Thank you for giving me so much of your time,' the Tribune said, concluding the conversation.

'It's been a pleasure,' Pilate returned easily, yet caution kept him watchful. He could not forget that the tall Laticlavius beside him was the Emperor's special legate.

CHAPTER TEN

CAPERNAUM

Tullus had hired fast two-wheeled carts, three in number, pulled by pairs of quick-stepping mules, and alongside was an escort of cavalry. The plain outside Caesarea was well wooded, and the morning air was fresh, but it soon grew hot. Twice they passed men felling trees, and twice Tullus grumbled to Drusilla that few ever bothered to replant. Were they Jews? she asked. Tullus shook his head – mostly Greeks and Samaritans. The Jews, he said, were concentrated to the south in Judaea and over the Carmel range in Galilee.

By midday they had passed through the range of hills that divided the coastal plain from the fertile valley of the Esdraelon, the range that started with Mount Carmel. At the edge of the plain they changed mules at the legionary camp near Caparcotna, taking time to inform the Prefect of the Tribune's imminent arrival. It was a modest Roman presence, well placed between the hills of Samaria and the great plain, a camp waiting to grow, Tullus believed.

A patchwork pattern of cornfields filled the view as they headed towards the valley of the Jezreel. The area was well populated and the villages frequent. Some were Greek in nature, some Jewish. They were not yet in Galilee.

'Is there trouble between the villages, between the Greek and the Jew?' Drusilla asked.

'Mostly they keep to themselves, and no doubt our presence helps.'

'Are punishments harsh?'

'More insensitive than harsh, but when a soldier is killed or injured, then harshness is a mild expression!'

'You speak from experience, sir.'

'Yes, my lady.'

The heat was relentless as they progressed towards

Scythopolis, and Drusilla was continually busy with her fan.

'It's cool today!' Tullus joked. 'Wait until tomorrow when we're in the valley of the Jordan.'

'You are a comfort,' she returned, her rich, beautiful laughter captivating him.

They reached Scythopolis before dusk, and went directly to the house of the Centurion's friends. Their hosts were of modest means, but their welcome was unstinted, and Drusilla could see that they held the Centurion in the highest regard. They were Jews, as Tullus had explained, though with the Greek manners and dress of their adopted city. They lived at peace with their neighbours; still they were Jews, devout in their belief. There was something else, however, something deeper, a bond of trust between them and the Chief Centurion, and what was more, she felt included.

By first light their escort had arrived and it was time to leave. As the sun rose it grew quickly hot and humid. Tullus had been right, Drusilla thought. The buzz of insects filled the air, and the lush, abundant green of the valley contrasted dramatically with the lifeless hills to their right. It was a strange, strange landscape. On they went, taking the western coast of the Sea of Galilee, and there to the east were the same bleak hills, redeemed, however, by the subtlety of pink and blue that mystified their contour.

By now, Drusilla thought, Lucius would be racing with his cavalry escort down the same road that they had covered yesterday. It would be a hard journey, but he would hide his tiredness, just like Father. Father! at once her mind filled with pain and worry, returning to the well-worn round of its imagination – her father's stoical will, his abhorrence of dishonour, and the honourable solution. Visibly she shrank from the thought.

From the corner of his eye the Centurion noticed her shudder.

'Is anything wrong, my lady?' he asked, his speech still bound by outward formality.

She told him plainly of her fears.

'It is inconceivable that the Emperor will uphold the charge,' Tullus responded firmly. 'For one thing it would be politically unwise, and according to your brother the Emperor is not a stupid man.'

His words carried conviction, and in gratitude she stretched forward and touched his arm – a gentle touch, but powerfully received.

The Centurion's eyes returned to the road ahead, but his mind was full of his companion. They were growing closer with slow inevitability, yet caution dragged upon his purpose. She was a high-born, graceful lady, and he of simple farming stock. He hoped it would not end in misery, as his few attempted friendships had before.

They reached the city of Tiberias in the early afternoon, and the Centurion immediately sent a message to his contact in Herod's palace before proceeding to the small Roman garrison. There he awaited a response on the pretext of changing mules. It came immediately – they were still awaiting news from Machaerus.

No one wished to linger in Herod's capital. Indeed, Drusilla found the ornate buildings gross, deadened, as it were, by lavish decoration. An ambitious prince, wishing to impress, was her conclusion.

They were quickly on the road again, and by late afternoon they had arrived in Capernaum.

At once Drusilla felt at home in the villa that Tullus had recommended all those days ago in Antioch. It was cool, so very cool inside, and she was captivated by the charm of her elderly hosts, the Ben Josephs. In turn they were equally charmed by her. She was a Senator's daughter, yet there were no extravagant demands. Her requirements were simple, her behaviour considerate. It was what Tullus had expected.

Satisfied that Drusilla was happy with her rooms, he made for his garrison quarters. The smallish fort was nearly half a mile away, and he strode the distance quickly, arriving to find Felix and the rest of the party still unloading baggage.

Inside, awaiting his arrival, was Cornelius, his Optio. Squarely built, strong and young, Cornelius was devoted to the Centurion, and had modelled his life on the example of the older man. They first greeted each other formally, and then, on the lead of the Centurion, warmly and informally.

'You received the message from Antioch, I hope,' Tullus enquired. Delay was always possible, even with the army post.

'Yes, sir. Quarters for the Tribune and his party have been prepared.'

'He wears the broad stripe, Cornelius. I hope his room is not too basic.'

'We got some extras. It looks better than yours, sir!'

'That's no recommendation, Cornelius,' Tullus responded with a laugh. 'What else have you to report?' he added.

'Little has happened in your absence, sir. We were called once to quell an alleged riot in a village close to Ginnesar. When we got there, all we could see were frightened villagers. Apparently a number of spirited youths had chased one of Herod's tax collectors. You will be proud of me, sir, for I behaved in true Tullus fashion. I gathered the whole village together, lectured them on the importance of respecting the law and directed the soldiers to help with some unfinished road work. I had wine with the chief men of the village, and we parted amicably.'

'Herod's taxgatherers are worse than ours!' the Centurion returned. 'No wonder the young bloods chase them. Just think how easily some wooden-headed officer could have caused an incident. 'Teaching them a lesson' they call it,' he added abrasively. 'I remember seeing a village disappear because there was some whisper of rebellion – but I talk too much. What more have you to tell?'

In the courtyard Felix was still busy with the baggage. He felt inexplicably at peace. Strange, for the place was hot and dusty and his quarters plain, yet he was happy. Beside him was Sarah, soon to be his adopted daughter. From their halting conversation – he knew some Aramaic, she some Greek – he had learned that her parents had been part of a Jewish community that had fallen victim to a frontier skirmish, and that she had been the booty of the victors. Her fearfulness, habitual at first, was lessening with the growing awareness of her good fortune. She was grateful, clearly so, and eager to serve her new-found father. Felix liked her.

He stood at rest, his eyes ranging round the long, rambling courtyard. One soldier was busy repairing harness, another buffing his armour. A few knots of men were gathered here and there talking casually, and of course there were those on their spell of guard duty. This was the Centurion's world, but it puzzled Felix why a man like Tullus, who had reached the position of Primus Pilus and had served his year as Chief Centurion, could prefer such a minor posting. Indeed, the cattle sheds at the Villa Valerius were more imposing than the fort at Capernaum. Strange, he thought. There had to be some explanation, not least why the authorities allowed him to remain in his 'retirement'.

The sun was beginning to set and the air had grown balmy. Suddenly the soldiers froze, and Felix knew the cause at once. The Tribune had arrived.

Valerius raced straight to the old servant and embraced him.

'Did my sister survive the journey?' he asked.

'Yes, she seemed to enjoy the adventure. She certainly looked happy.'

'Gazing at Tullus, I suppose,' the Tribune quipped.

'A little.'

'What do you think, Felix?' Valerius questioned.

'I think he's one of life's patricians, Master Lucius, and the Equestrian order awaits him!'

'Yes, Felix,' Valerius answered, a sigh betraying his underlying weariness. They were miles apart, he thought, and such a match, even if allowed, was frowned upon. Nonetheless, he had no will to stop it, for Tullus was a man, a man indeed.

The soldiers in the courtyard were still rigid in salute, and the Tribune was quick to acknowledge their respect. For a moment he talked to the man repairing the harness, and then he made for the main building. At the entrance he was met by the Centurion, his posture fixed in formal salute. The salute was returned, but there formality ended.

'Any news?' the Tribune asked.

'We're expecting word very soon – it could be tomorrow.'

'Cursed delay!' Valerius reacted. 'Surely he'll release her when she tells him who she is!' he added forcefully.

'Well, if he does we'll have immediate tidings of his generosity, and all the world will praise his graciousness – he'll see to that.'

'So we're still at the mercy of this polished savage!' The Tribune spat his words out bitterly.

Tullus nodded, but said no more. He had no wish to feed the Tribune's anguish.

Being engrossed in conversation, they did not notice the bent figure of a man burdened with baskets moving towards them across the yard. His clothes were of a dark, coarse material, but spotlessly clean.

'Beloved James!' the Centurion's greeting sounded strongly in the evening stillness.

'You're back, Master,' came the terse reply.

'Tribune, this is James,' Tullus said, turning to his tall companion.

Two Galilean eyes looked at the Tribune intently. 'The Master's friends are my friends,' he said, his voice carrying the roughness of the surrounding hills.

'James, there will be seven for dinner this evening: will you need help?'

'Are the two old folks coming?' the servant asked, referring to the Ben Josephs, who were about his own age.

'Yes, and also their guest, the Tribune's sister.'

'Well, Master, if the old ones are coming I must do it myself.'

'Of course, I'd forgotten.'

James nodded abruptly and went inside.

'That's the real commander of the station,' Tullus said with humour. 'He prepares his food after the Jewish fashion. You'll enjoy it; his cooking skills are famous – now let me take you to your quarters.'

Felix, too, was making for his quarters when the huge form of Venio engulfed him. The big man bubbled with the story of his journey.

'The faster we went, the more the Governor liked it,' he enthused. Then he switched to another topic.

'You must show me how to fold the Governor's toga, Master Felix.'

Felix laughed. 'Your energy matches your dimensions. Come with me now; I'll teach you while we have some wine.'

Apart from the guards at the gate, the courtyard was empty.

The dinner party was almost over before the Tribune introduced the topic of the Nazarene.

'I've forgotten to mention this before,' he said, turning to the Centurion, though his remarks were addressed to the party in general. 'I've been asked to report on the activities of a Messiah cult in Galilee. Pilate told me the leader was probably the figure known as the Nazarene.'

Valerius stopped, for the change in atmosphere was too obvious to ignore: the immediate barrier of caution in Ben Joseph's eyes; the sudden halt in James the servant's movements; and the Optio Cornelius, too, looked ill at ease. The Centurion, however, remained motionless on his couch, his head lowered. All eyes were upon him, but it was the Tribune who spoke.

'I must apologise if I have offended this noble gathering. I can assure you . . .'

'Valerius, my friend, it is we who should apologise,' Tullus responded quietly. 'The Rabbi, or the Nazarene, as you call him, is greatly respected by many of us here in Capernaum, but he is also much misunderstood. So we have grown suspicious of outside enquiry, especially when officialdom is involved.' The Centurion stopped, drank slowly from his wine cup, and then continued, his voice deep and steady.

'To be honest, you caught us unawares. Indeed, our considered response must be one of gratitude that you, of all people, should be the one selected to investigate the Rabbi's activities. Reason can only be at peace with reason, so what need we fear from you?'

'So the Nazarene is more than a mere prophet of phantasy?' the Tribune said enquiringly.

'Much more.'

'And you fear he may be subject to some unjust Roman censure?'

'The Rabbi is subject to his Father in heaven!' The loud mutter of James the old servant was clearly audible. The Ben Josephs turned to face his stubborn features, but James was unrepentant.

The Centurion laughed, and all could see his mirth was genuine.

'James never dallies with diplomacy, for what he thinks he speaks!'

The Tribune was glad to match the mood of the Centurion. Clearly the subject of the Nazarene troubled the Ben Josephs, and there was no point in pressing for information he could learn privately from Tullus.

'James,' he said, turning to the old servant with a smile. 'I may not rightly understand the meaning of your words, but I do appreciate your deeds. Your cooking has been excellent.'

The Centurion's servant nodded in embarrassment, as Drusilla and the rest of the party added their approval, but he was obviously pleased.

The question of the Nazarene lingered on, however, and this the Centurion openly acknowledged.

'I think a meeting with one of the Rabbi's disciples would be instructive,' he suggested. 'I'm sure my good friend Ben Joseph could arrange that easily.'

'I'm in your hands,' Valerius returned casually, and the conversation passed to other subjects.

Drusilla's eyes were often on the Centurion, not from narrow infatuation, but in simple admiration. As host, he conducted himself with ease and dignity. Indeed, equanimity was his predominating quality. She noticed that he treated Felix with great respect, and this touched her deeply. As at Scythopolis, there was a strong feeling of trust in the gathering, and as at Scythopolis its focus seemed to rest in the Centurion.

Marcus Tullus, she thought, was not a big man in the accepted sense; even so he was larger than average. She liked his firm chin, his straight and definite nose, even his greying hair, but there was something else, something intangible, a breadth of being, in fact the very equanimity she had first discerned. It was compelling.

Next to Marcus Tullus was the tall reclining figure of her brother, talking to the Ben Josephs in his amiable way. An aristocrat who actually behaved like one. Just like Father. At once the deep-lined round of worry rose to cloud her thought, but straight away her mind chose trust.

Cornelia's rescue was never far from the Tribune's thinking. Notwithstanding this, the evening had carried a sense of peace, a rest before the action of the morrow drove him forward. Indeed, it was a quality of which the guests made ample mention as they took their leave.

In the vestibule two legionaries stood guard, one from a troop replacement just arrived from Syria. His name was Marius, a new and eager agent of the Tribune Gallo. Marius listened keenly to the guests as they departed, but he heard no Latin, just Greek and the local barbarous tongue. He was disdainful, and who ever heard of a simple Optio dining with a Laticlavius?

In the morning, before the sun reached its blazing height, Felix, Sarah and the protective Venio walked into the town. Already the elders were seated on the stone paving of the market place, there to receive complaints and arbitrate in disputes. The place was crowded and extremely noisy.

'There's James,' Sarah exclaimed, pointing to the old servant buying for his master's pantry. It was obvious that everyone knew him, and no doubt hoped for his business.

They did not enter the main press of people, but stayed watching from the outside. They in turn were being watched; in fact Felix sensed enquiring eyes at every step as they moved towards the synagogue.

At the door of the synagogue cripples and beggars had placed themselves strategically – hoping for the alms of the faithful, Felix guessed. A Rabbi with his pupils passed by and stopped at the doorway. The teacher's clothes were of a fine woven material, a mixture of light and dark textures. He and those conversing with him were not as the general townsfolk. Professionals, Felix conjectured, but why so many?

As he sought the shade of a large overhanging tree close by, the sound of voices grew strident behind him.

'Damned Romans . . .' Felix heard amidst the rising bitterness. He sensed the hatred rather than the meaning, for his Aramaic was not as good as that of either Lucius or Drusilla.

'All talk . . . talk. . .' Felix listened intently. 'They came by the knife.' The rhythm of the words added menace. They were young voices, but they kept their distance. Having no wish to provoke them, Felix turned casually and moved away. At his side Sarah was rigid with fear, for unlike Venio, who knew no Aramaic, she had understood every word.

No one followed them, and the street, now opening out to its dusty end, was quiet. Close to the crumbling walls of the old town Felix looked back. He could see the synagogue quite clearly, but the scene had completely changed. A large crowd had gathered, and it looked like trouble. They had got away in time. Suddenly he remembered – the Nazarene. Was it him? he wondered. Tentatively he turned, cautiously retracing his steps, but half way down the street he was met by the Centurion's servant.

'You're too late,' he said bluntly, 'he's gone!'

They accompanied the Galilean back to the garrison fort. Venio offered to carry the servant's baskets, but received a sharp refusal. The big man was more hurt than angry, and James, seeing how his blunt words had offended, offered an apology.

'We've got laws about food, my friend. It's nothing to do with you.'

Venio caught the meaning, even though he did not understand the words.

'Will the Nazarene be staying long?' Felix asked. He had been deep in thought.

'The Nazarene! – you mean the Rabbi, the Rabbi Jesus!'

Felix waited without answering.

'When he's here he usually stays a while. Do you want to see him?'

Felix nodded.

'Well, Master Felix, I know the times he appears, so if you come with me in the morning you'll be all right.'

'I should like that,' Felix said simply.

The Galilean took a long, searching look at the dignified grey-haired Roman as they continued towards the fort, but said nothing.

News from Machaerus was imminent, and as the day advanced the Tribune became progressively ill at ease. He was with the Centurion, trying to concentrate on the routine of the garrison, when Ben Joseph arrived, breathless after rushing. It was midday.

'I have arranged a meeting for this afternoon. The Disciple John is coming,' he said, his excitement just under control.

Valerius looked blankly at Ben Joseph, the previous evening's conversation forgotten.

'Oh! Good!' he said, suddenly remembering.

'This is indeed an honour,' Tullus responded. It was plain that Ben Joseph's words had made a considerable impression, and the Tribune's eyes looked for an explanation.

'The Disciple John is one of the three closest to the Rabbi Jesus,' the Centurion explained. 'You are to be congratulated, my friend,' he added, turning to Ben Joseph, 'your agency has been most fruitful.'

'It is what I expected,' Ben Joseph replied. 'The personal legate of the Emperor must be treated with respect, and honoured in the manner proper to his station.' He paused. 'The meeting will be at my villa. I also mentioned that the Tribune's sister, the Lady Drusilla, and the Master Felix may wish to be present.' Then he excused himself. Certain preparations needed his attention.

For the Tribune and the Centurion it was time to take the midday meal, and together they climbed the steps to the roof of the garrison fort, where under a canvas canopy food and drink were waiting. Normally the roof was impossibly hot, but a fresh breeze from the lake had made it practical.

Their vantage point was just a little higher than the surrounding buildings. Valerius could see that apart from the dazzling white of the town every plot of land was cultivated to the full. Towards the hills, however, the earth was rocky and unyielding. There was a liberal planting of trees, but what captured his attention was the deep, deep blue of the lake.

'It is difficult to believe,' the Centurion began, 'that we have violent storms on that watery paradise, but we do. They come from nowhere, it seems, and disappear with an equal mystery.'

'There are plenty of fishermen braving the waters at present,' Valerius commented.

'They have a nose for storms, but even they are caught – here's Felix,' he added. 'Now we can eat.'

The food was simple – local cheeses, with bread and a

generous quantity of fruit. To drink there was either wine or water with lime slices, but Valerius had little appetite. There was too much on his mind, not least the approaching meeting with the Rabbi's disciple. Why, he wondered, did Tullus and Ben Joseph treat the subject with such profound respect? There had to be a good reason, yet men could be strangely illogical in matters of belief. He looked across at Tullus, busy in conversation with Felix. He was always the same, he thought, stable, yet wholly free. It seemed impossible that Marcus Tullus could be prey to any narrow cult. The whole matter was best left until he met the disciple.

'What is the topic today?' he asked, joining the conversation.

'That knowledge is simply recollection,' Felix replied, his eyes sparkling with humour.

'Socrates – the 'Phaedo'!' Valerius responded in mock triumph. 'You see, I still remember – your tuition was not in vain, after all!'

'Yes,' Felix said slowly, pretending reluctance, 'but I'll agree more readily if you defend the premise!'

'A powerful premise, for if all knowledge is recollection, then all knowledge is within us. Am I right?'

'Well,' Felix responded, a wide grin hovering on the brink of laughter, 'you've made a statement. Are you willing to defend it?'

'Willing, yes . . .'

'And able, if I know a father's son.'

All three found the resulting exchange exhilarating, and, for Tullus, a fascinating precursor to the imminent meeting with the Disciple. How would Valerius and his sister respond, he wondered, and Felix, what would his opinion be?

'Felix, you know about the meeting with the Rabbi's Disciple?' he asked.

The old servant nodded. He had met Ben Joseph in the yard, he said.

'Good, we can walk over to Ben Joseph's place together.'

'The Grace of Peace be with you,' the Disciple said as he entered the room.

All rose to welcome him, and the Emperor's legate was careful to follow the example of his host, though for a Tribune of the broad stripe it was unusual behaviour. People rose for him.

The Disciple John was a young man of medium height. His hair and beard were dark, and his finely woven clothes well cared for. Valerius found the total simplicity of his every movement and utterance compelling. His eyes were at peace, and there was something else, something potent, full of qualities yet without a quality, a deeply quiet presence. If this is the Disciple, the Tribune thought, what must the Master be like?

Lime water and sweetmeats were offered, and the Disciple thanked the Ben Josephs for their kindness. He also hoped that the noble Tribune and his party, especially the lady, were not too exhausted after their long journey from Rome.

How gracious, Drusilla thought, how appropriate his behaviour. This was no rough fisherman or farmer. She looked at the Centurion, sitting quietly, his eyes intent upon their guest, and at Felix, who was clearly fascinated by the young Jew. The Ben Josephs, of course, were shining with devotion.

The conversation paused for a moment. It seemed the room itself was waiting.

'Sir,' the Tribune began, 'our good friend Ben Joseph will have explained the nature of my brief concerning your Master the Rabbi Jesus. I might stress that my sole instruction is to enquire. The Emperor, I know, cares little for provocation. So all I need to ascertain is that the activities of the Rabbi do not pose a political threat. And if I may say so, the nature of the Rabbi's Disciple tells me that such fears are groundless.'

The Disciple smiled, the peace in his eyes undisturbed.

'Unfortunately,' the Tribune continued, 'a written report is called for, and, as you know, reports need to be factual. So if you could help me with a description of your Master's work it would aid me considerably.'

The Disciple John looked straight at the Tribune.

'My Master's kingdom is not of this world. Therefore my Master's work is not as the princes of this world.' The Disciple spoke with a simple directness. There was no sense of assertion in his voice, yet his words shocked the Tribune. He had expected the 'other-worldly' answer, as Pilate had described, but he never dreamed he would believe the words he heard. Determined to distrust his feelings, he proceeded.

'May I ask the nature of your Master's kingdom?'

'My Master's kingdom is within you. It is within you and without you. The Kingdom of the Father is spread upon the earth, and men do not see it.'

'Who is the Father?' the Tribune forced himself to ask.

'He who is Absolute.' The answer was immediate, and cut through the Tribune's surface thought to hit a chord of recognition within him. His mind flashed with the Socratic premise he had so recently defended, that knowledge was simply recollection.

He sat upright on his couch, his jaw tight and determined. He did not look at the Disciple as he posed a further question.

'May I ask, what is the relationship between your Master and the Father?'

'My Master has often said, 'I and my Father are one."

The Tribune sat without speaking, the turmoil within him raging. He looked across at Felix, hoping for some lead, but Felix only smiled approvingly. All this happened in the briefest of moments, though to the Tribune it seemed an age. He felt compelled to speak, but still he avoided the Disciple's eyes.

'It is clear that the thrust of your Master's work is in the realm of the gods. Your words hold no compromise, and the claims you make on behalf of your Master are at the frontier of this man's thought,' he said, pointing to himself. Valerius's mind was in turmoil. He had no idea from where his words were coming, but he continued.

'I see no need to trouble you further. The few comments you have made have given me the inner meaning of your Master's message – the outer details I can easily glean for myself.'

He looked up, and again there was shock, for love surged within him as he met the quiet gaze of the Disciple. Managing to control himself, his speech continued involuntarily.

'Sir, the power of your message will not rest easily in some minds. Indeed, there could be violent opposition, and if there are commotions my duty is to act. Meantime, I shall do nothing.'

The Tribune's response was stark, yet strangely appropriate. He knew it was imperative to speak the truth without apology, for the man before him had no use for platitiudes. This course had set him free. He had betrayed neither reason nor the interests of Rome.

'The Tribune is a man of honour,' the Disciple said as he rose. 'I hope that grace will allow us to meet again.'

Their eyes met, and once more love rose within the Tribune, but the turmoil had gone.

The Disciple spoke to each one in turn. He stopped before the Centurion for some time, emphasising how much the community had appreciated his help in the building of the synagogue. Finally he took his leave of the Ben Josephs who were waiting by the door.

'This is a blessed house,' he said, and then he was gone.

They were quiet for some time before the Tribune eventually broke the silence.

'If that was the Disciple, what must the Master be like?' he said, voicing his earlier thought.

Again they fell quiet.

'Marcus, have you heard the Rabbi speak?' Valerius asked, the use of the first name adding emphasis.

'Yes, a few times, though my function in respect of the garrison makes it difficult. However, I have long discussions about the Rabbi's teaching with my friend Ben Joseph and his circle.'

Ben Joseph nodded in affirmation.

'Well, undoubtedly I need to discuss the subject further. Perhaps we can do so over dinner. – Felix, what did you think of the Disciple?'

'I had a strange feeling that he was actually living in his Master's kingdom,' Felix answered reflectively.

A servant entered suddenly, interrupting the conversation. First acknowledging Ben Joseph, he hurriedly informed the Centurion that a messenger was waiting.

Cornelia! the Tribune thought, with instinctive certainty.

Silently they listened as Tullus walked through the door to the outer portico, each footfall clearly discernible. In the stillness the words of the messenger, one of the Roman guards, were plainly audible.

'There is a half-clothed savage demanding to see you, sir. He will not wait, and is full of stubborn insolence.' The sneer in the voice was obvious to Ben Joseph and his guests.

'Soldier, I will decide who is insolent and who is a savage.' The power and authority of the Centurion brooked no argument. 'Bring the man to me at once!'

'Sir,' was the only reply.

Valerius smiled. 'Tullus doesn't miss his target,' he said, looking across at Drusilla, but her eyes were lowered. He could not blame her for her attachment.

Meantime the Centurion had returned.

'Ben Joseph, my friend, you'll have to excuse the noble Tribune and myself. News has arrived from Machaerus!'

As so often at a time of crisis and decision, the Tribune felt calm, and a strong self-awareness accompanied his movements as he rose to follow Tullus. Outside he was briefly introduced to the dishevelled messenger, before all three made for the garrison fort.

Deeply quiet, Valerius had space for questions unrelated to Machaerus.

'Who was that opinionated soldier you spoke to?' he asked the Centurion. 'He seemed uncommonly articulate.'

'Yes, he has a cleverness above the average legionary standard. His name is Marius – a new man, not long arrived from Syria. He also owns a personal slave, which is unusual for a young recruit.'

'Does this not cause resentment amongst the other men?' the Tribune asked.

'No, he shares his advantages liberally, especially with his own tent party, and he never seems to be short of money.'

'Perhaps he has a paymaster!'

'I've thought of that. He's being watched.'

Tullus missed little, Valerius thought. No wonder he had reached the post of Primus Pilus.

The legionaries on guard became as statues as they passed inside the garrison walls, and at the entrance to the main building James was waiting.

'Do you need anything, master?' he asked, with characteristic sharpness.

'Yes, James, this good man needs a generous beaker of wine, and food as well.'

Once they were inside the coolness of the building the messenger was quick to tell his story.

'The beautiful lady is at Machaerus,' he began wearily. 'Herod had arrived a day or so before me, and was already fascinated by his 'new lady', a fascination heightened by the lady's resistance, for she refuses either to speak or to eat.'

'Why?' the Tribune exploded. 'Why hasn't she said who she is?'

'We don't know, sir,' the messenger answered quietly. He was obviously exhausted.

'Then tell him who she is!'

'No, sir – not Herod! – he could loose her in the desert and deny he ever saw her – no!' The messenger shook his head sadly.

'Marcus, that was what you warned – curse him!'

Valerius sprang suddenly to his feet, his arms tightly folded, his lips compressed.

'Continue, continue!' he said absently.

'She is of course held in seclusion, so all my information is from the mouths of others.' The messenger spoke slowly, as if each word had to wait for energy.

'What can we do?' the Centurion asked.

The messenger drank deeply from the wine cup that James had set before him.

'Herod at Tiberias and Herod at Machaerus are two different men. At Machaerus he admits of no ruler other than himself. His whims have full play, and to thwart him is dangerous. It was there the holy 'Baptist' met his end.'

Valerius had heard about the prophet figure from Tullus, but only in the briefest terms. Get to the point, man! he shouted inwardly.

'The only hope is in the person of the noble Tribune himself,' the messenger resumed. 'I see no other way. Only you, sir, have a valid reason to visit Herod. Indeed, you have two reasons. Firstly, there is your function as the Emperor's special representative; secondly, you are renewing an acquaintance – the Centurion told us in his note that you had met Herod in Athens.'

The Tribune nodded.

'It would seem strange for the Tribune to call at Machaerus rather than Tiberias,' Tullus said reflectively, 'though I suppose we could make the excuse of being in the area and wanting to see the famous fortress.'

'There is a large garrison near Jericho which could be a suitable reason for your presence, sir,' the messenger suggested, looking straight at the Tribune.

'It's not that close!' Tullus interjected.

'Leave it to the army. Blurring edges is their speciality.' The Tribune smiled thinly.

The messenger breathed deeply, his exhaustion evident.

'I suggest only a small escort. Herod is very sensitive about such matters.' He paused as if summoning up further energy to speak.

'When you get to Machaerus, sir, you simply allow the normal pleasantries to proceed. Herod likes entertaining his guests, and in the evening, when it is cooler, there will be dancing and music. It is hoped that the girl will 'inadvertently' join the musicians or the dancers. Hopefully she will run to you, or you will simply claim her. Herod will be powerless, for he dare not touch a hair of your head. To injure a Tribune of the broad stripe would cost him his kingdom. He will be furious, of course, and the urge to vent his anger will be boiling fiercely.'

'Yes, and those charged with Cornelia's keeping could suffer the full venom of Herod's rage,' Valerius responded sadly. 'The price of her rescue could be high.'

The messenger sighed. 'We hope not,' he said quietly, but the sense of poignancy was strong. 'You see, all Judaea, if not the whole Empire, will know of the girl's release. Now if her keeper should be punished and the rumour spread abroad, Herod's posture as both a magnanimous and innocent party would be seen for what it was. We will make sure the Tetrarch is advised of the diplomatic dangers, and we'll also tell his wife, Herodias. Her jealousy will be useful, for she will revel in her husband's dilemma.'

'Yes, Herodias is a power to reckon with,' Tullus responded, while replenishing the messenger's cup. 'Tell me, do we suggest advising Herod of the proposed visit? For the Emperor's legate cannot simply arrive.'

'I know. I'm against sending a prior despatch, but if you feel you must, make it short notice. Say it was an impulse.'

The messenger paused, looking at both men in turn.

'The feeling is that Herod is much too astute to be a knowing party to Cornelia's kidnap, and we are certain he left Athens before the news of her capture. What we don't know is how he would react if he should discover, suspect, or be prompted to suspect her identity. As I've said before, he could loose her in the desert all too easily, and then we would be powerless. There are many uncertainties, not least a gossip-filled despatch from Athens, so we have planned to intercept the post deliveries; luckily we have friends in a position to do this.'

The messenger sat back slumped in his chair, his face lined with tiredness.

'You have thought of everything, my friend, but now you need to eat and rest,' the Centurion emphasised.

The Tribune was generous in his thanks, while promising an ample reward.

The messenger smiled and shook his head. 'Success will be reward in plenty,' he said quietly. 'Now,' he added, 'all I can think of is a bath and sleep.'

'Come,' Tullus beckoned, 'James will have a tub prepared.'

Left alone, Valerius was soon busy with plans. The moon was full, so he could travel through the night. An escort of four legionaries would be enough; any more would hold him back, for speed was of the essence. He would take Venio, of course, and a pair of fast two-wheeled carts would serve them well. Most important, he would need gifts for Herod and his wife; that he dare not forget. He could probably address the garrison at Jericho with little prior notice, a useful and necessary cover which would make his 'sudden impulse' to visit Herod just plausible, but only just!

He stood in the centre of the room. In a moment the whole effort of his journey and its preparation would begin. He thought of the Jewish messenger. Who would have guessed at such erudition from the rough, travel-grimed exterior? He and his friends were risking much, and for a Roman! What was more, the word of Marcus Tullus, a Roman too, had been enough to set it all in motion. Tullus was bound in trust to these people. It was self-evident, and Valerius knew the secret. He had been told it, not in words but in experience; the remarkable meeting, just past, with the Disciple of the Rabbi Jesus. The benign force that was helping him was the so-called Messiah cult. The very cult he had been asked to investigate.

Two carts were loaded with food and baggage within the hour, and the horses, fresh and restless, stood waiting, jerking at the reins. The four-man escort and Venio were already seated when Valerius, flanked by the Centurion and Felix, strode from the main building. Without ceremony he climbed into the first cart beside Venio, and at once they were off. He stopped briefly at the Ben Josephs' to see his sister, and soon the carts were rolling again.

At the garrison Felix stood watching by the courtyard gate long after they had disappeared from sight.

Inside the messenger lay asleep.

That evening the Centurion and Felix dined with Drusilla and the Ben Josephs. At first the meal was subdued. The full current of action ran with the Tribune, and it was not unnatural that they should feel, in the waiting, a mood of becalmed impotence. No one mentioned Herod or his fortress Machaerus in front of the servants. Thus the conversation was confined to general speculation about the Tribune's rate of progress and his possible time of arrival at Jericho.

It was Felix who turned the subject to the Disciple and his Rabbi.

'Sarah tells me of the amazing miracles the Rabbi has performed. They appear to defy the natural laws,' he said, looking at Tullus and Ben Joseph for an explanation. They did not respond immediately, and it was Drusilla who spoke first.

'I've always consigned miracles to the realm of the super-natural, but now, as I say it, I'm not at all sure what the word 'supernatural' means!'

'Your father always described it as a pointless play upon the natural, an unnecessary diversion.'

'Like a magical additive.'

'Exactly – and dangerous too, but such practice seems incompatible with the Disciple we met this afternoon.'

The Centurion nodded vigorously.

'You're right, the power of the Disciple and his Rabbi is well beyond the realm of magical tricks,' he said firmly, 'yet the Rabbi's power is awesome. He who was blind now sees; the cripple by the door of the synagogue walks, and the Elder's daughter – wholly cured.'

'Sarah says that faith is vital to it all,' Felix prompted.

'That's true; more than once I've heard the Rabbi compliment the faith of those he healed,' Ben Joseph confirmed.

'How can he do these wonders?' Drusilla questioned.

'By the grace of the spirit,' her host answered quietly.

Drusilla did not seek further explanation. For some instinctive reason she felt it inappropriate.

Felix was the first to leave the gathering. He had an early appointment with James in the morning, he said. They were going to the market. A little later the Ben Josephs discreetly withdrew, leaving the Centurion and Drusilla alone together. It was the first time, and Drusilla was visibly nervous.

'You enjoyed the evening, my lady?' he asked, immediately despising the triviality of his words, and even though his steady voice disguised his feelings Drusilla detected a note of shyness. A surge of warmth flooded through her.

'Marcus, my name is Drusilla.'

Their eyes met, and the unspoken language that flashed between them was too powerful to deny.

As if unseen hands had lifted her she rose and came to him, and immediately they were in each other's arms. She repeated his name. That was all she could say, and the words 'Beloved Drusilla' were his only response.

He pushed her gently from him and looked into her eyes. She was hopelessly lost, and at once they held each other close again.

'Marcus, I hope with all my heart that nothing will ever come between us.' Her voice was muffled against his chest.

'What in the world could come between us?' he said gently.

'Oh, Marcus, I manufacture doubts and make them solid obstacles' She squeezed her arms more tightly round him.

'Let doubts be banished, my lovely Drusilla – come, we'll sit a moment, but I need to go presently, for it's getting late, and I must neither offend your honour nor embarrass your kindly hosts.'

They lingered for a while, and then, kissing her gently on the forehead, he took his leave.

He walked slowly towards the fort, the moon lighting his way. His love for a cultured and graceful woman was requited. He felt complete, and profoundly happy. Above him the myriad stars seemed close and immediate, their twinkling light paling only in the small area about the moon's magnificence. This evening would ever be a beacon in his memory.

He thought of Valerius, driving hard in his desperate haste, and the misery of the girl trapped in Machaerus arose to temper his elation.

CHAPTER ELEVEN

JERICHO

At the selfsame time when the Centurion was returning to his quarters the Tribune was approaching Scythopolis. The same moon, the same canopy of stars felt close, like one vast witness in which it seemed his every thought was under observation. Occasionally the whine of a jackal magnified the stillness. The sound was like a crying child – disturbing, full of distress.

'They come down to the Jordan to drink,' one of the soldiers said.

When changing horses at Scythopolis the soldiers did not reveal the Tribune's identity, and they resumed their journey quickly. Venio seemed tireless, and the four legionaries were excellent material, he thought. Tullus had given him his best men.

The sky was tinged with the first light of dawn when they stopped at Alexandrium for the next change of horses. Again the Tribune kept his presence secret, and again there was no delay. As they left, the sun rose in all its splendour, covering the distant hills with a shimmering mantle of pink. The scale and majesty of the scene was magnificent, and for a moment Valerius forgot his tiredness.

The heat grew with the rising sun, until by mid-morning it was oppressive. The bleak, rocky terrain, reflecting the intensity of the light was merciless on their eyes, and the water-bags, reflecting their thirst, were almost empty.

The horses' pace was slow, and their efforts painful; nevertheless they reached Jericho before midday and went straight to the garrison headquarters. At this stage Valerius was at the mercy of circumstance. He could not force his will. In any case, parading soldiers in such heat was inadvisable. It was a pity, though, for his review of the Jericho garrison would have been a useful talking point with Herod. Visiting Jericho was one thing, but addressing the legionaries quite another, and a much more valid reason for his presence. Notwithstanding, he was resolved to leave for Machaerus within three hours.

The garrison Commander was a man of few interests outside the army. He did not like his posting and he did not like the Jews. At best they were sullen, at worst ungovernable fanatics, he told the Tribune, but when pressed he knew little of their customs. The wrong man for such an area of sensitivity, but Valerius was grateful for his lack of prying curiosity and his ready compliance with the wishes of a senior officer.

The Tribune could address the men immediately if he wished, was the Commander's reaction when Valerius broached the subject. There was a large shed open on all sides, he explained, used as a general area of shade. It would be ideal.

Valerius was amazed. Indeed, everything seemed perfect, until the Commander revealed that Pontius Pilate was present in the town.

'The Procurator has promised to visit us this afternoon, so we are doubly honoured, sir. Have you met him?'

'Yes – only a few days ago in Caesarea,' the Tribune answered tersely. 'I must send my respects at once.'

Pilate's presence in Jericho was disastrous, for he knew he could not leave for Herod's fortress without paying him due respect, especially when relations between the Procurator and the Jewish prince were strained.

To the Commander the Tribune's preoccupation seemed natural, a moment's reflection, for Valerius disguised his turmoil well. In fact he had decided to act. He would address the legionaries at once. Again, a message would be sent to Pilate suggesting an immediate meeting, and when that time arrived he would decide a course of action.

The conditions for the Tribune's address were poor, as the bright sunlight surrounding the large, pillared canopy made men like silhouettes. Yet it went well, and there was little restlessness. He was beginning his conclusion when the shouted interruptions came, just as at Cyrrhus, the same timing, but being weary and preoccupied he had forgotten his past

83

troubles, so when the shouting came his reaction was spontaneous.

He laughed. It was involuntary, a bursting release of tension, but to the assembled legionaries convincing and articulate in its unspoken language. In the sudden absence of tension he felt almost drunk with weariness. The journey from Capernaum, the anxiety and now the dilemma over Pilate's presence had all combined to sap his energy.

'In this job you get all sorts of questions and assertions,' he said, thumping the wooden rail of the podium. 'The hazard of the platform!'

A feeling of ease and detachment pervaded him as he scanned the rows of faces close to the podium. Then he began to speak, his words free and certain.

'To slander the personal legate of the Emperor is to slander the Emperor, and to slander the Emperor is to slander yourself, for the Emperor, as Princeps, stands for us all. You, the Army, are the guardians of his rule, your order and discipline the sinews of the state, but the true bond of Rome is the bond of honour. Behave with honour and you will serve the Emperor and the people under your protection. The Empire is not an armed camp – long live the Emperor!'

Suddenly his address was concluded, and immediately he began descending from the platform.

'That's a real Roman,' someone said, loud enough for most to hear, and at once cheering echoed round the pillared canopy.

There was much on the Tribune's mind as he walked quickly to the Commander's quarters. For one thing, the charge against his father was common knowledge; Gallo no doubt had seen to that; but his chief concern was the presence of Pilate.

He soon learned that the Procurator had not acknowledged his greeting. The discourtesy angered him, and at once he sent Venio with a second message. Then he waited, listening distractedly to the Commander's polite conversation, all too well aware that precious time was slipping past. The Commander must have noticed his impatience, but he made no comment and asked no awkward questions. He was discreet, Valerius thought, even to the point of eccentricity; not even a mention of his father's treason charge or the shouted interruption of the address.

At last Venio returned with a note from Pilate's assistant. The Procurator was unwell, it said, and regrettably unable to meet the noble Tribune.

The Tribune's first reaction was one of unbounded relief, and his second one of amusement. Pilate's illness was diplomatic; otherwise he would have sent Maximus or one of his close aides in person. Certainly the tone of the message was curt. He guessed that Gallo's persuasive powers had been at work when, no doubt, he had reminded the Procurator of the help he had received from Sejanus.

After instructing Venio to prepare for their departure he returned to his conversation with the Commander.

'Perhaps you can send a message on my behalf wishing the Procurator a speedy recovery.'

'Of course, sir.'

'By the way, when did you last see Pilate?'

'This morning, sir.'

'And he seemed well?'

'Yes, sir.'

'I see,' Valerius said dismissively, his mind on other things. 'I hope to return to Jericho,' he continued, 'either tomorrow or the following day. However, I may decide to go north by way of Philadelphia and Gerasa. Should the need arise, I can be contacted through the Chief Centurion Marcus Tullus at Capernaum.'

'Tullus!' the Commander repeated in recognition.

'You know him?'

'Everyone knows Tullus. He was the hero of a near-disastrous ambush three or four years ago, when his presence of mind and courage saved many lives. I expect you know of this.'

'No, I don't. Tullus wouldn't say, of course, and I suppose everyone else assumed I knew.' The Tribune's voice was full of interest.

'After the incident he was called to Athens or Rome, I can't remember which, and when he returned he settled in

Capernaum. By right he should be retired in some administrative post, but again, you'll be aware of this,' the Commander concluded hurriedly, as if he had overstepped some limit of discretion.

'Well, thank you, my friend. My admiration for Tullus has new food to feed upon.'

It was mid-afternoon when they left the ancient oasis of Jericho. Almost at once the wilderness and its heat surrounded them. Journeying south to join the road from Jerusalem to Philadelphia they were able to move quickly. Then, as they crossed the Jordan with the Dead Sea on their right, the road began to deteriorate, becoming little more than a track. One of the soldiers knew the route and was explicit in describing the difficulties, but the most relentless enemy was time, and the Tribune soon abandoned hope of arriving before sundown.

There were still uncertainties and impending decisions that would not allow Valerius to rest. Would the carts stand up to the relentless battering of the journey? Could they change horses at the approaching oasis? There were no reports of brigandry in the area; he had learned that at Jericho, but the doubt remained. When should he send a messenger to Herod advising him of their arrival? He would make a decision after they passed the oasis. By all the gods, he was tired! His health, he concluded, was the one uncertainty he had not considered.

CHAPTER TWELVE

THE JUGGLER

A t the very time when the Tribune's cart was bumping along the ill kept road towards the oasis, Drusilla, escorted by the Centurion, was exploring the centre of Capernaum.

'You're popular,' she said to Tullus, after seeing the many times he was greeted.

'We work closely with the Elders, and often act on their advice.'

'And you built their synagogue.'

'We Romans are never happy unless we're building.'

Drusilla laughed. 'There's truth in that.'

'And there's our handiwork,' he said, pointing at the white stone of the synagogue. 'Do you see that tree?' he added, continuing to point.

Drusilla nodded.

'That's where I heard the Rabbi for the first time. I'll never forget it – never!'

'What's he like?'

'In the ordinary sense – ordinary, but there it ends, my dear Drusilla, for when he feels the need to speak, or even look, you sense a being of enormous power.'

'After seeing his Disciple yesterday, I can understand!'

'Good evening, sir,' someone called as they passed.

'Who was that?'

'Zechariah, one of the Elders,' he replied.

They stood for a moment watching the bustle of the market. It was best seen in the morning, Tullus said, when it was full of fresh energy. For Drusilla, however, the market suddenly linked with Athens and Cornelia's abduction, bringing back the full horror of the situation. She shuddered, but intent on the scene before him, the Centurion did not notice.

They walked on to the small, simple harbour, to find little activity other than children playing noisily, and a few fishermen mending their nets. Some fishing boats were lying off the shore, the chatter of their crews drifting across the mirror-like lake. The smell of fish was strong.

'Marcus,' Drusilla said very gently, 'can we go home now?'

Tullus looked at her anxiously, but she smiled reassuringly. They were in the public eye.

James was there to welcome them.

'Five despatches have arrived, Master. I've left them on your desk. There are four for the Tribune and his party, and one for yourself. That's what they told me.' His voice was as usual sharp and quick, but there was warmth in his smile for Drusilla.

She said nothing until they were alone.

'Dear Marcus, I'm sorry, but the market reminded me of Cornelia.' She put her arms round him and squeezed tightly, almost desperately.

'Is there anything else, Drusilla?' he asked, feeling the dampness of her tears.

'No, Marcus,' she answered innocently as her emotion subsided.

'Are you sure?' he pressed.

'Yes,' she murmured, comfortable in his arms.

'I wonder where Lucius is now.' she continued.

'If he escaped from Jericho promptly he'll be about two hours from Machaerus,' he answered quietly.

Her arms tightened round him. The very name Machaerus was full of menace.

'Your brother carries the mantle of the Emperor. He's quite safe.'

Gently they released their embrace.

'Trust, Drusilla, trust is our ally.'

'The very thing I find so difficult,' she said sadly. 'But you help greatly, Marcus,' she added, the light of her smile suddenly brilliant.

'When you smile like that the sun grows dim!'

'Flatterer!' she chuckled.

She watched as he sorted through the five roll despatches lying on his desk. There was one for her.

'It's from Father,' she mouthed. She hesitated, afraid to open it, and then she did, tearing the seal aggressively. Quickly she scanned the content. It was the last item – trust Father! The Emperor had graciously dismissed the treason charge as ridiculous.

'Marcus, Father is safe,' she said, sighing with relief.

He turned to her; again her face was full of light.

A firm knocking at the door demanded their attention. It was Cornelius.

'The messenger who brought the despatches from Caesarea is still here, sir, and would speak with you. He came with an escort, so it looks important.'

'I'll see him immediately,' Tullus answered. 'Perhaps you can wait next door for a moment,' he said to Drusilla. 'When I've seen the messenger I'll escort you to the Ben Josephs'.'

She kissed him on the cheek and turned to leave. As she did so she saw the Centurion's own despatch lying open on the desk. It was from Rome, she noticed, but she made no comment. It was her secret.

The messenger was direct and specific. He had an urgent despatch to deliver into the hand of the Tribune Valerius or a responsible officer where the Tribune was quartered. He had merely obliged the army by bringing the other letters.

On receiving the roll, the Centurion looked carefully at its cover, but there was no hint that revealed the identity of the sender – Tiberius, he guessed; it was his style. At once he placed it with the others in his letter rack, taking special note of its position. No one else could possibly find it, he concluded.

After escorting Drusilla to the Ben Josephs, he returned quickly to his quarters. His course of action was simple. He would send the special despatch through the night to Jericho. Three mounted soldiers would suffice – with the garrison so dispersed there were few to spare – and with a frequent change of horses they could reach Machaerus by mid-morning. Thankfully, the Tribune would also get the news about his father. Vital news to sway a wavering Herod.

Summoning the men, he sat down and absently scanned the room. Suddenly he sat up, stunned with shock. There was an empty space in the message rack. The special despatch was gone. For a moment he looked unbelievingly at the slot where the roll had been.

He called immediately for James, but James had seen no one enter; neither had Cornelius. He looked at each man in turn, including the three soldiers chosen to make the journey to Machaerus. They were men to trust, so he told them what had happened.

'Someone was watching me, and saw me put the roll into that space,' he said, pointing to the empty spot. 'How else could they have known which roll to take?' He gestured loosely at the maze of paper and roll messages. 'I want the new recruits from Syria watched and their movements investigated. Whoever took the roll had less than half an hour in which to do it – no one is to leave the garrison without my permission, and we'll have to watch the boiler furnace; the thief may try to burn the message once he's read it. If there's anything suspicious, let me know immediately – who's at the gate?'

'Marius,' Cornelius answered.

'That lets him off.'

'A pity,' muttered James, bringing smiles to their faces.

'Wait a moment!' the Centurion interjected. 'In that position Marius has power to let people in and out – is anyone with him?'

'Old Quintus,' one of the soldiers said.

'Good – Cornelius, have a word with him, and make sure it looks casual.'

'How could the thief have seen you, master?' James asked, when Cornelius and the soldiers had left.

'Through that loose trellis,' Tullus answered, pointing to the opening into the courtyard. 'Keep your eyes and ears open, James,' he added. He could see that his old servant was concerned.

'They'll blame you, master!'

'Perhaps,' the Centurion responded quietly. 'James!' he added briskly, 'I need to send a messenger to the Tribune, but with this new situation I can only afford one man. Whom should I send?' The Centurion was almost playful in his attitude.

'Someone young, master – Septimus, maybe, the one who's always practising the javelin?'

'Right again!' the Centurion responded, his laughter close.

With deliberation James sat down opposite the Centurion, his habit when a pronouncement was imminent.

'We've just lost a message from some head man,' he began, his eyes burning amidst his sun-scorched features. 'It was brought by three horsemen, and that doesn't happen every day. It must be important – probably from the old man on the island. I'm a Galilean, so I don't know why I'm worrying, but you just sit there with a wide grin on your face. You're mad, master!'

'Don't be fooled, James – there's a devil inside me!' he said, moving towards the door. 'I must organise the Machaerus despatch immediately.'

Once alone, James began to search his master's office. Maybe he had dropped it on the floor. It could well be, he thought in his salty way, for that woman had turned his head. He crawled about the floor, searching diligently for some time, but he found nothing except a small spherical piece of marble, which he pocketed automatically.

The Centurion was at the Ben Josephs' and just about to eat when James was announced by one of the servants.

'Marius's slave is missing, master!' was his terse message.

'Of course! Of course! The very one we forgot,' the Centurion said, slapping his couch with exasperation. 'I'll come with you at once.'

Master and servant walked quickly.

'Is Marius's slave the one I've seen amusing the men with tricks and juggling?' the Centurion asked.

'He is,' James answered bluntly. Suddenly he stopped and dived into the midst of his rough clothing. 'I've got proof, and here it is. I found it in your office, master – one of the trickster's bits!' In his hand lay the small ball of marble he had picked up from the floor. He smacked his lips with satisfaction.

The Centurion fingered the little stone pensively as they continued.

'James!'

'Yes, master.'

'I'm concerned about Master Felix. He seemed unusually quiet and withdrawn this evening. You were with him in the morning. How was he then?'

'He saw the Rabbi! That's what's wrong with him,' James said tartly, confident of his diagnosis.

CHAPTER THIRTEEN

MACHAERUS

The Tribune and his escort were now on the track that spiralled upwards to the fortress Machaerus. The last hint of evening light had all but gone, and the dark mass of the mountain on which Machaerus sat rose before them. Totally exhausted and walking by their carts, they grimly started the ascent. Some time earlier the Tribune had sent a soldier ahead to herald his arrival. It had been an arbitrary decision, for his tiredness had left no energy to debate the points of possibility. Furthermore he had been overcome by an attack of dizziness. It was his old complaint.

The track was well defined by the moon's light, and there was no need for torches. Half way up they stopped to rest. The wind had freshened, carrying with it grains of sand and grit gathered from the parched, desolate slope. Valerius turned and looked back in the direction of the Dead Sea. He thought he saw the glitter of reflected light, the moon on the water, but it was probably imagination.

There were lights, though, when he looked again towards the summit; dancing points of light, moving down the slope towards them. Then they saw the torches blazing in the wind, and the shadowy forms that bore them.

The two parties were within hailing distance when the Tribune recognised Herod striding in front of his retinue. It was eastern hospitality at its best, he thought, and everything in his family training willed him to respond with equal generosity and reveal his purpose, but it was only sentiment. He knew such innocence would be utter foolishness, indeed a madness.

'My dear Valerius, what an honour!' Herod's greeting rang with enthusiasm.

'Noble sir, I am touched by your welcome, but I must apologise for this late arrival – an impetuous decision, I'm afraid.'

'Spontaneity, my friend – a happy quality!'

Herod was full of talk as they climbed the slope together, and in his weariness the Tribune was content to listen.

'It's just like Athens, and guess who's here as well,' Herod enthused. 'The Tribune Gallo!'

'Is he?' Valerius managed to say, barely disguising his shock. Gallo's presence was disastrous, for no doubt he would be a willing messenger of Cornelia's kidnap. Or maybe not, for if he were involved he might well hold his tongue. Another uncertainty, he concluded.

Herod must have sensed the Tribune stiffen when he mentioned Gallo. If so, he affected ignorance, and the words flowed on.

'He would have come with us to greet you, of course, but he was sleeping, and I didn't like to disturb him. You Romans can't cope with our rich Galilean wine,' he added jokingly. 'Well, my friend, you and your escort will need to bathe and rest. Later we will have some food, and then our dancers and musicians will be on hand to entertain.'

'That is most kind,' Valerius responded with pretended enthusiasm.

They had reached the top, and the dark bulk of the fortress walls rose before them.

Having bathed, the Tribune slept fitfully for almost an hour. Then, accompanied by Venio, he descended the stone steps from his quarters to join the gathering in the main hall. He had almost reached the foot of the staircase when a further attack of dizziness froze him immobile. He waited, holding desperately to the rail, until it passed.

The strong symptoms of his old illness frightened him. Would he collapse and ruin the chances of Cornelia's rescue? Would he be able to cope with Gallo's invective? Again, there was the wily Herod, and the need for vigilance. The Tetrarch would know about his father, for Gallo would have seen to that. Yet he had been given an elaborate reception. Perhaps Herod's clever mind had seen the treason charge as spurious. His body was beginning to perspire – another symptom. Doubts raced in triumph over reason. Then words from childhood rang in his mind. He could almost hear his father's voice.

'Step by step, Lucius. Each step will be a beacon for the next.'

At that moment Herod spotted his approaching guest. He paused in his conversation, and instantly the general buzz of talk was hushed. All eyes were on the Tribune. They saw him tall, restrained, striking in the simplicity of his toga. For a moment no one spoke. Herod's wife, Herodias, was fascinated. In a fluid movement she sat upright on her couch. A tremor of emotion ran beneath the surface of her poise.

'My dear Tribune, welcome! welcome!' Herod's voice boomed out.

Valerius was immediately engulfed by the gathering, and after the introductions were over he was escorted to his couch on Herod's right – the position of honour. Next to him was Herodias, and then the steward Chuza and his wife Joanna. Gallo was on Herod's left, and then came the Tetrarch's favourites, rich merchants and landowners from Galilee and Perea. The couches were in a shallow arc, facing the ornate tiles that marked the centre of the hall, and all about them flickering tongues of flame danced from the myriad lamps and torches, their light giving a blazing life to the rich tapestries that hung on the high walls.

Only Valerius wore the toga, as Gallo, his fellow Roman, displayed a brilliant robe similar to the courtiers' apparel. It was a gift from Herod, a flattering and princely gift appropriate for the friend of the great Sejanus. The Tribune noticed that the steward Chuza and his wife were alone in the modesty of their dress. They reminded him of the Ben Josephs, and instinctively he felt them as his allies in Cornelia's rescue, though he was careful not to show his feelings.

Herodias quickly engaged the Tribune in conversation. She found him fascinating, knowing that he came from the highest level of Roman society. Gallo was nothing, and, if she wished, an easy prey to her advances, but Valerius was a prize fit for any woman. His patrician manners were measured with quiet dignity, and his aloofness was modified by an underlying warmth. Herodias was excited.

The sophisticated intimacy in her voice and movements did not leave the Tribune unaffected. However, to encourage her was unthinkable, yet he knew that any blunt rebuttal of her charm could spell danger. He had no wish to make an enemy of such a wilful woman.

Tables laden with food were placed before them, and a stream of carriers continuously added to the abundance. Under Herodias's sharp eye the servants fluttered nervously as they bore dishes of lamb, freshly cut from the sizzling carcase.

Herodias nodded, indicating that all was ready, and the Tetrarch acknowledged the grace of the great God in words acceptable to his Roman guests. With a flourish he sampled his first sliver of meat. The banquet had begun, and praise for its bounty was on every lip.

The silver plate handed to the Tribune was beautifully wrought, and his gilded goblet, full of Galilean wine, a wonder. A wonder, too, was the spread of food before him; abundance heaped upon abundance, but he was not hungry, for a feeling of nausea had accompanied his dizziness, yet he had to play the grateful guest.

His indifferent gaze scanned the mound of pomegranates, the grapes in their generous heaps, the greens glistening with oil, the olives, the dates and figs. The round flat loaves of bread were still hot from their baking. Close to the bread was a large dish of olive oil. There were cheeses, of course, and sweetmeats to tempt the palate, as well as honey from every corner of the Tetrarchy. All this fuss for a few mouthfuls, he thought. Nevertheless, he allowed himself to be guided by Herodias, who suggested lamb, along with bread briefly dipped in oil.

Slaves with wine beakers were constantly in attendance, and as the meal proceeded the general clamour of the conversation grew.

'Valerius, any news about your father? I hope that all is well.' Gallo's voice sounded above the rest.

Anger, rather than words, rose within the Tribune. He made to speak, but a flurry of dizziness stopped him. He gripped the couch tightly, and the large figure of Venio moved even closer to his master. The delay in his reply had drawn the attention of the guests, and all were waiting for his answer.

'No news, I'm afraid,' he said, as graciously as he could, but an atmosphere of awkwardness remained, and at once Herod moved to smooth the matter over.

'The charge against your father must come from some eccentric source,' he said easily. 'I'm sure the Emperor will dismiss the charge as foolish.'

'My sentiments entirely, sir,' Valerius responded, and with that the general conversation resumed. As usual, he thought, Gallo had sown his seed of doubt, but with little real effect. Indeed, for a time the Tribune was puzzled, until he realised the simple fact – Gallo's audience was Herodian, not Roman. For them the intrigues within the Senate were on a distant stage.

The dizziness had passed, and questions from Herod and Herodias, along with polite interjections from Chuza, kept the Tribune engaged in conversation. There was no mention of Cornelia's abduction, and Valerius assumed that either Herod did not know, or if he did he had resolved to keep it secret. Certainly it was not public knowledge, otherwise some expression of sympathy would have been obligatory.

On the opposite side from Valerius, Gallo had attracted a circle of attention. Laughter was frequent, for the friend of Sejanus was entertaining. Gallo, of course, displayed no overt opposition to the Tribune. Like Valerius, he said, he too was the servant of the Emperor.

Herod applauded the professed unity, though he was well aware of the forceful undercurrents. It was not his place to take sides, for he, as a client prince, would have to deal with Rome, regardless of the ruling party. He had shown Valerius, as the Emperor's legate, every honour, making him first in the hierarchy of guests. With Gallo, however, he played the bosom friend, the friend of long nights and late drinking, and the friend of the whispered confidence.

Herod's even-handed approach was not lost on the Tribune. Indeed, he admired the Tetrarch's skill. Herod was politically astute, yet not a man to always calculate, for the partner to his cleverness was passion.

'I believe your sister is staying at Capernaum,' Herodias said, interrupting his thought. 'She must be our guest at Tiberias when we return.'

'She would be pleased,' the Tribune replied, knowing the opposite to be the case.

'It must be very quiet for her,' Herodias continued, 'that is, except for the saintly troublemakers.'

The Rabbi and his disciples, Valerius surmised.

'And who are they?' he asked, pretending innocence.

'Oh, there is a Rabbi who claims he's God, and he excites the people with Messianic hope. I keep telling my husband he should rid himself of such troublemakers, but he won't listen!' Herodias emphasised the last words.

'Herod never listens! – what slander is my good wife perpetrating?' the Tetrarch asked, joining the conversation. His manner was full of humour, but his words contained a bitter edge.

Diplomatically the Tribune outlined Herodias's opinion, but as he spoke he caught a fleeting look of fear in Herod's eyes.

'He is a Rabbi, my dear, and when you strike a Rabbi you strike the people. You had your way when we struck the Baptist down, and little good that did!'

'It stopped his raving!'

'Herodias, my dear, you simplify things,' he returned with studied tolerance, though he was obviously annoyed. 'You see, Tribune,' he added, 'our tradition is full of prophets and preachers. It's in the blood of the people.'

'Superstitious blood,' Herodias retorted disdainfully. 'Tribune, there are some who actually believe that the Rabbi just mentioned is the Baptist reborn.'

The Tribune nodded politely. The messenger at Capernaum had mentioned the 'holy Baptist'. Obviously he had been a strong religious figure.

Herod did not react to his wife's provocation. Instead he turned to the steward Chuza.

'Chuza, you have met this Rabbi; what is your opinion?'

'He has performed many good works, I'm told,' the steward said quietly, but he ventured no further opinion.

'My treasurer is, as always, circumspect.' At that Herod laughed, and took the chance to change the subject.

What a complex character Herod was, the Tribune thought. A clever and able politician, modern in his perception, yet a man still swayed by superstition, for he had been troubled by the mention of the Baptist's second birth.

The main meal was over, and the servants had cleared the

tables, but the wine still flowed. The crucial time was fast approaching, he judged. He felt his heart beating strongly and tension began to grip his stomach. So far no dizziness. He beckoned Venio.

'Tap my shoulder when you see,' he breathed. There was no need for further explanation.

'You're not too weary, Venio, I hope,' he said aloud.

'No, master.'

As the musicians assembled, Herodias seemed to grow more talkative, but he dared not show impatience. His eyes scanned the harpists, while he nodded and made appropriate responses. Next came the horns and trumpets, then the flutes. Cornelia had learned the flute.

He felt a light tap on his shoulder, and there was Cornelia, plainly visible. Her eyes turned towards him. He stood up.

His cry, 'Cornelia' and her rush towards him were simultaneous.

'Master Lucius,' were her only words, as she clung to him and he held her until her sobbing ebbed away.

'My dear, sweet girl,' he said, looking at her intently. Each seemed to drink the other's joy.

Suddenly the Tribune was aware of the silence.

'Tribune! what does this mean?' Herod's voice sounded distant, as if from another world.

Valerius turned at once to face his host's black anger, but now that Cornelia was safe his full power came to him.

'This sweet girl is my sister's companion,' he began, his gaze unflinching. 'She was criminally abducted in Athens, and now by the grace of the mighty gods I've found her.' He continued to focus on the Tetrarch, his eyes unwavering as he watched desire battle with political reality on Herod's face. Slowly the darkness began to lift.

'My dear Valerius, we had no thought of this!'

'Of course, my friend, you were not to know,' the Tribune said dismissively.

'Why all this concern for a slave?' Gallo's drunken words were heard by all.

The Tribune froze, his anger boiling. Slowly he turned to face his enemy. Again there was no sound.

'The Lady Cornelia will be adopted by the good merchant Demetrianus of Antioch.' The Tribune's clipped words rang defiantly.

'In the circumstances a better wager than Valerius,' Gallo reacted dully, his eyes glazed with excess drinking.

The Tribune's anger turned quickly to disgust, but it was Cornelia's renewed distress that made him turn away.

'Master Lucius, I'm grateful, very grateful, but I'd rather be a slave than leave my lady or yourself,' she managed to say, her voice choked with emotion. Clearly her terrible ordeal had left her weak and vulnerable, for it was not in her nature to be demonstrative in public.

For a moment he held her closely, feeling the warmth of her shaking body.

'Dear Cornelia, no one will force you to do anything. You'll be with Drusilla in a few days' time.'

Standing back, he looked at her for what seemed a long time. She was very beautiful. It was as if he was seeing her for the first time.

The whole assembly was mesmerised by the drama taking place before them. Both conversation and movement were stilled, and tears ran down Venio's cheeks unashamedly.

Herod broke the spell at last.

'My good steward's wife Joanna will see that the lady is cared for according to her wish.'

The Tribune nodded in approval.

'Rest well, my dear. I'll see you in the morning,' he told her gently.

As she walked away she turned to look at him, her eyes full of adoration.

Suddenly everyone was talking.

The Tribune returned to his couch and the knowing smile of Herodias.

'That was a fortunate coincidence, Tribune,' she said with a note of amused detachment. 'I've often noticed that the Roman stoic is much more demonstrative than we hot-blooded easterners.' Her look was not unfriendly.

'Madam,' he said, bowing slightly in acknowledgement. She was a clever woman.

Herod's mood was no mirror of his wife's urbanity. He failed to hide his coldness, and his eyes had the same frozen fixity the Tribune had observed in Athens.

Behind his frozen look Herod's mind was busy. Had he been tricked? He had, he thought angrily. Yet it had appeared innocent. Too unusual to be innocent! he countered. But who had let her out? – for no one had been able to make her talk, eat or co-operate. Who, then, had persuaded her to join the musicians? Were there traitors in the fortress? If so, he would make them plead for death. His mind raced on. Now he understood the so-called impulsive visit, but he kept returning to one basic question. Why had Valerius not asked him directly about her whereabouts? Either the Roman did not think he knew, or he did not trust him! Would he have released her? He smiled to himself. She was a pretty thing, and the desert was large. Yet there were many creatures just the same. Yes – he would have let her go! He inclined his head towards the Tribune.

'I suppose you never dreamt you would find the girl in this place, Valerius,' he said easily.

'I knew she was transported to the east, or so I was told in Athens. However, knowing her origin, I assumed her captors would sell her beyond the borders of the Empire.'

Herod pretended not to understand and asked the Tribune to continue, and he, sensing that the Tetrarch was testing him, reacted not with caution but with annoyance. Yet he restrained his impatience.

'The writ of Rome is more sacred within its borders than without, or at least it should be,' he said briskly, shooting a quick, involuntary glance at Herod. The effect of the unthinking gesture was instant, making the Tetrarch switch to the defensive. Had the Tribune questioned his loyalty to Rome? Immediately he made his position clear.

'I am a loyal friend of Rome. That is well known, and if I'd guessed her identity . . .' He gestured elaborately with his hands. 'But she wouldn't speak or eat! How someone persuaded her to join the musicians is a mystery!'

'My friend, don't worry. What happened happened,' the Tribune said reassuringly. He had no wish to antagonise the Jewish Prince, for even though he was a fox, he was a useful fox to Rome. 'If I'd not been here this evening,' he continued calmly, 'you would have realised the truth when news of her abduction reached your ears. But even if Cornelia had not joined the musicians I should naturally have sought your help and advice at tomorrow's formal session.'

The Tribune's voice had a note of finality, which Herod accepted.

The musicians were in place, waiting. The Tetrarch nodded lazily, and they began. He sat back, reclining deep into the rich, patterned cushions, his mind in turmoil and oblivious to the music. The whole event was grossly embarrassing, and soon would be the gossip of Rome, and any punishment of the girl's keeper would belie his generosity. Damn! he thought, would he ever be his own master? His fists tightened in exasperation.

The first strains of music had hardly begun before the Tribune was almost overcome by sleep. He pinched himself, ate grapes, but the heaviness in his eyes was overpowering.

'You're tired, Tribune.' The voice of Herodias seemed to come from a tunnelled distance.

'Forgive me, the magical modes are much too soothing.' He smiled, grateful for the stimulant of conversation, but the music seemed endless and the effort to keep awake painful. Through his glazed half-vision he noticed that Gallo and Herod were exchanging confidential whispers. Meaningless mutterings, he surmised, for Gallo looked incapable of anything else.

Then all at once the music stopped, and the musicians filed out, except for a drummer and a single flautist. Herodias excused herself.

'The dancing is about to begin, Tribune. You will excuse me? I find the eager eyes of the men distasteful. I can tolerate one man's eagerness, of course!' Her thin smile was like a wisp of silk. Then, acknowledging her husband, she retired.

Gallo began to revive as the dancing grew more spirited. He sat on the edge of his couch, clapping and foot-tapping to the rhythm, his eyes glistening as he followed the lithe movements of the dancers. Impulsively he rose to imitate them, his interpretation vigorous and passionate.

Herod was greatly amused, and tears of laughter ran down his cheeks. He turned to Valerius to share his amusement, but he was fast asleep.

'Tribune!' The Tetrarch nudged his sleeping guest, 'you cannot sleep while such talent plays!'

Valerius shook himself. 'Your hospitality and your Galilean wine, my good Tetrarch,' he murmured in excuse.

By now Gallo was in full cry, whoops of support echoing in the high roof. Then suddenly he collapsed onto his couch, totally exhausted.

'A prodigy!' the Tetrarch shouted. 'More wine!'

Once more the cups were filled.

It was time for the last solo dance. Herod quickly scanned the circle of his guests, and on seeing the lined weariness on his steward's face he dismissed him with a casual wave. Chuza bowed to his master and the Tribune and withdrew, but no one seemed to notice except Valerius. There were good points in the complex mixture of Herod's personality, he thought.

A girl stood in the centre of the hall, vibrant with energy, her posture defiant as she waited for Herod's sign to start.

She began with a slow, deliberate beat which she articulated with a pronounced stamping of her foot and a jerked movement of the arms. Gradually the beat accelerated. All attention was on her supple figure, fashioned to near perfection. Naked desire lit the men's eyes – Herodias's aversion was well-founded. The pace quickened, until the girl's body glistened with perspiration. Then came the frenzy, and the last impossible peak. Suddenly it was over.

The girl collapsed at Gallo's feet, drained of energy. There was no surrender in her eyes as she looked at the man before her. Her act of submission was the will of Herod, not hers. She was Gallo's prize.

The adulation of wine-loosed tongues drowned the sound of her gasping breath. Then quickly she rose and left the hall.

The dancing and the girl's submission had filled Gallo with a new, bellicose energy. He wanted to practise his invective, and to him Valerius was the obvious target. The desire was boiling, explosive.

'My generous friend,' he began, addressing Herod, 'we

must allow Valerius some time for a blissful couch with his lady flautist.'

Herod's response was thin and frozen.

'Easy, my friend, easy,' he said quietly.

The Tribune just managed to restrain his anger, but Gallo was undeterred.

'You ought to enjoy yourself while you can, Valerius, for fortune is a fickle thing. Your father knows that well.'

'To Hades with you, Gallo, hold your tongue!' the Tribune exploded.

'Ha! I've drawn blood. The paragon can speak.' Gallo was growing reckless, a wine-soaked recklessness.

Valerius made to speak, but another fit of dizziness checked him. Encouraged by the Tribune's hesitation, Gallo staggered to his feet.

'Come, let's dance, my paragon,' he taunted, leering at the Tribune.

In an instant the huge figure of Venio stepped before his master.

'Trust Valerius to hire an ox as his servant,' Gallo muttered, swaying wildly, but the arms of Herod were there to steady him.

'Calm, calm, my friend,' Herod said, while guiding Gallo to his couch.

'I want to dance with my paragon,' he protested, but he sat down listlessly in dull obedience.

The Tribune's dizziness had begun to clear when he heard the welcome sound of Herod's voice bringing the proceedings to a close.

'This has been an evening to remember,' he boomed. 'We've seen both the dignity of Rome,' he said, bowing to the Tribune, 'and her playfulness.' His elaborate gesture indicated Gallo. Then a servant interrupted him. It was obviously something urgent.

'Send him in at once,' he responded loudly to the servant's whispered message. Then he turned to Valerius.

'Tribune, a rider has arrived with despatches for your hand only.'

The Tribune watched uneasily as the messenger walked

stiffly towards him. Long hours of hard riding had taken their toll, he guessed. He was one of Tullus's men – he had seen him with the javelin – but what were his messages, and who were they from? His father, Lamia, maybe, or even Tiberius, and one from Tullus, perhaps? A quick glance showed that the main roll was from Rome, the Governor Aelius Lamia, the other from Tullus. Quickly he scanned Lamia's brief message, then he read it aloud to Herod.

'This is great news, Tribune, but not unexpected. May I tell my friends?'

Valerius nodded.

'The Emperor has dismissed the treason charge against the Tribune's father,' he announced loudly in Greek, and shouts of congratulation echoed round the hall. 'There's more, there's more,' Herod bellowed, holding up his hand.

'It's the Emperor's joke. He says 'he's no longer worthy to live if Valerius hates him.' Clearly the great man's way of ridiculing a spurious charge. My friend, congratulations!' he added, slapping the Tribune on the back. 'Wine! more wine! We must raise our cups to the Senator and the wisdom of the Emperor.'

The toasts were noisy and enthusiastic, and Gallo played his part with surface charm. The news had sobered him, but it also left him cold and angry. Valerius was an intolerable obstacle to his plans.

It was late and dawn was not far off, and after thanking the Tetrarch for his generous hospitality the Tribune withdrew to his quarters, followed by Venio and the messenger. He would read Tullus's letter in his room, he thought, then sleep at last.

At the insistence of Joanna, Venio woke Valerius after what had been a few hours' fitful sleep. She was concerned for Cornelia, whose nightmares had been constant.

'She's had little rest, sir,' she emphasised when the Tribune received her. 'Such a reaction often happens when an ordeal is over. I've tried to calm and reassure her, but you, Tribune, can do more than any number of strangers.'

Valerius nodded, watching Joanna intently. She was a good deal younger than her husband. A motherly lady, he thought,

104

whose round, placid face exuded calm, yet there was something else very familiar in her voice and actions, but he could not remember what it was.

They went to Cornelia's room immediately, and as soon as he entered she ran to him, obviously distressed.

'Master Lucius, please take me away from here!'

In his arms she grew calmer, and quickly the awareness of her longing grew to dim her nightmare memories. She moved from him, her face flushed.

'Master Lucius, this good lady stayed with me all through the night,' she said, looking at Joanna.

'Madam, that was most kind.'

Joanna said nothing, but her open tranquillity had an eloquence deeper than words. A sudden welling of love rose within him, and the strong sense of familiarity returned. Yes, of course, he almost said aloud, the Disciple.

His heart was open as he turned towards Cornelia, and she, adoring him, was full of light. The feelings that engulfed him were impossible to deny. Embarrassed and confused, his eyes sought refuge in the patterned rug covering the floor.

'We will leave as soon as possible after the formal talks with the Tetrarch are over – about midday, my dear,' he added softly.

The Tribune excused himself, leaving the two women alone, and for a moment nothing was said. Then Cornelia began to weep silently.

'Oh, madam, what am I to do? What am I to do? I love him. I cannot help it. I love him. I love him,' she cried, abandoning her pent-up secret to expression. 'I am a slave, and even if I were a freedwoman it would make no difference, for he is . . .' her sobbing choked the rest.

'My child,' Joanna said kindly, 'be patient, he will find a way.'

The talks between Herod and the Tribune were jovial and friendly. Herod was pleased with himself, for he had played his part well. Thankfully, Gallo's glib advice had not influenced him, as Valerius was anything but politically dead. The letter in the night was ample proof of that. Frustrating though it was, he had accepted the loss of the girl as an irreversible fact. Anyway, it was a small price to gain the confidence of the Emperor's personal legate.

He was even more gratified when the Tribune stressed his key position in the area.

'Tetrarch, you know the border well, and what is more, you know its politics, and again, you are an excellent representative for the Roman cause – a role that could expand.'

The eyes of the two men met, and Herod knew the Tribune meant his words. He was elated.

As Valerius had anticipated, the meeting ended at midday. Gallo had already left, and the Tribune, Herod and his steward Chuza shared a light meal together.

'I expected Gallo's eyes to be like pomegranates this morning,' Herod said jokingly amidst the general conversation, 'but no, he was full of energy as usual – what a character!'

'Did he say where he was going?' Valerius asked.

'Not directly, but I gathered from one of his aides that it could be Philadelphia.'

At last it was time to go, and Valerius excused himself to prepare for his departure. In the courtyard of the fortress his two carts were waiting, along with a four-wheeled covered cart provided by Herod for Cornelia's transport. It was the final irony.

His mission was complete, but the Tribune was under no illusion. Without the mantle of the Emperor he could have done little.

CHAPTER FOURTEEN

QUMRAN

They were accompanied by Herod's cavalry escort during the descent from the fortress mount – it was the Tetrarch's last gesture of hospitality – then suddenly, almost brutally, they were alone amidst the barren scrubland. Already it was oppressively hot, and already the Tribune regretted pledging his word to leave in what was the heat of the day. Yet there was little alternative if he hoped to reach Jericho before night-fall.

The party was divided over three carts. In the forward cart were two of the soldier escort. Then came Herod's covered wagon carrying the Tribune and Cornelia, with Venio in the driving seat, and in the following two-wheeled cart were the other two soldiers and the messenger, his legs still raw from his hard ride to Herod's fortress. Because of this, the Tetrarch had insisted on sending his own messenger to Capernaum with the good news concerning Cornelia.

In the covered cart the Tribune and Cornelia had much to talk about. She told him the detail of the kidnap and the jour-ney east, and he listened with obvious aversion. They looked after her well, she said.

'Thank your beauty, Cornelia, not them!' he reacted bit-terly. 'You were valuable merchandise! But tell me, why did you not tell them at Machaerus who you were?'

'They threatened to do terrible things to my lady your sister if I spoke about myself.'

'Your kidnappers?'

'Yes – they said they had eyes and ears everywhere. I should have said, Master Lucius, my lady may be in danger – I had an awful dream about it last night!' The distress of the morning had returned to her face.

'Don't worry, Cornelia. They've got their money; that's all

107

they wanted. The threats were meant to keep you quiet in case Herod took cold feet, but once he parted with his silver . . .' He shook his head. 'Drusilla's not in danger – what else did they say?'

'They said I would be isolated in a solitary place if I revealed my origin!'

'That wasn't idle,' he grated.

'My position was so hopeless that I wanted to end . . .'

'Cornelia!' he interjected. The thought of her taking her life horrified him.

'Master Lucius!' she reacted, startled by the power in his voice.

'Don't call me Master Lucius!' he said sharply, but he apologised immediately. 'I'm sorry. My name is Lucius. 'Master Lucius' on your lips makes me feel like some . . .' he hesitated. 'Like some slave-minder!'

She looked at him, her eyes full of love, but he did not dare to meet her gaze, as his feelings of affection were too powerful, too new, and in the circumstances much too dangerous, for the law forbade their union. To many, of course, the answer would be simple. She could be his mistress, but he shrank from the thought. How could he even contemplate such a relationship when she was little less than a daughter to Drusilla. It was unthinkable. The gods were conspiring, he thought, but there had to be a way – there had to be. She was so beautiful, so sweet in nature, yet he had taken her for granted. She had been Drusilla's girl, always there, though never really noticed. Now it was different – wholly different.

He sighed. By all the gods, he was tired. The heat, the jolting of the carts, the strain of the days just past, and above all the lack of sleep, were having their effect, but the muzzy agitation in his mind would not give him peace to rest. He was worried about the missing despatch reported by the Centurion. It was embarrassing, to say the least, for in its loss the overtones of incompetence were obvious.

At the oasis by the Dead Sea they changed horses as before. Valerius and Cornelia, glad of the break, at once alighted from their cart, but it was much too hot to walk about. They refreshed themselves with well- diluted wine, their every movement watched by curious villagers – Cornelia's broad-brimmed hat exciting giggles from the girls.

'They're like a prince and princess,' Venio said to one of the soldiers.

'Ay, it's natural to them,' he responded.

There was no time to linger, and soon the carts were rolling again. They had not long started when Cornelia asked Valerius about his journey from Athens.

'And you must tell me all about your speeches to the legionaries, Mas – Lucius,' she added shyly, blushing with embarrassment It was the first time she had addressed him without the prefix 'Master', and it carried powerful emotions.

He laughed, hoping to ease her awkwardness.

'I'll certainly tell you about my various follies, but before I begin there's one curiosity I should like to satisfy. How did they get you to join the musicians? You were apparently not given to co-operation.'

She did not answer immediately, and he, assuming an indiscretion, quickly added his apology.

'No, no, I was only wondering where to begin.' She paused again. 'I think I sensed something a day or so before you came, for the lady who stayed with me last night visited me in my room. She said nothing, but I knew she was different from the rest. Then another came and asked me if I played a musical instrument. She seemed very kind, so I said I played the flute. That was all that happened, until the same lady came, handed me a flute and whispered 'Gracchus' in my ear. I had no difficulty in co-operating then!'

'How are you feeling now?'

'A little tired.'

'I'm amazed you survived the ordeal so well.'

'The Valerian stoicism!' she quipped. She could not tell him that her energy came from the joy of being in his presence.

He laughed lightly.

'Our secret weapon – that explains it!' He laughed again, watching her wide-brimmed hat with affectionate amusement as it flopped with the movement of the cart.

Suddenly Venio reined the horses as the two-wheeled cart in front toppled to the side, its right wheel shattered. A legionary was lying injured, his face twisted with pain, and at once the Tribune was at his side. His arm was broken, and there was little Valerius could do but firm it with splints. Cornelia dressed his abrasions, and then, after a generous mug of wine, he was helped onto Herod's four-wheeled cart. They were ready to go, but waiting for Venio.

'There's something strange, Master Lucius,' the big man said as he climbed into the driving seat. 'Wheels don't break like that – too clean,' he added.

'They've taken an awful pounding.'

'Even so, it's odd, Master Lucius.'

Venio had moulded his behaviour around the example of Felix, and the use of 'Master Lucius' was a case in point. He had asked permission, though. In one way it amused the Tribune, but in truth he was impressed by the sensitivity and devotion of his physically large servant. The once rough dock-hand from Ostia had changed dramatically.

The pace of the carts was slow and frustrating to the Tribune, but he could not force the horses in the heat of the wilderness. His impatience was a symptom of his tiredness, a painful tiredness in which his responsibilities felt oppressive. The suffering of the soldier beside him, the roll despatch lost at Capernaum, his relationship with Cornelia. Thoughts circled endlessly. Then came a moment of dizziness. He gripped the bench seat until it passed. He despaired, for the dread of his debilitating illness drew on well-worn mental patterns. In the past it had taken months to recover. Gods, preserve me from disgrace, he pleaded fiercely, from his mission ending before it had begun. He winced at the thought. A little pressure, they would say, and Valerius gets a headache.

Again the dizziness returned, but this time he came to with his head in Cornelia's arms and the anxious face of Venio looking down at him.

'Keep going, Venio,' he urged, 'it's this stupid dizziness, that's all.'

He tried to get up, but his swimming vision forced him back. They made space for him, and he lay cushioned against the erratic movement of the cart, yet the dull excitement that possessed him would not let him sleep.

110

Suddenly there was a crashing noise behind them, accompanied by shouts and the sound of frightened horses.

'What's the matter, Venio?' Cornelia reacted. She could not see behind because of the piled baggage. But Venio had gone already to investigate, and there was no reply.

Valerius, aware of trouble, tried to rise and failed. Frustration surged through him until it seemed his head would burst.

'Trouble with the other cart,' Venio reported briefly. 'We'll not be long.'

Cornelia could hear the big man's voice sounding above the rest, but her main concern was focused on Valerius and the injured soldier – getting them to drink, wiping the Tribune's forehead. She was fully occupied, a blessing in its way, for with the weeks of stress she herself was close to breaking point. It was best that she was busy.

'What happened, Venio?' Valerius asked from his horizontal position when the big man climbed once more into the driving seat.

'We've lost the other cart, Master Lucius.'

'The other one!' he interjected, but his voice was weak and thin.

'Yes – one of the pins failed and the wheel came off – the cart's wrecked, but no one was injured, and the men are riding as cavalry.'

'But we checked the pins!' the Tribune reacted.

'Yes, but there are certain tricks,' Vanio returned. 'The carts were tampered with – I'm sure of it, Master Lucius.'

'What about the wagon?'

'Perfectly sound, sir.'

Even to the tired and troubled mind of the Tribune the conclusion was obvious. Herod was innocent, for why offer a perfectly sound wagon to transport Cornalia and at the same time tamper with the other two. It failed to make sense. Gallo, of course, had left early and would not have known that Herod had offered the four-wheeler. As usual there was no firm evidence, but if Venio was right, and he probably was, Gallo – or a Jewish zealot, though he doubted that – was very anxious to stop him. If it was Gallo, why the violent urgency?

Then he remembered the missing despatch – stolen for the same urgency, he guessed. Gods! His mind tightened with frustration. The humiliation of the loss and its implied incompetence was unbearable, but he did not blame Tullus. He could not bring himself to criticise the Centurion.

He lay back, exhausted. Then, like a taut, leathery veil, something seemed to pull down on him, dark and unseeing. He struggled to be free, his efforts desperate. The same thing had happened once before in Rome.

'Lucius! Lucius! are you all right?' he heard Cornelia saying.

'Yes,' he mouthed, opening his eyes to see her anxious face. He was dripping with perspiration. Suddenly he shivered. She heaped clothes on him, but soon he was perspiring again.

'Dear Lucius, what am I to do?' she said inaudibly, her tears falling freely.

A moan from the injured soldier made her turn. Poor man, she thought, he was close to delirium and his arm was very inflamed. Carefully she dried his face and neck.

'Venio!' she called desperately.

The big man swung round on his driving bench.

'We can't go on like this – we need help!'

'My lady – leave it to Venio, but hold on, hold on!' He could see she was close to collapse.

Immediately, he beckoned one of the mounted soldiers, the old and experienced legionary Atticus.

'Where's that Jewish community you were talking about? Is it close?' he shouted above the noise of the wagon and horses, but it was impossible to hold a conversation as they were.

'I'll get down and lead the horses, then we can talk easily,' he added, jumping from the wagon.

'What's happening?' the soldier asked, jerking his head in the direction of the four-wheeler.

'The master's ill, and our injured friend is beginning to rave. What's more, the lady's at the end of her strength. We need to get them out of this furnace. That's why I asked you about the Jewish place you mentioned. Is it close?' he questioned, looking down at the soldier from his commanding height.

'It's over an hour away.'

'And Jericho?'

'Longer – another half hour, maybe. We don't go as straight as the raven's flight.'

'Too long, too long. What's this Jewish place like?'

'It's clean and it's got guest quarters. I went there once on a routine patrol. It's run by a strict cult. They're not violent, but most think they're crazy, including the Jewish leaders.'

'How crazy? – would we be in danger?'

The soldier Atticus shook his head. 'They're harmless!'

'What's the place called?'

'Qumran – it's down the west side of the Dead Sea.'

'Well, what do you think, Atticus? You've the oldest head amongst us.'

'If things are desperate.'

'They are!'

'It could be the answer, but there's no physician there, and that's vital.'

'But we must get them out of this heat. What if we sent a rider to Jericho now? He'd be much faster than the four-wheeler, and if the physician used a chariot he could be at this Qumran place not long after us.'

Atticus nodded. Up ahead he could see the outline of the ruined toll-house by the Jordan bridge.

'We'll send a man when we've watered the horses – by all the gods, it's hot! If the underworld is worse than this we'd better mend our ways.'

Atticus did not laugh, and neither did Venio.

After they had watered the horses, the young legionary who had ridden through the previous night from Capernaum joined Venio on the driving seat. His legs, still raw from the effort of the journey, had been unbearably aggravated by the mounted spell since the second cart had collapsed. He too needed medical care.

'What's happening, Venio?' the Tribune asked when he felt the wagon move again, and Cornelia, who had thought him asleep, was startled by the weakness in his voice.

'We've just watered the horses, sir, and we hope to find shelter from the heat within the hour. We've also sent to Jericho for a physician.'

The audible delirium of the injured soldier filled the space before the Tribune spoke again.

'Where is this place of shelter, Venio?'

'It's a Jewish religious community, Master Lucius. Atticus knows the place.'

There was another long pause before the Tribune spoke again. He did not seem to have the energy to think.

'They may have their own physician. Tell the old soldier to enquire when we get there.'

'Yes, Master Lucius.'

The journey dragged on, and to Cornelia only the Tribune's face seemed constant in the swimming confusion. Desperately she held to that.

They turned from the main road and headed south. To the east was the Dead Sea, or the Sea of Asphalt as it was officially called, to the south-west the haze-blurred outline of mountains. The waves of searing heat grew worse, and for a while Venio questioned their decision. In front the two mounted soldiers had wrapped their heads with cloth like the desert people, and round about there was no life to be seen. Still they pressed forward, until eventually the shimmering outline of a low-set building became visible beneath a cliff-like escarpment.

At last the horses drew to a halt, and from his recumbent position the Tribune could hear Atticus explaining their position. The old soldier spoke well, Valerius thought.

'We have sent to Jericho for a physician,' he was saying, 'but the Tribune asked if you could help in the meantime.'

A steady voice answered in perfect Greek. 'Your need is our duty.'

Venio and Cornelia were mesmerised by the scene in front of them. The sun-bleached white of the buildings, the gravel foreground and the escarpment behind blended as one with the flowing robes of the three men waiting to greet them. Their hair and beards were long yet well groomed. They had great dignity, Cornelia thought, a strange authority. Instinctively she felt that they could help.

Their spokesman, clearly the eldest, was grey-haired and the tallest of the three. On his instructions the wagon was drawn closer to what he called the strangers' rooms. His directions were simple and precise. There were no unnecessary

114

words, no elaborate deference as Venio carried the Tribune into the cool of the building. Cornelia followed.

They were ushered into a small room off the main reception area where Venio laid his master down on the bed provided. As he left to fetch the injured soldier, the tall grey-haired man entered – a high-ranking member of the community, Cornelia guessed.

He smiled in greeting, his eyes placid yet keenly observant, and again, as with Joanna, the Tribune was reminded of the Disciple.

'Sir, I am the son of my teacher, and a priest of this community. I have been told you wish our help.'

'That is so,' Valerius said. He could not summon the energy to be explicit.

'The lady needs rest and nourishment,' the priest continued. 'I would recommend the care of one of our families.'

Startled, Cornelia looked anxiously at the Tribune, and he, lifting his hand towards her, closed his fingers over hers.

'Have no fear, my dear Cornelia,' he said quietly, 'you're in the hands of kind and careful people.'

She smiled hesitantly, and then obediently followed after the priest, leaving the Tribune alone, but only briefly, before the huge figure of Venio filled the doorway.

Valerius took some time to collect his thoughts.

'Just one thing, Venio. See there's no trouble when the physician arrives; I don't want these people insulted. And, Venio . . . visit the Lady Cornelia when she's rested. She may need reassuring.'

'Yes, sir.'

'Venio, you've been magnificent . . .' He wanted to say more, but the effort of concentration had exhausted him. Yet he could not rest, as the shame of failure, like a cloud, hung over him. His mission was over. There was no point in thinking otherwise, for he knew his illness too well.

Venio waited uneasily at the Tribune's side, wondering if he had acted rightly. It was a strange place, he thought, and the people even stranger. Nevertheless, his master seemed to trust them, and that, he decided, was good enough for him. When he heard the footfall of the priest returning, he slipped quietly from the room. The priest smiled as he passed. He had kindly eyes, Venio thought. There was no badness in them. At once he felt much more content, even hopeful.

The priest had learned enough facts about the Tribune's illness from Cornelia to proceed without explanatory questions. As he approached, Valerius made to move, but an easy gesture indicated rest. For a time he stood quietly beside the bed. Then, out of the Tribune's vision, he slowly extended his hand until it hovered over the Roman's forehead. Valerius felt its warmth but not its touch. It was soothing. He closed his eyes, and the tense knot that had held his head in active agitation began to loosen and to drift away. Slowly sleep advanced, until of a sudden he dipped into its healing rest.

For some while the priest remained noiseless at the Tribune's side before drawing a light rug over the sleeping form. Then, quietly, he left.

Venio's small room was next to that of his master. It was stacked with the Tribune's baggage. Some items had been dropped as they were carried from the cart, so he thought it best to make a final check in the reception area. There was nothing, however, other than a small leather bag, and not the Tribune's according to his memory. Yet he looked inside. It was better to be sure. The only content was a roll despatch. It was his master's, and plainly addressed to him. Strange, he thought, for he could not recall ever seeing the bag before. Still puzzled, he put it with the rest of the Tribune's papers. He yawned, lay down on the hard bed and was instantly asleep.

In just over an hour he was awoken by Atticus. The Jericho garrison physician had arrived. Venio rose immediately, still feeling drugged with sleep as he waited with the grey-haired priest in the reception area. All at once the physician burst through the door, full of purpose, with Atticus following, doing his best to be respectful.

'We are grateful for your speedy response, sir. The Tribune, I know, will be most appreciative.'

The physician gave a perfunctory nod. He had little interest in the words of a mere legionary.

'Soldier, where is the noble Tribune? I should like to see him now.' He did not disguise his impatience.

116

'I'm afraid our noble master is asleep,' Atticus replied, maintaining his note of deference.

'That is a natural process most people engage upon – soldier, may I repeat myself – I want to see the Tribune now!'

'You can certainly see the Tribune, sir, but I know it would be most unwise to disturb him at this time,' the priest intervened.

'Do you?' The physician's voice was thick with disdain. 'There are four doors here,' he added, turning to his aide. 'Let's start here!' It was the Tribune's room, and Venio, inarticulate with rage, stopped before him.

'You listen . . . to the . . . grey-haired one.'

His voice came in short bursts, and the physician backed away. Venio enraged was a frightening prospect.

'You are obstructing a medical officer in the course of his duty,' he said, but his anger was more pretended than real. He had made a fool of himself, and he knew it. What was more, the big man before him was the servant of the Tribune. He had seen him in Jericho the day before, and the personal servant of a Tribune Laticlavius was best heeded.

'Where is my room, soldier?' he asked Atticus, withdrawing with as much dignity as he could muster.

'The end door, sir. Refreshments are already there for you and your assistant.'

'Right!' he returned sharply, glancing quickly at the priest as he strode off. Peddlers of fakery, he muttered to himself.

Atticus winked at Venio, still simmering with anger, and the priest smiled.

The Tribune slept soundly until the following morning, when he awoke wholly refreshed and without the slightest sign of dizziness. He was amazed and profoundly grateful, and, like unto his nature, he planned to move immediately, but the priest argued powerfully against it.

'You need two days at least, sir, to consolidate your strength.'

The Tribune closed his eyes as if lost in decision.

'The last time I had this trouble it took two years and the best physicians in Rome before it cleared.. You, sir, have cured me overnight. I'd be a fool not to heed you. It goes without saying that I'm most grateful to you and your colleagues.'

The priest smiled, but said nothing. Just like the Disciple, the Tribune thought. The same quiet presence.

'How can I avoid this trouble recurring, sir? – I'm sorry, I don't know your name.'

'My name is Raphael,' he answered. 'Now, as to your first question – you need to punctuate your activity with rest.'

'The very thing I find difficult!' Valerius interjected.

'I mean mental activity, of course, and the rest needs to be regular. For you this is important.'

'How does one achieve such rest?'

'The noble Tribune questions well.' Raphael smiled. 'One needs to rise above the clouds of thought – but there will be time to talk of this within the next two days.'

Valerius nodded.

'My good man Venio tells me that both the Lady Cornelia and the injured soldier are much better – I really am most grateful.'

Raphael's placid eyes responded warmly. 'No doubt your servant informed you of the physician's presence.'

Valerius smiled. 'He did. I've asked to see him.'

'Your servant Venio is a good man, Tribune.'

'Worth his weight in gold – and that would be a ransom,' the Tribune added jokingly.

As the elderly Raphael left the room, the Roman physician entered.

'Well, Lentius,' Valerius began briskly, 'we owe you both our thanks and our apology. Our thanks that you responded so quickly to our call of distress, and our apology that your journey has been rendered unnecessary. We were not to know the proficiency of these good people in medical matters.' The Tribune's tone was matter-of-fact. Again he spoke in familiar terms, having met the physician two days before in Jericho.

The physician was uncomfortable under the Tribune's direct and steady gaze, and felt obliged to confess to a measure of impatience in his behaviour the previous evening.

'Understandable, Lentius, understandable, especially after a long and hard drive from Jericho.' Valerius had no wish to hold an inquest. To him men like Lentius were poor candidates for reformation.

118

'I was fearful, as the reputation of these Essenes, or whatever they call themselves, does not breed confidence,' the physician said in justification.

'The world knows rumour, not their reputation, Lentius – by the way, how is the noble Pilate? I hope he's recovered from his illness.'

Lentius was clearly embarrassed. 'He's quite well, sir, and has returned to Caesarea.'

'Well, Lentius, as you can see, I'm fit and well, and most grateful to these people. If, however, you wish to examine the injured soldier and set your mind at rest, you are, of course, at liberty to do so. But no doubt you will consult with the priest Raphael in the event of any instruction you may wish to give.'

That was enough for Lentius. He had no wish to consult with any long-haired magician.

'I rather feel I should return to the garrison at Jericho. It is, as you know, sizable, and I am kept busy. If I stayed here I should be overseeing the healthy.'

'A sensible appraisal, Lentius. Well, once more, thank you for your prompt response. – Lentius, we hope to arrive in Jericho tomorrow evening, and I wonder if you could arrange that two fast carts be here in time for us to make the journey before nightfall. And another thing, what of the soldier who told you of our trouble?'

'He was exhausted, sir. I told him to rest.'

'Good. Tell him to await our arrival. So, hopefully, Lentius, we'll meet again tomorrow evening.'

The physician bowed in acknowledgement, amazed at the Tribune's graciousness, for he had expected the opposite after the incident with his ox-like servant. Here was a chance to realise his hope of transfer and escape from the nightmare hole called Jericho.

He made his case as plausible as he could, and the Tribune listened, disguising his annoyance. This was the curse the Emperor suffered every waking hour.

'Lentius, my friend,' Valerius began airily, 'put the matter to me when I'm with the garrison Commander tomorrow evening – that's the best way,' he added, certain he would hear no more about it.

As soon as the physician had left, the Tribune went to see the injured soldier and the messenger whose legs had suffered badly. Both were recovering well, and were voluble in praise of Raphael and his fellow priests. Then it was time to visit Cornelia.

She was overjoyed to see him, and quickly introduced him to her hostess. The lady was in her early thirties, and dressed in a similar fashion to the men – a long robe with a girdle. Her hair, caught up in a plain knot, seemed to reflect the simplicity of her small dwelling, where Valerius could see that nothing was superfluous to practical need.

Apologising for her husband's absence, she discreetly excused herself, leaving the Tribune and Cornelia alone.

'Venio sent word that you were better. Oh, Lucius, I'm so happy!' Love shone from her eyes. She turned, walked a few paces and retraced her steps. The liquid grace of her form, the line of her back and her slender waist captivated him, and deprived of expression, the tenderness he felt was painful in its intensity. He closed his eyes. This was not the time.

'My dear, let's take a walk. The morning sun's still low in the sky.'

'Everything here is held in common,' she chatted lightly by his side, 'and it's very disciplined.'

'The spartan dwelling of your hostess spoke of that.'

'They don't go out to seek new members, but should they come there is a long probation,' she continued.

'Your hostess told you this, no doubt.'

'Yes, but I didn't like to ask too much in case it embarrassed her – I wonder why they choose a wilderness like this?'

'Possibly the only place the authorities would allow them land. Though more probably because it's private. No trouble with prying visitors – except for the occasional Tribune Laticlavius and his lady!' he added lightly.

His last words shocked Cornelia, and he saw it. He had made a foolish mistake, as their relationship was so delicately poised that any slip, however minor, could upset the balance. He dared not encourage an impossible dream, for the law forbade their union, a fact they both knew well. Yet he could not dismiss the hope, however tenuous, that he would find a way.

His father would be sympathetic, he would understand, for he had always named Cornelia special.

Cornelia's company was delightful, and he could have spent all day with her, but it was prudent to keep his visit short. So he took his leave, pleading the need to draft despatches to both Capri and Rome. This need was real enough, as it was expedient to tell the story of Machaerus before rumour did it for him. Also he would have to write to Tullus, as he did not intend returning to Capernaum, but hoped instead to tour the border garrisons.

The Emperor's mission was pressing, and now that Cornelia was free, his father vindicated, and by the gods' goodwill his illness cured, there were no impediments. He would tell Tullus of his intentions, and of course there was the missing roll. A decision was required, a simple decision – admit the loss. He could see no other way. Then finally he would draft a letter to his father telling him of Cornelia's rescue and of his son's dilemma, and that he wished, against the dictate of the law, to marry her.

The Tribune was writing when the priest entered the small room. As ever, Raphael showed him all deference due to his position, but with no sense of seeking favour. It was the person, not the broad stripe of the Senate, that received Raphael's attention. The same sense had been self-evident with the Disciple at Capernaum.

'Sir, you were to tell me the secret of finding rest,' the Tribune said with characteristic directness.

Raphael smiled. 'Straight, like the roads of Rome – stillness is the way to rest.'

'Falling still is difficult when thoughts are raging.'

'Practice works wonders, Tribune.'

'You're setting me a task, it seems,' Valerius responded with humour.

Raphael nodded, his eyes reflecting the Tribune's mood.

The bond of respect between the Jewish ascetic and the high-born Roman was tangible, and for the period of the Tribune's stay they met regularly. On each occasion there was a brief discussion, and at each meeting Raphael reiterated the same conclusion. Man had the choice of living in the light or in the dullness of his own proud thought. Light and darkness were Raphael's repeated imagery.

They parted warmly on the evening of the second day, when Raphael apologised for failing to conduct the Tribune round the settlement.

'Community laws, Tribune,' he concluded.

The Tribune was dismissive, while producing a silver goblet from amidst his baggage.

'Raphael, I know you have little use for trinkets and the like. Nevertheless, I hope you will accept this plain and simple cup as a token of gratitude, for, sir, without your help my mission would have ended.'

'The community will find your gift most useful.'

Raphael stood watching and alone as the carts moved off, their wheels crunching their way over the brittle surface. As the noise grew distant he returned to the strangers' building, where he was immediately confronted by another of his patients, a man found near to death in the wilderness.

'I've lost a bag, a leather bag!' the patient said in agitation. 'A small leather bag – like so,' he added, indicating with his hands.

'I haven't seen it, but the party just left may have picked it up in error.'

Raphael watched as the slight, wiry figure before him grew more ill at ease.

'Servius, your recovery has been sudden,' the priest said evenly, 'for only an hour ago you were pleading exhaustion.'

The slave of Marius ignored Raphael's insinuation as he busily searched the reception area – his name was not Servius.

'How can I get to Jericho?' he asked sharply.

'A cart passes the community every morning on its way there.'

'They have a passenger,' the slave returned abruptly. Then words of gratitude slipped smoothly from his tongue.

The Tribune had ample time to formulate his plans and priorities on the journey from Qumran. Paramount was his need to tour the border areas, for both Tiberius and Lamia would be expecting his reports, so the sooner he was there the better. He

122

would need an escort, though – the four-man guard on the way to Machaerus had been a desperate exception. Indeed, the whole question of security needed care, as those who had sabotaged the two carts at Machaerus could try again. He, of course, was not the only one in danger, for Capernaum could be a target. So the garrison would need a supplement of men, especially with those required at the Ben Joseph villa. Again, there was the question of Cornelia's transport. She could not travel on the roads unguarded. So in all, his demands on the Jericho Commander would be substantial.

There was little space for social leisure when the Tribune arrived at Jericho, for the detail of his plans required attention, particularly as he intended to leave by first light in the morning. So supper with the Commander was necessarily brief. The surgeon Lentius was there as expected, and pleasantries were exchanged, but, as Valerius had anticipated, he made no mention of his much desired transfer.

The Tribune excused himself about the twelfth hour, the advice of the priest Raphael still active. The measure of his rest needed to be regular.

The first light of dawn was colouring the sky when Cornelia, accompanied by the Tribune, made her way to Herod's cart. There she was greeted by the old soldier Atticus and an eight-man guard, her escort for the journey to Capernaum.

Helped gently by Valerius, she climbed into the four-wheeler. She turned, and barely holding back her tears, watched him looking up at her. They would not meet again for months. She made to speak, but nothing came.

'I'll write,' he said above the noise of the wagon as it pulled away. They waved, and then he turned towards the train of two-wheeled carts awaiting him.

Cornelia had requested nothing for her journey, and had obeyed the Tribune's wishes without question. Now that she learned of the elaborate arrangements for her comfort, her girl companion, and the number of her escort – she had thought the soldiers were a guard of honour for the Tribune – she was astonished.

'Who arranged all this?' she asked Atticus.

'The master, my lady.'

Valerius had not compromised: he had catered for the one he hoped to be his future wife, and in the letter to his father he was equally direct. She was beautiful, he wrote, regal in her dignity, and more of a patrician's daughter than any he had met in Rome. He wished to marry her, even though the law forbade it. There had to be a way.

CHAPTER FIFTEEN

CAPERNAUM

What the brother had done, the sister had failed to do. Drusilla had hesitated, and a fear that her father would forbid her union with a low-born soldier had trapped her thinking. As the days passed, her fear grew more obsessive. Then guilt entered. She should never have encouraged the attachment, for misery was its only end. Yet, for the moment, any thought of breaking with Marcus ceased each time that he appeared, and each time she resolved anew to stand against her doubts, but they came again, clinging, carrying belief, and using reason, it appeared, to make their case.

She should have confided in Felix, but the stoical habit of fighting alone prevailed, leaving her isolated until she was ashamed to speak. She felt different from others, and their capacity for simple enjoyment seemed out of reach. It had been the same in Rome, though now, in Capernaum, there was a new intensity, spurred by her love of Marcus Tullus. Happiness was present, enjoyment within her, yet it was barred. The strong belief clung, sickly sweet and familiar. She hated it, and to be free she knew she had to sacrifice her love for Tullus, but that she could not do.

At times, especially in his company, she saw the madness of her thoughts. Indeed, something deep within her knew their falsity. Fear, however, held them close; fear of being over-whelmed, and that she could not cope. A grace was given, though; she did not panic.

The Centurion had noticed Drusilla's agitation, but had thought it understandable, as awaiting word from Machaerus had not been easy, and even though the good news had arrived two days before, there was sure to be an aftermath. Weeks of tension did not vanish overnight.

Tullus was about to leave for his usual evening visit to the Ben Josephs when he heard the sound of marching soldiers and a heavy cart grinding to a halt. At once he guessed it was Cornelia.

Atticus was the first to climb from the wagon, and then, with his assistance, Cornelia alighted. Drusilla and Felix had not exaggerated, Tullus thought; she was beautiful. Her features, framed by blond hair, would still be striking in middle age. She had poise and grace, not unlike Drusilla, and with a note of restraint in her bearing that added maturity to her youthful years.

Tullus, realising that the Tribune was not present, moved forward.

'Welcome to Capernaum!' he said in greeting, his deep voice sounding large in the evening air.

'Sir, I'm most grateful to be here, and I'm especially grateful to you, for clearly you are the noble Centurion to whom I owe so much.'

He smiled in acknowledgement, noting the richness of her voice – just like Drusilla's.

Immediately she saw Felix she ran to him. They embraced warmly, tears streaming down the old servant's cheeks.

'My dear, you've changed. You're a beautiful young woman!'

'You've changed too, Master Felix.'

'Are the wrinkles so obvious?' he chuckled.

'No! No! – you're so – so – open.'

'Seeing you, my dear,' he said quickly.

'It's the Rabbi! He's seen the Rabbi five days running!' The mutterings of James the Galilean were discernible only to the Centurion.

'James, meet the Lady Cornelia.'

'James,' she said graciously.

His twinkling eyes acknowledged the greeting.

'Master, Capernaum has a princess,' he added, with his usual flint- like sharpness.

Cornelia laughed lightly.

'We had hoped the Tribune would be with you,' Tullus said, his concern for the missing despatch still paramount.

'Alas, no, he was anxious to start his tour of the border areas, but he's sent you a long letter, and there's one for my lady, too – where is my lady?'

'I'll take you to her. She's staying in a villa close by, which will be your home as well.'

The joy of Drusilla and Cornelia was beautiful to watch. Emotions ran strongly, yet withal there was a gentle dignity about their greeting. This was no meeting of a mistress and her slave. On the contrary, Tullus thought, more like a mother and her long-lost daughter.

Drusilla was full of questions, to which Cornelia responded modestly. Tullus was impressed, for he would have understood if her answers had been breathless and indulgent. However, when it came to describing the Tribune's role in her rescue, her adoration was plainly obvious. Had something happened? for the high drama at Machaerus was a potent setting. Had the seeds of tragedy been sown? Tullus knew the law. An Equestrian could marry a freedwoman, but such a course was not open to the Senatorial order, and he knew of no exceptions.

The news that two carts had been sabotaged jolted Tullus into the present. Battle was engaged in earnest, he thought, but why the violent urgency? He was alerted again, if not astonished, when Cornelia spoke of the visit to Qumran.

'And they cured my brother overnight?' Drusilla reacted, knowing the trouble he had had before.

'Yes, my lady.'

'What sort of people are they?'

'Very disciplined – like super stoics in a way.'

'Do you know about this sect, Marcus?' Drusilla asked.

'Yes – the Community of the New Covenant is a name I've heard them called, and 'super stoics' is a good description. They're noted for their healing powers.'

'Your thoughts are deep, Marcus,' Drusilla observed, sensitive to the Centurion's mood. 'Are you worried about my brother's connection with these people?'

'No, not worried; they and the Essenes further down the valley at En Gaddi are a profound people. There could be some political embarrassment, however, as the Temple authorities in Jerusalem have little love for Qumran, and with cause, for the New Covenant was originally founded by priests who broke away, disgusted by corruption at the Temple.'

She did not question further, for he knew about the strange world of Jewry in a way she did not understand. Then, as if defeating her guard, a shaft of doubt struck her, almost physically, it seemed. Who was Marcus Tullus? Was he one of them? – and working for them? Trying to influence her brother? She shuddered with aversion. What gross ingratitude, she thought, after all his help in rescuing Cornelia. Idiocy, she said strongly to herself, but the stain of doubt remained, and it distressed her greatly. The fear of her inability to cope was gaining ground.

'Are you well, Drusilla?' The Centurion had noticed her discomfort.

'Yes! Yes, thank you,' she answered with embarrassment, but he sensed otherwise, though it was not the time to press the matter.

The Ben Josephs arrived. There were introductions, and the conversation continued, with Cornelia as its natural focus. Suddenly Tullus realised that the Tribune's roll was unopened and firmly clasped in his hand. Excusing himself, he broke the seal and began to read.

'An eight-man reinforcement, and more to come.' Good, he thought, as he extracted the main points. Herod's cart to be returned to Tiberius – a simple task, but what an irony. – The Tribune's itinerary was detailed, an exhausting programme that ignored his recent illness, but the main issue was the missing despatch. Here the Tribune was direct: 'Write, admit the loss, and request a copy urgently.' The Centurion admired the honesty. Nevertheless, the loss of the Emperor's despatch was a devastating admission.

Since the message had been lost his men had scoured the countryside for information, but to no avail. A horse had been taken from the stables, after which the missing slave had seemingly vanished. His owner, Marius, maintained an unperturbed, if not arrogant, confidence. The slave was useless anyhow, he maintained, and not worth pursuing. He would buy another.

The Centurion decided to act on the Tribune's instructions immediately, and bowing to the company he took his leave, but the anxious look of Drusilla troubled him. Something was wrong.

Once in his quarters he drafted despatches both to the Emperor's secretariat and to the Governor Aelius Lamia, writing simply as the Tribune had directed. Two horsemen were selected to take the messages to Caesarea and the Imperial post. It was dark, but the star cover, hanging brilliant in the sky, gave a faint light, enough to follow the road. They could leave at once, but his report to the Tribune could wait till the morning.

He was busy writing to Valerius when Felix entered, breathless with exertion.

'I've found the missing roll, but you must know of this!'

'I certainly don't!' the Centurion reacted incredulously.

'You don't! That's what they said at the Ben Josephs', and I didn't believe them. It's a mystery, but I've found it – I'm certain, for it's addressed to Capernaum, and carries the correct receipt date, no doubt recorded by you – and it's from Capri.'

'Where did you find it?'

'Amongst the Tribune's papers that arrived from Jericho – and he didn't say!'

'No – on the contrary, he lamented at the loss – you're sure, Felix?'

'Certain, Marcus.'

'Was the seal broken?'

'Oh, yes, someone's read it all right, and I read it too, for in the circumstances I saw no point in standing on ceremony.'

'What does it say?'

'Very little, mostly pleasantries, that is until the last line – here, read it for yourself,' Felix added, handing the roll to Tullus.

Tullus mouthed the words until he reached the last sentence which he spoke out loud.

"Make sure the Navy and their ports are loyal to the Principate." – a general directive concluding a rambling and casual despatch – purposely casual, no doubt, but what does it imply, that's the question?'

Felix shook his head. 'Why single out the Navy?'

'Perhaps he wants to use it,' the Centurion said, looking quizzically at Felix.

'For what?'

'To escape!'

'By the gods!' Felix reacted, 'I see what you mean – Sejanus is poised to usurp power, and the Emperor is securing his retreat!'

'Exactly – Syria with its four legions is a perfect power base for an exiled Emperor, as access to the army on the German border would be much too difficult.'

'Pannonia would be difficult as well, and there's no other major concentration of the legions – Hispania, maybe, and there's Egypt of course, with two legions, but Germanicus was the idol of Alexandria, so I doubt if he would choose that option. Yes, Syria, with its four legions, is the obvious place,' Felix concluded.

'It certainly puts the Tribune's role within a different context.'

'A dangerous context, Marcus. We must warn him.'

'Two men will leave by first light . . .'

'It's worrying,' Felix interjected, anxious for his master's son.

'Yes, but Gallo would not dare attack the Tribune openly, for the friend of Sejanus cannot implicate himself in any crime against the Emperor's personal legate. Sejanus would disown him if that happened.'

'Accidents can happen, Marcus – like the carts from Machaerus.'

'Even an accident suffered by the Tribune could spell trouble for Sejanus.'

'He's very powerful, Marcus.'

'But what's his power based upon? – the Praetorian Guard and the so-called friendship of the Emperor, for beneath the smiles the Senate see him as an upstart.'

'He can manipulate the Plebs, and he's got his place-men everywhere.'

'He has power all right, but it's precarious. He's on a pinnacle, a knife-edge, and a feather-weight could push him either way, and if the Emperor reached the legions here in Syria the purple would rest but briefly on his shoulders.'

'That's if the Emperor got here – it's a long, uncertain sea journey.'

'It's a desperate option for a desperate situation, Felix, for if Tiberius left Capri there could be civil war, though I doubt it, as I can't see the German border legions having any love for the Praetorian or its mighty Prefect, but you never know – the promise of a Consulship works wonders!'

Felix smiled wryly. 'What a brood we've hatched from one small sentence – we're better than the Oracle!'

'And without the mystic vapours!'

Tullus bent down and pulled two cords hanging close to his writing table.

'I've just called James and Cornelius, for we've got to move quickly, as it's vital that the messages to Capri and Rome are stopped.'

'Will you send Cornelius?'

'No, I'll go myself,' Tullus answered, adding that he would remain in Caesarea, renew his old contacts, and give them a watching brief on all new navy personnel, including the established staff who showed the signs of sudden affluence.

'Felix,' he continued, 'I'll not have time to write to the Tribune, but you can detail what has happened, and also could you tell the ladies that my stay at supper will be less than short?'

Outside, the stars with their flint-sharp points of light seemed to reach down, close and intimate. The sense of witness was strong, calling Felix from his thoughts, but the thoughts persisted. Tullus was well informed, very well informed, and far above the standard needed for his role in Capernaum. Again, the practised ease with which he planned to set up agents in Caesarea was impressive and certainly not the thinking of a novice.

Felix had reached the villa. 'Good night, sir,' said one of the guards as he went inside.

Not long after, the Centurion arrived, but he had only time to eat a few mouthfuls before his two-wheeled cart drew up outside the villa.

'That's the indomitable Atticus, my usual companion on journeys,' Tullus said with a smile. 'Age and tiredness are unfamiliar words to him – he insisted on coming.'

'A true son of the Army,' Felix responded. 'Never a truce!'

Drusilla accompanied Tullus to the door where she clung to him desperately, as if trying to blot out her doubt and its attendant misery.

'You're troubled, dear Drusilla – what's wrong?'

'Nothing, Marcus, nothing – I'm just a silly woman.'

He looked at her closely, the flickering light of the lamps illuminating her face. There was something wrong, but Atticus was waiting.

'If your trouble does not pass, speak to Felix.'

They embraced again, and then he left her.

Standing alone, she listened to the sound of the cart receding until the faint noise faded into stillness. She was tired, very tired, and all she wished for was rest; to go to bed and sleep, and to forget.

The Tribune abandoned his hope of visiting Palmyra when he received the Emperor's despatch. Instead, he headed for Antioch, and as the days wore on messages from Damascus and Apamea spoke of his progress. Then three weeks passed without communication, and Cornelius, troubled by the lack of contact, sent a three-man team with despatches to the Villa Demetrianus.

It was over ten days before the weary messengers returned, their number swollen by a further three from Antioch. The Tribune and his party were safe and well, they reported, and billeted at the Legate's residence.

A message had been sent to Capernaum, and its non-arrival meant that two of the soldiers were missing. He was greatly saddened, the Tribune wrote, as one of the missing men had been with him since Machaerus. Clearly the roads from Antioch were dangerous, and in future messages would be both infrequent and heavily guarded.

The Centurion had no such trouble. His messages arrived on a near- weekly basis, but he did not use the army as a carrier. Sometimes he employed a merchant, and at other times a simple labourer. He even used a Rabbi once. It was the mark of the professional, and for Felix further evidence that Tullus either was or had been an agent. James had told him that his master had been called to Rome three years before – some

132

time after the famous ambush – but Marcus Tullus never talked of this.

If Tullus was an agent, his work and that of Master Lucius seemed to be as one, for there was not the slightest hint of conflict. This area of the Centurion's activity, although intriguing, was to Felix peripheral to the steady strength that was constant in his nature. To walk with Tullus in Capernaum was an experience, for he seemed to know everyone from the Elder to the street vendor. He did not stand apart from the people, yet he did not forget his dignity, and he never pretended to be other than a Roman, but the townsfolk saw more than a Roman Centurion; they saw a friend, the friend who had helped them build their synagogue. Felix saw ample evidence of this. In the case of the Rabbi Jesus and his disciples, Tullus was wholly tolerant.In fact, he publicly adopted a protective role, not surprisingly, considering his faith in the Rabbi's teaching. Now Felix shared this faith as well.

The first time he saw the Rabbi he was struck with awe. The teacher's message was direct, starkly direct, without concession or compromise. To the proud and self-important he was harsh, but even though his words cut through their ignorance he himself seemed unaffected. It was speech that spoke, not he. He was gentle with the meek, and those with faith received his blessing, but what struck Felix most was the change that he felt within himself. It amazed him that by simply being in the Rabbi's presence a weight of thought was lifted from him, and what was more, his step was lighter.

The day after the messengers returned from Antioch Felix and his daughter Sarah went as usual into Capernaum. It was a beautiful morning. The heat of summer had mellowed to the gentle warmth of autumn, and a slight breeze from the lake brought a touch of freshness. It was idyllic.

As they approached the centre of the town they could see a crowd gathered round the entrance to the synagogue. It was the Rabbi. He was earlier than usual. They quickened pace, and his words became discernible as they moved nearer.

'Why call me Lord, Lord, and do not the things which I say?'

Felix smiled to himself. The Rabbi was very practical.

Slowly he and Sarah edged themselves towards the centre, and for a moment the noise of a nearby farmer's cart drowned the Rabbi's words. Felix could see him now. He had finished speaking and was sitting silently on a stool, his look inclined towards the gravel surface before him. Behind, the Disciple John was standing, alert and watchful.

There was something ever new about the teacher's presence that defied description, yet paradoxically the newness was constant, stable, unshakable, always the same. His eyes lifted and looked straight at the grey-haired Roman. Felix felt exposed, as if his thoughts were visible to all, and, conscious of his awkwardness, his eyes sought refuge from the steady gaze.

'Come!' The Rabbi's voice was irresistible. Felix looked up, full of inner panic, but the teacher's call was not addressed to him. He was beckoning someone else, a crippled woman, bent almost double.

'She's been like that for eighteen years,' someone whispered.

The Rabbi waited while she was helped forward, and the crowd, expecting a miracle, were hushed.

'Woman, you are loosed from your infirmity,' he said when she was close. There was no sentiment in the teacher's voice, none whatever. Then he laid his hands on her, and she rose straight, full of wonder and gratitude.

At once the crowd erupted in exultation, yet Felix remained quiet. True, the healing he had witnessed was a miracle, but the real miracle was the man before him. What he had seen was the natural expression of the Rabbi's power, or his Father's power, as no doubt he would say.

It was difficult to hear amidst the hubbub that followed. Felix could see a rigid-faced man, an elder perhaps, confronting the Rabbi. He heard the word 'Sabbath', and as the crowd grew quiet the man's speech became discernible. There were six days in which to work, and in which time healing should proceed, but not upon the Sabbath.

The Rabbi waited until the indignant outburst had finished, then he slowly raised his head. There was no sense of anger, but his words were arrows, sharp and pointed.

'You hypocrite, do not each one of you on the Sabbath

loose his ox or his ass from the stall and lead him away to watering?

'And ought not this woman, being a daughter of Abraham, whom Satan has bound these eighteen years, be loosed from this bond on the Sabbath day?'

The man, visibly ashamed, did not answer; in fact no one answered. The Rabbi stood motionless, but he did not give the sense of waiting. He was there, Felix thought, just that. Then suddenly he was gone, moving quickly through the crowd.

Felix held Sarah's hand and led her from the gathering. They were a familiar sight to the townsfolk; the grave, grey-haired Roman and his young adopted daughter, vivacious at his side.

'Hello, Senator!' said one of the young bloods as they passed. He laughed and waved at them, and they saluted gravely, at which he laughed again. The townsfolk had accepted him.

As he walked, Felix was aware of a new clarity in his mind. Something had been shifted at the time he met the Rabbi's gaze. He was full of questions, pressing questions. Who was the Rabbi Jesus? Was he god or man, and if a man, what kind of being? What did he mean by 'I and my Father are one' – that he, a Jewish Rabbi was one with the Father, the mighty Jupiter himself? It was too gross an arrogance for flesh and blood, yet there was no arrogance in the Rabbi; authority, yes, but never arrogance. Indeed, his reason had the penetration of a Socrates, and when he spoke it seemed as if the truth itself had uttered.

The Rabbi, of course, was not always in Capernaum, and to Felix this was a growing frustration, so much so that he had resolved to follow him, for why rest idle when the living truth was walking in the land?

That evening at the Ben Josephs' he revealed his intention of following the Rabbi on his journeys outside Capernaum, but Ben Joseph discounted the idea as impractical and danger-ous. A Roman wandering about Galilee unprotected was simply ridiculous. Ben Joseph was adamant. Felix, however was equally determined, and continued to outline his plans. He would need a cart, he said, ideally a covered one, with enough sleeping space for Sarah and himself.

'You can't put the little girl at risk, Felix,' Ben Joseph protested.

'We'll be in the company of the Rabbi. No harm will come our way,' Felix returned simply.

The Roman's plain statement of faith silenced Ben Joseph, and the two men sat quietly for some time before being joined by Drusilla and Cornelia.

'Marcus has arrived,' Drusilla announced. 'He's paying a lightning visit.'

The Centurion looked tired when he entered, Felix thought, though his manner gave no hint of this. As usual his presence seemed to fill the room, and Drusilla could not keep her eyes away from him, but Felix was disturbed to note her look of fearfulness. He had seen the look before during her childhood when doubt and indecision used to freeze her movement.

She laughed, however, when Tullus joked about his experiences in Caesarea, but a sense of humour had always been her saving grace, and as the stories continued, no doubt for her benefit, her laughter grew more free. As usual, Felix concluded, Marcus Tullus was master of the situation. He was wrong. The Centurion was not in control. Indeed, he had been hurt, deeply hurt, by the coolness in Drusilla's eyes.

Wrongly believing her fearfulness contained, Felix's attention returned to the Rabbi and the powerful desire to follow him. Quickly he reiterated his plans to Tullus, while summarising the reservations of Ben Joseph.

'I want to go, Marcus, but I must respect reasonable advice.'

'Our friend Ben Joseph is right. It is dangerous, and the Tribune could be against it.'

'Master Lucius would refer the matter to you, Marcus,' Felix returned quietly.

Drusilla nodded in agreement. 'My brother would never oppose Felix on such an issue.'

'There's a political consideration, Felix, for in the people's eyes the Tribune and yourself are one.'

'I could be investigating the 'Messiah cult',' Felix responded with a knowing smile. 'After all, it is the Emperor's wish!'

'You rogue, Felix!' Tullus reacted. Then he fell quiet, his head bent in reflection.

'I would be loth to prevent any man from following the Rabbi,' he said eventually. 'James could go with you. He would like that, and would be the perfect guide. A legionary guard would isolate you, and reduce you to a figure of ridicule. Indeed, that option would be intolerable. However, to have a knowledge of the people and their customs is a great security, and James has that knowledge, but the greatest security is the presence of the Rabbi himself.'

'If any of my countrymen tell me ever again that Romans are without faith I shall laugh them to scorn,' Ben Joseph said emphatically.

Drusilla had been listening intently. She had heard about the Rabbi from Felix many times in the past weeks, but his descriptions had been distant, like a story. Now, with his decision to journey in the Rabbi's following, a new sense of the Teacher's proximity arose in her mind. It held a strange attraction, but the narrow, loveless world of her isolation soon returned. This isolation had grown acute during the Centurion's absence in Caesarea, when the fear of having to choose between Tullus and her father began to dominate. In fact, her fear had grown to belief. How could a Valerius marry a Tuscan farmer's son? It was not possible.

The conversation over supper was lively, and Drusilla disguised her misery well, but not completely, for Tullus was well aware of her unease. Again, when it was time to leave, he was conscious of how she engineered their parting to be public. The hurt of her rejection was sorely felt. It had happened before, of course, but never with a woman like Drusilla. Their estrangement would be painful, for she was much too close to his heart's desire to be easily forgotten.

By first light the Centurion left for Caesarea. As he passed the Ben Joseph villa he turned and looked intently, but he did not see Drusilla standing in the half-light, there to watch him start his journey. She stood motionless but tearful, bitterly regretting her behaviour of the previous evening. Then, when the last sound of the cart had gone, she went inside.

The following day, Felix, Sarah and James also left. Capernaum was empty, Drusilla moaned inwardly. She felt very alone.

Cornelia, on the other hand, was not oppressed by loneliness. True, she longed to see the Tribune, yet there was a measure of contentment in her waiting, for she remembered clearly the words of the kindly Joanna – 'Be patient, he will find a way'. They still sounded prophetic. However, she was not without uncertainty. How could she hope for union with one who came from the highest level of Roman society? It was an incredible presumption, but hope remained, rooted deeply in those moments of affection that had happened from the instant of her rescue.

She was deeply grateful for the miracle of her deliverance. Indeed, when she reflected on it, her life was little other than a miracle, in its sudden changes from dark despair to fairest fortune. She still vividly remembered the day the Senator brusquely snatched her from the slave market in northern Gaul – the picture of herself shivering on the platform was etched deeply in her memory. She had been bewildered and frightened, a sudden orphan by the curse of tribal warfare. Then there were the Senator's angry words with the merchant. She had been terrified, but this had quickly passed as her amazing change of circumstance unfolded. At that time she had felt, just as now, an overwhelming sense of gratitude.

CHAPTER SIXTEEN

ANTIOCH

As soon as he arrived in Antioch the Tribune renewed his contact with Demos, and each morning they met to formulate their plans and policy. Valerius was direct about the Emperor's instructions to keep the navy loyal, but Demos showed little surprise, behaving as if he knew already. He was also quick with advice, suggesting that the Tribune should become acquainted with the junior officers, both at Seleucia Pieria and at the Legate's Residency. Such men could be bribed by men like Gallo. Again, such men could stir up trouble at the port amongst the sailors and marines – simmering resentment over pay and late retirement were always easy to exploit.

The Tribune acted on the advice of his friend and arranged a series of supper parties, with Demos playing the servant. It proved a useful exercise, and the Tribune's view of things grew clearer.

He was happy with the situation at the naval port. The Squadron Commander and his deputy were steady, reliable men, friends, in fact, and their staff reflected the same sturdy qualities. It was a different picture at the Residency, however. This was the focus of power, the headquarters, a draw for the ambitious, or the sons of the ambitious. The place was full of sycophants, with one notable exception, the Equestrian Tribune Largus – the same Largus who had caught the edge of Valerius's anger when he had first entered Antioch. Largus spoke his mind, though never bluntly, for if he disagreed he did so with a natural charm. The Legate liked him, preferring his independence to the time-serving smiles of his other aides.

Largus was the perfect contact, and the Tribune wasted little time in cultivating his friendship. In doing so he learned much about the Legate. Largus respected the grey, wizened, tense-lipped administrator. The old man, as he called him, was scrupulously fair and not given to bribes, an uncommon virtue well suited to his frugal habits. The Legate was cautious, though – perhaps over-cautious, but there was ample cause for circumspection, Largus said, knowing the rivalries that played within the Residency.

The Tribune Largus became a regular visitor at the Villa Demetrianus, along with the Naval Commander and his deputy. Indeed, all three had come to be close confidants of Valerius. One evening when they were relaxing together they were suddenly interrupted by Demos the Greek. Demos, by now well known to them, did not stand on ceremony.

'Gallo has arrived,' he said directly, 'and has rented the Villa Rufus. His progress through the streets was grand – marked by smiles and compliments for all, and even silver, which he scattered at the gaping Plebs,' the Greek added with flippant cynicism, but his private words with the Tribune were blunt and urgent.

'Tell the Commander to double his guard, for he's an obvious target.'

Valerius relayed the message to his naval friend, but it was too late, for that evening on their way from the Villa Demetrianus the Commander and his deputy were attacked by a gang of apparent robbers. Clubbed from behind, the Commander fell instantly, but his deputy escaped amidst the confused battle between the naval guard and their assailants.

The next morning Antioch was buzzing with the news. All seemed to know before daybreak, and rumour spun fantastic tales. The facts, alas, were harsh enough. The Commander lay unconscious at the Legate's residence, but his deputy was nowhere to be seen.

All day the Tribune sat by the Commander's bed, his feelings a mixture of grief and anger; a frustrated anger, for the attackers had escaped without trace, and again there was no proof of Gallo's involvement. In the evening the Commander regained consciousness, looking at Valerius with transparent openness. There were no words spoken, no thoughts to disturb the powerful sense of unity. For a moment Valerius dropped his vision, but when he looked again the Commander was dead.

The Tribune sat stunned, his eyes closed. Then, rising

slowly from his chair, he went out into the main hall, to find the Legate and Gallo talking.

'How's your slave-girl, Valerius?' his adversary called, his voice puffed up with its usual confidence.

Still shocked by the Commander's death, the Tribune made no reaction, and ignoring Gallo he stopped before the Legate.

'The Commander is dead, sir,' he said flatly. Then, without waiting for a reaction, he strode from the hall.

Valerius went straight to the Villa Demetrianus, and was met by both Demos and Largus.

'The Commander's dead,' he announced in the same feelingless tone he had used at the Residency.No one spoke, for the night before all three had shared his company.

'By the gods, Gallo will pay for this!' Largus said with intensity.

'There's no evidence against Gallo,' Valerius cautioned.

'It's him all right!' Largus returned bitterly.

'Largus, you mustn't be seen to associate with me. It's too dangerous!'

'Don't worry, sir, I cover my tracks well.'

There was a period of silence before Demos spoke.

'There is good news, sir. The Commander's deputy is alive, and here in the villa recovering from a knife wound.'

Again there was silence. Events seemed to be moving in a way that outstripped commentary.

'May I say something, sir?' Demos asked.

Valerius nodded.

'I suggest we keep the deputy's presence a secret – let the Residency believe he's still missing.'

'Demos, what's your plan?'

'It's simple, sir – Largus tells me that Gallo has suggested a well- favoured nominee from Rome as 'acting Commander', that is until the fate of the deputy is known – let him nominate his 'acting Commander', for we'll have the obvious benefit of knowing who he is, and when we know, we can produce the deputy and effect maximum embarrassment.'

The Tribune pondered for a moment. 'Why not allow Gallo's man to take up his post on the flagship – let him go to sea, and then arrest him, far from his sponsor's care?'

'Who would arrest him?' Largus interjected.

'The Deputy!' the Tribune and Demos answered simultaneously.

'By what miracle? – he's here!'

'That's Demos's department!'

'Easy,' the Greek reacted, grinning widely, 'smuggle him on board and keep him there in hiding until the galley's safely out to sea.'

'Where would he hide on a galley, Demos!?' Largus questioned sceptically.

'Disguise him as a sailor,' the Tribune suggested.

'Perfect, sir, perfect – and with picked men on his section.'

'What about his wounds?' Largus pressed.

'Superficial,' Demos returned.

'And his hands – they'd see he was no sailor!'

'Tell him not to wash them for a week!'

'All right,' Largus conceded, 'say the plan succeeds and we arrest Gallo's puppet. Then what? What do we do with him? for ships must come to land!'

'That's the Tribune's department,' Demos said mischievously.

Valerius smiled. 'The longer Gallo believes his plans are working the better – that's the aim,' he began. 'We could bring the captive back to Antioch, of course, and hold him secretly. However, if that was discovered we would look like fools, with Gallo exploiting our embarrassment to the maximum – again, we'd have to hold the puppet's aides as well, and keep that secret!!'

'Yes, that wouldn't be easy,' Largus said pointedly.

'My instinct favours Rhodes,' Valerius continued, 'for I know the Governor would be a ready ally. We could hold him there in mild confinement pending an investigation, and there's cause enough for that. I didn't tell you that the Commander was found with gold on his person, and that any self-respecting robber would have seen it.'

'What will Gallo do when he discovers what has happened?' Largus asked. 'He could be vengeful.'

'Probably, but what could he do? His man is far away in Rhodes, and the new Commander will be guarded like a king. Again, there'll be the inquiry into the late Commander's death.

My guess is that he'll disown his wretched nominee, for his mighty patron wants results, but not publicity.'

'And I thought I was devious,' Largus reacted. 'Beg pardon, sir,' he added, bowing to the Tribune.

All their arrangements proceeded perfectly until the day the 'acting commander' was scheduled to join the flagship for manoeuvres. It was then, on a sudden impulse, that Gallo asked his nominee to transport him by war galley to Caesarea.

The idea greatly amused the friend of Sejanus as he joked with his close aides.

'It's neat, sir. It's neat,' said one of his assistants admiringly.

'With your gift for words, sir, you'll have the sailors and marines eating from your hand within the day,' another said.

'A little longer, maybe!' Gallo returned lightly. 'Think of it – if Valerius wants to follow me he'll have to hire a grain ship,' he added, doubling up with mirth. 'Wine! Wine! let us celebrate!' His hands gestured with enthusiasm.

The elation at the Villa Rufus contrasted sharply with the gloom at the Villa Demetrianus. The Tribune was both furious and frustrated, for his plans were now in ruins. It was his own fault, he muttered to himself. He had tried to be too clever.

He was pacing restlessly when Demos joined him.

'Demos, where's the Deputy?' he asked at once.

'On board the flagship, sir.'

'We must get him away from there immediately.'

'So the plan is off?'

'Of course it's off!' Valerius snapped. 'We can't touch Gallo!'

'That's a pity!'

'Be serious, Demos!'

Both men looked up as Largus entered, but there was no greeting, as the preoccupation was too intense.

'I think our plan still holds,' Largus cut in.

'How can it!' Valerius reacted.

'The 'acting commander' is at Seleucia Pieria preparing for his departure and for the arrival of his patron, but Gallo is still here at the Villa Rufus and won't be leaving for another hour, and what's more, he's celebrating!'

'At this time of the morning!' the Tribune reacted.

'He's got a copper stomach – but his aides haven't!'

'Who told you this?' Demos questioned tersely.

'I've just come from there! I've been drinking with them!'

'Brilliant! – what a man!' the Greek exclaimed admiringly.

'What's your plan, Largus?' the Tribune barked.

'Send false orders to the 'acting commander'. Tell him to go to sea immediately, and inform him that the Tribune Gallo is now travelling by road.' Largus continued filling out the detail until Valerius eventually nodded his approval. 'If we could delay Gallo in some way. In fact we must delay him,' he said finally.

'Leave that to me,' Demos said confidently.

'Remember, Demos, no violence to the person,' Valerius cautioned. 'The battle is beneath the surface!'

'He'll only have a headache, sir. – there's just one passage from the Villa Rufus. I'll organise a festival to block the street.'

Both Demos and Largus rushed off, leaving the Tribune to agonise. There were many uncertainties, and Largus in particular was putting himself in considerable danger.

Largus looked, as he was, a handsome Equestrian officer from a wealthy family, but his youthful, boyish face belied a steady nerve, a penetrating mind and a will like steel. Gallo, though he did not know it, had an implacable enemy, as Largus blamed him unreservedly for the death of the Commander, a man he had revered. Certainly appearances were misleading, and Largus was the perfect proof. He was an incredible find, but so was Demos, though it was the other way – Demos had found him!

The Tribune had long since assumed that his Greek friend was a secret agent, serving the sleepless eye of the state. There had been many knowing looks and inferences, but silence had become the rule on the subject.

Time was slipping past, and the Tribune's anxiety was mounting. What was happening? he wondered desperately as he paced the room, watched by the ever attentive Venio. Then he sat down. There was nothing he could do but wait.

Demos had gambled on Gallo's love of pleasure, and he was

right. A garland of flowers presented by a pretty girl was enough to capture him, and at once his angry impatience at the crowd blocking his way evaporated. Accepting a beaker of wine, he stepped from his chariot, and his assistants, ever anxious to please, did nothing to restrain him. Only one of his confidants persisted, and he dismissed him casually.

'Don't worry, my friend. There's time enough, and it's good public relations.'

'What public relations can you have with the dregs of Antioch?' the aide muttered in exasperation, but Gallo was beyond the reach of common sense.

Demos, fearful that the drunken celebration might not work, had also enlisted the help of a wealthy merchant, a man grateful for past favours. The merchant was well known, and Demos had further gambled that Gallo would be gracious should he meet him casually. Luckily the merchant's villa, the Villa Sidon, was nearby, and the meeting did occur, exactly as Demos had anticipated.

When the waiting had become almost unbearable, the boyish face of Largus appeared at the door of the Tribune's quarters. The messages had been sent, he said, and their authorisation forged.

'By whom?' Valerius asked.

Largus pointed to himself. There had been no time to find an expert, he said.

'Will it work?'

'It has to, sir. Well, I'm off to join Demos's party and to play at drunken friendship with the enemy!'

The Tribune smiled to himself. Gallo had met his match. He sighed deeply, discovering his tiredness as his tensions eased. He thought of Capernaum, and the image of Cornelia was at once before him. The strong desire to see her quickly moved to a decision. He would turn off for Capernaum on his way to Caesarea, but his journey south depended on the movements of Gallo, for he was determined to keep the friend of Sejanus within his view, and this very day was no exception.

'Venio, prepare the covered cart and assemble the guard for immediate departure. We're going to the port.'

The Tribune arrived at Seleucia Pieria well ahead of Gallo, to learn, with much relief, that the squadron had put to sea, but the news that one of the galleys had hoisted a flag elated him. This was the pre-arranged signal. The plan had worked, and the Deputy was now in charge.

Valerius kept well within the dark interior of his covered cart, allowing a servant of Demetrianus to ask his questions. Venio, of course, would have been recognised. The Tribune was also well clear of his guard, whom he had posted close to the Navy administration building. In fact his covered cart was anonymous amongst the transport wagons of the quayside.

It seemed a long time before Gallo eventually arrived, leaning heavily against the rail of his chariot, and sullen from his excess drinking.

The chariot and the following line of carts came to rest on the narrow quayside, dwarfed by the tall warehouse buildings. The Tribune had placed himself well, almost too well, he thought, but he and Venio were safely out of sight, and the servant of Demetrianus looked innocent enough.

Immediately on stopping, one of Gallo's aides approached the sailors on guard at the entrance to the Navy's pier. The sailors held back, except for one who wore a head bandage that covered an eye.

'They've gone, sir,' the sailor said respectfully, in a heavy Greek accent.

There was something familiar about this sailor, Valerius thought, as he watched intently. The covered cart was catching the words well, and he could hear easily.

The sailor's message passed back through the inebriated ranks until it reached Gallo.

'Gone!' Gallo's voice was unmistakable.

The Tribune tensed.

Suddenly awake to the situation, Gallo jumped from his chariot to confront the sailors. His powers of recovery were amazing.

'Where have they gone?' he demanded.

'To the sea, sir,' came the naive reply.

'Sailor, your grasp of fact has a devastating profundity.'

146

'Thank you, sir.'

'The Navy are always courteous.' Gallo shot a sidelong glance at one of his men, who exploded with suppressed mirth. Gallo had an audience, to him an irresistible trap.

'Sailor!' he continued. 'Can you concentrate the incurious expanse of your vast and virgin mind?'

'I'll try, sir.' Lines of effort appeared on the seaman's face.

'You're doing well, sailor.'

'Thank you, sir.'

'It's Demos,' Venio whispered in the Tribune's ear as they watched from the dark interior of their cart. 'The sailor's Demos!'

'You're right – by the gods, this is pure theatre! – but have you seen Largus?'

'No.'

'Look, he's with Gallo's assistants!'

'I see him now – he's a cool one, Master Lucius.'

'He certainly is.'

'Sailor!' Gallo's voice boomed again, 'you've had sufficient time, I trust, to focus your attention,' his sarcasm feeding on the humour of his men.

'I think so, sir.'

'Good – now, can you tell me when the squadron will be back, for they should be here to be our transport.'

'I don't know, sir.'

'You don't know – do you know where they've gone?' Gallo snapped, his anger rising.

Demos, appearing eager to help, turned to consult the other sailors.

'We think they've gone to Sidon, sir.'

'Sidon!' Gallo exploded.

Demos pointed to the south.

'I know where it is, you idiot! – Largus!'

'Yes, sir.'

'Go to the Navy Office in the forum and find out what's happened – I don't believe this Sidon nonsense.'

'I think the sailors may be right, sir – it looks like a very unfortunate mix-up,' Largus said, in a voice full of concern.

'What mix-up?' Gallo snapped.

'Well, sir, the festival of celebration that delayed us took place beside the Villa Sidon, and the messenger you sent had been rejoicing for some time. Words and wine react strangely . . .'

'Spare me the philosophy, Largus,' Gallo barked.

'Sorry, sir.'

'Check with the Navy Office – I want to know what's really happened.'

Largus ran off with a show of instant obedience, and Gallo began to pace about the narrow area of the dock. Sensing trouble, the Tribune and Venio crouched low and out of sight. Valerius was furious with himself, knowing that his presence served no purpose, and knowing that discovery could spoil everything. He could hear Gallo's footsteps approaching. They stopped. Valerius listened, afraid to breathe and perspiring with tension.

'What are you doing, driver?' Gallo's voice sounded close.

'Waiting, sir,' the servant of Demetrianus answered.

'A profound answer,' Gallo exclaimed dramatically. 'Profound in its simplicity.' The laughter of his assistants was audible in the background.

'Now, my wise friend,' Gallo continued, 'who is your fortunate employer?'

'The merchant Demetrianus, sir.'

The Tribune heard the admission with alarm. It was bound to excite Gallo's curiosity.

'Ah, Demetrianus – a philosopher employing a philosopher and with a paragon as a guest. You have met the mighty Tribune, I assume?' The sarcasm was honey-sweet.

'He has no dealing with the likes of me.'

A good answer, Valerius thought.

'You're right, my friend. He's much too high above such common folk as you and me – Largus, you're back – what's the news?'

Thank the gods, the Tribune mouthed, hoping Gallo might forget about the servant of Demetrianus.

'They know nothing, sir,' Largus began in a voice of guileless honesty. 'No one told them of any change in arrangements. However, one man remembered a drunk swaggering through the doors and asking for the new Commander . . .'

'Typical, typical,' Gallo interjected, the sound of anger waiting to explode.

'The squadron may have gone for a brief training exercise, sir,' Largus suggested with a note of helpful innocence.

'Don't be stupid!' Gallo snapped – no doubt the reaction Largus had anticipated. 'They'd have training in plenty going to Caesarea,' Gallo continued, his voice sharp with annoyance. 'No, this Sidon business has the ring of fact, and if the gods would have us go by road, we will! – turn the carts about!'

The Tribune, still crouched low in his cart, listened to the welcome sound, but he did not move until the receding noise grew distant.

'That was a close run thing, Venio!'

'Yes, master.'

'You did well, my friend,' Valerius called forward to the driver.

'It was nothing, sir – your man's a puffed-up frog,' the driver returned, in rough-spoken Greek.

Valerius smiled, amused at the description, but there was more to Gallo than the surface show. He had a sharp, vindictive mind, a mind to seek revenge. Vigilance would be vital in the weeks ahead, not least for Demos and Largus; Largus especially, as, unlike Demos, he could not lose himself amongst the alleyways of Antioch. His place was at the Legate's side.

Tullus also would need to be careful and not walk about unguarded as if his life was charmed. Hopefully he would see him soon in Capernaum and warn him personally.

CHAPTER SEVENTEEN

'FOR I ALSO AM A MAN SET UNDER AUTHORITY'

To Drusilla, Capernaum was empty. Marcus was in Caesarea; Felix was following the Jewish Teacher; and Lucius was in Antioch. Occasionally Cornelius the Optio would call and speak politely, but otherwise there were no callers. The weeks seemed long and endless.

Drusilla's treatment of the Centurion during his last visit had filled her with remorse. She had written warmly in apology and he had replied with equal affection, but with her sense of guilt assuaged the whole dark area of doubt returned. Cornelia, however, was elated, having received a message from Lucius that he was soon to be in Capernaum.

Three days after Cornelia had received the Tribune's letter a covered cart stopped outside the Ben Josephs'. It was Felix. With uncharacteristic haste he rushed into the villa, his news distressing. James was in a piteous state with the palsy, and, knowing Drusilla had some knowledge in medical matters, he appealed for her advice.

One glance at James was enough for Drusilla. The paralysis was obvious and severe. She looked straight at the torment in his eyes, reflecting his desperate efforts to speak. Slowly she discerned the main word he was trying to say – the word 'master'. He was calling for Marcus.

'The Centurion, your beloved master, will be here soon,' she said reassuringly.

His look softened and the hand that he could move reached out in thanks. Tears welled in Drusilla's eyes.

Once James was out from the dull interior of the cart, she spoke urgently to Felix.

'Get him to bed as quickly and as gently as you can – there's little we can do, but, Felix, he must see Marcus. Tell Cornelius

150

to send for him at once. We can only hope that he arrives in time – . Has James been able to drink?'

'Very little,' Felix answered as he lifted himself back into the cart.

'I'll be over directly,' she called.

Cornelius acted instantly, and a two-horse chariot raced from the fort even as Drusilla arrived at the gate.

Marius, Gallo's watchman at the Centurion's camp, witnessed the commotion with disdain, angered at the effort wasted on one bad-tempered Galilean. Yet what else could he expect? For when it came to Jews, Tullus and his Optio were lenient to the point of treason.

Resentment and frustration burned in Marius, but he could not act; in fact, he dared not, knowing that his every move was watched. One day, though, his time would come, when at last he would reveal himself and purge this nest of treachery with its traitorous Centurion. Then the Jews would know who ruled. Marius's narrow, obsessive mind conjured his imagined triumph endlessly, until no doubt disturbed his self-delusion.

There were no delusions held at James's bedside. The old servant was sinking fast, and when the town's physician came he merely shook his head. Drusilla rarely left the dying Galilean, hoping against hope that Marcus would arrive in time. 'James, stay alive, please stay alive until he comes,' she whispered to herself.

In the morning, about first light, the Centurion arrived, his desperate journey apparent as he entered James's room. He looked Drusilla full in the face before moving close to the bedside – there was no need for words. Slowly his hands reached out to hold the head of his faithful servant. Gently he kissed him. James tried to speak, his hopeless efforts distressing to watch.

'James, James,' the Centurion said quietly, in an effort to calm him, but the eyes of Tullus blurred with tears.

For a time Tullus sat motionless and, to Drusilla, a presence seemed to grow about his person. It was almost visible, she thought. Suddenly he turned to Cornelius who was by the door.

'Ask Ben Joseph to come immediately. I can only hope he's at the Villa, but hurry, Cornelius.'

Drusilla turned enquiringly towards him as Cornelius left.

'The Rabbi,' Tullus said simply.

'Has he returned to Capernaum?'

'Ben Joseph will know. I don't know why I didn't think of it before, but now that I have – I must try!'

'Could he?' she wondered aloud, contemplating the incredible.

'If the Rabbi wills it, yes, it will be so.'

Cornelius was an efficient messenger, and only a short time passed before Ben Joseph arrived. The Rabbi was in the district of Capernaum, he responded, and he would do his utmost to locate him. Then, bowing his head in his self-effacing way, he rushed off.

As they waited there was little conversation, and to Drusilla the silence was oppressive. Beneath her calm exterior emotions raged, fed by the presence of a dying man, the presence of Marcus and the incredible suggestion that a Rabbi could cure the palsy. It was superstitious nonsense; all her family training said it was, yet part of her believed it to be possible. For a time the scene about her seemed unreal. What was she doing here? Who was Marcus? Who were his Jewish friends? Who was she? There was nothing still or constant in Drusilla's mind. She wanted to rush from the room, yet something kept her rooted to the spot.

Tired of her thoughts, she looked across at Felix. Dear Felix, she thought, always there, always reliable, and so like her beloved father. The same stature, the same grey hair, the same grave, contemplative manner and the same love of learning. He could be forgetful, though, but that was more a family joke than a reality. He was so stable, she concluded enviously.

Felix, however, felt anything but stable, for an old habit of self-criticism, vicious self-criticism, had returned. Why had he forgotten? What monumental stupidity, and what must Tullus think? They had been with the Rabbi, amongst his train of followers, and he had left the Teacher's presence. He had seen the Rabbi cure many, indeed the most amazing things had happened, yet when it came to James he had forgotten. It was unforgivable, he thought bitterly, for a human life was in the balance.

Sooner than they all expected, they heard the distinctive step of Ben Joseph returning. The next moment he stood before them.

'The Rabbi is on the Tiberias road on his way into Capernaum. He should be here at any moment,' he announced.

The Centurion rose to his feet. 'Ben Joseph, it is not right that we should approach a prophet of your people publicly without due deference and introduction. Will you go before us and explain our hope?'

Ben Joseph nodded and immediately headed for the door.

Before following his Jewish friend, Tullus took a final look at James. He was lying peacefully, his distress gone. No doubt he had heard the conversation, and faith had brought its calm.

In the open space before the garrison fort they began to assemble. Ben Joseph was out in front, with the Centurion a few paces behind, and behind him to the right stood Drusilla. Cornelia was on his left, with Felix further to the rear but on Drusilla's side – Sarah had remained with James.

Slowly the Rabbi and his following drew near, their progress interrupted by those seeking the Teacher's blessing. The waiting seemed endless to Drusilla, yet she was held by the scene before her as if it were a drama on the stage. She watched as Ben Joseph approached the Rabbi; the exchange was not audible, but it was clear that the Rabbi Jesus had not dismissed his plea.

Behind, from the direction of the town, the sound of approaching carts grew louder, yet no one turned to look, for all attention was focused on the Rabbi. Suddenly the crunching of the cart wheels stopped. The Tribune had arrived.

Sensing the compelling drama before him, Valerius silently alighted from his cart. His hand held high was enough to keep his guard in place, and another gesture towards Cornelius, at rigid attention by the fort entrance, put the Optio at ease. Then, followed by Venio, he moved forward noiselessly. At first his eyes could only see Cornelia. Then they included his sister, Felix, and the rock-like figure of Tullus. Clearly something intense was holding their attention, and to disturb them was out of the question, so he stopped a few paces behind Cornelia.

He looked ahead to the party in front of the Centurion. First he recognised Ben Joseph, and at that the man Ben Joseph was addressing turned towards him. At once he knew it was the Rabbi. Simultaneously he remembered to be still, as the priest Raphael had told him, and stillness came, deep and all-pervading. He had never known the like before.

The Rabbi and Ben Joseph began to walk towards the Centurion, and Tullus, holding steady, felt stripped of all pretension. There were no familiar props, it seemed, no supports to grasp. All that was constant was a strong and potent presence.

Ben Joseph was the first to speak.

'The Master has graciously agreed to help.'

The Centurion had not planned his response, but his words came without hesitation.

'Lord, I am not worthy that you should come under my roof: but speak the word only, and my servant shall be healed.' Tullus watched his speech emerge as if it were another speaking. 'For I also am a man set under authority, having soldiers under me, and I say to this man, Go, and he goes; and to another, Come, and he comes, and to my servant, Do this, and he does it.'

In an unhurried way the Rabbi turned to those that followed.

'Truly I say unto you, I have not found so great faith, no, not in Israel.'

Felix, listening intently, was full of wonder at the Centurion's understanding, for he had described the lawful nature of the Rabbi's power so aptly.

The Teacher moved to face the Centurion again. His voice was powerful, yet strangely gentle.

'Go your way; and as you have believed, so be it done unto you.'

The Centurion bowed to show honour and gratitude, and when he raised his head the Rabbi's steady gaze was still upon him. Then, for a moment, the Teacher's eyes focused on Drusilla, and at once her heart-felt cry for help was answered. Light flooded through her being; a melting within reflected in an outward melting, in what seemed an endless stream of tears. Spontaneously she fell to her knees in gratitude.

When she looked up the Rabbi was already on his way and the outstretched hands of Tullus were waiting to help her to her feet. They looked at each other without speaking, the joy evident in her tear-stained face. Their old intimacy had returned.

By turning in the direction of Drusilla, the Centurion had missed the presence of the Tribune, and as he passed through the fort gates the guard failed to attract his attention. His single-minded purpose was unheeding of distraction, and it propelled him straight to his servant's sick-bed. Drusilla had also missed her brother's arrival, but she was too bewildered, too awed by events and too happy to have noticed much, other than the Centurion. Now she was beside him in James's room, and at once an all-embracing calm began to still her running energy.

James was lying on his bed as they had left him, but Drusilla saw at once that his state had changed dramatically. There was a light about his face and he looked as if he was resting deeply.

For James, it seemed as if he had departed from his body. His being was free and an inexpressible peace pervaded his consciousness, its depth beyond dimension. James had no wish to leave this blissful state; notwithstanding, he began to cognise his surroundings.

As his eyes opened he saw Sarah and Ben Joseph at the foot of the bed. Slowly he turned his head to the left, and there in his vision was his noble master, with the lady that he loved beside him. It seemed to James that he was returning gradually, very gradually, from the depths of his being, yet to those who were watching his recovery was quick and spontaneous.

'Master, it was the Rabbi?'

'Yes, James.'

James sat upright on his bed, his mind humbled before his amazing fortune.

'I must give thanks!' he said urgently.

'Thanks are of the heart. The formal act can wait until you're rested.'

'Master, I've not felt so rested for twenty years. There's only one thing wrong – I'm hungry!'

'Sarah can prepare something. Is that all right?'

'Of course it's all right. I've trained her.'

The Centurion laughed heartily, turning to Felix who had just entered.

'As you can see, the real master of Capernaum is back in charge!'

Felix responded with words of wonder and praise. Not only had James fully recovered, he concluded, but he looked ten years younger.

Felix was much relieved, but for himself as well – a gross selfishness, he thought. Nonetheless, he was relieved at James's recovery, and blame for his forgetfulness was no longer a burden. Yet all this was petty thinking in the light of what had happened. As Tullus had said, the Rabbi had not entered under his roof. 'Speak the word only,' the Centurion had said. Amazing – not least Tullus's faith and understanding. Amazing, he repeated to himself. Nevertheless, Felix held to his conviction that the miracle had been lawful, the working of a higher knowledge.

Felix's reflection and the general buzz of conversation was interrupted by the entry of Cornelius.

'Sir,' he interjected, addressing Tullus, 'do you know that the Tribune has arrived?'

'No! Where is he?'

'At the villa – he arrived just as the Rabbi and our good friend Ben Joseph were speaking. You must have missed him as you rushed back to see James.'

'A significant arrival.'

Tullus did not go to the villa directly, but, accompanied by Drusilla and Ben Joseph, went to his own quarters. There he handed his Jewish friend a large silver dish, a gift for the Synagogue, as a token of gratitude. He also wrote a brief note to the Disciple John asking him to convey the heartfelt thanks of all to the Rabbi.

'We have been greatly blessed,' he said simply.

'Can I give something, Marcus?' Drusilla asked.

'Of course, my dear.'

When the Rabbi approached the Centurion, Cornelia remained open and receptive. Her experience of Qumran had made her trustful. She saw at once that the Rabbi's hair and dress were similar to Raphael's, but he was much younger. For a moment the Teacher's gaze rested on her, and she was filled with a sense of total contentment. All was well and would be well. Again there was something fine, like a light within her being.

She saw the same fineness in the Tribune when she turned to discover him behind her, and after a moment's wonder she was in his arms, embraced by his tender greeting.

Felix saw their joy, but he knew it held the seeds of tragedy. He would have to speak to Lucius, but resolution weakened with the warmth of the Tribune's greeting.

'Felix, Felix, I haven't seen you for weeks, and there's so much to talk about – what's been happening here?'

The old servant explained the significance of the drama they had just witnessed, and the fantastic fact that the Rabbi, or God, or whatever he was, had cured an incurable illness by fiat of will, without even seeing the patient.

'It's unbelievable, but I've no doubt that James has recovered – listen, the cheering of the soldiers is already evidence!'

'Amazing, but after what happened at Qumran I'm not wholly surprised. What does it all mean, though? What have we stumbled upon?'

Felix shook his head. 'I wish I knew – I've listened to him often, and always he speaks with complete authority. There are no exceptions. His words are close, somehow, and real; peace on his lips brings peace. It's as if the truth itself were speaking.' Again Felix shook his head. 'We've found something rare, very rare indeed.'

They looked at each other without speaking, the mystery of the Rabbi tangible and hanging in the air, it seemed.

'Master Lucius,' Felix interjected, 'I've an urge to see James and the fulfilment of this wonder.'

'Of course, Cornelia and I will go to the villa – are there any despatches?'

'There are – I'll bring them over.'

Felix walked quickly to the garrison. As he approached, the guard dutifully opened the heavy gate, but there was hostility in the soldier's eyes. It was Marius, his anger burning and active. Without reaction, Felix walked on briskly.

Upstart freedman, Marius muttered to himself, Jew-lover, self-styled philosopher, but just as gullible as the rest. Miracle, indeed! A Jewish trick, with one bad-tempered servant a chief actor. No one could do what had been claimed. Fools, he thought bitterly, as he listened to the soldiers' shouts of celebration. A dark magician was igniting Galilee and a Roman garrison was applauding, but why was nothing done? For despite being watched he had managed to send warning after warning to the Tribune Gallo. Marius was almost frantic with frustration, possessed as he was by hatred of the Jews, of Tullus and his Optio, and by the firm belief that a Jewish uprising was imminent. Trapped between the narrow walls of his belief there was little space for reformation, yet he had wit enough to keep his counsel private. Thus he waited, certain that his day would come.

Supper was at the Ben Josephs' villa, and the note of rejoicing was clearly evident. Only the Tribune was subdued, and this quickly prompted Cornelia's concern.

'Are you well, Lucius?' she asked confidentially, amidst the general noise of conversation.

'Yes, I'm fine – the road from Antioch is long.' He smiled reassuringly, but Cornelia, sensitive to every facet of his nature, knew that he was troubled; a fear confirmed when he and Felix abruptly withdrew to an adjacent room.

'We'll only be a few moments,' he apologised generally, again smiling at Cornelia.

Once alone with Felix, the Tribune was direct. He wished the impossible, for he wished to marry Cornelia. He had written to his father on the subject, and now the reply had arrived. Valerius made no comment on his father's words, but handed the roll to Felix.

Watched intently by the Tribune, Felix unrolled the despatch and began to read. The gentle buzz of conversation coming from the room next door seemed to emphasize the silence.

'The Senator is not unsympathetic,' Felix said without looking up from the text. Then he began to read aloud.

"Only yesterday forty slaves were executed and the freedmen exiled, in the household of an ageing Senator who had committed suicide. This piece of so-called justice rested on the suspicion that the suicide could have been contrived by the slaves as a cover-up for murder. My protests in the Senate had no effect; the ghost of Spartacus and his uprising still haunts us – violent rebellion is always counter-productive.

"All my life I have fought against such barbarity. So perhaps I can claim some understanding when it comes to the eccentric behaviour of the family in respect of their slaves and freedmen."

Felix passed over the next few words, which referred to himself.

"I have treated Cornelia idealistically instead of practically. The fact that she carries the name that blessed the mother of the Gracchi is proof of my excess. I allowed Cornelia to become a lady, when in law she is a slave. Again, I hoped by her slave status to protect her from the lusts of Rome until I found a worthy companion for her. Little did I think that my son would crave that companionship.

"So you can see how the idealism of this Senator has created a dilemma for his son. For in truth the law forbids it – a Senator's son cannot marry a freedwoman, and freedwoman she is. This I formally grant.

"Lucius, the law is the law. You are the legate of the Emperor, and your name is ancient."

Felix looked up at the troubled face of the Tribune.

'It's a long letter. Most unlike your father.'

Valerius said nothing, but continued to lean forward on his couch, his elbows on his knees. He looked tired, but there was no sense of bitterness.

Felix continued to read.

"About a month ago I asked permission to travel to the east and visit our estates. I also mentioned a father's intention of seeing both a son and an elder daughter. The Emperor responded warmly and invited me to visit him on Capri. In his despatch he was full of praise for your conduct, including your rescue of Cornelia – the facts of which are common knowledge over here. I will say no more, but let us hope that there may be an opportunity to raise the subject of Cornelia, and with the gods in favour, who knows, some form of Imperial dispensation may be granted."

Felix looked up from his reading.

'This is hopeful, and the Emperor's permission would counter the jibes and petty slanders.'

'You forget the matrons of Rome!' Valerius reacted cynically. 'Felix, read this first before you continue; it's from Capri,' he added, handing the despatch across. 'You will see that Tiberius hopes the rumours about marriage and Cornelia are untrue.'

Felix did not respond for some time.

'Gallo's rumour?' he suggested eventually.

'Maybe, but the Emperor has ears everywhere.'

'Don't lose heart, Lucius.' Felix only used the plain praenomen when speech was intimate and private. 'Tiberius likes your father – all is not lost.'

'I know, but the uncertainty is hard to bear – it could be months before we know, and my doubts are rampant – I fear Tiberius may baulk at a slave's blood mingling with our ancient family.'

'Your father didn't!'

'But there are few like him. Anyway, he knows her worth.'

Felix nodded. 'We'd better inform the master of the Emperor's words. Shall I write?'

'Yes – thanks, Felix,' Valerius responded wearily.

When they rejoined the supper party the conversation was still on the subject of the Rabbi and the miraculous events of the day. The Tribune did not look at Cornelia immediately, but he knew that she was watching him; so he played his part with casual ease, as if his talk with Felix had been routine. He feigned a yawn.

'You're tired, Lucius,' she said.

'A little, my dear,' he returned. By all the gods, she was beautiful, beautiful in every sense.

'Nothing can happen without trust.' The words of Tullus rose above the general conversation. 'Trust'. Valerius almost said the word aloud. It was what he needed most. Unbidden, his mind recalled the uncanny stillness he had experienced earlier in the presence of the Rabbi, and trust came, not trust in anyone or anything, but trust itself, total and without limit. His worries and concerns vanished. They simply were not there. It was a powerful experience that he could not readily forget.

Felix left the gathering early. He was anxious to write to the Senator, and he also wished to call on James. The urge to follow the Rabbi was still paramount and James was vital to his plans. He would bring the matter up casually, of course; any hint of pressure would be wrong. Nevertheless, Felix was impatient to rejoin the Rabbi's following. No doubt James would speak his mind. He never stood on ceremony.

Soon after Felix's departure the Ben Josephs retired to their private rooms, and after that the Tribune excused himself. He was finding it impossible to stay awake.

'I'll see you in the morning, my dear,' he said to Cornelia, 'and we'll go walking as we did at Qumran.'

She was obviously pleased.

The Centurion rose to his feet as the Tribune left, and after a smile and a quietly spoken 'good night' from Cornelia, he and Drusilla were alone.

'She adores him,' Drusilla said wistfully.

'Your brother?'

'Yes, she adores him; she always has.'

'And he?'

'Took her for granted – didn't really notice, I suppose, but Machaerus has changed all that. Now he looks at her with obvious affection.'

'But, Drusilla, what future can there be?'

She did not answer, but instead began to speak reflectively about Cornelia's youth.

'After Father purchased her in northern Gaul he spent the journey to Rome teaching her Latin – so like Father. He was impressed by her intelligence, and when he arrived at the villa he told me to take special care of her, and so it happened. She grew up with Junia, and in truth became one of the family.

'As you can appreciate, Cornelia's kidnap was an awful shock to us, not least to Lucius, and when he rescued her in circumstances of high drama his eyes were opened to her beauty.

'You question rightly, for the law is clear; there is no future, except she be his mistress, but that would be . . . un . . . unthinkable.'

'There may be no alternative.'

'There must be, and after what happened today, I'm full of hope. We have been blessed, Marcus – all of us.'

He held his arms open, and she nestled within his embrace.

'What happened today was a great grace, and your resultant faith is beautiful, but, my dear Drusilla, we must be practical.' He spoke gently, yet she could feel the vibration in his chest.

'Beloved Marcus,' she said softly, 'all will be well.'

'And what of us, my sweet Drusilla?'

'Marcus, that is for you to say.'

'A humble soldier begs permission to approach the father of a gracious lady for her hand in marriage.'

'A grateful lady – Oh, Marcus, yes! Yes!' Her arms squeezed tightly.

'Dear Drusilla. Only yesterday I believed that I had lost you.'

'Forgive me, Marcus, but my cruel doubts have gone – vanished! The Rabbi's power did that.'

He kissed her.

'Drusilla, my origins are humble.'

She put her fingers across his mouth. 'A noble and courageous soul needs no laurel from the games.'

'My dear, as with your brother, the world will have its way.'

'Marcus, you are a citizen. An Equestrian post is yours by right, yet for some odd reason your promotion's been delayed – probably your own doing. Indeed, I'm certain it's your doing, otherwise who would defer your elevation? Certainly not the Legate, for according to my brother he respects you.'

Gently he released his embrace.

'The Rabbi Jesus is often in Capernaum,' he said simply, 'and one does not leave such an influence lightly. I think you understand.'

'I do! I do!'

'There is another reason, my dear – an army matter, but temporary,' he added casually.

She did not press for detail, knowing that if he had some secret work he would be pledged to silence. Drusilla had not forgotten the roll she had seen on his desk, its origin Rome.

She smiled, and they embraced.

'I'm so happy, Marcus. So very happy.'

He kissed her again. 'I don't want to return to the garrison,' he whispered, 'but I think I should.'

'Yes, it would be wise,' she murmured.

After two days the Tribune and Tullus both left for Caesarea – the reported activities of Gallo had hastened their departure. They were soon followed by Felix, Sarah and James, in their case to join the Rabbi, who had suddenly left Capernaum. James had suffered no reaction and was fully recovered, but most commented that the flint edge of his character had softened.

Once more, Drusilla and Cornelia were alone.

CHAPTER EIGHTEEN

CAESAREA

When the Tribune and Tullus arrived at the Procurator's palace they learned that Gallo had been in residence for seven days. He was a dominating presence, and Pilate was impressed by his oratory and wit.

Gallo made little pretence at road surveying, and more and more he spoke openly of Sejanus – the ageing Emperor's great friend. The failing powers of the old man were set against the vigour and vision of the Praetorian Prefect. The message was clear, though Gallo was careful not to criticise Tiberius. He knew that slander was best magnified in the tavern where vulgar stories of depravity on Capri could be easily spread.

In many ways Gallo's task was easy, yet he was far from satisfied, knowing that Valerius and 'that cursed Centurion' – his appellation for Tullus – were always there to thwart his plans. So when the Tribune arrived in Caesarea and captured the immediate enthusiasm of both town and army, Gallo was furious. He was also mystified. How could that humourless block of ice stir any sentiment? Gallo knew about Sarah's purchase, and again, he knew about Machaerus, but he was disdainful. The follies of a slave-lover meant nothing. He had missed the point, for both events had added to the magic of the name Valerius. The Emperor's legate was a friend of the oppressed, and the constant stream of pleas that he received was ample proof of this.

Blind to the Tribune's personal success, Gallo focused blame on the Centurion, for according to his men, Tullus had been active in Caesarea over the past two months. It was Tullus and his agents who had fired the people to support Valerius.

Gallo was tired of the recurring frustration caused by the Centurion. He knew he could not touch the Tribune, at least overtly, but he could contrive to have Tullus arrested for collaboration. Marius, his agent, kept pestering him with evidence to this effect, and he might as well use it. Marius was a fanatic, of course, full of exaggeration, and he doubted if a charge against Tullus would stick, not that that mattered; what mattered would be the resulting confusion in the Valerian camp; for if Tullus were arrested Valerius would rush to his aid, while he, Gallo, would be left unhindered. Gallo liked the plan. All sorts of 'accidents' could happen, and if it became embarrassing he could always blame Marius's fanaticism.

These plans were buzzing in his mind as he drank with Pilate. Very soon, he mused, Valerius would join them with his ox of a servant; at least, that had been the pattern for the last four evenings.

'I suppose Valerius will be here soon with his tame bull thrilling us with his silence.'

'Yes, the Tribune is very restrained,' Pilate answered carefully.

'Constipated, more likely!'

'He's the personal legate of the Emperor.'

'Personal legate of senility.' Gallo looked pointedly at the Procurator. 'You owe your post to Sejanus; you know who rules the Roman world, and it's only a matter of time before the purple is official.'

Pilate made ambiguous sounds of agreement, but the turn in Gallo's conversation troubled him. He had no wish to be pressured into any factional camp, yet he dared not offend the powerful friend of Sejanus. Sejanus was powerful, that was true, but so was the Emperor. What was more, Pilate did not believe that the old man was senile. Indeed, the official papers he received were full of evidence to the contrary. Nevertheless, the power of the Praetorian Prefect was awesome. To support Gallo was dangerous, and to refuse support was equally hazardous.

Gallo looked at Pilate defiantly. 'Come, Pilate, grasp the sword of decision!'

At that moment Pilate gratefully noticed the arrival of Valerius. His uncommitted world was still intact.

'Here's the slave-lover,' Gallo said through the side of his mouth. 'Valerius, my friends tell me you've found a new

Prophet of Israel,' his voice boomed as the Tribune approached.

The Tribune did not answer, but took his couch with due acknowledgement of the Procurator.

'Are you in his magic circle?' Gallo pressed.

Again the Tribune made no reply.

'Valerius, you are coy this evening. What does your magic circle do? Make frogs into horses or horses into frogs?'

'For the gods' sake, Gallo, talk sense!' Valerius snapped.

'I thought I was! – that is, judging by the stories that I've heard, fantastic stories. This Nazarene of yours is growing popular, but his Jewish bosses don't like it!'

'Who do you mean?' Valerius asked bluntly. He was well aware that Gallo was baiting him.

'Who do I not mean – he labels all as hypocrites! You ought to tell your pious friend to be more careful.'

'Would you have him praise pretension and corruption?'

'He'll have to if he wants to lead a quiet life!'

'Gallo is right, Valerius. The Nazarene is fast becoming a problem; not only for the Jews, but for us as well. He needs to modify his language – tone it down. We cannot let him wreck the balance.'

'Send him down the mines!' Gallo's rounded words were definite.

'Gallo, my friend, the Jews may fight amongst themselves. That is their affair, but for us to lay a hand upon their prophet would be idiocy. Their whole nation would blow up in our faces.' It was evident that Pilate meant what he said.

'Pilate, how serious is the problem concerning the Rabbi Jesus?' Valerius questioned.

'It will be all right as long as he keeps out of Jerusalem. Should he go there on a feast day, though, it could be very difficult; for his enemies are there; we are there and the emotional crowds are there; and if he should perform one of his so-called miracles in that madhouse, anything could happen.'

Valerius nodded. There was much in what the Procurator said, and his scepticism was understandable, as throughout the Empire frauds and fanatics were ever claiming that they knew the spirit world.

'Get rid of him,' Gallo boomed, 'and dress it up in law if that's your wish!'

'Is that your usual practice, Gallo?' the Tribune exploded, the death of the Commander vividly remembered.

Gallo smiled thinly, restraining his invective. He did not want an open conflict with Valerius, at least not yet.

'One day your sneer will freeze upon your lips,' the Tribune barked, his anger imperious. 'And, Procurator,' he continued, turning to Pilate, 'do not stain your hands with the Rabbi's blood. He is innocent.'

Pilate nodded thoughtfully. It was prudent to respect the fury of a Laticlavius, especially when he was the Emperor's legate.

Still angry, Valerius rose abruptly to his feet. He had had enough of Gallo for the evening, and after briefly taking his leave of Pilate he strode from the hall.

'The Emperor's errand-boy is touchy,' Gallo said casually as Valerius left. 'Maybe his slave-girl has rejected him.' He stifled a yawn, but Pilate did not seem to hear. The anger of the Tribune was still fresh in memory.

In the morning the Tribune was unrepentant of his outburst. It cer tainly had affected Pilate, who was most solicitous when Valerius called to announce his imminent departure. Certainly in respect of the Rabbi a little anger had done much, much more, he suspected, than any amount of patient reasoning.

Valerius had decided that the measure of his stay in Caesarea was complete. Again, there was a balance to be struck between watching Gallo and being his nursemaid. In any case the Centurion would remain to keep him and his agents under observation.

Gallo still did not know about the reversal of his fortunes in Antioch. Because of this, and because of Tullus's patient work in Caesarea, the Tribune felt the time was ripe to visit Palmyra and the north-east. Once there, of course, he would return to Antioch.

Not long after the Tribune left Caesarea Gallo also departed from the city, heading for the court of Herod at Tiberias. The

Centurion remained at Caesarea, but he was wary, and immediately sent two of his men to Tiberias on the pretext of ordering stores for Capernaum. He also sent instructions to Capernaum that Marius was to be watched closely and certainly not allowed to leave the garrison. Again, he ordered that the guard at the villa be further strengthened. Gallo at Tiberias made him uneasy, yet he felt it necessary to remain in Caesarea. Experience had taught him that times of apparent release could be full of danger. Menace did not leave with Gallo. Indeed, violent events could well be planned to happen in his absence.

CHAPTER NINETEEN

THE SENATOR

At the time his son was travelling north from Caesarea the Senator Marcus Gracchus Valerius was preparing to leave for the Villa Jovis on Capri. He did not know what lay before him, but age had tutored him to take things as they came.

The Senator's travelling party, in keeping with the Valerian custom, was modest and included two loyal freedmen and a scribe, as well as drivers and assistants for the carts. Arria, his loving freedwoman, had remained behind to keep a watchful eye on Junia, Drusilla's sister.

The winter weather was mild and the journey south, which included stops with friends, was pleasant. He was six days on the road, and on the seventh he made the crossing to Capri. Once at the Villa Jovis he was taken immediately to the Emperor's private quarters, and there, facing the tall twin doors, the same doors his son had stood before, he paused, his tension mounting. What awaited him? How would Tiberius receive him? Only a Socrates could stand against such pettiness, he thought.

Suddenly the doors opened, and there was the Emperor, peering at a pile of despatches.

'Valerius!' he called in greeting, while rising to his feet with unusual briskness.

'Noble Princeps, you haven't changed a bit since I last saw you.' The Senator, relieved at the warmth of his reception, spoke with a disarming honesty.

'The winter comes, Valerius, even if the autumn lingers!'

'But the winter snow falls gently when not disturbed by wind.'

The Emperor's shoulders heaved with laughter in their characteristic way. 'And you haven't changed – no! – not a jot! – Come, let's recline at the portico.'

Wine was ordered, and as the Emperor took his seat he beckoned an attendant.

'See if you can find our friend Nerva. Tell him the Senator Valerius has arrived.'

The conversation began in a general way, with the Senator thanking his Emperor for squashing the treason charge. Tiberius was dismissive.

After the wine was served the attendants retired out of ear-shot. The Senator waited, knowing that the Emperor would steer the conversation. They sat for some time before Tiberius spoke.

'Who is it to be, Valerius – Sejanus or the boy 'Caligula'?'

The question came like a shock of cold water, and for a moment fear gripped at the Senator. This was dangerous ground, but there were no witnesses; the servants had retired. He spoke quietly.

'On that stage to choose is to condemn. The Princeps has a lonely task.'

'You have spoken prudently, Valerius. Each day I sacrifice to the divine Augustus, but he is slow with guidance. Is it to be the brats of Germanicus, poisoned against me by the lies and bitterness of their mother, or should it be Sejanus, with the hounds of the Praetorian at his heels?'

'Our Princeps has many years of rule before him. Why not let the gods decide your heir in their good time?' the Senator suggested, but he knew it was a weak response.

'Valerius, I'm past seventy!' Tiberius snapped. 'The Senate and the people need to have all doubts about our heir removed.'

'What about your grandson Gemellus?'

'He's a boy and he'd need a regent – guess who that would be!'

Sejanus! the Senator did not need to guess.

'Valerius, you have been party to imprudent words.' The Emperor's hands worked nervously with his toga.

'No breath of this shall pass my lips.' Shock had made the Senator alert. Tiberius was not himself. His behaviour was most uncharacteristic.

'I'm an old man, Valerius. I'm exhausted, yet I'm forced to labour; but let me keep my senses . . . pray the gods may grant me that!'

Tiberius's hands continued to twist and pull at his toga.

'Why was Drusus taken from me?' the Emperor continued bitterly. 'I know he was no Scipio, and I was hard on him, but Valerius, he was my son! I could have trusted him. Now there's no one!' He paused for a moment, his weariness obvious. 'Caligula,' he added distastefully.

Tiberius was disturbed, if not unbalanced, for he had revealed his thinking in a way he never did. Valerius watched with alarm.

'What is your advice, Senator?'

Valerius swallowed.

'Do nothing, sir. Even a short passage of time can move an intractable circumstance into a position of obvious resolution.' He had said little and he knew it, but what could he say? The whole question of Tiberius's heir was a pit of scorpions.

The Emperor sighed. 'Perhaps you're right. Perhaps the time is not yet ripe.' The heaviness seemed to lift from his features and Valerius breathed deeply with relief.

'Now, let's talk of happier things. Your son's a credit to you, Valerius. He's made quite an impression. And the rescue of the girl, that was a coincidence, or was it!? I've heard he wants to marry her. Fanciful, but hardly practical. No doubt the rumour is untrue.'

'I'm afraid not, sir.' Felix's message had failed to arrive in time, and the Emperor's comments had taken the Senator by surprise. Nevertheless he faced the situation squarely, describing Cornelia's sweet and intelligent nature, while adding that she had been a chieftain's daughter.

'The chieftains of the north are not exactly kings,' the Emperor reacted as if he were grumbling.

'I know, sir, but I strongly hinted to my son that his only honourable course was by the special dispensation of his Emperor, and now I appeal to you. I can assure you, my noble Princeps, she would make the perfect Roman matron.' Valerius did not flinch from Tiberius's quizzical look.

'You Valerii are incorrigible!'

The Senator was grateful for the humour that flickered on the face of the Emperor as his troubled and capricious manner was disconcerting to say the least.

The Emperor did not answer the Senator's appeal directly. Instead, as was his habit, he talked around the subject. This was more like the old Tiberius, Valerius thought.

'Lamia is full of praise for your son,' the Emperor continued, 'and seems amazed at the extent of his influence. He has apparently joined up with a Primus Pilus by the name of Tullus. A Primus Pilus or an Equestrian – Lamia was vague on the subject.'

The Senator did not suppose for a moment that Lamia had been vague. It was pure Tiberius.

'A good man, by all accounts,' he proceeded, ' – has been appearing in my reports for the last three years – was the hero of a rather nasty ambush. Now, I've heard from another source that this same Tullus and your daughter are, shall we say, friendly. Tell me, Valerius, why does the ancient patrician house of the Valerii shun the nobility of Rome?'

Another shaft of fear struck at the Senator, but he remained outwardly calm. He had not expected a controversy concerning Drusilla, and was nonplussed, yet he was compelled to speak.

'Drusilla has mentioned this soldier in her letters. She obviously admires him. I suppose her father should have been more perceptive.'

The Senator paused to look at his Emperor, hoping for a sympathetic response, but Tiberius reacted with an air of languid indifference, as if he were enjoying the Senator's embarrassment.

'Come, Valerius! You must answer my question. Why have the Valerii turned from the aristocracy of Rome?' The note of playful banter was obvious. For a moment Tiberius had forgotten his dynastic worries and their capricious twists.

Taking heart from the Emperor's mood, Valerius decided to speak without apology.

'To turn from aristocracy would be to turn from excellence, the description of the Greeks for this level of society. Now, if the Valerii have turned from excellence they are foolish, but my knowledge of Cornelia and your description of Tullus do not lead me to conclude that we have transgressed the natural law. The problem lies with customary law, and the Valerii turn to their Emperor for help.'

Humour flickered at the corner of Tiberius's mouth.

'Perfect, Valerius! Perfect!' he chuckled. 'Shades of the divine Plato – I knew you would answer like that.'

Propped up with cushions, the Emperor lay back on his couch.

'You want to journey to the east, Marcus?' The subject had changed, and the Senator, amazed at his good fortune, felt as if he had survived a long and uncertain cavalry charge. He was also aware that the Emperor's use of the praenomen was a rare compliment.

'A long journey,' Tiberius mused. 'You have my permission, of course, but why not stay here and send for the rest of your baggage? After all, Capri's well on the way to Brindisium; that is, assuming you're going that way. I'm sure your favourite freedwoman could look after all the necessary arrangements.' Tiberius shot the Senator a knowing look. So he knows about that as well, Valerius thought with resignation.

'Your offer is very generous, sir, and I'm greatly tempted, but my library is the problem; for if I go to the east without some part of my roll collection it would be little better than exile. As you can appreciate, I would need to select the rolls I wish to take personally.'

The Emperor's laughter exploded as if smashing through a fortress wall.

'Other men take dancers and concubines, but Valerius takes his library. I bend before the logic of your case.' He laughed again before leaning forward with an air of confidentiality.

'Does your son have to marry the girl?'

Again Valerius was shocked, but the conversational manner of Tiberius was disarming.

'Cornelia as his mistress is . . . it's unthinkable, sir.' The Senator's reply was heartfelt. 'It would soil the honour of my son.'

The heavy figure of Tiberius seemed suddenly inert. 'Yes,' he said in a drawn-out way, the sound carrying a lifetime of disappointment and regret. 'Yours is a strange family, Valerius, but you're right. Love without honour is empty.'

The words seemed incongruous on the lips of the Emperor, for they did not accord with his reputation, and certainly not with the vile rumours currently circulating in Rome.

Tiberius had disappeared within himself, it seemed, and the Senator, alert and waiting, sensed a heaviness, as if a burden of tragedy were clinging to the ponderous bulk of the Princeps.

'Your son deserves to have his plea considered,' the Emperor said eventually. 'I'll think about it – yes! I'll think about it – a northern chieftain's daughter.' His last words were muttered, and again he seemed to go within himself.

The Senator Valerius knew Tiberius well and he knew the signs were good, but even though he was elated he held his peace. It was not done to interrupt the thinking of an Emperor.

Tiberius had lost his capricious look, but his fingers, still active with nervous energy, twisted and pulled at the fabric of the couch; their distracting play a trap for the Senator's attention. The burden of the Principate was taking its toll on the ageing Emperor, and little wonder, Valerius thought. It was no mean feat to have preserved and consolidated the heritage of Augustus, but there was a price to pay, for his awesome responsibilities allowed little peace of mind. Indeed, some maintained that the force of absolute power had deranged him. A premature judgement, Valerius thought, but what if the terrible pressures of his office grew unbearable. It was a frightening prospect, yet Tiberius was experienced, immensely capable, and he was a Claudian. The long tradition of his house was rooted in him.

Changing position on his couch, the Emperor looked up, his face reflecting a shift in mood.

'Marcus, your library cannot keep you from staying overnight, so we will expect you at our supper table. Nerva, if we can find him, will be joining us. We can do a little drinking, and talk of better days; the better days now past – to talk about the future would sour the wine!'

The Senator accepted graciously. He had no alternative, for only men of little sense would slight the sovereign power. Not that he anticipated the evening to be difficult, as Tiberius, he was certain, would leave the cares of state aside. Nevertheless, the Emperor was the Emperor, and in his presence it was prudent to be watchful. Valerius was also certain that the question of his son's marriage would not be raised again during his stay at Capri. Tiberius, after due consideration, would send a letter. It was his style. All the Valerii could do was wait.

With well-practised deference one of the Emperor's freedmen approached and spoke quietly to his master. Tiberius rose to his feet and lines of worry thickened on his forehead.

'There's someone waiting, Senator. Gnaeus here will show you to your rooms. We'll meet again this evening.' The Emperor's voice had lost its relaxation and the quick capricious glint had returned to his eyes.

The audience was over, and Valerius took his leave with customary formality. Once through the twin doors, he found himself face to face with the Emperor's next visitor, the Praetorian officer Marco, the deputy of Sejanus.

Marco was careful to acknowledge the respected Senator, and Valerius responded with civility, but he was watchful, for he found it difficult to trust any officer of the Praetorian. Too much power rested in the ranks of their exclusive cohorts. They were overpaid and greedy still, and the fear they engendered made them disdainful and arrogant. To most they were a curse, yet they were needed as a counter to the border legions – not the massed legions, an unlikely combination, as the generals were sure to disagree – but rather to deter crack cohorts being sent to coerce the Principate.

The army was at once a friend and an enemy, and the balance of power was ever a concern. Another constant concern was the large slave population. Spartacus and his rebellion were fearful Roman memories.

Rome needed protection and the price of that protection was the Praetorian Guard.

CHAPTER TWENTY

FOREBODING

The Tribune's progress was slow, reflecting the bitter weather of the northern frontier. Neveretheless, he was determined to reach Samosata. This self-imposed pressure was typical of his nature and was fuel for his illness, though he did not see it.

Relentless activity, of course, was one way to forget what he feared to be his doomed relationship with Cornelia. His earlier hopes had faded, as had the powerful impulse of trust at Capernaum. Yet he could not abandon hope completely. That was impossible.

At Samosata he suffered a momentary attack of dizziness, a brief reminder, but enough to curb his will and send him back to Antioch.

At Antioch he quickly gleaned the current news from Largus. The former deputy commander of the naval squadron was now fully in charge. Doubtless Gallo would have heard the news, but the present investigation into the death of the previous commander had produced embarrassing implications for his nominee and Largus felt certain that Gallo would abandon his man.

There was other news, innocent, it seemed, yet Largus was suspicious. Two young men of Equestrian rank had just arrived from Rome full of praise for Gaius 'Caligula' – too full, Largus thought. Nevertheless, their praise for the third son of Germanicus pleased the legate well. It blinded him to their sycophancy, Largus grumbled. There was something patently false about the new arrivals, and in time he would uncover their pretence. The Tribune had little doubt he would, for Largus was determined. It was best not to be his enemy.

The Tribune met frequently with Largus and Demos during his month-long stay at Antioch. Then near the end of

February he left for the south, prompted by news he had received from Tullus.

The Centurion's letter was long and detailed, and at first there was nothing apparently urgent. Gallo, he reported, had spent almost two months at Tiberias. The official reasons were unquestionably sensible, as there was no denying that winter was the best time to survey roads in the Jordan Valley. After his stay at Tiberias he had left for Palmyra in the company of Herod. A trade mission was the official motive. More like a drinking party, the Tribune thought cynically, remembering his visit to Palmyra on the way north.

Tullus also reported that Gallo had enlisted further 'assistants', and that Marius's slave was now amongst the number of his servants.

The situation at Caesarea was unchanged, but the conflicting words 'brooding stability' emphasised the Centurion's unease, for some undetected plan of Gallo's making could well be lying dormant.

The Centurion's unease became much more evident when he turned to the subject of the Rabbi and his followers. He was disturbed, he wrote, by the growing conviction amongst his Jewish friends that the Rabbi could be in considerable danger if he visited Jerusalem for the Passover, due in a month or so. The Tribune would be well advised, Tullus suggested, to spend some time in the city of the Holy Temple.

'Your influence,' he wrote, 'would moderate any Roman reaction, should trouble arise.' The Centurion did not elaborate on the theme, but it was quite clear that his main concern was the safety of the Rabbi.

'What worries me most,' the Centurion's text continued, 'is the stupid emotionalism rampant amongst his popular supporters. Even men who should know better are voicing hopes of a political triumph in Jerusalem and seem determined to ignore the essentially spiritual nature of the Rabbi's teaching.

'I sent a message to James, urging him to breathe some sense into the fanatical fringe, but the hope of a national saviour is strong. In short, emotion rules, a dangerous emotion and one that Rome is sure to purge if it continues.'

The Tribune stopped reading. He fully appreciated the

Centurion's concern, and knew all too well that the safety of the Rabbi and the interests of Rome were two very different things. The Rabbi's kingdom was not of the world, the Disciple John had said, and he believed him, but the world would not believe. It would judge the Rabbi by its own standards.

The Tribune sat back in his chair in the now familiar room at the Villa Demetrianus. Close by was Venio, but the Tribune was oblivious to his surroundings, for his mind was focused on the image of the Rabbi.

The Rabbi Jesus was no ordinary man. The recovery of James and the transformation in Drusilla was proof of that. A Socrates with godly powers, Felix had said, but even that was limiting, he had added. That Valerius understood, for the peace he had experienced in the Teacher's presence had been beyond dimension.

The idea of cautioning the Rabbi and of suggesting compromise seemed utterly incongruous, yet it appeared to be the only course. He could bar the Rabbi's entry into Jerusalem, but that could cause the very trouble he was trying to avoid. Indeed, to restrict or confine a popular Rabbi could ignite the passions of the Jewish community – especially the Zealots.

'Trouble?' Venio questioned.

There was a delay before the sound of Venio's words was registered by Valerius, after which he briefly explained the dilemma concerning the Rabbi.

'We can't control the Rabbi's destiny, Master Lucius.'

The Tribune looked at his servant for a moment without speaking. They had grown close during the long months of winter travel; even so, the sensitivity of the big man always amazed him.

'You're right, Venio, but imagine admitting that to Rome.'

The Tribune sighed with resignation, and picking up the Centurion's despatch began to read again.

Both ladies, Tullus said, were anxious for his return, 'and your sister and I would like your blessing on a matter you may readily anticipate.' The Tribune smiled at the measured discretion.

The Centurion's letter ended, suddenly, it seemed, on a different and disturbing note. There was a growing lawlessness in Galilee and Judea, he wrote. 'Take every precaution, and if you journey south, avoid sending heralds unless you find it necessary.'

The Centurion had not mentioned the trouble he had encountered from bandits, or was it Zealots, on a recent journey from Caesarea, when only the speed of his horses had saved him. This brush with banditry added to his mounting concern for the safety of the Rabbi, knowing well that increased lawlessness could be blamed on the Teacher.

Soon after his escape, Tullus learned that Marius had been redrafted. Such transfers were not uncommon, but the news fuelled his unease.

He revealed nothing of his fears to Drusilla, yet she knew that he was troubled, and she knew it was the Rabbi. She too felt an uneasiness, a strange foreboding, even though her own happiness seemed inviolate. She confided in him, voicing an instinctive feeling that the Rabbi would not return to Capernaum.

In response he embraced her tenderly.

'Felix is the wisest of us all, for once he recognised the Rabbi's worth he followed him. – I fear you may be right, my dear,' he added quietly. 'Alas, I do.' But he did not voice his worst fear, that in going to Jerusalem the Rabbi Jesus would be going to his death.

CHAPTER TWENTY-ONE

'WHOSOEVER SHALL SEEK TO SAVE HIS LIFE SHALL LOSE IT; AND WHOSOEVER SHALL LOSE HIS LIFE SHALL PRESERVE IT.'

The doubts that troubled the Centurion were nowhere discernible in the Rabbi's popular following. News of his progress ran before him, and at each village he approached excitement mushroomed. Expectation hung in the very air, it seemed, for the hope of a deliverer was strong and in the fabric of the Jewish faith.

As his master the Centurion had urged, James cut through the unreasoning emotions with stinging Galilean sharpness, but it made little difference. The passionate, both young and old, were unheeding and full of intensity. A call to arms would have ignited them, but no, there was no call to arms, no ranting spleen directed at the Roman power. Instead, the Rabbi lashed the Jewish leaders: the Pharisees, the scribes and lawyers. They were whited sepulchres, beautiful on the outside but full of dead men's bones, and more directly, they were vipers, serpents; the Rabbi gave no quarter to hypocrisy. His words amused many, for they saw the truth in them, but it was not what they had come to hear and see. They wanted a dramatic miracle and the restoration of the dream of Maccabean power. Most of this instant following fell away, yet a hard core of followers remained. Some were hopeful of a final triumph in Jerusalem, while some, a few like Felix, listened faithfully to every word the Rabbi uttered.

The grey head of Felix could be seen mostly at a modest distance from the Rabbi. Felix was a Roman in a Jewish world, and even though the power of Rome was master he felt it proper to conduct himself with tact. He was a guest and needed to behave as such. The Disciple John was always quick to greet him, but Felix did not push himself. Nevertheless, his connection with the Disciple brought a welcome benefit, in that he was invited to attend some private gatherings at which the Rabbi spoke. At such meetings the Teacher was more direct, and largely dispensed with the 'story' in his answers. Felix kept silent on these occasions, careful of offending some Jewish sensibility. He was also awed by the Rabbi to the point of being tongue-tied.

For Felix, every day he spent in the Teacher's presence was a wonder, but the day of the ten lepers was remarkable. The astounding event happened as they were entering one of the villages. It was morning and the cool air was invigorating. Felix's cart with its two mules was some way to the rear. James was in the driver's seat with Felix and Sarah walking beside the slowly turning wheels.

They were at the outskirts of the village when Felix noticed ten men standing afar off to his left. They were lepers, keeping their distance for fear of being stoned.

An involuntary shudder ran through the whole scattered number of the Rabbi's followers, for the terrible reminder of such abject suffering was resented.

'Master, have mercy on us!' the lepers cried, their voices loud and desperate.

Slowly the Rabbi turned and moved to where he could see them clearly. There was a sudden stillness, as if everything in nature held its breath.

'Go, show yourselves to the priests.' This was all the Teacher said, and Felix marvelled, as he always marvelled at the sound of absolute authority in the Master's voice.

At once the Rabbi resumed his entry into the village, apparently unmoved by the eruption of excitement that surrounded him. Felix watched the lepers until he saw their unmistakable gestures of joy. Then he turned and continued walking. He had no doubt that the ten men were cured, but how!? How!? – Felix had seen the Rabbi work many wonders of healing. James, of course, was living proof of this, but somehow these lepers, ten of them, all healed, caused total confusion in his mind. Who was the Rabbi? Who was this remarkable being walking a few paces in front of him? Was he working with universal powers? He had to be. Felix felt very close to the answer.

While Felix was engrossed in his thoughts, one of the cleansed lepers rushed by, the warning bell of his terrible malady still sounding. Its ringing scattered the people in front of him until he fell before the Rabbi in gratitude. A whisper rustled round the gathering. The healed leper in his filthy rags was a Samaritan, a stranger to the laws of Israel.

The Rabbi spoke.

'Were there not ten cleansed? But where are the nine?'

He turned to his disciples.

'There are not found that returned to give glory to God, save this stranger.'

His eyes returned to gaze upon the Samaritan.

'Arise, go your way: your faith has made you whole.'

And the man arose, taking the bell from his neck as he went.

They walked on. The centre knot of the village was visible in the distance and the scattered dwellings of its perimeter were becoming more numerous. The poverty was visible, but so were the signs of vigour and industry.

The sky was clear and cloudless, and on the ground wild flowers spread their beauty with generosity. March was a colourful month. A particularly vivid bunch of red anemones caught the attention of Sarah and impulsively she stopped, plucked the blooms and ran with them to the Rabbi Jesus. There, caught in sudden shyness, she held the flowers up awkwardly.

'The blood of the Maccabees,' James muttered close to Felix – James had left his driving seat to lead the mules into the village.

The mutterings of the Galilean were meaningless to Felix, but the blood-red flowers were vivid.

The Rabbi smiled, receiving Sarah's offering with perfect grace. Gently he patted her head, and overcome by emotion she ran back to Felix. At that the full, undivided gaze of the Teacher fell on the grey-haired Roman. The faithful servant of the Valerii was overwhelmed, and tears ran from his eyes, but he was unashamed.

182

Felix walked as if in a dream, yet he felt himself keenly alert. Suddenly knowledge lit his mind.

'The Rabbi is universal.' He spoke the words half audibly.

'What did you say, father?'

'Nothing, dear, nothing.' He would try to explain later.

'He is what he says he is,' he mouthed. Why had he taken so long to understand the obvious? 'I and my Father are one' was a statement of fact.

Felix stumbled and almost fell, and the hand of James went out to save him.

'You're not looking where you're going, Master Felix.' As usual, James was blunt.

Felix laughed, for James's manner of speaking greatly amused him.

When they arrived at the village they parked the cart and took the mules to be watered; after which they made their way to the central market place. The village was small, but news of the Master's approach had attracted many from the surrounding countryside. The Rabbi himself was not visible, as he was taking refreshments in the house of a local elder.

Felix, his adopted daughter and James took their places on the paved area close to the synagogue, for all the stone benches were already occupied. It was warm, pleasantly so, and the March sun had still to reach its zenith. Excited conversation buzzed round them, the miracle of the ten lepers dominant. Felix watched the eager, animated faces. Why had they come? What were they seeking? What was their view of the Rabbi Jesus? He could see a number of lawyers, more than usual, he thought.

'There are a lot of experts around today, James,' he said, anticipating a humorous reply.

'We're not far from Jericho,' the Galilean returned, his eyes twinkling. 'I always like it when they try to catch the Master out. He never misses them!'

The crowd in front stood up, heralding the Rabbi's approach, and all were silent as he and his close disciples took up their position near the entrance to the synagogue.

It was not long before the questions came, and, as often happened, they centred on the imminence of God's kingdom. Some of the questions were more like statements, others were naive. The Rabbi remained silent, his head bowed, until one Pharisee asked bluntly when the kingdom of God should come.

The Master lifted up his head and answered.

'The kingdom of God comes not with observation.' His eyes scanned the gathering before he continued. 'Neither shall they say, Lo, here! or Lo, there! for the kingdom of God is within you.'

This was not the triumphal prophecy the crowd desired. There was no promise of a victorious Jewish theocracy, but the Pharisee who had asked the question was thoughtful.

Almost imperceptibly, the Rabbi entered the synagogue, where, according to James, he would speak more privately to someone, or to his disciples.

Felix watched the crush of elders and lawyers follow the Teacher, but most, including the three from Capernaum, remained outside. The synagogue was small.

After some time the Rabbi reappeared, followed closely by the Disciple John and other prominent adherents. The Master stopped close to where Felix was standing, and he could hear his words clearly. They were obviously directed at one of his disciples.

'Whosoever shall seek to save his life shall lose it; and whosoever shall lose his life shall preserve it.'

What did he mean? Felix pondered. To lose the little life and gain a greater? – but the Master had used the word 'preserve'. How could you lose something and preserve it? It was hopeless, he thought, giving up the struggle. Then at once the answer came. You could lose a cover and preserve the reality that was covered. The kingdom of heaven was within, but it was covered. Felix was animated, but suddenly he realised he had stopped listening to the Rabbi.

'Two men shall be in the field; the one shall be taken and the other left.' The Master's words were straight and powerful.

'Where, Lord?' someone asked.

'Wheresoever the body is, there will the eagles be gathered together.'

It was powerful imagery, but what did it say? There was much more to the Rabbi's words than the surface meaning.

The questions continued, and James's mood grew almost carnival when the Rabbi exposed the hypocrisy of the falsely pious. The parable on the subject left no one in doubt.

'Two men went up into the Temple to pray; the one a Pharisee and the other a publican.' The Teacher's words rang clearly in the market place. Felix had been quick to learn that the tax-gathering publicans were despised, while the Pharisees were great upholders of the Jewish law. It was a well polarised picture.

The Rabbi Jesus continued:

'The Pharisee stood and prayed thus with himself, God, I thank you that I am not as other men are, extortioners, unjust, adulterers, or even as this publican.

'I fast twice in the week, I give tithes of all that I possess.

'And the publican, standing afar off, would not lift up so much as his eyes unto heaven, but smote upon his breast, saying, God be merciful to me a sinner.

'I tell you this man went down to his house justified rather than the other: for everyone that exalteth himself shall be abased; and he that humbleth himself shall be exalted.'

Although James enjoyed the parable, Felix could see that the use of the tax-gatherer analogy was most unpopular, for hatred of the publican was deep and bitter, and nowhere more so than in these poverty-stricken villages. On the other hand, the lawyers and scribes resented any attack on their piety. They were the conscience of Judea – clearly the Rabbi did not court popularity.

There was one Pharisee, however, who had obviously been impressed. He had remained attentive throughout. It was always like that, Felix thought. There was always one at least who heard.

CHAPTER TWENTY-TWO

CAPERNAUM

Spurred by the trouble anticipated in Jerusalem, the Tribune travelled south, to arrive at Capernaum in the latter part of March. He was strained and tired, and behind the first pleasantries of the Centurion's greeting he was sharply aware of the question he would have to ask. Were there any letters from Capri or Rome? He hesitated before bursting through his fearfulness.

'Any rolls delivered for me, Marcus?'

'There's one from Rome,' Tullus answered, leading the way into his office.

Once the despatch was in his hands, the Tribune unrolled it with studied slowness, his fingers awkward with tension. The content could mean joy or misery. He began to read.

'It's from Father. He's coming to Antioch,' he said aloud, 'and hopes to be here within three months. My younger sister Junia will be with him – says he needs to calm the new madness in his children.' The Tribune looked up at Tullus and forced a smile. 'Don't worry, Marcus, he's quite complimentary.'

As he continued to read, his brow furrowed and lines of strain deepened on his face.

'It's Cornelia,' he said quietly.

The Centurion nodded, but said nothing.

'Father has been to the Villa Jovis, where he asked the Emperor for special dispensation.'

Tullus moved his head discreetly.

'Tiberius was not unfriendly, but as usual would not commit himself – probably thinks the infatuation will pass. Father has done all he can, and all we can do is wait. This endless waiting is maddening!'

Valerius began to pace the small room, his frustrations raging.

'Just think, one petty blemish on my record could destroy all hope!'

The Centurion remained silent. Valerius was not one to appreciate a baseless reassurance.

The Tribune sighed, his tiredness again apparent.

'Well, Marcus – the Rabbi – your words I read at Antioch worried me. Tell me more about it.'

For some time Tullus elaborated on the various passions the Rabbi's presence in Jerusalem would inflame.

'The Master will speak the truth on all occasions, not a popular practice,' he said knowingly, 'and predictably some of the Sadducees and Pharisees, the forceful ones, being jealous of their power and privilege, will be out to stop him. They'll listen to his every word, not to hear the truth, but to snare him with the law. He'll be accused of blasphemy – even a Roman can prophesy that! There are good men amongst the Jewish leadership, but as usual they are few, and there are the moderates, doubtful allies, I fear. There are some, the Zealots, for instance, who would welcome the Rabbi, though for the wrong reasons, violent reasons.'

'What about Herod Antipas?' Valerius interjected.

'He'll be there all right, but the Fox is out for himself, and there's us, of course, the Roman presence. All we want is a quiet life and our taxes,' Tullus added with a note of cynicism. 'What does one obscure Jewish preacher mean to us? An easy sacrifice if it keeps the peace; though I must say Pilate does respect the law.'

'And I thought Roman politics were a maze of knives!' Valerius reacted.

'Yes, it's complicated. Nevertheless, we as Romans have the Sadducees to bargain with – we have little hold on the Pharisees and none at all on the Zealots, but the Sadducees need us to keep the peace, to keep the status quo and so to keep the Temple running, for that's the basis of their power.'

'So I can use my rank to shape their will. At last the Emperor's personal legate may be of some use!'

'Of continuing and considerable influence, sir – the Sadducees must listen and so must Pilate, too!'

'I'll need you to advise me, Marcus.'

Tullus nodded. 'Cornelius is more than capable of looking after Capernaum – it's time he was promoted.'

'Put the recommendation through and I'll support it – we'll have to move carefully,' Valerius added, thinking of Jerusalem.

'Very!'

'Well, my noble friend, I must visit the altar and remember the gods, otherwise my men will think me wholly irreligious!' The Tribune smiled wearily. 'Then it's the baths, after which I must visit my sister and Cornelia.'

'Cornelia is . . .'

'I know – weary of waiting and uncertainty. By all the gods, what can I say to her? And my sister, how is she?'

'Well and happy – your sister and I are very happy.'

'Marcus, you have my unreserved blessing.'

At that the two men gripped each other firmly.

After visiting the altar and bathing, the Tribune set out for the Ben Josephs' villa, escorted by three legionaries. His guard commander was ever vigilant. He almost bumped into Drusilla as he entered the portico, and at once they embraced warmly.

'My dear Drusilla, you look radiant.'

'I've had good news – Father has given his blessing to Marcus and me, and the Emperor approves as well. Father wrote that Tiberius, Nerva and he had had an old men's drinking party, and that in the midst of the nostalgic chatter the Emperor leaned across to Nerva and said that I was marrying a real soldier.'

'Amazing, but Father has always fared well with Tiberius. Did he tell you he was coming to the east?'

'No!' she exploded, propelling herself into her brother's arms. 'He'll be present at our wedding?'

'I hope not – you are marrying Tullus.' He emphasised the 'are', and Drusilla laughed.

'My darling brother, I am so happy, and I hope, I so very much hope, that you will be happy soon.'

Grateful for her sympathy, the Tribune held his sister tightly.

'How is she?' he asked quietly.

'Cornelia is a stoic, Lucius. She says little, but I know her hope is fading. I'm sorry, but it's better you should know.'

'Where is she?'

'In her room – shall I fetch her?'

'No, I'll go myself.'

Cornelia was sitting close to an open trellis. She was sewing and did not hear the Tribune approach. For a moment he watched her silently. She was thinner, much thinner. It shocked him, and he caught his breath involuntarily.

She turned to see him, and for a moment of unbelief she sat watching. Then, in the instant, they were in each other's arms. There was no point in pretence of any kind. They were in love.

'Beloved Lucius,' was all she said, leaning back to look up at him.

'I'm sorry, but I cannot propose any formal . . .' The Tribune's words came awkwardly, and she put her fingers over his mouth.

'I know what you're going to say. I know it's impossible.' Her eyes were wide, and in their depths there was no shadow of reservation. 'Lucius, I don't care what my status is.'

'No! not that!' The violence of his aversion startled her. Again he took her in his arms.

'Don't you see, my dear Cornelia, that the heirs of the Valerii need to be lawful, and the only heir I desire is from our union.' He had done and said everything he had determined to avoid.

She was weeping almost uncontrollably, and he gathered her with an infinite tenderness into his arms.

'Don't cry, my lovely Cornelia.' His voice was very gentle, and slowly she grew quiet.

'Beloved Lucius, it's impossible; you know it is, but you have said it; you have said you want me as your wife. Lucius, dear Lucius, you have made me very happy.'

He looked at her for a long time without speaking. Then he told her of his father's visit to Capri. There was hope, he told her. She brightened, but he knew her doubts still lingered.

'The spirit of the Gracchi lives, and you carry the name of their blessed mother.' It was a strange statement, and he did not know why he had said it.

CHAPTER TWENTY-THREE

THE REVENGE OF MARIUS

After two days in Capernaum the Tribune was on the move again, taking the same road as he had done before on the journey to Machaerus. He had slept badly at Capernaum, and the tiredness he had felt on the road from Antioch had not lifted. Nevertheless, he stopped to address the small garrison at Scythopolis. The event itself was satisfactory, but it left the Tribune in a state of exhaustion. He rested overnight, and again there was little sleep. However, he pressed on the next morning, but even though he took every precaution, the gathering mesh of confusion in his mind grew more pronounced.

Slowly and inevitably, the pattern of his illness repeated. First came the short spells of dizziness; then they grew more severe, until he was unable to stand up without support. They were close to Jericho when Venio forcefully suggested a return to Qumran, and the Tribune could do little other than nod his assent.

The priest Raphael was not at the community when Valerius and his guard arrived, but he was due back in the morning. As before, the Tribune was carried into the strangers' reception area and put in the same small room he had occupied previously. A three-man team had already been sent to inform Tullus of the situation.

The Tribune had a restless night, and it was not until midday that Raphael arrived. At once he went to see Valerius, and after what seemed a long time to Venio, he emerged.

'It may take some time,' he said without elaboration.

Within three days the Centurion arrived at Qumran, and after seeing Venio he was introduced to the priest Raphael. At once each man knew the merit of the other. Trust was immediate, but it was obvious from what Raphael reported that the Tribune's illness would prevent him from being in Jerusalem at the crucial time. It was unfortunate, to say the least, for even though he knew he could go as the Tribune's deputy, he also knew that his impact on the rulers of Jerusalem would be as nothing compared with that of the Emperor's personal legate and son of the Senator Valerius.

The next morning at first light the Centurion left for the city of Jerusalem, using three of the Tribune's guard as an escort. When he reached the junction of the Qumran track with the main Jerusalem road he found a troop of soldiers waiting and approached to exchange greetings. Before him, in the uniform of a military tribune, was Marius, the agent of Gallo.

Marius's soldiers closed in and then, correctly, but with vindictive relish, Marius pronounced the Centurion's formal arrest.

'This is idiotic!' Tullus exploded, as he listened to the charges levelled against him. He was accused of collaboration with a fanatical religious sect bent on rebellion, and caught, Marius added, on his way from one of the rebel strongholds.

'No one will believe this rubbish. The Procurator Pilate is in Jerusalem. I demand to be taken before him.'

'The charges are well documented, sir.' The words were sharp and cold, like icicles. 'I'm afraid I cannot comply with your request, sir,' he added, 'as I have orders to take you to Palmyra.' The beginnings of a smile played about his mouth.

'Whose orders?'

'That is not for me to say, sir. May we proceed?' Behind the frozen formality, the obsessional mind of Marius was gloating over its success. He noticed the Centurion scanning his uniform sceptically, and reacted with imperious satisfaction.

'I was waiting for my official posting in Capernaum. My family thought I should taste life in the ranks before receiving my commission. I was told you were the best soldier in Syria, so I chose Capernaum!' The words were coated with sarcasm. 'I suggest you and your companions ride in this open cart,' Marius added, pointing with exaggerated grace at a two-wheeled vehicle drawn by mules. He was enjoying his role to the full.

Rage overwhelmed the Centurion.

'Stop this idiot playacting and take me to Jerusalem.' The

soldiers standing close to him stepped back involuntarily at the force of his anger, but Marius was unmoved. His eyes narrowed with hatred.

'I will decide who is playacting and who is not.' His words came with bitter satisfaction.

The Centurion's mind flashed back to the time when the dishevelled messenger had arrived from Machaerus with firm news about Cornelia. He remembered it clearly, and could almost hear the arrogant sneer in the voice of Marius as he described the messenger. He recalled his own words, too: 'Soldier, I will decide who is insolent and who is a savage'.

'The cart?' Marius prompted. The gauze of polite pretence had slipped away, leaving the bare sinews of hatred.

The Centurion climbed into the cart followed by his escort. He had little alternative, for Marius had two full tent parties, sixteen men and mostly young recruits. They were clearly enjoying his humiliation, for the legionary recruit had no love for the harsh discipline of their Centurion masters. The attitude of the older soldiers was plainly different. They were visibly uneasy, knowing Tullus wore a Chief Centurion's uniform. To them such men embodied the very spirit of the army.

Somewhere Gallo was behind this, Tullus thought frustratedly, but if Gallo supported Marius privately he doubted if he would do so publicly, as he found it difficult to imagine the devious friend of Sejanus backing such a clumsy move. If he was right, and he believed he was, Marius was expendable. He could be dropped as quickly as a hot cinder from the altar. It was Gallo at his cynical best, and Gallo it was, for he had just been to Palmyra, Marius's declared destination. Tullus knew Palmyra, and the Camp Prefect, a drunkard, easy to manipulate. Why the army kept him in such a key position was a mystery.

Marius was anxious to get moving, and soon the soldiers were marching at a fast pace towards Philadelphia. Soon after crossing the Jordan bridge they branched north, leaving the main road for what was little more than a track. At once the Centurion was deprived of the one hope he had envisaged. That was the possibility of meeting another troop of legionaries on their way out of Philadelphia, when he could have appealed to their commander and at least sent a message to the Tribune. Marius had obviously anticipated this. The man was both fanatical and clever, a dangerous combination. Gallo was playing with fire.

Their progress was slow, but Marius appeared to be in no hurry. In fact, he ordered a halt as soon as they were invisible from the main Philadelphia road. The Centurion and his escort were given well-diluted wine by one of the older legionaries, the soldier who had shown disgust at the Centurion's treatment.

'I know you, sir,' he said to Tullus. 'I served under you in that campaign near Sura.'

'We were both younger then,' Tullus smiled, but the scowl of Marius hurried the legionary away.

It was growing hot, and every stone of the wilderness floor was beginning to magnify the heat. They were travelling north and were obviously going to miss the town of Livias Julias. After bypassing the town they began to veer east towards the hills and slowly climb from the valley floor. The Centurion had no precise idea of his location, though he felt they could be somewhere due west of Philadelphia, if not a little to the south.

They stopped again, this time for food, and Tullus noticed that there were two baggage carts full of provisions. His conclusions were immediate; they were meant to eat on the road and not in the towns or settlements. Marius had reduced the possibility of public contact to the minimum, for his captor had the sense to know that once he, Tullus, was before a Roman garrison commander, he would be freed.

He was being kidnapped rather than arrested, for while Marius might believe his action fully justified, Gallo, his patron, would know it to be spurious. This being so, why had he been captured? There could be only one answer, he concluded. He was not the prize. It was at the Tribune that the schemes of Gallo were aimed. What would happen, he asked himself, if the news broke that Marcus Tullus was missing? There would be an extensive search around the Qumran and Jericho area, and for a few days the event would be prominent in conversation, but rolling time would quickly find another drama. One man, though, would not give up the search for his friend and proposed brother-in-law. Indeed, such a search could distract the Tribune for a month or even two. If he was right, it was a clever plan, for in one simple move Gallo had neutralised both the Tribune and himself. If the scheme failed or lost its usefulness, Gallo could disown Marius as a fanatic, and few would disbelieve him.

After eating they continued to climb away from the Jordan valley. They were following a dry river bed into the mountains, where the desert bleakness was giving way to scrub and rough grassland. It was early afternoon when they stopped again, and as before he was offered diluted wine by the same soldier as previously. He was grateful for the veteran soldier's discreet attention. Titus was his praenomen, and he knew he had an ally.

Once more they were on the move, and as they climbed into the hills they passed their first isolated tree. The going was rough and the path poor and pitted.

Until then Tullus had tended to look upon his situation like a visitor to the theatre. He was deeply involved in the drama, but it was not quite real. He was frustrated and angry, yet somehow he felt he would get to Jerusalem. There was time enough, and even if the present lunacy continued for another two days there would still be time. Nevertheless, as the hours passed his pessimism grew, for escape was well-nigh impossible.

The Rabbi would probably be in the area of Jericho by now, he mused, with Felix, James and Sarah in his following. At once he was filled with a powerful desire to be in their midst. He had always wanted to follow the Rabbi on his journeys, but his army life had made it impossible. Again, it was difficult, to say the least, for a Chief Centurion to be the sudden private citizen.

If the Rabbi did journey by way of Jericho he would face a bleak, dry climb to Jerusalem. There was only one well between the oasis at Jericho and the high ground before Jerusalem. There the robbers waited, but the Rabbi's followers would be safe. It was the lone traveller who had most to fear.

What would happen when the Rabbi reached Jerusalem? What would be the outcome if he spoke within the Temple

Court? The Centurion could easily imagine a group of lawyers exhibiting their erudition before the Master. Their pride would resent his obvious authority, and some of their number would turn to hatred, for there was no one more blind than the priest or the philosopher when their theories and beliefs were questioned, and when the question was powerful the blind defence grew passionate. The Centurion had convinced himself anew. The Rabbi's power could breed bitter opposition. In fact, this opposition already had advocates in the Sanhedrin, the central council of elders, for the Master's discernment of Pharisee hypocrisy had annoyed the dignified ranks of the Jewish leadership. Who was this pretentious Galilean? they asked. Could anything good come out of Galilee!? Tullus had learned of their attitude from Ben Joseph.

The Sanhedrin, of course, were always ultra-careful of their relationship with Rome, and if a popular Rabbi disturbed the public order while they remained inactive, Rome could see them as unable, or worse, unwilling to remedy the situation. For them the Rabbi's presence could be most unwelcome.

The Centurion's thought was abruptly terminated when one of the cart wheels suddenly lurched into a deep rut. From then on he and his escort walked behind the cart.

According to the Centurion's reading of the sun they were travelling almost due north. Trees, either solitary or in small clumps, were becoming more numerous. In front of them was a raised flat table of ground well above the river bed, an ideal camp site, and, as it was late afternoon, Tullus fully expected Marius to stop. Up in front the veteran Titus was busy in conversation with his officer; a heated conversation, Tullus guessed, probably about the night stop, he anticipated, but the troop marched on. Marius had other plans.

They had been climbing constantly for some time. It was cooler. There was a trickle of water in the river bed, and the trees, now much thicker, were beginning to narrow in upon the track. The Centurion looked at his escort and then at Titus who was walking beside him. Titus's response was immediate.

'I told him, sir, but he wouldn't listen. He says there's a good place up ahead.'

'It will need to be soon!' was all the Centurion said.

The climb continued until they were walled on each side by trees. Up ahead, about half a mile, the track appeared to broaden out, or so it seemed to Tullus. Was this the camp site Marius was seeking? Suddenly the light began to fail and on each side the dark presence of the trees danced with phantom shadows. Sensing trouble, Marius bound his prisoners' hands and roped them to the cart as the temptation to escape was obvious.

Tullus knew they were in mortal danger; a lifetime of experience told him so. An isolated troop of soldiers had been visible all day and hostile eyes could well have seen them. If that were so, they had time enough to organise and plan, and the temptation to attack in what was perfect cover would be overwhelming. Tullus was resigned rather than afraid. Nevertheless, he was tense, expecting imminent trouble, yet vividly before him was the image of Drusilla.

Titus was busy watching the black anonymity of the flanking trees. Like the Centurion, he knew they were as silhouettes and hopelessly vulnerable, while a potential attacker would have the blackness of the trees as cover.

Slowly they moved on. Only a hundred paces separated them from the opening in front. Marius, now fully aware of the danger, had his men in total readiness; their shields held between them and the forest. They were almost at the clearing when Marius, who was leading his horse, stopped and looked about him. Then, feeling the danger to be past, he mounted.

At that very moment they were attacked from both sides. The hail of arrows was thick; their effect deadly. Shouts and screaming rent the evening air and shadowy figures sprang as if from nowhere. The young legionaries, their numbers halved, were hacked down as they tried to form a shield wall.

Titus cut the ropes that held the prisoners and turned to rally the remaining soldiers, but there was no one standing. He retreated towards the open space, at every step expecting the fatal arrow. A javelin glanced off his helmet and landed behind him. He was retreating backwards, his progress slow. Cautiously he edged himself towards the forest fringe, all the while expecting the greeting of a sword. Once below the covering branches, he stopped. All he could hear was his own breathing and the slight rustle of the wind. Titus had escaped.

Back at the scene of the ambush numerous shadowy figures were moving to and fro in the half light. Their leader was bent over the fallen figure of a soldier, his ear close to the Roman's chest.

'It's him all right.'

'Is he still alive?' asked another voice.

'Yes, his heart's still at work. He's not wounded,' the leader continued, peering at the fallen figure. 'Just a cut on the back of his head. Here, give me a hand.'

They laid the soldier on the grassy edge of the forest, spreading the cloak of the dead officer over him.

'Give me that goatskin bag of wine,' the leader said, 'he'll need it later.'

'You're mad – what about his breastplate; it's encrusted with silver, and there's gold . . .'

'Leave it,' the leader barked.

'But he's a Roman unbeliever!'

'Leave him as he is,' the leader returned, the menace in his voice undisguised. 'We owe him this one.' He made a mock salute. 'Sleep well, Marcus Tullus.' The accent was Galilean.

In the morning, at first light, Titus skirted the edge of the trees until he arrived at the scene of the ambush. There he waited, vigilant, until eventually he ventured into the open. The soldiers still lay where they had fallen, but they had been stripped of almost everything except their tunics. There was no spade to dig a grave, but even if there had been one, the task was much too great for one man. Nevertheless, he dragged each lifeless body to the edge of the trees and lined them up in one ordered row. Two missing from their number. They were the Chief Centurion and, of course, himself. He was very tired, but he forced himself to search the area again, but Tullus was nowhere to be found.

Titus sat down for a moment's rest. A snake slid through the grass close to his feet. The Centurion could have escaped, yet he did not think so. There had been no Roman standing when he retreated from the field. Marcus Tullus might have dragged hinself clear, though. He sighed wearily. When he had rested he would search a wider area. This he did, but still without result.

After covering the dead bodies of his comrades with branches and foliage, Titus began to walk down the slow incline that led eventually to the Jordan valley. The news he had to tell the world was bitter.

CHAPTER TWENTY-FOUR

JERUSALEM

The Rabbi approached Jerusalem by way of Bethany and Bethphage with the three from Capernaum still present in his following. At Bethphage James left the cart and mules in the care of an innkeeper and from there the three proceeded on foot, along with the swelling number of the Rabbi's admirers.

Pressing crowds did not appear to trouble the Rabbi. Indeed, it seemed to Felix that he never left his inner kingdom of peace. Circumstances might play with the instrument of his human nature, but the inner kingdom was never forsaken.

They were at a place called the Mount of Olives when the Rabbi stopped. Then something happened which Felix found very strange: two of the disciples were instructed to bring a colt, which the Master said would be found tied at the entrance to the village close by. It was a colt on which no man had sat before, and they were to loose it and bring it to him. If anyone questioned them they were to answer: because the Lord had need of him.

The colt was found, as the Rabbi had foretold, and brought to the Master. Whereupon coats and various garments were draped over the animal, after which the Rabbi was helped onto its back.

Felix was mystified. Why was the great Teacher bothering with such trivialities? he asked James.

'The fulfilment of prophecy, Master Felix. The prophet Zechariah. See your king comes to you: he is just and having salvation; lowly and riding on a donkey, on a colt, the foal of a donkey.'

'You know your scriptures, James.'

'Most do.'

Felix nodded pensively. In truth, he was alarmed, for Jewish prophecies, seen to be fulfilled, could be dangerous. Certainly the authorities would look on such events at best with grave suspicion. The gods be praised that Lucius and Marcus would be there to bring restraint.

They were on the Mount of Olives and about to descend when a wave of emotion seemed to engulf them. Felix could feel its power surging within him, and all about were shouts of praise and thanksgiving. 'Blessed be the King that comes in the name of the Lord,' they cried, and although Felix was bewildered his face shone with the same happiness as those about him.

Some of the Pharisees amongst the following asked the Rabbi to rebuke his disciples. They were no doubt alarmed, as Felix had been. Felix was close to the Rabbi and could hear plainly. The advice of the Pharisees was prudent, he thought, for such a display could well get out of hand, but the Master's reply took him by surprise.

'I tell you,' he said, 'that if these should hold their peace the stones would immediately cry out.'

Felix looked at James for an explanation, and the old Galilean reacted bluntly.

'We've been waiting since the time of Moses for this day!'

Felix nodded, but that was not the full story, he surmised.

As the Rabbi Jesus progressed, many spread their garments in his path and others cut down branches of the trees and strewed them on the way.

Suddenly, but with ease, the Rabbi stopped the colt and gazed at the city before him, and to Felix's amazement the Teacher's eyes filled with tears. Why? Why was a man of such enormous stature weeping? Nothing seemed to make sense. Then the Rabbi began to speak, his words strange and magnificent.

'If you had known, even you, at least in this your day, the things which belong unto your peace! but now they are hid from your eyes.'

He was speaking to Jerusalem, the Holy City, the focus of Jewish sacrifice. Here the great and invisible Jehovah had been worshipped for centuries.

'For the days shall come upon you, that your enemies shall cast a trench about you, and compass you round, and keep you in on every side,

'And shall lay you even with the ground, and your children within you; and they shall not leave in you one stone upon the other; because you knew not the time of your visitation.'

"Because you knew not the time of your visitation" Felix repeated. What visitation? What did he mean? and why the prophecy of tribulation? He clenched his fists, for he felt close to the answer, not a manufactured explanation, but the inner meaning.

The press of the Rabbi's following, so lately rejoicing, began to ebb away. They had come to hear of triumph, not of doom, yet many remained.

As they drew closer to Jerusalem, the surrounding crowds grew dense. Many had with them doves in cages and numerous lambs were being pulled or carried. There were calves too. All were the Temple offerings for the day of deliverance, the passing over from Egypt. The crush of the crowd squeezed round Felix, but it was a good-humoured throng.

In the busy, bustling streets of Jerusalem it became difficult to keep close to the Rabbi and his disciples. The Master's ability to slip unobtrusively through the tightest mass of people compounded the difficulty and eventually they lost him. In any case, the need to find accommodation was a necessary diversion. To this end they called at the Antonia Tower, hoping that the Tribune or the Centurion could help, but neither was present. After this James tried endlessly for lodgings in the crowded city, but without result, and eventually they became resigned to the long walk to their cart at Bethphage.

They were about to leave when they heard that the Rabbi had cast out the moneychangers and traders from the Temple, saying that they had made the house of prayer a den of thieves. The news danced around the excited crowds, growing with exaggeration, until at last James found an actual witness of the scene and questioned him. It was true, the man reported. The Rabbi had cast out the traders, and no one had touched him.

'He doesn't seem to court anyone's favour,' Felix said to James on their way to the cart.

'What did you expect?' As usual the Galilean's voice was sharp and quick.

'I wonder where tall Master Lucius is, Father?' Sarah asked as they continued on their way.

'Yes, I wonder,' Felix responded pensively.

'Women!' James muttered.

'I'm serious, James. I find it strange that neither he nor your master the Centurion is here. Tullus was emphatic in his message that they both intended coming – perhaps they'll be here tomorrow.'

Sarah skipped happily between them as they walked. Dusk had fallen, but there was ample light from the moon and the houses that lined the way. Many families were sitting in the open. Some were reciting the Exodus, and common to most was the baking of unleavened bread and the eating of the Paschal lamb. An atmosphere of quiet joy had descended on the city.

The next day they found the Rabbi Jesus in the outer court of the Temple, surrounded by a crowd reflecting the different levels of society. Among them were Temple priests, scribes, Pharisees and a group of richly clad figures, merchants, Felix thought, but their presence angered James.

'Herodians! damned camels pretending to be sons of Judah!'

Felix nodded briefly. Obviously James despised them.

'Half-baked Jews!' the Galilean added, continuing to mutter inaudibly.

One of the Rabbi's audience began to speak and Felix's attention quickly returned to the scene before him. The man spoke easily.

'Master, we know that you are true, and teach the way of God in truth, neither care you for any man; for you regard not the person of men.'

This was a fair appraisal, Felix thought, but James continued to mutter angrily.

'Tell us therefore what you think,' the speaker continued. 'Is it lawful to give tribute unto Caesar or not?'

It was a trap, and at once Felix understood James's anger.

'Why tempt me, you hypocrites?' the Rabbi returned, cutting through the clever sham of the speaker and his supporters. 'Show me the tribute money,' he added.

A number of hands stretched forward with a coin, and he took the nearest one.

'Whose is the image and superscription?' he asked, looking round the gathering.

'Caesar's!' came the answer in chorus.

'Render therefore unto Caesar the things that are Caesar's; and unto God the things that are God's.'

The smooth tongue of the speaker and the mocking eyes of his supporters were stilled, and all marvelled.

There was a brief silence before the Sadducees, conscious of their dignity, began to test him, but Felix found their convoluted questions difficult to follow. James, however, was quick to prompt him. The Sadducees, he said, denied the resurrection. Almost gleefully he summarised their question. If a woman had seven husbands, who would be her husband in the resurrection?

'The question of a child,' Felix reacted. 'Are they blind? Do they not know the stature of the man that stands before them?'

'To them it is a serioius question, Master Felix!'

'What did the Master say?'

'In resurrection they neither marry nor are they given in marriage.'

'And . . .'

'Listen to the Master!'

'As touching the resurrection of the dead,' the Rabbi was saying, 'have you not read in the book of Moses how in the bush God spoke to him, saying, I am the God of Abraham and the God of Isaac and the God of Jacob? God is not the God of the dead but of the living.'

Felix knew the three men mentioned were the ancient Jewish patriarchs, and according to the Rabbi they were living; for God, their God, was a God of the living. The Rabbi's words were plain enough, but what was their meaning, the real meaning? Again he felt close to something, something almost magical, but he could not grasp it.

At last a scribe who had remained silent and pensive throughout the previous exchange asked the Rabbi what was the first commandment.

Without hesitation the Master answered:

'The Lord our God is one Lord.'

James gently elbowed Felix in the ribs.

'One, Master Felix – the secret of Israel!'

'And of Plato, too,' Felix answered, using his elbow in return.

The Rabbi continued:

'And you shall love the Lord your God with all your heart and with all your soul and with all your mind and with all your strength: this is the first commandment.

'And the second is like, namely this, you shall love your neighbour as yourself. There is no other commandment greater than these.'

'Well, Master,' the scribe responded quietly, 'you have said the truth; for there is one God; and there is no other but he:

'And to love him with all the heart and with all the understanding and with all the soul and with all the strength and to love his neighbour as himself is more than all whole burnt offerings and sacrifices.'

The Rabbi's face shone with light as he looked at the speaker, and his face, too, was full of light, the same light.

'You are not far from the kingdom of God.' The words of the Rabbi seemed to live.

For Felix the sense of closeness he had experienced earlier was even more intense. 'The Lord our God is one Lord': 'You are not far from the kingdom of God': 'Neither shall they say lo, here! nor lo, there! for the kingdom of God is within you'. The words, vivid in his memory, repeated involuntarily. Suddenly it came to him. The kingdom of God was in everyone, not just the Rabbi and a chosen few, but everyone – even himself, he thought wryly. The Master had said it time and time again. How strange to hear and yet not hear. The kingdom was within and the living realization was a man's true end.

'What's wrong, Master Felix?' James had become used to Felix and his moments of oblivious thought. 'The Rabbi's moved on.'

'I was just thinking.'

'That's not unusual. Come, it's time to eat. Sarah's starving.'

'And a certain Galilean as well, no doubt, but before we eat let's check at the Antonia Tower again. Master Lucius and your master should be there by now.'

This they did, but their enquiries were fruitless; neither the Tribune nor the Centurion had reported to the garrison.

Felix was puzzled by their absence. They could be staying with some friend of Marcus, of course, but even so Lucius would surely have reported to the Tower. He decided to check first thing in the morning.

The next day they could not find the Rabbi. The crowds made it difficult to move quickly, and when they reached the place where he was reported to have been they found that they had missed him. So in the evening, when they returned to the cart, they were drained of energy.

There was still no sign of the Tribune or the Centurion. Felix was uneasy, feeling certain that something was wrong. Sarah and James were similarly troubled, their earlier carnival mood forgotten.

For two days they saw the Rabbi in the outer court of the Temple and on the following day they found him on the Mount of Olives, only to lose him quickly in the crowds. The general press of people was constant, though in general good-natured, but the three from Capernaum were troubled. Something had happened to the Tribune and Tullus. Of that they were certain.

The next day they were late arriving at the Temple mount. The news they learned stunned them. The Rabbi Jesus had been arrested, and bit by bit they gathered the details. It had all begun the night before, when a band of armed men from the chief priests and Pharisees had taken him. He had appeared before the Sanhedrin and had been tried for blasphemy. Some had spoken for him, it appeared, but his enemies had won.

'Where is he now?' Felix kept asking until he found an answer.

'He's at Herod's palace. Pilate sent him there to be judged. Herod being ruler of Galilee,' one man said.

'The rumour is he's sent him back,' another added.

James was dazed, unable to formulate his anguish. His master the Centurion had feared such a situation and had told him so, but where was he now? Where was his master Marcus Tullus? James looked at the grey-haired Roman at his side, his distress evident.

Felix was standing in a state of shock, the unheeding crowds milling about him, yet he felt alone.

'The trial of Socrates,' he whispered to himself. 'Does it always have to be like this?' he asked aloud, but no one heard.

Although they had arrived later than usual, it was still early. There was time for something to be done, Felix thought desperately, but what? He could check at the Tower once more, just in case, and if, as he anticipated, Lucius had not arrived, he could always ask where Pilate was.

As he thought, his enquiries at the Tower were fruitless. Some dangerous uprising must have prevented them from coming. Next he asked about the Procurator's whereabouts.

'He's at the halls of justice, sir,' was the polite reply. 'Trouble with some of the pilgrims, I'm told, but he should be finished by mid-morning. I'll tell him you called, sir.' The young guard was well-mannered and friendly. 'The Tribune Valerius addressed us at Jericho. Are you a friend of his?'

'Yes, his personal servant,' Felix answered, subduing his impatience.

The friendliness of the young soldier contrasted vividly with the harsh drama of the Rabbi's arrest and spurred Felix to action. Quickly he took his leave, rushing back to where James and Sarah were waiting. He was going to try and see the Procurator, he told them.

The guards at the halls of justice were neither polite nor reasonable. Felix met a wall of refusal, but contrary to his nature he persisted, so much so that he attracted the attention of a nearby Centurion.

'Soldier, who is this man?' the Centurion asked.

'He says he's the personal servant of a Senator.'

'Does it look like it?'

'No, sir!'

Felix suddenly realised that his dress and appearance had become more Jewish than Roman, yet he did not think to remove his Galilean headdress.

'Take him in. He's a trouble maker.'

'Yes, sir!'

The Centurion walked away with a casual swagger and the

two soldiers by the door obeyed his orders, disregarding Felix's constant protests.

Once locked in what was a cold, dimly-lit cell, he remembered that he had spoken solely in Greek. Why, he could not think, for the Latin tongue, especially his Roman accent, would have set him apart. He clenched his fists in exasperation. Why had he been so stupid?

There was a rough wooden stool in the corner of the cell, and above there was a small shaft of light coming from what appeared to be a grating. He sat down and in resignation leaned against the wall. It was cold.

James had expected Felix to return with a message of failure; such was the hopelessness he felt. So the continued absence of his Roman friend was to him a herald of success.

'He must have got in to see Pilate. I never thought he would,' he said to Sarah, restless at his side.

'There's Father!' she said for the third time. They both looked, but it was someone else.

'Maybe we should go and check at the entrance gate. Father might have left a message,' she suggested.

'No! I don't trust soldiers!'

'Master Lucius and your master are soldiers.'

'That's different,' he returned, smacking his lips stubbornly.

A sudden surge in the mass of people close to James and Sarah swept them involuntarily towards the open forum.

'Father will never find us,' Sarah reacted anxiously.

'Don't worry; if we lose him we'll meet him at the cart later on.'

'I'm frightened, James!'

Sarah was walled about by adults and could see little, but there was nothing James could do other than comfort her.

In front of him he could see a line of soldiers guarding an open-sided building. The recessed platform area which stood above head level was limited in size, though it was large enough for a number of people to present themselves to the crowd. Soldiers stood vigilant in both wings of the recess, and he could see other figures deeper in the shadow, although he was too distant to distinguish detail. Even so, he could see that there were elders and lawyers close to the platform. One of their number, a young, well-dressed man, climbed the steps and disappeared within the shadow of the recess. In a few moments he returned; the soldiers were allowing communication.

James was a Jew in the midst of Jews, but he felt like an alien. He was apprehensive. Indeed, he feared the worst. The Rabbi Jesus could save himself, he had little doubt of that. He had the power, but would he use it? James feared the opposite, and his mind returned to the day of the ten lepers. He could almost hear the Rabbi speak.

'Whosoever shall seek to save his life shall lose it; and whosoever shall lose his life shall preserve it.'

Felix might tell him he was taking the words too literally. That could be, but they were good enough for him – too good! It was hot in the pressing crowd, but James felt his body shiver.

Felix's claim to be the personal servant of a Senator was enough to warrant investigation by those higher in the pyramid of command around the Procurator. The soldiers had described him as a Greek-speaking native and had labelled him a crank. Nevertheless, his claim to be the servant of a Senator needed to be checked.

Felix was surprised to be taken from his cell so quickly, but he was much relieved.

'They want to see you up above,' one of the guards said.

Felix nodded but said nothing. There were two guards, and he walked between them along the corridor from the cell, then upstairs to a small ante-chamber. A heavy, elaborate wooden screen formed two of its sides, which suggested that a corner of a room or hall had been partitioned off.

He removed his Galilean head-piece and addressed his guards in perfect Latin.

'Whom am I waiting to see?'

The effect on the soldiers was instant. Felix without his head-dress and with the accent of an educated Roman was a convincing transformation.

'We don't know, sir,' one of the guards responded.

'Tell them what I've got to say is urgent, very urgent!' Felix pressed.

'Yes, sir.'

One of the soldiers left at once, while the other stayed behind to watch. Felix was still a prisoner, but he held his peace, confident that on seeing one of Pilate's aides he would be given access to the Procurator.

He was tired The shock of the Rabbi's arrest, his own imprisonment and the crowded days of the Passover had taken their toll. He could find no clarity in his thinking.

Some people had entered the room on the other side of the screen which, being solid up to head-height, blocked his vision. There were loud whisperings, but he could not distinguish the words. Then there was the strong, deliberate step of someone approaching.

'Bring the prisoner in.' The words that came from the other side of the partition were full of authority and Felix expected the guard to obey instantly, but he remained immobile. Clearly he was not the prisoner. There were more footsteps, and then there was a moment's silence.

'Are you the King of the Jews?'

Felix froze. The Rabbi was the prisoner.

'Say you this thing of yourself or did others tell it you of me?'

'Am I a Jew?' Felix recognised the voice of Pilate. 'Your own nation and chief priests have delivered you to me: what have you done?'

The colour drained from the face of Felix, but the features of the guard remained as stone.

'My kingdom is not of this world: if my kingdom were of this world, then would my servants fight . . .'

The door of the ante-room opened and another soldier entered, then after a whispered conversation with the guard he left.

Felix listened desperately through the interruption.

'Are you a king, then?' The words could just be heard.

The silence deepened before the Rabbi spoke.

'You say I am a king. To this end was I born, and for this cause came I into the world, that I should bear witness unto the truth. Every one that is of the truth hears my voice.'

'What is truth?'

There was no real question in the sound of Pilate's voice, and the Rabbi did not answer.

Again the door to the ante-room opened. This time Felix heard the whispered message. He had been taken to the wrong place.

'They never admit their mistakes,' his guard muttered as Felix was transferred to another waiting-room. 'That was the place I was told!'

The new waiting-room was smaller, with one wooden bench on which Felix took his seat. His mind was in a turmoil. Why had he not intervened while he had had the chance? for his words could easily have been heard. At that a contrary thought argued that his intervention would have been undignified and of little help to the Rabbi. The mental argument continued, bringing his state to one of anguish. He rose, and forgetful of his guard, began pacing up and down.

'It's all right, sir, you'll be released soon. It's only a formality.' The Roman accent and bearing of Felix had convinced the soldier.

Felix smiled and expressed his thanks, and only a few moments elapsed before he was in front of one of Pilate's aides. It was Maximus, the young man he had met when the Valerian party had first arrived at Caesarea. Maximus was immediately friendly.

'I'm sorry, Master Felix!' The young aide paused, inclining his head. 'Am I right?'

'Yes, you're right, sir. That is my name.'

'This has all been a stupid error. The guards will be censured, I assure you.'

Felix held up his hand in protest. 'They were doing their duty,' he emphasised. Then he put his head-dress on. 'You see – I do look like a native!'

Maximus laughed. 'Yes, you are convincing!'

Maximus talked on, recalling his friends from Venusia who were also known to the Valerii, and enquiring politely after the Tribune and his sister. Felix waited, disguising his impatience as best he could.

When the moment came to ask for an audience, Maximus was co-operative, though practical.

'The Procurator is engaged on a very tricky case. The Jews are explosive about one of their Rabbis, or prophets, or whatever he is. They say he is defying their laws and leading the people astray – which wouldn't be too difficult,' Maximus added cynically. 'They say he poses a threat to Rome – an exaggeration, no doubt. The Procurator could find no wrong in him and has been trying to release him, but the chief priests and their friends have been howling for his blood. The soldiers are scourging him at present, so perhaps they'll be content with that.'

Felix stiffened, tension gripping his stomach.

'That is why I want to see the Procurator. The Rabbi Jesus is a good man.'

'Well, Master Felix, it may be difficult, but rest assured, I'll do what I can.'

Felix was ushered into a more expansive waiting area and was offered wine, which he refused. He was unable to rest or concentrate his thought. He stared at the floor, his gaze fixed, immobilised by anguish. In the distance he could hear the muffled sound of shouting.

Where James and Sarah were standing the shouting was not muffled. 'Crucify him! Crucify him!' Bitter, vicious and unreasoning, the sound of the inhuman chant, it seemed, reverberated everywhere. It was well orchestrated, James concluded. Some dark souls would do anything for money.

Tears were running down James's cheeks, for beneath the rough exterior there was a strong sensitive streak. The brutal mockery of the Rabbi's crown of thorns and his scarlet robe had enraged the Centurion's servant. James had shouted the Rabbi's innocence, but his cry was nothing set against the hateful, grating chant.

He had been able to see the Rabbi clearly each time he was presented – the crush of people had pushed both him and Sarah closer, but he did not hear the Procurator's words, for the crowd was much too noisy. The Rabbi did not speak, and to James's eye he looked reflective. There was a quality of sadness in his gaze and a peace about him much more real than all the madness raging round him.

It was a mercy, the Galilean thought, that Sarah was not tall enough to see, surrounded as she was by pressing crowds –

curious, eager crowds, hungry for a drama but heedless of the cost. How could it happen? How could they be so blind?

The trial was almost over, the sentence inevitable. A bowl of water was produced, and the Procurator washed his hands deliberately before the people. It was a clear indication that Roman law had not found the Rabbi guilty.

The advice of Maximus was always well received by Pilate, but when he suggested a meeting with the servant of the Valerii on the subject of the Rabbi Jesus, Pilate's response was violent.

'I want to hear no more about the Rabbi Jesus and the Jews and their inane laws and their mad religion. Why was I ever sent to this barbaric province?'

Maximus was used to the Procurator's outbursts, and he persisted. The servant of the influential Valerian family was not one to be slighted.

Pontius Pilate sighed, called for wine and nodded to Maximus.

'Bring him in,' he said with resignation.

Felix was ushered in at once.

'Welcome, servant of the Valerii,' Pilate said in greeting, while mustering a smile.

Felix bowed and thanked the Procurator for granting him an audience. Then he went straight to the subject of the Rabbi, putting his plea for the Teacher's release in his deft, quiet way.

Pilate lay back on his couch.

'My dear sir, I agree with much of what you say. I could find no fault in the man. In fact, I rather admired him. He was brave and amazingly quiet in himself, considering the punishment being urged by his fellow Jews.'

The wine arrived, and Felix accepted a cup, more out of deference to his host than from desire. Pilate, however, drank deeply, and once his cup was empty it was quickly filled again by an attentive slave.

'I needed that,' he said, breathing deeply, 'for the gods have been at war this morning. They certainly upset the Jews. Indeed, I've rarely known them quite so rigid and unreasoning. Usually Caiaphas's priestly aides approach with honeyed words and knife-thin smiles, but this morning all their practised deference was forgotten – ha! – they were demanding, not asking for, blood. The unfortunate Rabbi Jesus was accused of blasphemy and claiming to be God, which is an unforgivable perversion in Jewish eyes. He was also accused of poisoning the people with his doctrine and, to top it all, being an enemy of Rome – as if they were the friends. One thing I know, I wouldn't turn my back on them.'

Pilate drained his second cup of wine and Felix, alert and waiting, could see that he was much troubled in himself.

'It was like Greek theatre,' the Procurator continued, 'like men possessed by fate and blinded by the part they had to play.'

Felix sat upright. The Procurator's words had touched on something dormant in his memory. Could it be, he thought, that the total tracing of events, beginning with the strange entry on the colt . . .

Pilate continued, interrupting his thought.

'The agitation of the Jews was so intense that I feared for the public order – Jerusalem at the Passover – ' Pilate shook his head ' – anything could happen. Eventually I washed my hands of the matter. In fact I did this publicly in front of the crowd, showing that their prophet was not guilty in Roman law, and when I said that I was 'innocent of the blood of this just person', their prophet, they shouted back, 'His blood be on us and on our children.' – I tell you, it was like Greek theatre.'

Felix's senses were numb before the inevitability of the Rabbi's fate. There was nothing he could say, nothing. Anyway, Pilate wanted to talk.

'I indulged in my own little drama. I ordered "JESUS OF NAZARETH, THE KING OF THE JEWS" to be written in Hebrew, Greek and Latin and pinned as a title on top of the cross.'

Felix shuddered. The very thought of crucifixion horrified him, but Pilate was unaware of his guest's discomfort and his words rolled on.

'I thought that pinning such a message to the unfortunate Rabbi's cross was too good an opportunity to miss. A stark reminder that such claims were hazardous. The chief priests, of course, didn't like it. They wanted it to read 'He said I am King of the Jews', but I had great pleasure in telling them that what I had written I had written.'

Felix found the question of the title both cynical and petty. The prefect of a province had no business trading in such matters, but why had the Jews wanted to change the title? Strange, he thought. There would be a reason, though.

Pilate got up from his couch and Felix followed his lead.

'Now their King is on his way to be crucified like a common felon.' The Procurator's arm swung out in an illustrative arc, but there was no satisfaction in his eyes.

'Gods!' Felix exhaled.

'Life is brief and brutish for most of these people!'

'He's innocent. He's a truly good man. Can we not stop this awful tragedy?'

Pilate spun round to face his guest.

'Impossible! If I intervened at this late hour it would be interpreted as a miracle. Jerusalem would erupt. My wife was pestering me about this – some dream she had – but there's nothing I can do – nothing! What would Rome think if I risked a major riot to save one obscure and troublesome Jewish preacher?'

'The Tribune Valerius would back you.'

'Maybe, but he's not here, and that's what matters. – No! – the forces at work are beyond my control, and frankly, if Jerusalem did erupt, would we have sufficient numbers to contain it? – That I doubt!'

Pilate shook his head.

'No! the risks are too great, for there's a madness present in Jerusalem.'

The Procurator looked hard at Felix. 'What I have said I have said. There is no alternative. I am an actor, forced to play my part, just like Caiaphas.'

Again Pilate looked hard at Felix. 'Good day to you, servant of the Valerii. I have enjoyed our talk.'

Felix bowed respectfully and took his leave. He had failed, but one thing was clear: the day's events had left the Procurator troubled.

Felix was escorted out of the building, and once more he was back amongst the crowds of Jerusalem. Quickly he made his way to where he had left James and Sarah waiting, but he was not surprised to find them gone. Bewilderment, fearfulness and a sense of isolation were playing within him, demanding his attention. Felix did not give it; instead, he forced himself to ask directions to the field of execution.

Two Greek-speaking men knew a quick route, they said, that would avoid the crowds. Both were going to the field as well, and Felix followed them.

CHAPTER TWENTY-FIVE

GOLGOTHA

James and Sarah, trapped by the crowd, were swept down the funnel of the narrow street that led to Golgotha, the field of execution. Both were dazed and weary and had little strength to fight against the onward thrust, but when the press of people thinned they quickly stepped aside to wait the Rabbi's passing. They had halted beside an old couple who were waiting by their door and who lamented the tragic fate of the Rabbi. Would he, they asked, step down from the cross in triumph?

James shook his head doubtfully.

'He will obey Jehovah's will. That is all I know.'

'There's Father,' Sarah shouted, while running amongst the crowd to catch him by the hand.

The three were united again, but there was no time for talk, for the terrible procession was approaching. First came the soldiers. Next, a broad, strong man carrying the Rabbi's cross, and close behind him was the Rabbi Jesus himself, his body showing the considerable punishment it had already suffered. Sarah stood wide-eyed. Then, seeing a cup of lime-water on a ledge beside the old couple, she took it, and with the speed of youth handed it to the Rabbi. He drank most of it before a soldier intervened. Rudely Sarah was pushed back, and for a moment the Rabbi stopped; no one prevented him.

He smiled at Sarah as he had smiled at her on the day of the ten lepers, and she forgot her tears. Then he turned to James and after that to Felix, who again experienced an overwhelming feeling of love. He stood immobile, and the Rabbi passed on.

'Even now he's giving with the same totality,' he whispered to himself.

The old pair were full of praise for Sarah's action as they offered lime-water to their three visitors, but the cup from which the Rabbi had drunk was set aside. The two old folk were not strong enough to make the journey to the field and James, in his more fluent Aramaic, asked if they might care for Sarah while he and Master Felix paid their last respects. To this they readily agreed.

Neither James nor Felix wanted to witness the cruel barbarity of the crucifixion, yet both felt compelled to be present.

The Rabbi Jesus was already on the cross when they arrived. He was flanked by two felons: one to the right and one to the left. The field was crowded and all levels of Jewish society were present, from the chief priests to the beggar. Some expected a miracle, a final triumph, but as time progressed they began to drift away, like most of the merely curious. Those brutish people who seemed to relish suffering in others jibed and taunted the Master, and Felix was disgusted to see some of the priests along with the scribes and elders joining in the hateful chorus.

'They want to discredit the Master, for they're afraid of the people's sympathy,' James explained bitterly.

Their fear was well founded, Felix thought, as he looked about the crowd, for many were troubled by what they saw. He exposed corruption, that was why he was on the cross, one man muttered, but the angry look of a nearby priest silenced him.

'He saved others yet he cannot save himself,' a number jibed. 'Let him come down from the cross and we'll believe in him!' And so the taunts continued. There was little silence on the mount of Calvary.

To anyone who had a mind to think, the crucifixion was a savage spectacle. It was the deterrent, the visible and chilling reminder to both the rebel and the criminal. Felix abhorred the calculated cruelty. He was not the only one. In fact, he had heard of officers who, overcome with revulsion, had mercifully ended their prisoners' agony, but here on the field of Golgotha the whole slow, agonising cycle was observed.

The crowd was beginning to thin, but James and Felix waited on, for they had both agreed that their vigil would last until the Rabbi's passing. They heard the Master speak to the malefactors on either side of him and to the Disciple John, but from where they were standing it was impossible to hear distinctly. Felix wanted to move closer, but he suppressed his curiosity. He was at Golgotha to honour and to pay respect, not to be curious. He stood, head bowed, only looking at the crucified Teacher for brief periods. At such times he could see all the visible signs of torture; yet there was something else: the same inner peace he had observed so often. Each time he looked it was there, shining in the midst of his physical agony.

Dark clouds had grown to cover the sky, though Felix sensed it to be more than that – a kind of inner darkness. He shivered. Still they waited and the soldiers by the cross grew more and more restless. Few welcomed such a detail.

Felix let his eyes scan the field about him. The crowd had greatly thinned. He recognised many who were still present; the faithful ones, he thought. Beside the Rabbi's cross were three women, and standing with them the Disciple John.

Suddenly the Rabbi cried out, his voice powerful:

'Eli, Eli lama sabachthani?'

The soldiers were immediately quiet, but those about the field turned to each other, the buzz of conversation perceptible.

Felix was totally confused. The Rabbi had cried to his God, asking why he had forsaken him. Bewildered, Felix turned to James.

'I don't understand – I thought I did, but no, I don't! Why, James? What does it mean?'

James was almost too distressed to speak.

'He's in pain – can't you see!' James returned. The sharpness in his voice had gone.

'Yes! – but . . .' Felix cut his sentence short, for James was clearly not himself.

Quietly the Galilean began to chant; a psalm, Felix guessed, for it was his habit.

'My God, my God, why hast thou forsaken me? Why art thou so far from helping me and from the words of my roaring?'

James looked up. He was not reciting the psalm sequentially, but selecting certain verses.

'All they that see me laugh me to scorn: they shoot out the lip, they shake their head, saying,

'He trusted in the Lord that he would deliver him: let him deliver him, seeing he delighted in him.'

James stopped again and looked at Felix, before continuing with another verse, but in an absent way:

'For dogs have compassed me: the assembly of the wicked have inclosed me: they pierced my hands and my feet.'

Once more the Galilean looked at his Roman friend. Felix wanted to believe the allusion of prophecy, but he knew it was easy, all too easy to play with words. Again, the Rabbi had said the words. He had said, 'Eli, Eli, lama sabachthani?' and he always spoke the truth.

Someone in the crowd had soaked a sponge in wine or vinegar and was balancing the dripping sponge on the end of a reed. Slowly he moved it towards the Rabbi's mouth. At the same time Felix heard from behind the sound of horses' hooves crashing to a halt. Two soldiers ran towards the sound, but he did not turn to look. His eyes were on the Rabbi.

Then the tall figure of the Tribune rushed before him, with Venio following behind. Valerius drew his sword, holding it in salute, his head lowered. He had arrived too late.

At that moment the Rabbi spoke.

'It is finished.' The voice of Jesus filled the air about them, after which he bowed his head, giving up the ghost.

For what seemed a long time no one moved, the Tribune Valerius remaining at attention. Suddenly he staggered. Felix staggered. In fact all seemed to lose their balance.

'An earthquake, Master Felix,' James pronounced.

Then it began to rain, a drenching rain, yet no one ran for cover.

The Tribune acknowledged the Disciple John and bowed towards the ladies with him, but he did not think it right to intrude upon their grief. Slowly he walked across to the soldiers and their centurion officer standing to attention in the slanting rain. The broad stripe of the Senate could never be ignored. After a few words with the men he turned to leave the field. It was only then that he saw Felix and James. He embraced each in turn, but the sight of a high-ranking officer embracing what appeared to be two Galileans amazed the onlookers.

Drenched with rain, they left the field together and after they had walked a respectful distance there was a sudden explosion of questions. One question dominated. Where was Tullus? The absence of the Centurion was perplexing, for he had left Qumran with the sole intent of going to Jerusalem. Something had happened, something serious. The Tribune clenched his fists. Tullus always travelled with much too light an escort.

'Felix, will you wait for me at the Antonia Tower? My guard will recognise you.'

Felix nodded.

'And, Venio – we have some business with the Procurator!'

At that the Tribune and his servant mounted their horses and were off.

Felix and James walked slowly without speaking. The rain had eased and it had grown warmer. A humid mist hung about the city.

James was abject in his appearance, and the drenching rain had not helped. He walked in a shuffling way, his head drooping despairingly. The shock of the Rabbi's death had robbed him of his will and energy, and now his master, the Centurion, was missing. It was too much.

For Felix, however, the press of questions surrounding the Rabbi's death kept him from giving way to misery. If the Rabbi was at one with the Father, how could death sever their union? There was also the question of prophecy that James had often emphasised. Even Pilate had alluded to this in his talk of Greek theatre.

'You must recite that psalm in full some time.'

'Yes, Master Felix, but not now,' James reacted flatly.

'I wonder why the Master said 'It is finished'?'

'He meant what he said. Let him rest. He's dead!'

'He's not dead. He can't be. If the Rabbi's at one with the Father, how can he cease to be?'

'Master Felix,' James returned, managing a note of exasperation. 'Up there,' he pointed, 'his lifeless body's hanging on a tree!'

'But, James, even the barbarians know there's more to life than flesh and blood.'

At last they reached the place where Sarah was waiting. She embraced them both, but she did not talk about the Rabbi.

CHAPTER TWENTY-SIX

HEROD'S PALACE

The Tribune eventually traced Pilate to Herod's palace. Followed by Venio, he quickly climbed the steps to the main hall, where, surrounded by their slaves, he found the Tetrarch, Pilate and Gallo deep in conversation. They were drinking, and it was plain enough that all three were in a semi-drunken state.

Valerius approached with due deference, apologising for his unheralded intrusion.

'My dear Valerius, welcome!' Herod was expansive.

Valerius bowed. 'You are, as ever, generous, noble sir.'

'Have some wine, Tribune. We're celebrating having escaped a riot and disposed of an agitator.'

'A just man has been crucified – he knows it!' Valerius reacted bluntly, pointing at Pilate.

'Noble Valerius, you were not there. The public commotion was considerable,' Herod said smoothly. 'Have some wine, my friend.'

The Tribune declined politely, but he found it difficult to be civil. The scene of dissolute opulence before him clashed too harshly with the hideous suffering he had witnessed at Golgotha.

Herod sensed the Tribune's mood and immediately the familiar fixed, calculating coolness glazed his eyes. It was the look Valerius had observed at Athens and Machaerus. Again as at Machaerus, Gallo was lying sullen on his couch, his small eyes watching all, but unlike Herod and Pilate he had not bothered to rise in greeting. Pilate, though, was obviously uneasy. Wine had not dulled the memory of the day's events.

'The Tetrarch is right,' he said, feeling the need to justify himself. 'The chief priests and elders were outraged by the Prophet's claims. I've never known them so agitated.'

221

'He drove the traders from the Temple, and his words left few unmarked amongst our leadership,' Herod intervened.

A gross exaggeration, Valerius thought, but he held his tongue.

'Then there were the claims of kingship,' Pilate continued. 'Other-worldly, perhaps, but to the mob a king is a king!'

'Why, then, did the common people turn against him?' Valerius asked bluntly.

'They were manipulated, but I know the noble Herod disagrees with me.'

'The Passover crowds are volatile and fickle,' Herod interjected, 'and if they thought their laws defiled – need I say more?'

'No, my friend – I know too well,' Pilate returned.

Valerius smiled to himself. Obviously Pilate and the Tetrarch had patched up their differences.

'No one spoke for him,' Pilate went on, 'and they were chanting for his blood. The situation was tense and explosive and I could see no alternative other than give them their king to crucify. Clearly it was a Jewish matter pertaining to the Jewish law and not Rome's business.'

Herod nodded vigorously.

'I'll say this, though,' Pilate concluded, looking pensively at his wine cup. 'The Prophet was no ordinary man.'

'Stop moping, man!' Gallo said, bursting into sudden life. 'Leave that to Valerius. Let him be the nursemaid to slaves and prophets!'

The Tribune tensed with anger; even so he did not snap at Gallo's bait. Instead, he took the Procurator aside to enquire about the Centurion, but Pilate had heard nothing. Neither had the Tetrarch when he turned to him, and Gallo lazily shook his head; the faint smile that hovered round his mouth went undetected.

'Tullus is too good a man to lose,' Pilate said with concern. 'We'll put out a general alert.'

Valerius bowed in acknowledgement, and again apologising for his uninvited call, he left.

Once back at the Antonia Tower, he found the soldier Titus

waiting for him. Titus told his story factually, without elaboration: the Centurion's arrest, the ambush and his vain search for the missing Tullus. Valerius listened, anger and anxiety competing for ascendancy.

'Noble Titus, you have acted well,' Valerius responded, his face grim with determination. Firmly he grasped the veteran's arm. 'Wait here with my guard,' he added. 'I have some unfinished business with the Tribune Gallo – come, Venio, you may need to restrain me!'

With the minimum of ceremony he was readmitted to the hall where Herod and his guests were gathered,

'My dear Valerius, few men are honoured with two visits from the Emperor's personal legate in one day,' the Tetrarch said grandly, though with a note of caution, for ever since Machaerus he was wary of the tall aristocrat. Valerius could not be bought, and it was wise to treat such men with care.

'Noble sir, my apologies for this further invasion of your privacy,' the Tribune responded, matching Herod's play of words. 'I wish to speak privately with the Tribune Gallo,' he added, but his voice left no one in doubt. Anger spoke in his every syllable.

Gallo laughed, swinging his wine cup in a long, triumphal arc.

'Valerius, speak up – there are no secrets here.'

'With your permission, Tetrarch,' the Tribune said tersely, his anger boiling.

Herod nodded, his eyes alert and watching.

'Then, by the gods, I will.'

In an act of resolution the Tribune drew his sword, and immediately Herod's guards moved forward, but the Tetrarch restrained them.

'Where is he, Gallo? Where's Tullus? or should I ask where's your good friend Marius?' Valerius barked, pointing his sword with menacing emphasis. 'But of course you knew nothing when I asked before?' he added scathingly.

'How should I have known, dear boy?' Gallo returned easily, gesturing with his wine cup in another graceful flourish.

The Tribune was enraged. His sword flashed and the contents of Gallo's cup spilled red over his tunic.

223

'Let that be an omen, Gallo!'

'Of what, dear boy? – the demise of the Valerii?'

Gallo remained slouched on his couch, but his eyes were wide and darting.

Slowly Valerius moved his sword-point close to Gallo's throat. Herod's guards grew agitated, yet still the Tetrarch held them back.

'Listen, Gallo,' the Tribune began, spitting the words out slowly, 'and listen well – your friend Marius has been ambushed. He and eighteen men are dead, and Tullus whom he kidnapped is missing!'

Pilate and the Tetrarch gasped.

'Kidnapped, Gallo!' Valerius repeated. 'To use the word arrest would make a horse laugh – who gave Marius his orders, Gallo? – Who?'

'How should I know?'

The sword point drew closer.

'By all the gods, Gallo, if anything has happened to Marcus Tullus I'll return and hack you to pieces!'

'Master.' The voice of Venio sounded softly in the Tribune's ear.

'Tetrarch, my man reminds me of the civilities,' Valerius said in his clipped way, while sheathing his sword.

'Thank the gods for that,' Gallo muttered, but no one was listening. Shock had stunned both Herod and the Procurator.

'I'll organise a search from Jericho,' Valerius stated. 'Does that meet with your approval, Procurator?'

Pilate nodded.

'Eighteen men,' he mouthed inaudibly. 'No, nineteen men are dead, and Marcus Tullus missing. This will sound bad in Antioch and Rome, and as usual it will be the Procurator's fault.'

The Tribune was determined to leave for Jericho immediately and exploit what little light was left. Felix and Sarah, James and now the veteran Titus would travel with him. His guard were on foot, as he had left his carts at Jericho and had only brought two horses to the busy city. There was, of course, the covered cart that James had left at Bethphage.

There was no time to waste, and Valerius planned, come what might, to reach the Jericho garrison before the night halt, which would be brief, for Marcus Tullus could be lying injured.

Only one thing remained to be done: a note needed to be sent to Herod, something he had forgotten in his rage, for Tullus had gone missing in Perea, Herod's Tetrarchy. It was proper, and certainly prudent, to ask permission from the touchy Jewish prince before proceeding with the search. Due to the urgent circumstances, he wrote, he was leaving immediately, in the surety of the Tetrarch's assent, and hoped that the noble prince would forgive his presumption. He knew, of course, that Herod had no option. To refuse help in such an emergency would lose him his Tetrarchy.

They set out walking, with the Tribune's guard clearing the road before them. The watching crowds were curious yet resentful, for any presence other than a Jewish one was seen to be a desecration of their holy city. Valerius sensed the people's mood, but being engrossed in conversation with Felix he paid it little heed.

'Ben Joseph told me often that the Sanhedrin were a wise and prudent body,' he was saying. 'Why then did they condemn a just man? Why, Felix?'

Absently, Felix scanned the line of watching people as they passed.

'I suspect it was like most council meetings,' he answered, after a delay. 'You know – some for and some against, with other forceful men manipulating things. The truth is – I don't know. In fact, that seems to be my general cry of late!'

'I can well understand, Felix, for I find the whole tragic business of the Rabbi's death a paradox. Why, for instance, did he allow himself to be bullied and crucified? – when I'm certain his tormentors were little more than flickering candles before him. He had the power; you know he had, for you were with him daily. He could have snuffed them out, but no, by all accounts he did not even try to save himself! – for what end, Felix?'

'His Father's will. That's all that comes to mind. There's the question of prophecy, though.'

'Prophecy?'

'Yes; James knows all about it.'

Felix elaborated by describing the Rabbi's entry on a donkey as foretold by the Prophet Zechariah. He also outlined the psalm that James had gently chanted.

'But, Felix, if James knows this, so will the Sanhedrin, and that being so, why did they ignore it?'

'They didn't, Lucius. They would have viewed the Rabbi's actions as a gross pretension.'

'Of course, and that explains their bitterness. So the whole event could be viewed as a mighty sacrifice, but on whose behalf? The Jews'?'

'They're the cradle, the focus, but I cannot think there's a limit. The Rabbi's kingdom is universal.'

'Is?'

Felix nodded. "I and my Father are one.' How can that unity, that soul, be dead?'

'Whoever let a Plato lover loose amongst the Jews?'

The Tribune smiled, and Felix looked at his master's son with great affection.

'Master Lucius, don't question James – not yet, at least. He's not himself.'

'Understandably. We could use him as a guide on the Jericho road, for it will be dark soon, and that could take his mind off things.'

'Will it be dangerous?'

'I'll get James to hire some scouts at Bethphage. He'll know who to trust.'

Once at the village, Felix and Sarah took their seats in the covered cart, while James, playing the role of guide, seated himself beside Venio. The Tribune continued to walk, taking the opportunity to question Titus.

Titus was typical of his kind, Valerius thought, a solid and reliable veteran who spoke directly.

'Have you any idea yourself what might have happened to Tullus?' the Tribune asked.

'I think he must have been injured, sir, otherwise he would have made his way to Livias Julias, as I did. He's strong and resourceful; I served under him once.'

The Tribune nodded. Tullus was the most resourceful soldier he had ever met.

'If he was injured he'd have taken longer to get to Livias Julias. Maybe he's there now.'

'I doubt it, sir. When I came to the scene of the ambush in the morning, the Centurion was nowhere to be seen. I took some time to search the area, after which I covered my dead comrades with branches. He'd have been well ahead of me if he'd have been fit enough to walk. I would have seen him, for to my mind there was only one way out, and that was down the river bed.'

'He might have gone the other way – no!' the Tribune corrected himself. 'If the Chief Centurion had been able to walk at all, he would have done his best to get to Jerusalem.' Valerius looked grimly at Titus. 'He's either up there in the hills badly injured or he's been held as a hostage, a bartering lever against some cut-throat we're holding. There's no time to waste! – How many men should we take, Titus?'

'A century, sir.'

'We'll do that – providing the Jericho commander can spare the men.'

The old soldier looked at the tall, high-born officer by his side with some amazement. Few had ever asked his advice, and he did not know of any who had acted on it.

Valerius and Felix had already discussed the need to break the news about the ambush to Drusilla, and it was inevitable that the duty fell to Felix. It was a task he did not relish, not at all, for although no one had said it, the chances of finding Marcus Tullus alive were marginal. Poor Drusilla. She was truly happy, probably for the first time in her life, and now this.

It was arranged at Jericho that Felix and Sarah would return to Capernaum. They were given an eight-man escort, but there was no need to leave until the morning. Drusilla would hear the bitter news soon enough. James was not to travel with them, as he had begged to join in the search for his beloved master.

It was some time before the full century-strong complement of the Tribune's force was ready to march; even so, delay was

227

kept to a minimum. Sleep was sacrificed, and after writing briefly to both Cornelia and Drusilla, Valerius took his leave of the garrison Commander – a man he had grown to respect.

When the Tribune left Herod and his guests, there was a long and awkward silence. Gallo, amused by the situation, remained immobile, his sense of theatre forbidding any instant explanation.

'Valerius wasn't exactly pleased with you,' the Tetrarch said eventually.

'He'll get over it,' Gallo responded lazily. 'What did he expect me to do – weep for Tullus? I know the quick conclusions he's been jumping at. This Marius he mentioned – of course I know him. He kept bothering me with spurious claims that linked Tullus with militant Jewry. I told him that such complaints should go through the proper channels. No doubt they laughed him to scorn, and he, the idiot, then acted independently. But tell me, why should I be held responsible for the naive obsessions of those Valerius cares to call my friends? Young bloods like Marius are always writing to me. They know of my connection with the Prefect Sejanus and so they pester me.' Gallo leaned confidentially towards Herod. 'Ambition, Tetrarch, ambition! And Marius has paid the price.'

'And Tullus, too, perhaps,' Herod returned. Gallo was clever, but Herod knew that he was clever, and the Tetrarch's suspicion lingered. Gallo sensed this, and it amused him.

'Slandered by Valerius,' he said wearily, stifling a yawn. 'At least I'll be famous!'

He lay back amidst his cushions, feigning sleep.

'It would be nice to know what actually happened,' he added in a voice of studied boredom. 'I suppose the army will get around to telling us one day. Valerius certainly was upset,' he continued languidly, 'but at least we know that some blood courses in his veins. Funny, though, that he received the news before the Procurator.'

'That's not funny – it's the usual custom,' Pilate reacted, for once matching Gallo's sarcasm. 'Anyway, the information will come soon enough. There'll be enquiries and reports, for Antioch will want to know and Rome will want to know.

Why do such terror groups exist? They should be stamped out, they'll say, and of course there'll be the usual round of instant solutions. I've heard it all before!'

'It's not instant solutions you want; it's the final solution!' Gallo interrupted.

'What solution?' Herod asked sharply, expecting the usual hard-line answer.

'Retirement!' Gallo returned with sudden animation. 'It would solve all the Procurator's problems,' he enthused, while grinning widely at Pilate. 'Just think! No enquiries! No reports! No Judea! Bliss! Let someone else do the worrying. The Tetrarch here is short of a few troubles,' he added with a wink in Herod's direction. 'Back to Rome at last, my noble Procurator, and a villa on the Aventine – a gentle stroll from the races!'

'How could I afford the Aventine? My name is not Valerius!'

'The ruler of a province?' Gallo reacted, with a note of mild enquiry. 'You surely have a little gold put by!'

Pilate pretended a knowing smile, but beneath the surface he was apprehensive, as Gallo's words, however flippant, could be the thinking of Sejanus.

Gallo had been clever, though coolly ruthless. He had caught Herod with the hope of Judea and the glittering prize of being King. It was a golden dream that Gallo had little thought of honouring, but he knew it would keep him friendly. Pilate, on the other hand, was easy to control. A veiled threat now and then would be enough.

The conversation continued, with Gallo giving a witty description of a chariot race he had recently seen at Caesarea. One of his friends, he said, laughing loudly, had been so drunk that he had collapsed in his chariot on the last circuit – and he had still won, he added, slapping his thigh. How his friend had escaped injury was fit for listing as a wonder.

Gallo had just finished his story when the Tribune's message arrived from the Antonia Tower. Herod at once broke the seal.

'It's from Valerius,' he announced. 'He's asking permission to conduct a large-scale search in the Tetrarchy.' Herod read on. 'Gallo, this friend of yours actually arrested Tullus and was taking him to Palmyra. How did the idiot think he would get away with it?'

'I suspected his obsession about Tullus was fanatical, but I never dreamt . . .' Gallo shrugged his shoulders.

'Someone released the legionaries, for he could not walk away with sixteen men.' Pilate knew the administrative requirements.

'The commander of the Palmyra garrison can be manipulated – especially after the evening meal,' Gallo suggested, affecting a sound of knowing regret. 'There's another factor arising from all this,' he added, looking pointedly at the Procurator. 'The activities of Tullus will have to be investigated. The authorities will demand this, for they will require factual evidence as to whether Marius's accusations are true or false.'

'Yes, that's right,' Pilate sighed. His day had been long and full of trouble.

CHAPTER TWENTY-SEVEN

DYRRHACHIUM

The weather being propitious, the Tribune's father made the short sea crossing from Brindisium to Dyrrhachium in early April. With him were his daughter Junia, now seventeen, and Arria, his favourite freedwoman. The Senator had brought nine servants with him, including his drivers and his cook. His baggage was considerable, as he intended to stay in the east for at least two years. There was, of course, the precious selection from his library.

A personal note from Tiberius included in the Senator's papers made the city authorities instantly co-operative, and, careful of his safety, a small military guard was provided for his journey. The Senator's party was considerable, but noticeably modest for a man of his rank.

While he awaited the completion of his travel arrangements, the Senator was the guest of the City Prefect. A supper was arranged in his honour, at which he was quick to notice, as he had noticed in Brindisium, that both the military and civil leaders were highly nervous of political conversation. The uncertainties of Rome were not confined to the capital. Indeed, the mood of disquiet was tangible amongst the city's administrators, for Dyrrhachium was the the gateway to the east. They could not stand aside and watch should civil war break out. Sejanus or Gaius 'Caligula'? That was the unvoiced question. Some, by their conversation, were in favour of a new direction, a strong hand; though they were careful not to mention names. Sejanus had support. In fact, many felt his obvious experience was necessary to the welfare of the Empire, but how would Lucius fare under the proud Sejanus? It was a chilling thought.

There was the powerful enigma of the Emperor himself. Most, though they rarely said so overtly, felt him old and senile. His freedmen ruled, not he, but the Senator Valerius knew differently, and what was more, Sejanus would know differently. It was the Senator's fear that the powerful Prefect, goaded by frustration, might act precipitately, but the one thing he could not do, even if he wanted to, was withdraw. He had gone too far for that. His enemies, though quiet now, would never let him rest.

Valerius had decided to use the Via Egnatia to Thessalonica, after which he would either go by land or sea to Athens. His choice of route had been to please his daughter Junia. She wanted to travel on the great road so famous in history. Had not the father of the Empire, Julius Caesar, as well as mighty Pompey, Brutus, Antony and, of course, Augustus marched their armies on its length? She had to see it.

Junia was strong-willed. She was strong in body, too, though not as tall as her elder sister. She liked having her way but had learned to hold her tongue when in her father's presence. Learning restraint and discipline had been hard, and still it was a battle. Junia respected her father, and a father loved his daughter. She obeyed his rule but gained concessions through the mediation of the friendly Arria, whose wishes the Senator rarely refused.

After two nights in Dyrrhachium the Senator began his journey in the morning light. Step by step, and hour by hour, he was moving closer to that strange-sounding town, Capernaum – a town he was determined to see; but first there would be Athens.

CHAPTER TWENTY-EIGHT

THE SEARCH
AND THE WAITING

At the time the Senator was setting out from Dyrrhachium, his son, with his century-strong force, was passing through the oasis of Livias Julias on his way to the scene of the ambush. The Tribune allowed generous stops, with time enough to snatch some sleep, but in the main their progress over the rough terrain was steady and relentless.

They reached their destination just after midday, and passing by the line of dead soldiers they struck camp in the wide clearing beyond. Immediately every man was busy, their tasks already fixed. Most laboured to fortify their camp, while a burial party marched off to dig a grave for the ambush victims. This completed, the Tribune assembled the full complement of men to pay the last respects. For those moving the bodies the stench was almost unbearable, and cloths protecting their mouths and noses were essential. The body of Marius was the last to be lowered, and at that the Tribune performed the rites. To all it was a grim reminder of the potential dangers surrounding them.

At once the search began, though the Tribune's concern for his men's safety inhibited progress. Five days passed, and another five, but the widening circle of their search revealed nothing. Time rolled on, with pressure mounting to give up the search. The soldiers were growing restless. They were tired of the rough, wooded terrain, and the constant need for vigilance made them edgy. With the Tribune's own personal guard it was different; all twenty had met the Centurion, and all, like the Tribune, were reluctant to abandon the search. Valerius was grateful for their support, but he knew that time was running out; nor was there any news from either Livias Julias or Jericho. One more day of searching, maybe two, but that would be the most, he thought reluctantly.

It was the assiduousness of the Tribune's personal guard that discovered the first clue; an ornate dagger which James, who was with the party, knew to be his master's. Close to where it had been found the grass was flattened, as if by many feet, and moving away from the area were two parallel tracks, made by a litter, James maintained.

The temptation to follow the tracks was strong, but, as sunset was close, the Tribune ordered his men back to the security of the camp. Valerius was elated, for he felt the omens good, and even though reason urged restraint he ordered extra wine all round in celebration. That night he slept soundly.

The next morning eagerness sped them to the site of their find and the tracking began, with James clearly the expert.

'It's a litter all right,' he said, 'with a donkey pulling it – almost certainly a donkey – and the footprints of a man as well. It happened some time ago, Master Tribune, sir.'

Valerius made encouraging sounds, and James continued forward, peering at the rough ground. Gradually a gravel surface grew dominant, making the tracks difficult to follow. James fell to his knees, his arm pointing to indicate a new direction. The place was covered with goat droppings, and then, wonderfully camouflaged by rock and scrub, they found two caves. Both were facing east, with one showing all the signs of human habitation – earthen jars, flat iron cooking utensils, and a bed made from skins and woollen materials. There were rings for tethering animals and the smell of goats was everywhere.

James felt the embers of a fire outside the cave entrance. They were still warm, and at once he began looking for fresh tracks, which he soon found.

'They're going in the direction of that split in the hills, Master Tribune,' he said, pointing towards a narrow, wooded gorge. 'Left about an hour or so ago.' He was obviously keen to continue tracking.

'Two miles from the camp – right under our noses,' Valerius said, half to himself, but he knew the difficulties of combing such awkward terrain. He turned to Titus, who was standing close to him, and also the the century's Centurion, Aulus.

'I'm fearful of taking men into that trap,' he pronounced, looking at the gorge.

'Yes, sir, it's against all the rules,' Aulus responded. He had recently been promoted and was clearly relishing the experience.

'What do you think, Titus?'

The old soldier considered for a moment before answering.

'I agree the valley is a dangerous trap, but what if James and I followed the tracks, and you, sir, kept to the high ground? We could always signal if we were in any difficulty.'

Valerius nodded pensively.

'Dangerous, Titus, but sound. You'll have to be careful, though.'

'You mean you'll do it, sir?'

Valerius smiled.

'Titus, you don't have to be a Scipio Africanus to have a good idea!'

'I suppose not, sir,' the veteran returned, covering his embarrassment with a nervous laugh. This was the strangest Laticlavius he had ever come across. Imperious in his look, but wholly approachable, and when you spoke the truth he listened as if you were the Emperor.

The Tribune turned slowly towards Aulus the Centurion as he pondered the detail of his plan.

'Centurion, I have a feeling that the trail we propose following will lead us to the Jordan, or at least in that direction. If I'm right we'll not be returning to the camp. Nevertheless, it would be best to give us three days' grace, just in case, but after that you should proceed to Jericho. Now, I shall need some of your number – two tent parties, in fact, which will boost my guards' strength up to forty. Select experienced men, and the mules we brought should be loaded with provisions and driven here with all speed; and could you ask my servant Venio to join us? He need only bring the necessities of my baggage. I need hardly say, my friend, that speed is vital.'

Aulus saluted, glad to be tested with responsibility. He turned, and, with an eight-man guard, marched off briskly. Aulus having gone, the Tribune sat down amongst his men and propped himself against a tree. He was weary yet unable to sleep. He did his best, though, to be still, smiling as he remembered Raphael's emphatic words. In truth, he was greatly relieved, as the lead they had found appeared to be positive. It had to be. To believe that Tullus was lost was a nightmare in his mind, especially when he thought of Drusilla. She would know by now. He knew his sister well, and he knew her suffering would be sharp. Then he thought of Cornelia.

The night following the news about the Centurion, Drusilla did not sleep at all. Felix and Cornelia sat with her until the morning. The next night was the same, and, with the third approaching, Felix was determined that her wine-cup would be potent. Even a fitful doze would be better than nothing, as worry heaped on sleeplessness was dangerous.

'The demonic forces cannot win,' she said suddenly after the evening meal. 'Surely they cannot.' The Rabbi was crucified, Marcus was missing and the happiness of Lucius and Cornelia doomed. The issues in her mind were sharp-edged silhouettes.

'Marcus missing – the Rabbi crucified,' she mouthed, giving outward form to her thought.

Felix felt compelled to speak.

'The spirit of the Rabbi Jesus is not dead. No demonic force can usurp the good!' he said with force.

'The spirit of the Rabbi is not dead,' she repeated, her voice a whisper. Then she turned for help, as she had turned on the day James was cured. Her surrender was total, whole-hearted, and with the sudden easing of her body's tension, she fell asleep. Felix watched closely. She was weeping. She was weeping in her sleep, and a wave of pity swept over him. But Drusilla was not weeping with sorrow, for in a vivid dream the power of the Rabbi had returned, and when she woke her face was full of light. Then, almost immediately, sleep returned.

CHAPTER TWENTY-NINE

THE GOATHERD

When the Centurion regained consciousness after the ambush, it was dark. At his side he felt a leather water-bag, and, being thirsty, he pulled the stopper to drink. It was diluted wine, and cold, and a sudden wave of sickness made him retch. He sat until the sickness passed; then shakily he got to his feet, but as he rose the throbbing in his head grew worse. He had no idea where he was and was too confused to care. He looked up, but the keen, blinking stars were like knife-points, and the feeling of nausea returned. A sudden dizziness made him stagger, yet he kept upright. Slowly, com-pulsively, he began to walk. It was his body walking, cat-like so it seemed, testing every step. Soon his energy began to fail and with that the dizziness returned. Even so, he shuffled on, his weariness deepening and the desire to sleep oppressive. Suddenly he fell, a heavy fall, his cloak thrown forward cover-ing his neck and head, and there he lay.

After a time consciousness, alerted by his body's cold, set him moving. Half crawling, half walking, a dream figure to his confused perception, yet moving, pressing forward. He would rest at times; then he would start again. Time had no meaning. The night hours were almost over when again he fell, this time bumping his head. Once more his cloak was flung forward.

In time the dawn came, and with it the growing heat of the day. The Centurion lay where he had fallen. Mercifully his cloak still covered his neck and head. Only his tough, weather-beaten legs were fully exposed, but there was a limit to their hardiness.

As the peril of his situation grew, the first faint light of con-sciousness began to return, but it was far away and dream-like. There was a bell sounding in the distance and something was brushing against him, something pushing at his face. It, too, was far away. A voice called in a strange language, like a whisper from another world.

A goatherd, clad in coarse woven clothes, stood over the Centurion. His unkempt hair and beard were long and the sandals he wore were roughly made. Stiffly he got to his knees and put his ear to the Centurion's back.

'He's still alive,' he said quietly to the small herd of goats standing about him. In response the he-goat leader of the herd nuzzled close to him, his bell ringing dully.

'Come, Jacob,' he said, patting the creature. 'We've got work to do.' And after covering the Centurion's legs with rough grass he hurried off, the goats following behind like trained domestic animals.

The Centurion lay motionless, but the slow rise to consciousness continued. Eventually the instinct to move grew dominant, and as if in sleep he dragged himself a few paces. His dagger hilt had caught on the rough ground, and both dagger and scabbard, torn from his belt, lay behind him, but the effort had exhausted him, and breathing heavily he sank back into oblivion.

Out of the heat-haze the goatherd re-emerged, leading a donkey which was harnessed to a litter, and behind, folllowing like an escort, were the goats.

The goatherd was a small man, and he struggled for some time before the powerful frame of the Centurion was safely on the litter. He was pleased with his work and his eyes shone with innocent pleasure. Carefully he cushioned Tullus's head with strips of coarse woollen cloth. The litter, though sturdy enough, was bowed with the soldier's weight, and the goatherd viewed it anxiously before tapping the donkey gently on the shoulder.

'Well, my old friend, it's up to you now.'

As if knowing his master's words, the donkey jerked its head and began to pull.

The slow, careful journey took some time, but eventually they arrived at the goatherd's cave. It was a struggle to drag the solidly built soldier into the cave and onto the bed of skins and woollen rugs, but the goatherd did it, his innocent face full of pity for the stricken Roman. It never occurred to him to wonder what might be his fate if the soldier were to die and he, the compassionate goatherd, should be discovered with the corpse. The soldier's breastplate was worth a fortune, he supposed, as he unfastened it: enough to buy a thousand goats. The armour of a senior officer, he surmised. He wondered who he was, but it never crossed the goatherd's mind to conjure what reward he might receive.

What the Centurion needed most was water, but this was not possible until he was able to swallow, and to swallow he needed to regain consciousness. This the goatherd knew. There was little he could do other than sprinkle cold water on the soldier's forehead and wait.

It was not long before the soldier began to show signs of consciousness, and all at once he started asking questions, impatient questions, but the goatherd did not understand the language. However, seizing the opportunity, he gave the Roman water, which the man drank automatically, while shielding his eyes from the glare at the cave entrance. Then the incomprehensible talk continued until, exhausted, the soldier lay back, overwhelmed by sleep.

The goats, pressing in at the mouth of the cave, stood silent and curious, with Jacob their leader close to the bed.

'He'll be all right, Jacob,' the goatherd said, 'but he'll need much milk, and your wives will have to be bountiful.'

Jacob tipped his head in seeming understanding, and the goatherd's hand went out to pat him gently on the forehead.

Day followed day, measuring the injured soldier's slow progress. Food did not interest him; in fact, he seemed to suffer from a partial nausea. The goatherd watched and listened intently, but patient as his efforts were, no real contact was established.

The Roman seemed to have an infinite capacity for sleep, and when he woke he talked, sometimes with irritation, and at other times there was a note of resignation as he looked about him blankly.

On the fifth day there was a shift. His appetite returned, and in his look there was a new alertness. The following day he began to talk in Aramaic, and to the goatherd's joy he recognised the Galilean intonation in the Roman's words.

'Galilee!' he said hopefully, and encouraged by the interest in the soldier's eyes he continued. 'Tiberias?' he queried, but there was no response. He tried other names, as well as the Greek cities, again without result; even so, he still had the Roman's attention.

Pensively he poured two cups of milk, handing one to the soldier, and as he savoured the fresh liquid memories came of his last visit to market. There had been much talk of a Rabbi who hailed from Galilee, and a particular town had been mentioned.

'Rabbi of . . . Rabbi of . . . what was the town?' he muttered. Thinking aloud was the habit of his solitary life.

'Capernaum!' the soldier interjected. The key had turned and the door to memory had begun to open, but the effort had exhausted him, and, overcome with tiredness, he lay back on his bed, the word 'Drusilla' a whisper on his lips.

The next day Tullus learned how he had been found, and how the goatherd, Simon by name, had brought him to the coolness of the cave. Such conversations, it seemed, required enormous concentration, and were therefore brief.

With the return of memory the need to make his survival known grew pressing, not least for Drusilla's sake, and for her brother's, as doubtless he was searching, but how could he make the journey? – certainly not alone, not as he was, dogged by weariness and the never-ending wish to sleep. Again, too much bright light made his headaches chronic. On the other hand, if Simon went, the goats would follow, and if he tethered them who would give them water?

Such inner debates weakened Tullus, and soon he was asleep again, not to awaken until it was almost dusk. Another day was gone, he thought with exasperation. In the morning he tested himself with a longish walk. He overdid it, though, and returned exhausted, his headache thumping. The next day he was stronger, and in the evening he brought up the subject of making contact with the nearest garrison.

'We'll all go together,' Simon answered with enthusiasm. 'There's a donkey cart in the next cave which I use for the market. It's long and low, with high sides, and just big enough for you to lie flat if you get tired.'

'What about the goats?'

'They'll come with us – if need be, I can tie them to the cart,' Simon answered, his eyes full of playful excitement, but Tullus could not match his mood. He simply could not keep awake.

During the night a fever came upon him, and in the morning it was raging, though not violently. The gods were delaying him, he thought with annoyance as he sipped a brackish herbal cure concocted by Simon. The fever lingered for two days, to disappear as mysteriously as it had arrived. Reluctantly he rested for a day, but on the following morning he set out, walking behind the cart, with Simon leading the donkey in front and the goats flanking the way like guards.

The pace set by the herdsman was deliberately slow, and moving gently with his eyes half-closed against the glare Tullus managed well. Within the hour they had descended a steepish slope into a small valley whose wooded sides rose sharply above them. Suddenly Tullus felt too weary to continue. He had to rest, and climbing into the cart he lay flat on its grass-padded floor, while pulling a light woollen rug over his body as protection against the sun. The whole process, including a drink, seemed to take ages.

The Centurion fell asleep almost immediately, and Simon was careful to ensure that his face and head were covered from the sun before he moved on. The slow procession continued, with Simon extra careful in avoiding bumps, knowing sudden jolts could be dangerous for his friend.

Jacob walked ahead, the vanguard of the party, occasionally looking round, no doubt impatient at his master's snail-like pace. After an hour Tullus woke, and they stopped once more to drink. Jacob and his wives, in Simon's words, had found a trickle of a stream.

For a time the Centurion walked behind the cart until, feeling tired, he again took to the cart. As he did so, he became aware of flashing reflections of light from the ridge above. The sun glinting on the rocks, he thought, and hopefully not a symptom of his condition.

As the slow, patient progress started again, he found himself thinking of the Rabbi. A sudden stab of worry seized him.

241

What had happened? What had happened in Jerusalem? The sleepy vagueness in his mind had gone. His thoughts were stark, their images sharp. His body tensed; his head began to pound, and then, exhausted by the strain, he drifted off.

All at once, as if from nowhere, Simon was confronted by a grinning, mean-eyed man.

'Well, what have we here, eh? Lots of tough meat and pails of milk!'

The man's grin had the viciousness of one who relished cruelty. He roared with laughter, and with a deft flick cut the woollen cord round the goatherd's waist. Simon was frightened. He could make no contact with the reptile eyes. Suddenly he was surrounded by men. Bandits!

No one noticed Jacob make his charge. All they saw was the sprawling figure of the goatherd's tormentor.

With the instinct of innocence Simon moved to help the man, but with a snarl the help was pushed aside. The onlookers bellowed with laughter, and maddened by this, the bandit lunged at Jacob, his sword suddenly red.

Simon howled with pain and flung himself on the companion of his solitude. His anguish was pitiful.

'What is this?' The voice came from a magnificent specimen of a man.

Simon's tear-stained face turned round. He knew the man, and had seen him often.

The big man glared at Simon's tormentor. 'I have a mind to slit your throat – our enemy is Rome and not the innocent. Remember that, or by our father's God . . .' He did not finish the sentence. Instead he bent down, lifted the dead Jacob in his arms and carried him to the back of the high-sided cart. He paused, startled, for there before him, almost covered by a woollen rug, was the familiar face of Marcus Tullus. Gently he laid the dead goat beside the Roman, who, disturbed by the movement, opened his eyes. The big man put a finger to his lips enjoining silence, and luckily the Centurion, in his half sleep, understood.

'Drive on, old friend. You have nothing to fear from us,' the big man shouted.

Simon put his arm round the donkey's neck, and the cart eased forward.

The attention of the outlaws had been wholly captured by the drama of the goatherd and their leader's intervention. They did not hear the high-pitched whistle repeat itself three times, but on the ridge above the sound was clear. From the valley floor Titus had given his signal, and at once the Tribune barked his orders. With infinite stealth his guard began descending into the valley, the cover of the trees their ally. The whistle came again, imitating a bird call, and he returned the signal. Again the whistle changed its note, and again it was returned. The Tribune's men were close. Slowly they edged forward until their enemy were in view. Then the Tribune gave the signal to attack, and instantly a flight of javelins hissed through the air, each one with its target. The surprise was total.

Only one of the twenty-strong rebel force escaped, and their lookout sentries on the ridge had perished too. If the rebels had men on the opposite ridge, they did not appear. It was doubtful, though, for the terrain was impassable.

The Tribune had ambushed the masters of the ambush. It was a considerable victory, and achieved without any loss of Roman life.

The one outlaw who had escaped the slaughter crashed past the place where James and Titus had been hiding, and without a word Titus drew his sword and followed, but James did not move. He had no wish to watch the sword of Titus do its work.

Titus followed the noise of the fleeing rebel until it suddenly stopped. Then, with the stealth of a cat, the old soldier made a wide detour and began to approach the area where the sound had ceased. Fearing a trap, he edged forward until unexpectedly he found his quarry lying face down in an open clearing. It was the rebel leader. Titus lifted a small stone and lobbed it onto the outlaw's body. There was no reaction, and the Roman moved closer. The rebel was breathing heavily, and Titus guessed that he had fallen and knocked himself unconscious.

Along with James, Titus had witnessed the whole drama of the incident involving the goatherd and had admired the obvious nobility of the rebel leader, but there was more than that.

Titus had seen the big man hesitate before the cart as if surprised, and was certain of the reason. The powerfully built outlaw had seen the prostrate figure of a man, no doubt Tullus, for earlier Titus had caught a distant glimpse of someone other than the goatherd walking beside the cart. The question was, what had made the big man act the way he did? Some warrior code, perhaps.

Titus looked at the helpless figure at his feet. A perfect physique, ideal for the games and worth a fortune. He sighed. Slowly the old soldier undid the water bag that hung by his side, laying it noiselessly beside the outlaw.

'Why am I doing this?' he said aloud, though there was no one to listen or to answer.

'Did you find him?' James asked bluntly when Titus returned.

'Yes!' The answer was equally blunt.

Titus had still not sheathed his sword, but James could see no blood.

They were soon engulfed by the victorious legionaries, and without delay James approached the Tribune.

'We think the master's up ahead, sir.'

'How did he escape this lot?' Valerius shot back, indicating the rebel dead. 'What state's he in?' he added.

'We think we saw him walking.'

'Thank the gods for that, but no more speculation – let's go and see!'

They found the Centurion propped against the cart and trying to comfort the goatherd. It was not easy, for Simon's distress was one of the most pitiful things Tullus had ever seen.

The Centurion had heard the shouts and yells of battle and had assumed it was the outlaws celebrating, but when he saw the Tribune striding out towards him he knew the noise had had another cause. James, almost running to keep up, was at the Tribune's side, and behind was the unmistakable Venio; again, there was . . . it was on the tip of his tongue . . . yes, of course – Titus.

'You've given us a lot of worry, Master,' James blurted out, trying to be fierce, but tears welled in his eyes. He stepped back, and the Tribune, who had let James outpace him, greeted Tullus warmly. There were hours of conversation before them. Not yet, though, for it was clear to Valerius that the Chief Centurion was far from well. The greetings continued, and then for a moment the buzz of conversation stopped. At once the quietness of the hills surrounded them.

'I'm afraid to ask,' the Centurion started. 'What happened at Jerusalem?'

'The worst – crucifixion – I arrived too late.'

'Crucifixion!' Tullus gripped the side of the donkey cart tightly.

'Felix doesn't believe he's dead. He says the spirit of the Rabbi cannot die!'

The Centurion looked white. 'I'll have to lie down,' he said quietly. 'James, look after my friend Simon,' he added, inclining his head towards the bewildered goatherd. 'I owe my life to this good man, and, sir,' he continued, returning to the Tribune while pointing to the dead Jacob, 'bury this noble animal with honour, if you please. It's the least we can do – was the leader of the outlaws killed?'

'No, he escaped,' the Tribune answered instantly.

'The gods are just.'

Titus nodded, but no one noticed.

The leader of the outlaws came to himself almost immediately after Titus left him. He had fallen heavily and in the process had briefly knocked himself unconscious.

The deadly peril of his situation soon returned. Cautiously he looked about him. Thankfully there was no one in sight, but he could hear voices, Roman voices, in the near distance. Suddenly he became aware of a water bag at his side, its leather strap across his back. Amazed, he looked closely. It was a Roman bag, with the crest of the Tenth legion clearly stamped on the leather.

Clutching the bag, he rose noiselessly and began to slip away. On and on he walked, not daring to stop until it was almost sunset. Only then did he pull the stopper of the bag to drink.

The mystery of the water bag persisted in his mind. The fact that the leather strap had been lying across his back meant that the bag had been placed there after his fall. How could it be otherwise? There was the rare possibility that he might have trampled on a fallen branch which could have catapulted the bag, but there was no memory of anything like that. Incredible though it was, he was beginning to believe that a Roman had done for him what he had done for Marcus Tullus.

The big man ran his fingers through his generous crop of black, curly hair. He was troubled in himself and he turned to his God Jehovah in prayer.

He had first met Marcus Tullus five years earlier, when his village had been used as an example to a troublesome people. Every tenth man had been slaughtered and property had been destroyed indiscriminately. He had been only eighteen. He remembered how Tullus, arriving on the scene, had been appalled, and had written in fury to Antioch. In fact, his father had fondly believed that the despatch had gone to Rome. His father had been impressed, but more impressed when Tullus had stayed to help with reconstruction.

The outlaw arose from his prayer. An inner decision had taken root and could not be gainsaid – his days as a rebel were over. His men had been wiped out, but there was little sorrow in his heart. Passionately he had pretended they were patriots, but in the shocked aftermath of the ambush there were no heady dreams. His men had been cutthroats out for easy gain and little else. He himself had played the patriot: the great avenger of Roman butchery. Now there was nothing left; nothing inside to spur the hatred.

CHAPTER THIRTY

PILATE'S WIFE

The Procurator Pontius Pilate had returned to Caesarea, glad to be free of the dogma-ridden tensions in Jerusalem. Normally such agitation passed quickly, but this time it was different. Neither the winds of the Great Sea nor his visits to the theatre by its shore could erase the memory of the crucified prophet, and when he did forget, the depression of his wife reminded him.

Pilate was much concerned about his wife, for her troubled and lifeless condition had not altered since their return from Jerusalem. Indeed, a barrier had grown between them, but what was worse was the naked fear in her eyes when she looked at him. This was hurtful, wounding, and he had no answer to it other than retreat.

Pilate's private worries were well matched by the public row over the arrest of Tullus and his possible loss. This and the nineteen known deaths had aroused a fury in Antioch.

The Legate's demand for an inquiry was no surprise to Pilate, and in anticipation he had already sent to Palmyra for details, certain that the preliminaries would be delegated to him. What he had not expected was the interest of the Governor himself, but even more surprising was the note from the Emperor's secretariat. Tiberius wanted to know all.

The interest of Sejanus had also been aroused, but the tone of his despatch differed pointedly from that of either the Governor or the Emperor's secretariat. 'A convert,' he wrote, 'even if he is a Chief Centurion, could put his new belief before the welfare of the Empire. This is not impossible, so the matter should be investigated thoroughly and objectively.'

Pilate could almost hear the sound of the powerful Prefect's voice dictating to his scribes, for when Sejanus spoke he was compelling.

The arrest and possible loss of Tullus had certainly excited the interest of the great, and clearly the procedure of any inquiry would need to be conducted with meticulous care. This did not daunt Pontius Pilate, for in the area of administrative detail he was a master. However, with Valerius and Gallo present, as they were sure to be, a calm, factual analysis would be near impossible. Pilate had always considered their mutual dislike to be more personal than political, but with the intervention of Sejanus he was not so sure. As for himself, Pilate was determined to remain impartial.

He was dining with his wife and his aide Maximus when the news came that the Centurion had been found.

'This will change everything,' he said, handing the despatch to Maximus.

Maximus whistled through his teeth.

'Valerius has come out if it well,' he said, looking pointedly at his superior.

'And when the news reaches Capri and Rome they'll echo your sentiments.'

Pilate paused reflectively before continuing.

'The mode of the proposed inquiry will be transformed, for Tullus will have to answer the spurious charges levelled against him in person. 'Spurious' is our private opinion, Maximus!'

'Yes, sir!'

'It will mean delay, as Tullus will need time to recover – anyway, the law is rarely in a hurry!'

'I suppose the Tribune Gallo will have the right to question,' Maximus suggested.

'Yes, if the Legate allows – and he will. Gallo's friendship with Sejanus is persuasive!'

'Why, sir, does a man like Sejanus confide in such a creature?'

'Maximus, be prudent – he's useful – but I never said it!'

'I wonder how Tullus will stand up to Gallo's invective?'

'I would put your question in reverse. How will Gallo stand up to Tullus?'

Pilate's wife nodded in support of her husband; a response he was quick to acknowledge.

'You're looking much better this evening, my dear.'

248

'Yes, the news about Marcus Tullus has heartened me,' she returned, rising to her feet. Supper was over, and she did not have the will to carry on a conversation.

'You will excuse me, sir,' she said, smiling faintly.

'Of course, my dear!' Pilate responded warmly, relieved at his wife's turn for the better – even though it was slight. But any change, however small, was welcome, for the barrier that had risen between them was sharply painful.

Ever since the Rabbi's crucifixion an unreasonable sense of guilt had haunted Pilate's wife. She had warned her husband, that was true, but had she done enough? The dream had been powerful, potent, and its memory clung, colouring her every thought. Had she betrayed some godly messenger? Someone sent to halt a crime, a crime against some just and priestly man?

Night and day her self-accusing thoughts continued. There was no rest from it, and she was fearful for her reason.

Martha, her personal servant, was the only one who seemed to understand. The servant's patient listening and her words of comfort helped, but she did not have the knowledge and therefore could not still the anxious questions of her mistress.

Pilate's wife was quick to tell her servant the good news about the Centurion, knowing Martha was from Capernaum.

'I'm very pleased, my lady. He's well liked, you know – he helped to build our synagogue.'

The light in Martha's face was evidence of her sincerity.

'My lady.'

'Yes, Martha.'

'You ought to speak with Marcus Tullus. He could answer your questions, my lady, I'm sure he could, for they say in Capernaum that he knows the Rabbi's teaching better than most Jews!'

'Martha, you've given me hope, but will my husband let me go to Capernaum?'

'Could he not come here?'

'No, Martha, not after what he's just been through. No, I'll have to go to Capernaum myself. There's hope there – I know it; there has to be, for I can't go on like this much longer.'

She sat perched on a couch, looking blankly in front of her. 'I'm so tired, Martha, so very tired, and yet I cannot rest.'

'Can I get you . . .?'

'Nothing, nothing.' The reply was dull with weary resignation.

The servant looked on, full of pity. She was fond of her mistress, for in Martha's eyes she was a lady, a real lady.

'The Procurator will never let me go – he'll see it as a foolishness.' Again the words spoke of resignation.

'You could stay with the sister of the tall Tribune, my lady. You liked her, you said.'

Pilate's wife nodded with sudden animation. 'You're right! I could stay with her! Why did I not think of it myself? This weariness has robbed me of my senses.' She shook her head. 'But will my husband let me go? That's the question!' Uncertainty had returned.

'But you'd be staying with the Tribune's sister!'

'Martha dear, there's more to it than that – much more!' She sighed knowingly.

Pilate's wife was right, her doubts well founded, for at first the Procurator was adamant in his refusal. Such a direct connection with the Valerii would compromise his neutral position. It was out of the question, he emphasised. So the days sped by with his wife's condition worsening, something he could not bear to watch, and at last he assented to her wishes. There was one condition, though, an unavoidable condition. She would have to call on Herod and his wife at Tiberias.

CHAPTER THIRTY-ONE

THE VILLA RUFUS

Gallo suffered only brief annoyance when he learned of the Centurion's rescue. As usual, he was quick to recover and realise the potential of the situation. Clearly, Tullus would have to testify in public as well as answer the numerous accusations Marius had listed.

Gallo, of course, had no intention of defending the foolish arrest which he had privately encouraged and which publicly he had been careful to disown. Only the drunken commander at Palmyra could be implicated, but that was his problem. Anyway, he was as slippery as a fish and could easily maintain that Marius had obtained the two tent parties under false pretences.

The public inquiry into the death of nineteen men would not be casual. On the contrary, every detail of formality would be obeyed. He would enjoy himself, he thought, imagining the embarrassment he could cause, and when he had finished with the 'celestial twins' from Capernaum, that cursed Centurion and his lackey Valerius, they would look like schoolboys.

Gallo smiled with cynical amusement, seeing the whole affair as a playground to enjoy and to exploit. The possibilities were many: Marius, for instance, could be painted as the lonely patriot battling the forces of subversion; a hero conveniently silent, Gallo mused, for death was one role that even Marius could play.

Gallo had received the news on his way to Antioch, and now, ringed by his cronies at the Villa Rufus, he had an audience. It was his constant need, and generally it mattered little who they were as long as he could dominate. He had no love for able men or those of equal mind to his. Such men were troublesome. They wanted reasons, while soft-heads did his will without enquiry. Because of this, his men in Antioch were weak, and even though he had sent directives little had happened in his absence.

One plan, the transfer and replacement of the galley captains, was proceeding without hindrance, but such changes were necessarily unobtrusive and therefore slow, painfully slow, for time was not a luxury Sejanus could indulge, as the old man could flee Capri at any time. If he did, his capture would be vital. Gallo had no illusions – it was either triumph or diasater. It was either Tiberius as a puppet of Sejanus, or Tiberius with the Syrian legions, and for him it was either the governorship of Syria or exile at Dura Europus beyond the eastern border – with ample gold to make it comfortable. The times were exhilarating and a fitting challenge for his powers.

There was much to be done, but how? How could he replace the squadron commander with his own man and keep above suspicion? How could he get more gold? For a plate or two were nothing to his needs.

He had two allies at the Residency, he remembered. Spineless wonders sent from Rome pretending to be friends of Gaius 'Caligula'. They had fooled the Legate, not a great accomplishment, and at times were party to secret information. At least they heard something, not like Largus, who for all his confidential whispering knew nothing. Gallo was sure of his judgement, for the 'baby-face' was much too innocent to keep a secret.

Largus, a frequent visitor at the Villa Rufus, had played his part well.

CHAPTER THIRTY-TWO

THE RETURN

The legionaries, with Cornelius out in front, stood waiting in their ranks. To the left were the town elders, Ben Joseph and Felix, their casual group contrasting with the ordered lines of the soldiers – Sarah was with the ladies at the villa.

It was morning, and the sun had yet to reach its scorching intensity. All were silent, listening as the distant sound of marching feet grew to a powerful rhythm. Then, close by Ben Joseph's villa, the vanguard of the Tribune's force swung into view – they had dismounted from their open waggons for the entry into Capernaum.

In the distance Felix could see the figures of Drusilla and Cornelia waving from the villa portico, and there it was, the canopied cart, no doubt carrying Lucius and Marcus. It was strange, he thought: both had left determined to protect the Rabbi, both had been thwarted, and now both were returning in what was little less than triumph.

At first the approach seemed slow, then, suddenly as it were, they had arrived.

The Tribune and Tullus saluted, after which the ranks of the garrison erupted with spontaneous cheering. The emotion was infectious, and the Tribune's guard quickly joined in.

Valerius held his hand aloft, and there was instant stillness.

'Noble sirs!' he began, bowing towards the elders. 'Men!' – slowly he scanned the silent ranks of the legionaries. 'The God of all men has showered his grace upon us. Your commander has returned.'

Cheering burst out again, and Valerius turned to his own guard.

'Men, you cheer yourselves! You won the victory. None are without honour, but there are two I must mention specially – the legionary Titus, and James the Galilean. We owe much to their skill and courage.'

James, who was standing behind his master, shuffled awkwardly as many shouted their agreement.

'There is one who does not travel with us – Simon the goatherd – you men do not know him.' The Tribune gestured towards the garrison ranks. 'But for him your commander would have perished. It was he who found the Chief Centurion and sustained him in his hours of peril. It is to Simon that I raise my sword. May the gods protect him!'

Valerius stepped back. Now it was the Centurion's turn. All listened intently, and though his voice lacked its usual power, it was still commanding.

'My heart is full of gratitude. I am grateful to you all, and in particular to those the Tribune named. There was one, however, whom he did not name – himself!'

An explosion of cheering was an instant acknowledgement.

'Respected elders, men,' Tullus continued, 'the Tribune Valerius does not only talk of honour – he lives it! – I am glad to be back,' he added simply, 'and glad to be with you. Thank you for your welcome.' Like the Tribune's, his words were brief. Then he turned aside to James.

'There is one who won't return, one whom Capernaum will never see again.'

James knew his master was referring to the Rabbi.

After the brief, formal speeches, there were personal greetings; Felix, Ben Joseph, the elders, Cornelius and his veterans; but Valerius was quick to extract his friend from the tiring round on the pretext of a confidential word.

'A Laticlavius has his uses,' he said with a wink. 'It's time you saw my sister, but first the altar. We must show due respect.'

After the ceremony, and after the Centurion had left for the villa, Valerius called Cornelius and Titus together to discuss such problems as billeting. As usual, his voice was clipped and brisk as he listed his orders.

'The men will want to celebrate this evening,' he said finally. 'Let them, be generous, yet keep control. I've no wish to sit in judgement over rioters – you're looking at me strangely, Titus!'

'Sorry, sir – you want me to . . .'

'To be my escort captain. I forgot to make that clear. You'll have the rank of Optio – don't look so startled, Titus, you've been acting as the leader since my previous man went sick at Jericho!'

'Yes, sir,' Titus reacted, trying to absorb his change of fortune.

The Tribune smiled. 'An Optio is better off when he retires!'

Cornelius laughed, and Titus, still bewildered, joined in.

'Are there any despatches for me, Cornelius?' the Tribune asked, his voice held at an unnatural pitch. The dilemma of Cornelia and the hope of the Emperor's dispensation were never far from his mind.

'One from Antioch, sir, delivered by a wiry Greek named Demos – a friend of yours, he said,' Cornelius responded, handing the roll to Valerius.

'Demos! – it must be urgent.'

The Tribune broke the seal immediately and began to read. It was from Largus and full of warnings and forebodings.

'Titus, we will be leaving for Antioch tomorrow afternoon and will be travelling through the night,' Valerius reacted bluntly. 'Don't tell the men until the morning light. Let their evening's ease be undisturbed.'

'Yes, sir.'

The Tribune mopped his brow. 'The sun is getting high. It's much too hot to stand about – ah, here's Felix!'

At that Titus and Cornelius felt themselves dismissed, leaving Valerius and the old family servant together.

'Come, Felix, walk with me to the villa, there's much to talk about.'

It was not long before the conversation centred on Cornelia.

'She needs to hear good news, Master Lucius.'

Valerius nodded, his lips pressed tightly in their characteristic way.

'Does she say anything?'

'No, I wish she would – she plays the stoic better than us all.'

'Yes, I know.' Valerius drew the words out slowly.

They walked on silently, their heads bent in a sightless searching of the dusty ground.

'Felix, I'm only here until tomorrow – trouble at Antioch. Look after her – maybe she needs a change to take her mind off things.'

The old servant of the Valerii assented, but his heart was heavy. He knew Tiberius to be a fastidious guardian of custom. Indeed, many viewed him as an old, unbending republican, wedded to the past. Felix could not see him giving his approval to a controversial union such as that of Lucius and Cornelia. It would be too much out of character. Yet there was hope; however faint, there was hope.

Cornelia was waiting on the portico, and as soon as Felix saw her he judiciously turned aside, pretending conversation with one of the legionaries who had been following as an escort.

Being under the eyes of the guards, Cornelia did not run to meet the Tribune, but once in the privacy of her quarters she clung to him, repeating his name until sobbing choked her voice.

'What's the matter, my dear?' His words were full of concern.

'Nothing, Lucius, nothing. I'm . . . I'm very pleased to see you.'

Again she clung to him, burying her face in his tunic. He knew she was still weeping, though her sobbing had subsided.

'We must be patient,' he said soothingly. 'I'm sure that Father will bring the news we want to hear.'

'Yes,' she said, but the sound had another meaning. The light of hope was low. Poor girl, he thought. The tenderness he felt was almost too intense to bear. He held her closely. She had been tutored in the best tradition and trained to be a lady. He had thought of her and Junia as sisters. They had played together, grown up together and had been educated together. Even so, for all her natural grace, she did not have the confidence of his younger sister. Junia was a Valerii, with the surety of the family name, while Cornelia, even though she had enjoyed the family privilege, did not have that inner rock of certainty. He kissed her. Her vulnerability made her even more attractive.

'Tell me what's been happening,' he asked. It was best to keep her mind on practical things. 'How is my sister? And what's the mood of Capernaum in the wake of the great Rabbi's passing?'

Cornelia brightened as she praised Drusilla's faith and courage.

'She never gave up hoping that Marcus Tullus was safe, and Master Felix was so attentive. He and Sarah are often in the town, seeking the Rabbi's disciples, Sarah says. Rumour has it that the Teacher has risen from the grave. The local interpretation is pictorial, but Master Felix does not discount these tales. He says that a man of the Rabbi's awesome power is capable of many things outside our common knowledge. He firmly believes that the Rabbi's spirit still lives, and so does my lady your sister. She told me it was the memory of the Rabbi that sustained her, and, Lucius, the Procurator's wife is coming to Capernaum!'

'Claudia!'

'Yes. Apparently, the death of the Rabbi Jesus has greatly distressed her and she wants to meet the Chief Centurion, the noble Tullus. The Procurator's letter was very circumspect.'

'I bet it was. I'm surprised he did not summon Marcus.'

'The Procurator mentioned this. He said that his lady would not hear of the Centurion making the journey so soon after his injury.'

'That's considerate, but it means that his wife's condition is desperate, too desperate to wait until Marcus has recovered, and desperate enough for Pilate to risk his aura of neutrality. He must have given his permission reluctantly – do we know what connection Claudia had with the Rabbi?'

'No, the Procurator's letter was not specific.'

Slowly the Tribune tightened his arm round Cornelia's shoulders.

'The Empire has not finished with the Rabbi Jesus – not at all.'

For a time she questioned him about his visit to Qumran and the search for the Centurion, while laughing happily at his humorous asides. She did not bring up the subject of his journey to Jerusalem. She had already heard the bitter facts from Felix. Valerius, too, avoided the subject. Crucifixion was a nightmare, and too horrible a subject for Cornelia in her present state.

'I forgot to tell you,' she said suddenly. 'We had a visit from Demos – said he was delivering a message. He's just the same. It was so good to see him and have an opportunity to thank him for all his help.'

Now was the time to tell her, he thought. She would not like it, but it was best to be straight.

'The message was for me, my dear. Not good news, alas.'

'I know. You have to leave. I heard it in your voice.'

He felt her body stiffen.

'I'm afraid you're right. There's trouble at Antioch. I have to leave tomorrow afternoon.'

Antioch! she moaned inwardly. His absence could be measured in months, and while he was in Antioch he could receive orders never to see her again. Her imagination was heightened by belief. She shuddered.

Valerius did his best to calm her, explaining gently how his journey was of vital importance. She nodded, listening only partially to his words, her mind occupied by the certainty that, if ordered, he would renounce her. He would do his duty regardless of the misery he would suffer.

'Lucius, if you have to turn from me I will understand. Your duty must come first . . .'

'Cornelia, no!' he reacted firecely. 'You must not think like this. The gods are wise. We must have faith!'

'Yes, Lucius,' she said defensively, but he knew her doubt remained.

'If Tiberius hesitates, I'll take you to Capri myself, and when he sees the lady of my choice he'll bow to reason!'

In response she put her arms about him, squeezing tightly, her face against his chest.

'And if he does not hesitate – if he orders, Lucius, what then?' The unspoken words were like hammers in her mind.

Valerius kissed her on the forehead, believing falsely that her spirits had been lifted.

'Come with me, my sweet Cornelia. It's time I saw my sister.'

Drusilla was sitting on the floor beside the Centurion's

couch when the Tribune and Cornelia entered. She was radiant as she rose to embrace her brother.

'Lucius, you've been magnificent.'

Valerius waved his hand dismissively.

'There'll be no dismissive gestures in Capri or Rome.'

'Drusilla, the defeat of twenty ill-fed rebels hardly constitutes a triumph!'

'Yes, but look who you rescued!' she quipped, smiling at the Centurion.

Tullus rumbled with an easy laugh.

'Marcus says he's going to retire and grow grapes!' she continued playfully.

'Pure invention!' the Centurion responded.

They all laughed, and Valerius was relieved to see Cornelia joining in the humour.

CHAPTER THIRTY-THREE

CLAUDIA

Although it filled her with loathing, Claudia called on the Tetrarch and his wife at Tiberias as her husband had insisted. He was right, of course, and she knew it, for the Procurator's wife could not pass the palace of the Tetrarch without paying her respects. So for three days she suffered the lavish Herodian hospitality.

Herodias was the mistress of palace intrigue and the clandestine affair. Innocence was a quality that had long abandoned her. She knew Claudia was going to Capernaum, and her questions on the subject of the Tribune and his sister, though deft and tactful, were relentless. The Valerii fascinated her. Drusilla had called once at the palace, and the contrast of her high aristocratic manner with the way she fussed about her rough-born servants' welfare was odd, to say the least.

'She did not bring the beautiful Cornelia, of course,' Herodias added, with a knowing smile. 'But imagine, Calpurnia, imagine someone like Valerius marrying a slave!'

The endless gossip and knowing whispers only added to Claudia's already agitated state, yet the gloss of propriety held, and on the surface Pilate's wife's behaviour was faultless, though understandably her relief on leaving for Capernaum was considerable.

The morning still retained an edge of freshness as Claudia and her escort approached Capernaum. Eagerly she looked about her as the outline of the town grew nearer. She was both hopeful and nervous, for the test was close. Would she find the answer to her questions? Would Tullus clear her of her guilt?

There were people up ahead, walking casually, with soldiers in attendance, though not in any formal attitude, and at once she guessed at who they were. The gap closed quickly, confirming her

260

assumption. It was Tullus and the Valerii having a morning stroll. As soon as it was practicable she alighted from her cart, an ornate vehicle: the Procurator's wife could not travel simply.

Drusilla ran ahead to greet her, and at once she felt at home. There was no elaborate fuss, just a simple welcome.

Tullus was his usual self, of course, strong and stable. He had survived the ambush well, she told him, and the name Valerius, she added, bowing to the Tribune, was regarded with even more respect. Immediately she saw Cornelia she understood the dilemma of Valerius. This was no slave; slave in law, perhaps, yet not a slave. Most assumed she was his mistress. She was young without being girlish, and beautiful, a beauty heightened by dignity. Claudia was impressed.

There was something almost indefinable about Tullus and the Valerii, like an inner stature. They were tall within themselves. Hope leapt within her. She had been right, she thought. She had been right to come. Her insistent promptings had been true.

Claudia gladly joined her hosts, leaving her escort to continue on towards the garrison. She walked between the Centurion and Drusilla, and for the first time since Jerusalem she felt content. Indeed, she knew with certainty that her stay in Capernaum would cure her. Why, she did not know. She only knew that the unredeemable guilt that had plagued her since the Prophet's crucifixion was lifting. Forgiveness was possible. What strange force was present in this place? Why Capernaum?

They stopped by the water's edge and looked across the lake, still retaining, as it were, its morning hush. In the distance they could see a knot of fishing boats, but the sun was growing hot. Soon it would be blistering in intensity, so necessarily the lakeside walk was brief. In normal circumstances Drusilla and Cornelia would have moved to higher ground or by the sea in order to escape the summer heat, but the restraints of security had made the Tribune cautious. The abduction of Cornelia was still immediate in his memory.

Once back at the Ben Josephs' villa the Centurion immediately excused himself to rest. The Tribune and Cornelia also took their leave of the Procurator's wife, thus leaving her and

Drusilla alone to talk. The Ben Josephs' villa was not the palace at Caesarea, Drusilla joked, knowing well that Claudia cared little for such things. Both women laughed, and their conversation continued easily, though there was an obvious hunger in Claudia's questions when they centred on the teaching of the Rabbi. She pressed her questions, and Drusilla told her all she knew.

'Wait until the evening, Claudia,' she kept repeating. 'Marcus will be joining us for supper, and Felix, too – you'll have your answers then.'

The Tribune and Cornelia had crossed over to the garrison fort, where she had playfully offered to scribe his reports. He, believing it would keep her occupied, had uexpectedly agreed. Nonetheless, tears were often close. His leaving was too imminent to be forgotten.

The afternoon passed all too quickly, and suddenly it was time for his departure. She watched him go, holding her composure well, but when his cart disappeared from view she fled to her room to sit vacantly in a kind of shocked dejection. Then, like an arrowshaft, the thought struck, potent with belief, that she was a hindrance, a barrier to his progress. She reeled, almost physically, before the new, sharp-edged doubt. She had no defence. Helplessly she watched her inner panic grow, its familiar pattern well established during her abduction. Even so, she gave no outward sign of her distress as Drusilla entered the room. It was time for supper.

Cornelia found it difficult to listen to the talk that circled the supper table. Her inner anguish was too persistent. It divided her attention, robbed her of her energy and left her with a sense of separation. Felix, aware of her isolation, was quick to involve her in the conversation.

'Cornelia,' he said directly, 'you met the priest Raphael. Was he similar in character to the Rabbi Jesus and his disciples?'

Cornelia stammered for a moment before collecting herself.

'Yes, Master Felix, he seemed to share the same order of being, but the Rabbi Jesus was . . .'

'Different,' Felix prompted.

'Yes . . . I cannot find the words.' She shook her head. 'I only saw him once; the day that James was cured.'

'Like yourself, my dear,' Claudia responded, 'I also saw him once – like a pool of stillness. I can see him now – a pool of stillness in the swirling Passover crowds. Can one see stillness? Maybe I imagined it!'

'The mind's eye sees in depth,' the Centurion said evenly.

The voice of Tullus, full of its old authority, was the sign for Claudia. At last it was the time to press her questions. Suddenly nervous, there was a tremor in her voice as she spoke.

'Was the Rabbi's death avoidable?'

The Centurion exhaled and looked at Felix.

'Felix tried to stop the execution.'

The grey-haired servant of the Valerii looked straight at Claudia, aware of his incongruous position.

'Your husband, madam, kindly granted me an audience and explained himself to be wholly trapped by circumstance, like an actor on the stage, he said. He also said that you yourself had pleaded for the Rabbi's life.'

'The whole question has almost driven me to distraction,' Claudia returned, glad to speak openly. 'There hasn't been a single night since the crucifixion when my sleep has not been disturbed. You see, I was warned in a dream. It was no ordinary dream – vivid – powerful – unforgettable – I feel responsible. I cannot rid myself of guilt.'

The room had grown silent, for the sincerity of Pilate's wife was obvious.

Uncharacteristically, it was Cornelia who spoke first. An instant sympathy prompted her, as she knew too well the misery that accompanied sleepless nights. Her abduction had afforded ample experience.

'The gods play with the strings of life,' she began. 'So Virgil and the ancients say, but I have a feeling that the Rabbi answered to a higher law – the father of the gods.'

She stopped self-consciously, aware that all were watching her. She rarely spoke at such a supper-party.

Claudia smiled warmly, her face suddenly younger.

'My dear, what you have said I'm sure is true, and it is a comfort, but may I press a further question on this gracious gathering. Who warned me in the dream? And if it was a god, did I fail in my agency?'

For a moment no one spoke. Slowly the focus of attention came to rest on the Centurion.

'I cannot believe,' he responded, 'that the Rabbi's life owed its continuance to the agency of a dream. The Rabbi is not dead. Ask Drusilla! Ask Felix! The man who said 'Before Abraham was I am' is established in the spirit. This is the truth. His body's death was but the shedding of a coat. The Rabbi and his Father are one. How could you be guilty of his death? How could that which has ever been cease to be? The Disciple John is in Capernaum. James, my servant, will arrange a meeting, and when you hear the Disciple speak, you will believe.'

Claudia wept openly. She was not ashamed of her tears, for her prayers had been answered.

The next day, in the company of Drusilla, Claudia met the Disciple. After the initial greetings Drusilla withdrew discreetly, and for a moment Claudia was shocked. How could she, the Procurator's wife, meet alone with a young Jewish rabbi? It was, to say the least, peculiar. Nevertheless, she showed no sign of her misgivings.

After the Disciple had gone, Drusilla was unashamedly curious. She did not have to question, though, as Claudia was eager to share her experience.

'He was very polite and respectful,' she related. 'He said very little, and listened to all I had to say, and when I asked him about the dream, he just smiled. There was a brief pause, and when he spoke it was so simple, as if he was confirming what I knew. He told me that the dream had brought me into contact with the Master's teaching, and also into the company of good people. A dream could serve no better end. I was told to have no fear, as the Master's destiny was his Father's will and no dream could alter that one jot.'

'Was that all?' Drusilla asked.

'Well, yes, as I said, he was very polite. He even apologised for the heat, saying that the winter months in Capernaum were much more agreeable.'

'Claudia, my dear, you've attended too many diplomatic receptions!'

'No, no, it wasn't like that. He was courteous, yes, but I was awestruck. He was so very much there, if you know what I mean.'

Drusilla nodded.

'As the noble Tullus said, I believed every word he uttered. Where can I learn about his Master's teaching?'

'Here!' Drusilla answered simply. 'Ask Marcus, ask Felix – or the Ben Josephs, for that matter – that is, when they return. They're away for a few days.'

CHAPTER THIRTY-FOUR

THE REBEL LEADER

At Drusilla's invitation Claudia continued her stay at Capernaum. Each evening there was conversation, and each morning they walked by the lakeside. On the third morning Tullus did not accompany the ladies. Instead, he joined his servant James on his early visit to the market. It was time to show himself in the town.

There were waves and greetings for him at every step. He walked at a slow, easy pace past the synagogue and then to where the fishing boats came in. At every corner there were well-wishers.

'Herod, that camel Tetrarch, would never be treated like this,' James muttered under his breath, but the Centurion did not hear him.

Suddenly, as if from nowhere, a tall, well-built man stood before them. He was a Jew, impressive in his size and bearing, with his youthful shock of curly hair uncovered. Behind, the Centurion's guard grasped his sword-hilt.

'Welcome, Marcus Tullus!'

The Centurion looked the big man in the eye, and neither flinched. It was the rebel leader.

'My old profession is ended, sir. I'm now a fisherman!'

James, his eyes unusually wide, stood motionless. He had recognised the man immediately. Quickly he looked about him. It seemed the whole of Capernaum was watching.

The Centurion continued to look steadily at the man before him. No words were spoken. Then, in a deliberate movement, his hand stretched forward. Firmly they gripped each other by the arm.

'Keep to the path of honour.' The Centurion's voice was resonant. He smiled. 'And fish well.'

The smile was returned, after which the one-time rebel

made for the lake's edge and the fishing boats.

'That was a bit public, Master. Half of Capernaum was watching,' James said through his teeth.

'He's not known in these parts.'

'I hope you're right, Master, but I doubt it. That fox Herod has agents everywhere. It could be very awkward, Master, if this business got to Herod's ears.'

'You're a comforting companion, James,' the Centurion returned. Amusement for a moment flickered on his face. 'But, as usual, you're right. Herod is only too willing to elaborate on any lack of Roman security, and the news of a Centurion grasping the arm of a known rebel would be perfect information to exploit. Anyway, James, what did you expect me to do?'

'What you did, Master!'

'Ah, well, if I've passed your censure, Capri and Rome should be easy!'

Tullus rumbled with a laugh, and James smacked his lips in his usual way.

Once they reached the market, Tullus left his servant amidst the vendors' stalls and returned to the garrison. He still tired easily.

CHAPTER THIRTY-FIVE

SPECULATIONS AND REFLECTIONS

After Tullus had rested from his walk in Capernaum he was told that a messenger awaited him. At once the man was ushered in and the roll handed over. It was from the Legate at Antioch, giving details of an inquiry into his so-called arrest and the subsequent ambush. The Legate had also enclosed a personal note in which he wished the Centurion a speedy recovery. He had delayed the inquiry, he wrote, until the cooler months, and was apologetic about the formal require-ment of Tullus's attendance.

The apology was polite and no doubt genuine, but the inclusion of Gallo on the list of those summoned left the Centurion wary. He knew too well that Gallo's golden tongue could easily exploit his known connections with the Jewish community. The inquiry could be awkward, very awkward, especially if the earlier meeting with the rebel leader were revealed.

Valerius was the target, of course, not him, and any censure he incurred would fall upon the Tribune – the Emperor's per-sonal legate. Against his every instinct he was trapped in a power struggle, a wholly desperate power struggle, between Sejanus and the Emperor.

He sighed. What would happen in Rome would happen. There was nothing he could do to alter that, but the effects of such a struggle could be disastrous for the Valerii. A tri-umphant Sejanus would mean a triumphant Gallo, and in that event the Valerian family would be little more than circus playthings. They would not be defenceless, though, for both the Capernaum garrison and the Tribune's guard were picked men. Tullus knew the east well, and a life beyond the borders, though incongruous for the Valerii, was not impossible.

The Centurion's thoughts, troubled in their mood, turned

to the Tribune and the urgent call from Antioch. Obviously the situation had worsened, and the fact that Demos had acted as messenger emphasised the urgency. Little specific had been said , either by Largus in his note or by Demos verbally. The wily Greek had left one warning, however. Tell the Tribune, he had cautioned, to be careful whom he ate with at the Residency. What was Gallo up to, he wondered? The friend of Sejanus was clever, and it was not beyond his wit to isolate the Legate and use him as a puppet, just as Sejanus planned to use the Emperor. Gallo could do it, but he would need money – gold – a substantial sum, to buy support about the Residency.

Tullus breathed deeply. If his speculation were correct, the Tribune's contact, Largus, would be treading on a knife-edge, and Valerius himself would be, to Gallo, an intolerable hindrance, a hindrance to be rid of. It was to be hoped that his fears were groundless. Nonetheless, it was both fortunate and timely that the Tribune had boosted his guard numbers to over thirty.

By now Valerius and his men would be well on the way to Ptolemais, where Demos had arranged for a grain ship to be waiting. A sea trip would be cool, he mused. He closed his eyes. A lot had happened since his first encounter with the Tribune at the Cyrrhus fortress. Who then could have foretold their close relationship? Certainly not Tullus.

His thoughts turned to Drusilla and their first meeting in the garden of the Villa Demetrianus. Her grace, her voice, the way she walked: her qualities had enthralled him. She was and remained everything that his expectation had ever desired. It had not been easy when he thought that he had lost her, but by the Rabbi's grace she had returned to him on the blessed day when James was cured. His mind grew still as he recalled his meeting with the Rabbi: a wonder that defied analysis. The stillness deepened.

All at once a vivid image of Simon the goatherd arose in his mind. The gentle-natured man had saved his life. He smiled, recalling Simon's innocent wonder when Valerius had brought him a replacement for Jacob, a magnificent animal, the best the Tribune's money could buy.

That had been less than a month ago. It was close in his experience, yet just under a year ago the pitiful plight of Cornelia had dominated. It seemed like yesterday. He had not known Cornelia then, but he knew her now, and it was not difficult to appreciate the anguish the Valerii must have suffered.

Yes! A lot had happened in the space of a year, and even now the Procurator's wife was visiting Capernaum: a notable event for a small garrison at any time, though it meant little to the townsfolk. The people of Capernaum had accepted himself and his friends the Valerii. Indeed, they treated Felix with affection – otherwise, Romans were Romans.

He had felt close to them this morning during his walk. They knew he had been stopped from reaching Jerusalem, and they also knew that Felix had pleaded for the Rabbi's life. There was a bond, the sharing of a loss, for they realised, as he realised, that something very special had been taken from their midst; yet they went about their business just as usual. Tullus felt it strange, although he knew his thinking was irrational; even so, the feeling persisted. It was clearly stupid, for he, too, was going about his business, his Roman business. He sighed. He was a human being, feeling human loss. Involuntarily, the Rabbi's words repeated in his mind, the same words he had used in answering Claudia: 'Before Abraham was, I am.' This was the highest truth.

He opened a drawer close to him, pulling out a roll of parchment that Ben Joseph had given him. It was an extract from the Rabbi's teaching.

'I am the true vine, and my Father is the husbandman,' the Centurion read slowly.

'Every branch in me that bears not fruit he takes away: and every branch that bears fruit, he purges it, that it may bring forth more fruit.

'Now you are clean through the word which I have spoken unto you.

'Abide in me, and I in you. As the branch cannot bear fruit of itself, except it abide in the vine; no more can you, except you abide in me.

'I am the vine, you are the branches: he that abides in me,

and I in him, the same brings forth much fruit: for without me you can do nothing.'

That was enough to reflect upon, more than enough! Again he lay back on his couch, and as his thoughts subsided he grew still, very still. Then sleep came.

CHAPTER THIRTY-SIX

ASSASSINS

The Centurion awoke as James entered his room. 'Master, something serious has happened. There's a soldier outside. He's caked with blood and dust and will only speak with you.'

Tullus got to his feet and was immediately alert.

'Send him in.'

When the soldier entered, he recognised him instantly as one of the Tribune's guard.

'You're soaked in blood! Are you all right?' was the Centurion's first reaction.

'It's the blood of the wounded, sir,' came the blunt reply, after which he quickly told his story. The Tribune and his guard had sustained a brief but vicious attack from bandits – or Jewish Zealots, some believed.

'They repeatedly assailed the person of the Tribune, but the wall of shields around him did not break and he remained untouched. The attackers did not stand to do battle. They had no stomach for a fight, for as soon as we advanced they fled!'

'Hired assassins!' The Centurion shot the words out quickly. 'The Jewish Zealot would have stood his ground – you said you formed a wall of shields; you acted quickly!'

'It was difficult country, sir; we were on foot and on full alert. Also, we received a warning.'

'A warning!' the Centurion repeated.

'Yes, sir – a young lad in his early teens – some of the men wanted to question him, but the Tribune let him go.'

'When did you get the warning?'

'In the morning after we left, sir.'

'Where was the boy from?'

'Here, sir, Capernaum.'

'Did he say who sent him?'

'A friend – he was told to say – the Tribune didn't press him.'

'He wouldn't. How many casualties?'

'Twelve wounded. The big man's badly hurt.'

'Shielding his master, I suppose.'

'Yes, sir. They think he's going to be all right.'

'Where did this happen?'

'Near Ramah, sir. The Jewish physician there helped with the wounded – a gift from the gods!'

'You'll need replacements.'

'The Tribune hoped for twelve at least.'

'Were the enemy numerous?

'Difficult to say, sir – about the same as us. They only lost four men, so they could strike again.'

'They will – assassins don't get paid unless they get their man. Is Titus all right?'

'Yes, sir – his defensive formation saved us.'

'The noble Tribune has a gift for picking men of worth. Well, my friend, you'd better get some rest as we'll be leaving soon,' Tullus concluded, dismissing the soldier with a nod.

The energy given by the emergency filled the Centurion with a false strength, and at once he decided to lead the relief force himself – only two tent parties, alas, the most the depleted garrison could afford. He would also take two of his expert scouts. They could prove useful and would bring the number up to eighteen men.

James protested vigorously when he heard his master's plan.

'Another knock on the head will finish you!' But he could see that Tullus was resolved. 'I'm coming with you, then!' he added defiantly.

'No, James! You're needed here. There are spies and criminals abroad in the town. Keep your eyes and ears open, but be careful.'

'What about the big man, Master?'

'I doubt very much that he's involved.'

'I agree.'

'James.'

'Yes, Master.'

'Tell our friend Felix to take an escort with him when he goes wandering in the town.'

'He'll be all right, Master. He's one of the blessed.'

'You've said that before.'

The Galilean nodded curtly.

'What do you mean, James?'

'Felix is blessed; you, Master are blessed; your beautiful lady is blessed. All who have felt the Rabbi's love are blessed.'

Master and servant looked at each other, united by an inner language.

Drusilla was shocked when the Centurion told her the news and when he revealed his plans. She knew, like James, that her protests would be fruitless.

'Promise me that you'll protect yourself against the jarring of the cart.'

'I'll float myself on feathers,' he joked as he embraced her, but the instructions he gave were precise and practical.

As long as Pilate's wife remained they could stay at the Ben Josephs'. Once Claudia left, however, they were to transfer to his quarters at the garrison. He was taking eighteen men, and the remaining soldiers could not adequately protect both the villa and the garrison, but while Claudia and her guard remained the villa was perfectly secure.

'I'm leaving the garrison in the charge of the veteran Atticus – he'll take no chances. For as you know, Cornelius is on his way to Caesarea to receive his promotion.'

'You forgot to tell me, Marcus.'

'I'm sorry.'

'Will he be leaving the garrison?'

'No! He's to be the new Centurion – that's the recommendation.'

'What is Marcus Tullus going to do?'

'Grow grapes!'

Tullus left Capernaum by mid-afternoon, when the heat was still intense. Soon he was asleep, bobbing on the cushions Drusilla had insisted he should take against the jolting of the cart.

Before he had left Capernaum another messenger had arrived with a second scroll from Antioch. Tullus had scanned the text briefly, noting it contained further details concerning the inquiry, and had decided it was something he could study

274

on the journey. It would help to keep him awake, he thought. So after an hour of fitful dozing it was the first thing he turned to.

The details of the proposed inquiry were routine and predictable, though the tone had changed. The reason for this was clear at the end of the message. The date of the inquiry had been brought forward on the recommendation of Rome, and was now fixed for early in August. This time there was no polite apology.

He had received two despatches from Antioch in one day; the first by the leisurely way of Caesarea; the second in haste and direct. Tullus was puzzled. Why was the matter suddenly urgent? Who was behind it? He did not think either Lamia or the Emperor, and if it was Sejanus, why? Why would Sejanus be interested in the timing of an army inquiry at Caesarea?

The Tribune was surprised to see the Centurion, though grateful for his counsel. Like Tullus, he anticipated a further attack, but was heartened by his friend's advice. Tullus knew the road to Ptolemais like the streets of Capernaum. The ambush points were predictable, and he had brought two of his best scouts.

'The assassins have lost the advantage,' Tullus maintained.

'Assassins is the right word, for they were clearly out to get me. It was very obvious.'

'Their paymaster is getting desperate,' the Centurion said quietly.

'Maybe Gallo over-confident!' Valerius returned.

'Or Sejanus over-anxious!'

'Marcus, you said the inquiry had been brought forward. I wonder why.'

'Yes, I wonder,' Tullus echoed, his head bent reflectively. 'I've got it,' he added, looking hard at the Tribune. 'You're one of those listed to be at Caesarea for the inquiry.'

Valerius nodded.

'You can't be in two places at one time!'

'I'm sorry about the inadequacy.'

'You're behaving like your sister. No, I'm serious. The change of the inquiry date could be a ploy to keep you out of Antioch at the crucial time.'

'Gallo will be at the inquiry.'

'Yes, and it's a point against my theory, but not a vital point, I think, for as long as you're not there Gallo may feel happy to leave things to his friends. If I were you, I'd plead the impossibility of attending the inquiry and delay the message till the very last moment. Gallo would never suspect your studied absence. On the contrary, he'd expect you to speak for your Capernaum friend against his inevitable attack.'

'I think my Capernaum friend may well need the testimony of the Emperor's personal legate,' Valerius returned in his quick, staccato way.

'You can send a written statement. Anyway, Titus will be there. The issue at Antioch is too important to be deflected by the discomfiture of one elderly Centurion.'

The Tribune made no reply. Nonetheless, his mind was busy.

'But, Marcus, why bother with the inquiry date when they planned to kill me?'

'The assassins are the creatures of Gallo, and the new inquiry date the idea of Sejanus – that could explain it.'

'It could,' Valerius nodded thoughtfully, 'and if true, Sejanus would have made his recommendation before knowing of your rescue – for it's less than ten days since we marched into Jericho.'

'Oh, I don't come into it,' Tullus reacted. 'It's you they want to stop.'

'I suppose so,' Valerius returned, his voice listless. He looked drawn, Tullus thought, like someone laughter had deserted. 'I'm worried about Venio,' he continued, 'even though the Jewish physician says he will recover. I don't like leaving him.' He sighed wearily, while leaning forward, his arms resting on his knees. Then, with a new resolve, he stood up.

'We'd better call Titus and plan tomorrow's march. And there's the question of the warning we received. It seems we have a secret friend in Capernaum.'

'And enemies,' Tullus responded. 'I've asked James to watch and listen.'

CHAPTER THIRTY-SEVEN

EPHESUS

The Tribune's father had reached the city of Ephesus and was installed at the Prefect's residence. He liked Ephesus and was encouraged to linger by the new and fascinating people he had met. One man, a prince from the valley of the Indus – that populous region beyond Parthia – was particularly interesting.

The Prince, who spoke Greek tolerably well, was on a journey of curiosity, he said. He was a wealthy man, as wealthy as any Senator, and had guards and servants in his retinue. Two merchants from his country also travelled with him, but he himself took no interest in matters of trade. In military affairs, however, he was obviously an expert, and was clearly fascinated by the Roman army's untiring thoroughness, especially their relentless training. Valerius gladly answered his questions – there were no secrets to betray. Discipline and punishment were harsh, but fear alone would soon destroy an army. It was the thread of honour, though sometimes tenuous, that sustained the Legions.

The Prince nodded his agreement, citing examples from his own tradition, and the Senator, sensing a rich and ancient culture, was enthralled. As quickly as civility would allow, Valerius steered the subject towards philosophy and religion. The conversation was intriguing, and readily they agreed to met again.

On the third day the Prince introduced his Roman friend to the rudiments of his traditional language. The Senator was captivated, as the Prince's teaching and his own Platonic training seemed to be as one. Truth, he said with a knowing smile, was not exclusive to either Rome or Athens! He was in his element, and the days passed quickly.

Each morning the Senator and his daughter Junia walked to the Forum, with two legionary guards in attendance. One such morning, while enjoying their habitual stroll, the Senator was almost sent reeling by a young man rushing through the crowds. Immediately the guards sprang to meet the challenge, but he was quick to disappear.

'That was strange,' the Senator reacted. 'His automatic apology was in perfect Latin, and he seemed to know me!'

'And me!' said Junia.

That a young man should look intently at his daughter did not surprise the Senator. Junia, though not as graceful in form as her sister, was attractive. He said nothing, and the moment passed.

Later, however, when they had returned to the Prefect's residence and were crossing the courtyard, Junia again spotted the same young man. He was in earnest conversation with someone, but she could not see who it was due to the deep shadows of the sunlit courtyard.

'There he is, Father.' Junia pointed.

'Who?'

'The young Greek, or whoever he is, who bumped into you.'

The Senator turned.

'That's a Roman face,' he muttered, but at his first step the youthful figure disappeared into the shadows. He searched and asked questions, yet strangely no one had seen or had remembered the wispy-bearded face or the lithe, athletic figure.

'It's like a child's mystery,' he said that evening when he was dining with the Prefect.

'It may have been a local trader,' the Prefect suggested.

'No!' The Senator shook his head. 'He spoke Latin like a patrician.'

'There was a naval galley in the harbour this morning, but they only called for supplies.'

Again the Senator shook his head.

'There's no one of that nature listed in the visitors' roll.'

'Well, it looks as if our 'iron-tight' security has been breached again,' the Prefect returned, with a note of knowing resignation. 'On the other hand, there may be some perfectly simple explanation. I'll look into it tomorrow.'

The incident was soon forgotten as the days passed, and especially as the conversations with the Indian Prince proceeded. The Senator had met Indians before, traders mostly. Their knowledge had been limited, but the Prince was wholly different. Indeed, Valerius knew he had chanced upon a profound system of philosophy. There was no time to waste.

The Prince was rarely assertive, and often his most profound comments were delivered casually, like an aside. Nevertheless, the Senator's trained and alert mind missed little. This was particularly so when the Prince began to quote from his ancient scripture, the Upanishads. Valerius could remember the first quotation vividly.

'Whatever lives is full of the Lord. Claim nothing; enjoy, do not covet his property.'

It was so utterly simple, the Senator mused. A child could understand it, but who could live it, other than a Socrates? That was the rub.

There was more, much more, and like 'Know Thyself', the famous injunction at Delphi, the Upanishads stressed the knowledge of the Self as paramount.

Junia was restless. She had seen enough of Ephesus and was impatient to be on the move again. However, while her father's Indian friend remained, there was little hope of that. She could ask her father once or maybe twice when he planned to leave. After that he would simply tell her to be patient, but if she could not shape her father's will she could always bully Arria. Arria knew Junia's ways, of course, and was adept at handling the Senator's strong-willed daughter; as well as that, the Senator always heeded her advice.

'I think we should give her some indication of time, my lord – that should calm her restlessness,' Arria suggested one evening after the Senator had returned from supper with the Prince. No matter how late, she always waited up for him.

'If you say so, my dear,' he responded easily. 'Tell her, within the next three days.'

'She wants to go by the coast,' Arria added quietly.

'I thought she was in a hurry!'

'She's just restless.'

'You're right, of course. Well, I see no harm in going by the coast. That is, if my Indian friend has no objection – he's coming with us to Antioch.'

'Your friend was very courteous when you introduced me.'

'He is a Prince in every sense, my dear.'

'Perhaps he sensed our . . .'

'Close companionship.'

'Yes, my lord,' she said softly.

CHAPTER THIRTY-EIGHT

THE ROAD FROM RAMAH

Soon after leaving Ramah, the Tribune's scouts, the men Tullus had brought from Capernaum, found the enemy lookouts in a drunken sleep. Then, moving in a wide arc, the Tribune's guard approached their quarry from behind to find them in an ambush position close to the first danger point the Centurion had mentioned. Titus and his men were hardened veterans, and the recent skirmish had stiffened their resolve. Their approach under cover of the wooded terrain was sure and stealthy, and when they struck no javelin or arrow was wasted. They counted twenty dead; if any had escaped they did not notice. They were not Zealots, that was plain enough, but criminals, nothing more, the dregs of Ptolemais or some such town.

In little over a month the Tribune had achieved two major victories against an elusive enemy and in difficult terrain. His reputation was established, and although he repeatedly emphasised the help of his advisors, no one listened. To the world, he was the victor. Strong in the Tribune's mind was the favour of the gods. The altar was not forgotten, but there was something more, both powerful and compelling – the memory of the Rabbi Jesus. It had happened after the attack, when for an involuntary moment a vivid recollection of the Rabbi's person had filled him with an incredible peace. In such a state it was unreal, if not laughable, to claim a sense of personal triumph. He welcomed the experience with equanimity. Indeed, it was the natural fruit of his stoical training.

On his arrival at Antioch he went straight to the Legate's residence, where much to his dismay he learned that the Tribune Largus was missing. The Legate, clearly concerned, had initiated a thorough search, but without result. At the Villa Demetrianus, however, his fears were allayed, as Largus had left a cryptic message, similar to the one Demos had left at Capernaum: – 'Trust no one at the Residency and be careful what you eat.' Valerius thought it very possible that his astute friend had gone into hiding.

For three days the Tribune waited at the Villa Demetrianus, but neither Largus nor Demos appeared. His concern grew, for if calling in person was hazardous, why were there no messages?

Gallo, he learned from Demetrianus, was at the Villa Rufus and apparently inactive – his parties neither as lavish nor as frequent as before. All was seemingly quiet, just as at the Residency. It was the heat, Demetrianus said.

Titus was a frequent visitor at the Residency because the Tribune's guard was stationed there. He was ever watchful, though he found nothing to arouse suspicion; nothing new, except for two men close to the Legate who described themselves as friends of Gaius. They did not use the popular name of 'Caligula'. The Tribune smiled knowingly. That would please the Legate, for Caligula was the son of Germanicus, and Germanicus had been his hero.

On the fourth day of his stay the Tribune decided to visit the Residency and see for himself. In the evening he dined with the Legate and his close aides. The old administrator was full of praise for his successes in the field, and the conversation proceeded casually, centring on the subject of aqueduct repairs. The Legate's two new men, described by Titus as pro-Caligula, agreed with all he had to say, but rarely volunteered an opinion. Typical sycophants, the Tribune thought.

With the warning of Largus before his mind, he ate only from the dishes in common view and refused all delicacies. He was a plain food man, he said, and an upset stomach had made him fastidious.

Supper passed without discussion of army matters, and politics were shunned. The Tribune, for his part, initiated no particular subject, preferring to leave it to his host, who, apart from a genuine concern for Largus, kept the topics light and on the surface. In private the Legate was equally cautious. Something was wrong.

As the days passed, the Tribune became more and more frustrated, for apart from Demetrianus there seemed no one he could trust. His chief allies had apparently vanished and his friend the Naval Commander was at sea.

All the while Gallo kept to his villa, behaving like an ageing nobleman who had turned his face against ambition. Yet something was wrong. Valerius seemed to sense it in the very air he breathed.

CHAPTER THIRTY-NINE

VENIO

After the Tribune had left for Ptolemais, and after he had
rested, the Centurion went to Venio's bedside. The big
man was greatly touched by Tullus's presence and wept
openly. He was badly injured and could move only with difficulty, but he was recovering slowly and was past the critical
stage.

For seven days Tullus continued to visit him and his
wounded companions. Some of the legionaries would never
fight again. For them an honourable retirement was the only
course. In this respect the army was not without compassion,
especially if a man like L. Gracchus Valerius signed their
application for benefit.

On the eighth day of his stay at Ramah the Centurion made
his routine call upon the wounded, and it was then that Venio
began to speak about the Rabbi Jesus. He recalled the day that
James was cured, and could remember every detail – for
instance, where he had stood in relation to his master the
Tribune. In fact the whole scene was crystal clear, but it was
the Rabbi himself and the unmeasured love his presence had
engendered that Venio held closest to his heart.

'When I was fainting from my wounds, sir,' Venio still
spoke weakly, 'it was that very love that saved me. That is the
truth, sir.' Perspiration glistened on his face.

'Yes, Venio,' Tullus responded.

'The Rabbi was very special – wasn't he, sir?'

'Yes, more special than our minds can comprehend.'

The eyes of the big man sought the Centurion.

'A year and a half ago I was a hired driver, living rough
about the docks of Ostia.' Venio smiled wanly. 'Getting drunk
too often and getting into trouble. The Tribune, my master,
changed all that.'

'You were willing to change,' Tullus returned, lightly touching the big man's arm. He was at once alerted; the arm was very hot. He felt his forehead. Venio was feverish.

'You need the physician!' he reacted, getting to his feet.

'Stay with me, sir.' The eyes of Venio did not plead, but they were compelling. Tullus obeyed and beckoned one of the guards.

'Get the physician,' he said, 'and quickly!'

The Centurion resumed his seat on the low stool beside Venio's bed and from time to time dried the perspiration beading on the big man's forehead. The physician lived at the other side of the village – he could be ages. Tullus was apprehensive, for there was a look of resignation in the eyes of the wounded man – a prophetic resignation – he had seen it often. Tullus grew still within himself. There was nothing to be said. Suddenly Venio lifted his arm to point.

'The light, sir. The light!'

Tullus turned. The face of Venio was blissful. Then there were the unmistakable signs. Venio was dead.

For a long time the Centurion sat motionless.

It was over twenty days before all the wounded were fit to travel. Their journey to Capernaum was slow, and their protection, an eight-man tent party, was meagre. This, however, did not trouble Tullus. Banditry was not typical of the area, and he believed it well beneath the Zealots' dignity to attack a wounded column. Again, he did not see himself as under threat. If anything, his political enemies wanted him alive. His sacrifice could await the inquiry.

At Capernaum he was greeted by a much relieved Drusilla, but she was shocked to hear the news of Venio's death.

'He was with us all the way from Rome. Lucius will feel it sorely, for they were close. Their shared experience, like Machaerus, is a potent bond.'

Tullus nodded pensively. One man will be taken and the other left, he mused, but who knew why?

'Claudia left six days ago,' she continued after a moment's silence, 'and Cornelia went with her. Felix thought the change might help. Marcus, I'm worried about her, for she was tearful when she left, as if it was a parting, not a brief vacation. She left a letter for Lucius to await his return, and I fear the probable content.'

'You mean she's trying to distance herself.'

'Yes – so that he may marry within his class.'

'He'll follow her.'

'Not if he's forbidden.'

They looked at each other without speaking. It was a nearly hopeless situation, yet Drusilla sensed a mood of determination in Marcus.

'Surely something can be done!' he said firmly.

She put her arms about him, and for a moment they were silent. It was she who spoke first.

'As you instructed, sir,' she began playfully, 'I moved to the fort immediately Claudia left – you may have noticed!'

'Dare I say I didn't?' he returned, pretending to defend himself.

'James has been very attentive. In fact, I've been very touched.' She smiled up at him. 'I'm his master's lady.'

He smiled back at her, but Venio's death and the misery of Cornelia had cast a shadow over them. Presently they were joined by Felix, and then James, following with a large jar of lime water. Both men were stunned by the news of Venio's passing, though for Felix the big man's dying moments were anything but mournful.

'He died well, Marcus,' he said quietly.

James smacked his lips, his usual herald of speech.

'The blessed, Master – one of the blessed!'

They all knew exactly what he meant.

Unobtrusively Drusilla slipped away from the company, leaving the three men to talk together.

'James, did you discover any suspicious characters in Capernaum?' Tullus was quick to ask.

'Yes, Master, two of them. They got me in conversation one morning at the market.'

The Centurion stiffened.

'What happened?'

'They didn't talk long, and wanted to know about my miraculous cure, as they called it. I didn't like them, but,

Master, when I turned away the big, curly-headed man came up to me. He didn't waste his arrows. 'Keep away from them,' he warned. 'Don't trust them – they're your master's enemies.'"

'Did you believe him?'

'Yes, Master – anyway, I checked with my other friends.'

'Could you point these vultures out to me?'

James nodded.

'Did I tell you that the Tribune received a warning?'

Both men shook their heads.

'A strange omission,' Tullus muttered in reaction. 'Well, he did – a young boy from Capernaum. The boy's warning was vital and probably saved the Tribune's life!'

James smacked his lips again.

'Are you thinking what I'm thinking, Master?'

'The big man sent the boy!'

'Yes, Master – but why did he not tell you? You could have sent a messenger. Maybe he didn't want to compromise you.'

'He already has; that one greeting was enough – anyway, he could have sent the boy. Things happen, James. I shouldn't look too hard for reasons.'

287

CHAPTER FORTY

CAT AND MOUSE

The day the Tribune heard of Venio's death his hopes sank low. He deeply mourned the big man's passing, and the memory of the many crucial moments they had shared was sharp and painful. Indeed, Machaerus brought tears to his eyes.

Machaerus, of course, was closely associated with Cornelia, and the death of Venio coupled with a possible, even probable ban on his marriage filled him with depression: a darkness in which all effort was deferred and in which the desperate play of Gallo and his chief seemed distant.

It was afternoon, but as the evening neared his mood began to change to anger and a cold determination that the big man's death would not go unavenged.

The Tribune was certain that Gallo's apparent inactivity was studied. Something was afoot, but what? And where, by all the gods, were Largus and Demos? His sense of impotency was maddening.

During supper with Demetrianus his frustration was boiling. He had to do something, as he could not wait forever on the whim of Gallo, yet what was there to do? He had sent men round the taverns, but the gossip that they heard was useless. Few had the art of Demos. However, just as he felt his pent-up feelings would explode his Greek friend appeared at the door. As usual, he had assumed a disguise.

'How do you like my widow's finery?' he joked.

'You'll find no husband here!' Valerius said quickly. It was the only humour impatience would allow.

'Demos, what's going on? Where have you been? Where's Largus? Why did you make the journey to Capernaum yourself? You only missed us by a day or two – why did you not stay?'

'Is that all, sir?!' Demos reacted lightly, while swinging on his heel with mock femininity. 'Largus was suspicious of the normal service,' he began to answer, his tone now sober. 'There were other ways, though untried, and as the message was vital I decided to go myself. I also knew that in your eyes it would emphasise the urgency.'

'Why did you not wait?'

'Cornelius didn't know for sure when you were returning, and I knew that if I left it would also emphasise the urgency.'

'It did!'

'Again, I needed to be back in Antioch – something's happening, but we don't know what it is.'

'We! Where is he? Where's Largus?'

'I wish I knew, sir – he's simply disappeared!'

'Do you think . . .?'

'If you're going to say they've killed him – no! – not Largus. He's much too wily.'

'I hope you're right. Now, tell me, Demos, what is the situation? You say that something's happening, but it's vague, to say the least, and vagueness never won a battle. What did Largus say before he disappeared?'

'He disappeared before I returned from Capernaum, so he may have discovered something.'

'Surely he would have left a message here at the villa.'

'I think he left in a hurry, sir – a sudden impulse, maybe.'

'What did he tell you before you set out for Capernaum?'

'He was sparing in his counsel. All he said was – 'Gallo hadn't retired'; that there was 'a knife in every smile' at the Residency, and that he had suspicions but he needed proof.'

'A bit secretive, surely!'

'He'd have a reason, I'm sure. I know he warned me, saying that the 'Road Surveyor', his name for Gallo, could pick me up at any time. Knowing that, he would also know that information could be tortured out of me.'

'A fat lot they'd get!'

'Gallo doesn't know that, sir!'

'I suppose not. Could you be picked up by the 'Road Surveyor'? Is Largus right?'

Demos nodded. 'I'm watched continually and they know of my disguises – hence this extremity. Largus is quite right; they could pick me off at their convenience. That's one reason why it took me so long to make contact. In fact, my usefulness here in Antioch has ended.'

'The Emperor's work is never ended – there are other cities!' Valerius smiled knowingly, but Demos only fluttered his eyelids in harmony with his woman's finery.

'There's more than Largus shy of information,' the Tribune returned pointedly. 'Well,' he added, 'if you're under threat you'd better don the uniform and join my guard.' He looked straight at his Greek friend. 'Now, by all the gods, what are we going to do?' His hand thumped hard against his couch in emphasis.

'If we don't know what to do, sir, it's better to do nothing – let the enemy make the mistake!'

'Or take the advantage,' Valerius snapped.

There were noises behind, and the Tribune turned to see Titus framed in the doorway.

'Ah! Noble Titus, don't be frightened by this fearsome widow. Her name is Demos – you may have heard!?'

The Tribune's mood only permitted a brief introduction.

'You have news, Titus?' he asked.

'Yes, sir, bad news from the navy. The Commander's deputy is five days overdue!'

The Tribune stood up.

'How many galleys?'

'Two.'

'Returning from where?'

'Ephesus or Rhodes – only the Commander knows.'

'And he's at sea as well. Two galleys missing – they could be sheltering from a storm somewhere.'

'Yes – the sea can be capricious round the islands,' Demetrianus said in support, his ageing, jolly face unusually sombre.

'Maybe pirates have . . .'

'No, Demos,' the Tribune interjected impatiently. 'Why would any self-respecting pirate attack a war galley? They'd be asking for trouble. Anyway, if they did capture her, what would they do with her?'

'All you say is correct, sir, but if a galley is separated from her squadron or sister ship and is carrying a special cargo for the legions, as they sometimes do . . .'

'But who would tell the pirates of the special cargo?'

'Deck hands, maybe.'

'I think we're being too obscure,' Valerius said bluntly.

Demos did not argue, for it was the habit of his world to hatch obscurities like chickens. The Tribune was right.

'There's another matter we need to address,' Valerius added, explaining the need to feign his departure to Caesarea. 'The new inquiry date,' he reflected, 'is seen by the Chief Centurion as a ploy to keep me out of Antioch. So when we know that Gallo's on his way we will return.'

'Had you thought that Gallo might have planned to do the same?' Demos interjected.

'No! But we should have – I assumed he would not miss the chance to air his oratory. Even so, I've got a feeling that you're right. One thing is certain. If he does remain, we'll know our instincts to have been correct. What a game of cat and mouse it is!'

The Tribune looked hard at his host Demetrianus before detailing his further plans. Then, in his usual quick, clipped manner, he began.

'With your permission, my noble host, I suggest leaving an eight-man guard at the villa during our temporary absence. You should proceed with caution, sir, and keep two strong men by your side when about your business.'

What did he need with guards and strong men, Demetrianus thought. He was an honest merchant. Nonetheless, he nodded, as there was little point in protest. He knew the son of Marcus Valerius too well, for once his word was given, it was given.

'Titus,' Valerius continued, turning to his guard captain, 'you, as chief witness, must attend the inquiry at Caesarea, and when you leave the body of the guard you'll need protection. Select a tent party – resourceful men, Titus, and take no chances! Who should act as deputy in your absence?' the Tribune asked, without slackening the pace of his delivery.

'Young Quintus, sir.'

'A good choice. Tell him that Demos here will be on hand to give advice, and, Titus,' he added, pointing at his Greek friend, 'get this man a soldier's clothes. I'm tired of looking at his widow's lace!'

Two days later, when busy with departure preparations, news came that one of the missing galleys had arrived at Seleucia Pieria, but it was not the galley of the Commander's deputy. Apparently, the two warships had been separated in a squall, and when the squall had passed the Deputy's galley had seemingly disappeared. The surviving ship had searched the area, but the sea was a big place, the message ran. Eventually the search was abandoned on the assumption that they had simply lost each other. Again it was assumed that the Deputy's galley would return in time with a similar story. Certainly the storms had not been fierce enough to endanger a quinquereme, though it could have blown her well off course. The Navy office, the report concluded, saw no need for alarm; even so, he wondered how the gossip ran in the taverns of Seleucia Pieria. It was a curiosity he could not satisfy, however, as his contrived departure for Caesarea was imminent.

It was morning, and an hour later, surrounded by his guard, he left for the south. A day later they disappeared into the hills; only Titus and an accompanying tent party continued south.

At the time Titus was passing through Sidon on his coastal journey to Caesarea, the Centurion began his preparation for departure. They were busy days, complicated by the need to draft a lengthy despatch to the Governor Aelius Lamia. Three reports in one, in fact, as events had disrupted his routine. A personal note was also included with the despatch.

Officially, no one knew of his connection with the Governor. The Tribune and Felix had sensed there was some commerce with Rome or Capri, and Drusilla was certain he had powerful friends, but the Valerii were discreet and nothing had been said. Tullus, in fact, had asked permission to inform the Tribune of his special work and still awaited confirmation. The Governor's replies, however, were often delayed.

Once on his way, the Centurion had ample time to preconceive the nature of the forthcoming inquiry. Soon he found his mind busy with the various possibilities, a futile game of imagination which was drawn short by the memory of the Rabbi's words: 'Take no thought for the morrow,' he had said, for the morrow would 'take thought for the things of itself.' It was a hard lesson to follow. Some preparation was necessary, of course, but clearly the eager play of anticipation was a fruit-less drain on energy.

It was a common problem and nowhere more evident than in the endless twists of political intrigue. What might happen? What could happen? The fears and stratagems were countless. He thought of Gallo, forever scheming. How much of it was necessary? How much of Gallo's activity had really advanced his master's cause? How many men had died for nothing? All Gallo needed was a few steady, well-placed men who would make no fuss. But the truth was that Gallo liked intrigue and revelled in the art of subterfuge. Tullus smiled grimly to him-self, knowing he would soon face Gallo's invective. He was not intimidated. To him, Gallo was a clever bully with man-ners suited to a tavern brawl. Such men made him angry.

The Centurion's progress to Caesarea was leisurely. He had decided to go by way of Nain, thus cutting off the long loop round by Scythopolis. The road to Nain was poor, but there was no hurry, and at the town a comfortable bed awaited him – his host a friend of Ben Joseph.

Not long after passing through Tiberias it became obvious that a cart was following him, for no matter how he changed his pace it came no closer. Whoever it was, he at once decided to confront them – or him – and with this in mind he hid with his guard on the blind side of a rocky spur round which the road bent in a sudden right angle.

He himself was cautious on rounding the bend, sending the soldiers before him. Such ambush positions required respect, but those following exercised no such precautions and ran straight into his trap.

Tullus held his vine rod out and the cart drew to a halt. There were three in the open vehicle. Two of them were the men that James had pointed out in Capernaum and the third was the slave of the late Marius, whom Tullus knew only too well.

'Well, my juggling friend, you had a speedy trip from Antioch.' Tullus pretended a smile.

'Yes, sir, three days.' The slave's answer was automatic, his wit frozen by the unexpected confrontation.

'Joining your new master, I assume?'

'No, I'm . . .!' The juggler stopped, suddenly awake to his mistake.

At that the studied smile left the Centurion's face.

'I know what you're about – all three of you! I suspect what you have done, and if I had the proof you'd be as cushions in the archery field. Don't let me see you near us again. My men get nervous when they're watched – go!'

The Centurion's stick hit out and the two-mule cart jerked forward. Men of little substance, he thought disdainfully, as he watched them go. The slave he found detestable. He had the narrow, cunning eyes that liked to witness cruelty – a cruelty that coupled well with Gallo's cynicism. Tullus smiled. So the juggler was not joining his master. Yet he looked as if he were headed for Caesarea. He laughed, attracting the attention of his men. Could it be that Gallo had remained in Antioch and was playing cat and mouse, just like the Tribune?

In the hills south of Antioch, the Tribune waited. The days passed slowly and his inactivity allowed the pain of Venio's loss full play. That and the worry of Cornelia became as one dull ache, robbing him of rest. Listlessly he waited for the dizziness to recur. Then, in the midst of his exhaustion, he recalled the priest Raphael, and with the memory, stillness came. Hope came too, lifting his spirit.

At last news arrived that Gallo had left the Villa Rufus, and, with his elaborate baggage train, was rolling towards the port of Seleucia Pieria. He was going by sea, the Tribune concluded.

At once the Tribune's guard assembled. It was time to return to Antioch.

CHAPTER FORTY-ONE

LARGUS

The progress of the Tribune's father was slow, and Junia was exasperated. It had taken three full days to reach Stratonicea, and the following day they did not start until the afternoon. It only took her father to ask the Indian Prince one question and another hour at least was lost in talk.

South of Stratonicea the road cut close to the inlet whose mouth was guarded by the island of Kos. It was late afternoon and still hot, though the smell of the sea brought a touch of freshness. Junia, her body swaying with the cart, screwed her eyes against the glare from the parched, dusty landscape.

'Father, there's someone on the road ahead of us.' A man's figure wavered in the heat haze.

The Senator looked up to see his guards move forward to surround him.

'Stop!' he shouted. 'Why ring a helpless man with swords!'

The man was young, Junia discerned, though the impression of abject vagrancy made it difficult to be sure. His hair and beard were matted, his tunic, once white, torn and streaked with dirt, and his body, where it was exposed, was raw and painful-looking.

With difficulty he held up his hand and tried to speak, but nothing came.

'Water,' the Senator directed.

The stranger sipped sparingly.

'Sir,' he said, his voice little louder than a whisper. Again he sipped.

'Sir, you are the Senator Valerius.'

'Correct,' came the abrupt reaction. 'How do you know me, may I ask?'

'Father, it's the man who bumped into you at Ephesus,' Junia interjected excitedly.

'That's right,' the man responded. He appeared to be making a tremendous effort to concentrate.

'Sir, my name is Quintus Sentius Largus,' he said slowly, 'and I am a friend of your son, the Tribune Valerius.'

Largus swayed, the scene before him heaving like the sea, and at once the orders of the Senator rang out. He felt hands lift him and he knew his desperate struggle was over. At last he could afford to rest and when they laid him on the cart he was already asleep.

When he awoke, the eyes of Arria and Junia were watching him. He smiled, though briefly, for the pain of his raw-burnt arms and legs was distracting. Nevertheless, the wits of Largus were ever keen.

'Do the daughters of the gods often descend from Olympus?' he said, his voice still weak and breathy.

The story that Largus had to tell was harrowing. He had been visiting Ephesus, he began, and was returning to Antioch in one of the two galleys that were making the journey. One day out of Ephesus a sudden storm engulfed them, and before it could be furled the galley's sail was ripped to pieces. Spray, whipped up by the wind, drenched everything and made visibility little more than arm's length. Yet through tunnels in the spray he did see things – the desperate chaos of the sailors; the other galley with its storm sail up; but more importantly, the unexpected nearness of some coastal craft. One, he thought, had something like a ramming spur. It was very close; even so, the glimpse was much too brief for certainty. There was a sudden jarring shock, enough to throw him off balance and shoot him overboard. Luckily, and with like alacrity, an oar was catapulted close to him. He grabbed it eagerly and in the flow of some unseen but powerful current he drifted clear.

The storm abated as quickly as its violence had arisen. Desperately he looked about him in the heavy swell, but apart from the outline of an island in the distance there was nothing. The galley had vanished.

The wind dropped as the light began to fade, and the noise of the water lapping about him seemed very present. He was alone, drifting at the mercy of the currents. How long could he last, that was the question.

Stars began to twinkle as the dusk closed in. Then all at once it seemed the heavens were alive with points of light. As the night wore on, he began to discern the dark bulk of an island rising up before him. He paddled desperately, but slowly he began to slip past. The current was too strong.

The first herald of dawn was beginning to dim the stars. It would be warmer, he thought – a small comfort, as his thirst would rise with the sun's heat. His position was hopeless, yet with a fierce tenacity he clung to the galley oar, even though his logic deemed it as a weakness.

His arms were aching. He could release his grip so easily and slip beneath the waves. Then, as if by magic, he felt the miracle of earth beneath his feet, and before him was a square of rock and sand just above the high tide level. The dimness of the light and the undulating swell had made it quite invisible.

Using the oar as a shield against the jagged rocks he scrambled out of the water. His legs were as jelly, and even though his body shivered in the cool breeze the relief was enormous. Gingerly, he laid himself flat on the rocks and out of the wind. He sighed, and with the sudden release of tension he fell asleep.

He awoke with the sun halfway to its zenith, his sea-softened skin a ready prey to the heat. He sat up, immediately cognising his position. Before him was the rocky face of the island he had passed the night before. It was close, close enough to make the crossing, though Largus knew that water could make the distance misleading. He had no alternative, of course: he had to cross.

He was parched with thirst and it was agonizing to move, but delay was pointless. So once more, with the aid of the heavy oar, he eased himself into the churning water about the rocky islet. In the event, the crossing was easy.

He told his story in snatches over the period of his recovery at the villa of a local estate where the Senator had already planned to stay. With Junia and Arria he was flippant and jocular, but with the Senator he was serious, if not grim.

'Sir, I need to get messages to both Antioch and Ephesus. It's urgent.'

'A messenger was sent to Ephesus within an hour of seeing you.'

'I know, sir, but there's another despatch that needs delivering. Tell me, sir, has the messenger returned?'

'Yes, Tribune – he was the first herald of the disaster.'

Largus sighed. 'I'm not surprised.'

'Tribune, you have more to tell me, it appears.'

'Yes, sir – the galley was carrying a large consignment of gold.'

'How many knew this?'

'Officially no more than six.'

'Officially!'

Largus nodded. 'The secret was betrayed. You see, sir, I was propelled overboard by the shock of impact. I saw it for a moment through the spray – a ramming spur – and then the crash. At first I didn't believe it. My eyes were playing tricks, it seemed: a fantasy fashioned by the dancing spray. But on the island I saw my so-called fantasy to be real. Three small coastal ships with spikes, drawn up on the beach. About them men were busy with repairs. What's more, they were dismantling the spurs.'

'Meaning they had first attached them!'

'And meaning, sir, they had the time – there must have been ample notice given!'

'But, Tribune, a storm is not a man's invention, even if he is a Greek. They couldn't have planned that!'

'The storm was a gift they exploited, for the Greeks can sail a boat the way we drive a chariot.'

'And if the storm had not occurred?'

'They didn't build the spurs for nothing, sir. They had some plan – separate the galleys, perhaps – and fire can be a potent weapon if it's used with skill.'

'Even so, to attack a war-galley –' The Senator shook his head. 'An extreme audacity. The rewards must have been . . .'

'Very substantial, sir,' Largus completed.

'It's ten days short of a month since the disaster, and you were its first herald. Are you sure the ship went down?'

'Certain, sir, for I looked both long and hard.'

'The conclusions are harsh – all may have perished.'

'The pirates would have seen to that – witnesses could unleash our vengeance, when simple decimation would be seen as mild. The islands would suffer sorely, sir. No, they'd have no wish for witnesses.'

'Did they not see you on the island?'

'No; I kept well clear – it delayed me, though, for I had to steal a boat from one of the villages, and that took time to plan.'

Again the Senator shook his head.

'A galley's full complement – all gone, and all for the sake of gold. My Indian friend maintains that crime is balanced on the scales of justice, if not in this life, then the next.'

'Well, sir, if I knew the serpent who betrayed the knowledge of a gold shipment I would save him the inconvenience of waiting.'

There was no doubt that Largus meant what he said. The cold determination in his voice was unmistakable.

CHAPTER FORTY-TWO

CAESAREA

Pilate looked reflective, his hand supporting his chin: in fact, the very picture of the practised official. An aide was reading the report relating to the Centurion's arrest, and having already studied the text in detail, his attention drifted to the gathering before him.

Tullus, of course. was in his place. A lifelong soldier; a man born of the ranks, yet without the moulded habit of his profession. Pilate admired him, and after Claudia's transformation owed him gratitude. Nevertheless, he found the Chief Centurion an enigma. He had deferred his promotion, preferring the obscurity of a small Galilean garrison. On the other hand, he had powerful friends. Pilate had sensed this well before Valerius arrived, but his proposed marriage to the Tribune's sister, confirmed by Claudia, was a final triumph: a dreamed-of prize, even for an established Equestrian.

Pilate smiled. Tullus was a force to be reckoned with, and a clash between him and Gallo promised to be interesting.

The languid gaze of Pontius Pilate moved to Titus, the Tribune's guard captain. There was no mystery about him – a veteran, the very marrow of the army. Close to Titus was the Palmyra Commander, by reputation a drunkard, yet sly enough to have his papers all correct. Marius, the Commander maintained, had acted independently, and had presented valid authorisation for the release of the soldiers destined to arrest the Centurion and subsequently to perish. The authorisation, he continued, concerned a routine transfer of men, and Marius, ever keen and eager, had volunteered to be the officer in charge. It was as simple as that, he concluded.

Pilate doubted the conclusion, but there was little he could do. The Palmyra Commander was much too wily to be trapped.

The official report droned on, and eventually the inquiry was adjourned until after the midday meal.

Gallo had yet to arrive. Predictable behaviour, the Procurator thought, being well aware of Gallo's propensity for the late and dramatic arrival. Once the official preamble was over, however, Gallo's absence became infuriating. For a time Pilate hesitated, then brusquely he signalled Titus to begin his evidence. When the veteran had completed his detailed statement he was questioned by the lawyers. Predictably, his answers were blunt and honest, and the Procurator had no doubt that his words were true.

Pilate was about to call the Centurion when a message was handed to him, and, immediately furious, he hammered the table before him.

'This inquiry is adjourned for one hour!'

The Procurator made no attempt to conceal his anger when reporting to his aides.

'The Tribune Gallo is not coming.' Pilate spat the words out bitterly, 'and suggests we adjourn the inquiry for two months. He regrets that vital business in Antioch makes it impossible for him to attend.'

Pilate said no more, careful not to criticise the friend of Sejanus openly. However, with his personal friend and confidant Maximus he was frank, if not reckless.

'He pressed for an inquiry and he pressed for a change of date, and now he has the arrogance to propose the original date, and not a word of apology! At least Valerius apologised and let me know in time.'

'Maybe Gallo has a valid excuse,' Maximus suggested quietly, but his master was not listening.

'It's no less than contempt of court.' The words exploded on the Procurator's lips. 'I'll halt the inquiry immediately. There's little point in remaining in this marble tomb longer than is necessary!'

'Your advice to the Tribune was correct, sir,' Titus said quietly as he and Tullus left the hall.

The Centurion nodded. 'If men's lives were not in danger it would be a situation of enormous comedy – you spoke well, Titus.'

'Thank you, sir.'

Titus left immediately for Antioch, but the Centurion had much to do before returning to Capernaum. There were trusted contacts to be seen. Men who sensed the moods and changing undercurrents of intrigue. That would take some time. It was also necessary to visit the Procurator's palace, for he could not leave without paying his respects to Claudia, and, of course, her guest Cornelia, though he had a stronger motive than mere courtesy, as one of his contacts had told him that the young and beautiful girl was ill.

Cornelia was not at the palace when he called. She had gone to Ptolemais.

'She accompanied one of my lady companions,' Pilate's wife explained. 'Apparently the girl's father, a rich merchant, has a villa overlooking the sea, and the girl pressed Cornelia to join her, saying that the air would make her well.'

'What's wrong with her?'

'Misery, sir.'

'Did she leave before it was known that the Tribune was not attending the inquiry?'

Claudia nodded.

'She's avoiding him,' Tullus said emphatically. 'Some stoical sacrifice – she left a note for the Tribune at Capernaum and we're suspicious of the contents.'

'It's worrying,' Claudia returned.

Tullus did not respond. Instead, he changed the subject.

'I've brought a present from Master Felix – some translations of the Rabbi's teaching.'

At once Claudia's eyes were eager and her thanks sincere.

The next day Tullus left for Capernaum, but he chose to go by way of Ptolemais.

CHAPTER FORTY-THREE

FELIX

Every morning without fail Felix and his daughter Sarah walked into Capernaum. Sometimes their stay was brief, but mostly they would linger until the heat of the day became oppressive. The two guards charged with their protection had long since abandoned cautionary advice, as Felix simply ignored any attempt to restrict his movements. No hovel was too humble for him to visit and no door was closed to him, and always the topic was the Rabbi Jesus.

It had all happened, as if by chance, one morning after his return from Jerusalem. An old lady had approached him in the market place and had started, with obvious sincerity, to thank him for his efforts to save the Teacher – indeed, the whole town seemed to know about his interview with Pilate. The old lady had continued by relating how she had been cured by the Master's touch. Encouraged by Felix's attention, her speech flowed on, and when he did not understand, Sarah was on hand to help. In conclusion, she suggested he should contact a certain herdsman who lived by the well at the north end of the town. He had a lot to tell, she said.

Felix did as the old lady suggested, and so began a pilgrimage of inquiry. Each afternoon he recorded his findings. It was a haphazard collection of notes that emerged, to which he added his own experiences. They were written in Greek, though much too weak in penetration rightly to reflect the stature of the Rabbi. In the right hands, however, they could live. Felix was not troubled by pretension.

His frequent visits to the town had another purpose. One he made obvious by his frequent enquiries after the Rabbi's disciples, and in particular the Disciple John. Some said John was in Jerusalem, others said Damascus, but in truth no one knew. Usually Ben Joseph was his source of information. He, however, was still in Cana, escaping the heat of the valley.

The dusty heat of the summer was worse than usual, the locals said. It was not surprising, Felix mused, that native custom was lenient on crimes committed in such a furnace. He was sorry for Drusilla, though, and for Sarah, trapped as they were in the cauldron atmosphere. Thankfully, the walls of the garrison fort were thick. In fact, it was one of the coolest buildings in Capernaum.

CHAPTER FORTY-FOUR

GALLO AND THE JUGGLER

The Tribune Gallo had acquired a villa overlooking the sea outside the port of Seleucia Pieria, and to the world he was the typical wealthy Roman escaping the heat of the interior. About the villa the general impression was one of inactivity, but inside his private rooms Gallo lived at his usual pace.

Supremely confident, he controlled every detail of his plans. Yet in the midst of his scheming the wine-cup and the slave-girl were rarely absent.

At first Gallo had been furious when he learned that Valerius and his guard had returned to Antioch, but his mood soon changed to one of uncontrolled mirth.

'Someone must have told him.' Tears ran down his cheeks as his laughter subsided. 'Such subtlety is beyond a schoolboy, though not beyond that cursed Centurion or the viper Largus!'

The ready audience of his aides echoed his mood with eager laughter, until his sudden scowl cut them short.

'If only I could get my hands on that 'innocent', that traitor Largus. He's made a fool of us. Anyway, Neptune's probably feasted on him. He's slippery, though. Be on the watch, for if he's roaming free, he's dangerous; much more dangerous than that love-sick Patrician at the Villa Demetrianus.'

'Sir, are we not in danger of underestimating the Tribune Valerius?' The speaker was one of Gallo's more cautious aides.

'How can you underestimate an emptiness?' Gallo touched his head. 'The man has nothing there.'

He laughed loudly as his mood switched to the jocular.

'Well, my juggling friend, I'm glad to see you back with us – what about a trick or two?' Gallo called, waving at the one-time slave of Marius.

The small, birdlike eyes of the juggler lit up with pleasure, and for almost an hour his dexterous tricks amused Gallo and his companions. Then, when he sensed a waning of attention, he announced his final and most mystifying trick.

Slowly he bared his arms, while making elaborate play that nothing was concealed on his person. He stood still, all attention focused on him. After which, as if from nowhere, a roll despatch appeared in the air and landed on Gallo's couch. The aim was nothing less than brilliant.

'My juggling genie, what wonder is this?' Gallo reacted, tearing open the seal. It was addressed 'L. Gracchus Valerius' and its origin was Capri.

'What a gift to bring me from the south – I do so like to hear of loving unions, but where, and how?'

'A tavern outside Caesarea explains the 'where', and a little . . .' the slave rubbed his forefinger and thumb together playfully . . . 'added to the richness of the grape – that was the 'how'.'

'Better and better, my friend. At last, a man of initiative. Come!'

Gallo arose from his couch and led the juggler from the hall. They walked outside across the courtyard and into the boiler room. Casually Gallo threw the roll into the flames, and, turning to the slave, assumed a philosophic countenance.

'Love is a delusion, and marriage confirms it,' he said with mock confidentially. 'We've done Valerius a signal service,' he added, as they returned to the courtyard.

'Tell me, did you deliver the message late, as I instructed?'

'Yes, sir.'

'What was Pilate's reaction?'

'He was furious.'

'As I thought. Pilate's like the seasons, fixed and predictable. Well, my friend, you are worthy of your hire,' Gallo emphasised, while slipping a pouch of silver into the slave's hand.

'Thank you, sir.'

'You returned from Caesarea quickly.'

'Yes, sir, we had a full sail almost all the way.'

The conversation continued as they walked back to the reception hall. The slave, eager at his master's side, was comprehensive in his description of the abortive inquiry, but he did not mention his humiliation at the hands of the Centurion.

CHAPTER FORTY-FIVE

CHANCE ENCOUNTER

The delay due to Largus did not trouble the Senator, as it meant more undisturbed discussion with his friend the Prince. Junia, also, was content to wait and chuckle at the wit of Largus as he convalesced. She quickly sensed, however, that her brother's friend could not be managed or manipulated. His eye was on some distant goal, and she, it seemed, was incidental. She was annoyed, even angry at times, but she did not show it, knowing there was nothing she could do.

Much to Junia's disappointment, Largus decided to travel separately when they reached the next town. He did not tell her why, and again she felt her anger rise, even though she knew that it was pointless.

Largus, however, was blunt and open with the Senator, and after a detailed discussion the agreed course was one of caution. The Senator would journey to the town of Tarsus, stay at the garrison and await news from Antioch. Largus, on the other hand, would go with all speed to the city and by carrying the Senator's official authorisation hoped quickly to negotiate any tolls or road checks, should his Greek disguise and peasant's cart arouse suspicion.

The Senator was troubled by what Largus had told him. There was danger at Antioch, and Lucius was in the midst of it. His instincts prompted him to intervene, but he knew his presence in the city would only add to his son's difficulties.

Gallo, by Largus's description, was wholly ruthless, much more so than his master, and the hint that he was behind the recent piracy was incredible. Sejanus would never stoop to that.

'What if the money's running out?' Largus prompted.

Valerius shook his head. 'Not Sejanus!'

'Well, sir, I doubt if Gallo shares the scruples of his master.'

'If you're right, Tribune – why would the islanders give up any of their gains?'

'An insurance against Roman punishment, for we could lay the islands waste.'

'What if Gallo failed to restrain the Navy?'

'The memory of an islander is long – they'd get him.'

The Senator nodded knowingly. Quintus Sentius Largus was not a fool.

Largus found the road to Antioch slow and difficult, and his impatience grew with each tedious hour. Eventually, at the port of Myra, he decided to abandon his cart and continue the journey by sea. The vessel he joined was a small coastal craft, and its master assured him of a speedy sail to the free city of Seleucia.

The Greek captain's conception of speed, however, was not that of Largus, and it seemed to the young Tribune that they stopped at every petty village on the coast. At last they reached their destination, when once again Largus bought a cart and pony. He pushed ahead as quickly as his sturdy animal would allow, and within five days he passed through Alexandria. Another day, he hoped, would see him in Antioch, though there was a mountainous ridge to cross before he reached the valley that led to the city.

Once out of Alexandria, he began to climb to higher ground. The terrain was dramatic. It had a certain openness, a freedom, and he began to sing to himself. Then suddenly, on rounding a bend, he found the road blocked by two boulders.

Grabbing his dagger, he swore aloud in Latin. He was not afraid. In fact, his chief emotion was exasperation. Alert and cautious, he looked about him to find two men emerging from their cover. One was elderly and wizened, the other young, his beard still thin. They were not practised criminals, and the knives they carried were fashioned for the field rather than the fight. Nevertheless, Largus was wary, for peasants could be cunning. Were there more of them? he wondered. He looked behind him only to meet the innocent eyes of a young boy. Quickly he shifted to keep all three well in view. A peasant and his sons, he guessed.

When the old man spoke, his accent was thick and blurred, and Largus was just able to make out his meaning. He wanted to borrow the cart.

'Borrow!' Largus exploded. 'By all the gods, what comedy is this? – you cannot borrow with a knife!'

The old man persisted. His wife was ill, he said. He had to have the cart.

'Why can't someone in your village help?' Largus barked.

'Our village has been pillaged,' the peasant replied, his knife still held resolutely.

'By whom?' The question was punched with force.

'They came from the sea and took our carts and food.' The wizened peasant had to repeat himself slowly before Largus understood.

'Islanders?' Largus prompted.

'Yes.'

'Had they a cargo?'

'Yes, heavy sacks.'

'Did you see the contents?'

'No – not even the children were allowed to look.' Again the peasant had to repeat himself until Largus realised his meaning.

'Tell me,' Largus began slowly, 'was one of the boats newly timbered at the bow?'

The old peasant shook his head. 'Our village isn't near the coast. We're in the hills.'

'I saw the boats,' the boy piped up. 'There was new timber!'

'We have no time to talk – we need the cart!' the old peasant blurted, trying to be aggressive. His wife was ill – he had to get her to the town. These were the words Largus translated from his halting speech.

'How long since they plundered your village?' he asked.

'Yesterday!'

'Gods!' Largus thumped the cart with the loose end of the pony's reins. The animal started, but quickly relapsed into apathy. He was furious with frustration. More than ever he needed to get to Antioch.

The old man moved closer. His uncertain peasant blood could erupt at any moment, Largus thought; and there were three of them.

'Take it!' Largus snapped, while jumping from the cart with his wine skin.

At once he set out resolutely towards Antioch, but the old man rushed after him, and Largus, for the moment fearful, turned abruptly.

'Your name, sir – we need to return to the cart – we're not thieves.'

'What joke is this?!'

The peasant persisted, and Largus shook his head angrily.

'Keep it!'

'No! no! – we're not robbers!'

Largus stopped, his frustration boiling, but he held his peace and looked squarely at the wizened face of the villager. The visible marks of his poverty were appalling.

'Nicos – Villa Maximus – Antioch,' he said bluntly. The Villa Maximus was not fictitious. It was close to the Residency and it could be watched. Who knows, he thought, the old peasant could prove useful.

The villager repeated the names slowly until they were firmly in his mind. Then he quickly left. Behind him Largus heard the cart being turned, but he did not look round.

It was hot, yet not unbearably so. The peaks of summer temperature had passed and walking was not difficult. As he strode out, Largus had plenty to muse upon. Indeed, the last month seemed like a thousand years. Nonetheless, the pressing need to get to Antioch kept him in the present.

Six carts passed him during the first hour of walking, and he could see another coming, but like the rest it was bound for Alexandria – the gods were extending their comedy. He thought of the peasant and his sons. Had he surrendered the cart too easily? He doubted it, for peasant emotion was not something to gamble with; even so, he would wager on the old man returning the cart. A clever man would never do it, no, not in a month of months. It would take an innocent – whatever that might mean.

On he trudged. The scenery was rugged and the road reflected its drama, but he saw little, consumed as he was with growing frustration. He had to get to Antioch, and in view of what the old man had revealed every moment counted.

At last there was a noise behind him; a cart was coming his way. Would it stop, though? that was the question.

He waved and smiled hopefully, and the driver, wary of trouble, drew the two-horse cart to a halt some distance ahead. The driver turned, his eyes suspicious, as Largus approached. Then suddenly he nodded.

The temples of Seleucia Pieria echoed with the sound of mourning and supplication. The naval men were baffled. What could have happened? For the fated ship was a quinquereme, a powerful vessel, and commanded by an experienced captain, the Deputy himself.

Only three survivors had been reported; two were sailors, the other yet unknown. It was a major disaster and an inquiry was imperative, but the Legate would not proceed without the Commander, and the Commander was still at sea. In fact, he was somewhere off the shores of Cyprus on a joint exercise connecting the main element of the fleet in the eastern part of the Great Sea.

This information, along with the loss of the galley and the missing Largus, kept the Tribune in a state of agitation. He felt impotent; a helpless observer watching his fears manifest, he knew the joint exercise was a perfect ploy to block the Emperor's escape. The order had been issued from Ravenna, the Legate had told him – a sweep to eliminate piracy.

Trusted veterans of his guard reported daily on the movements of Gallo, but all, including the activity at the Residency, seemed innocent. Gallo even paid him public compliments, a fact that fed his suspicions.

Whatever he did, he could not seem to penetrate the veil of secrecy. He missed Largus.

Largus had disappeared about the time the two galleys had set out for Ephesus, and Valerius feared the worst, that his friend had perished with the stricken ship. Demos, however, thought differently.

'Three survived, sir, and one remains anonymous – it's him – it's Largus. I was good, but he's the best.'

The Tribune looked at the Greek's twinkling eyes without reacting.

Exactly five days later a bearded and dishevelled Largus

appeared at the Villa Demetrianus.

'Quintus Sentius Largus at your service, sir,' he said, bowing with mock gravity. 'But not before a bath and wine.'

The Tribune hesitated for an unbelieving moment before embracing his friend. Largus, however, kept his word and refused to talk before he had bathed and changed. Then,with a cup of wine in his hand, he sat down opposite the Tribune on the open portico overlooking the garden.

'Well, sir,' Valerius began, 'may I assume a visit to the Oracle delayed you?'

'I learned a lot about myself, but not at Delphi.'

Largus looked hard at the Tribune.

'The friends of 'Caligula' and the friends of Gallo are the same.' His voice was forceful.

'Of course – it's obvious – why did I not think of it?'

'That's not all!'

The Tribune waited.

'Six men knew the Deputy Commander's galley was carrying a large consignment of gold.'

Valerius exhaled noisily.

'Six men, sir – the Deputy and myself were two. The Prefect of Ephesus and the Legate make four, and the two so-called friends of Gaius Caligula make six.' Largus was intense. 'The galley was holed, skilfully holed, in the midst of a storm by expert seamen – islanders. I'm certain the gold was plundered from the sunken ship and was landed south of Alexandria. In all probability it's safely hidden here in Antioch.' Largus stopped. His voice was emotional. 'The Archery Field is too humane for such a crime.'

The Tribune looked ahead, his features taut. A bird landed on the table before them and at once flew away again, but he did not seem to see.

'Gold to bribe the Legions,' he said grimly. 'The joint exercise – the gold – all is ready.'

DRUSILLA

The day that James was cured Drusilla's life was changed and, as if wiped clean, her cycle of obsessive worry disappeared. In fact, she had acquired a tranquillity of spirit which all remarked upon. Only in the few days that followed the Centurion's disappearance had she forgotten, but the vision of the Rabbi's power had restored her memory. It was this memory that sustained her through the waiting, and it still sustained her now.

She longed to be married. She longed to see her father. She cherished in her mind the picture of the family united together in Capernaum, but she knew from both Marcus and Felix that such a dream was distant. Indeed, the continuing state of uncertainty had gained a disturbing permanence.

Poor Lucius, he had never sought or bargained for such prominence in affairs. Thankfully, his health was holding well, and in this he had confounded all the fears of the family physicians. His visits to Qumran had saved him, and he had acknowledged this openly. Lucius had matured greatly, but in his love for Cornelia the shadow of tragedy lengthened at his side. It was a tragedy that the family had created unwittingly, and one too late to amend. The damage was done, and for Cornelia the wound was deep. In fact, Drusilla feared that the misery of her plight, coming so soon after her nightmare abduction, could unbalance her. Marcus, too, had similar thoughts and had acted on them. He had visited her at Ptolemais, and in his practical way had made her promise to refrain from any excess that would distress the Valerii. She wept. She did not want to go, but he made her swear before the altar to obey.

That Cornelia might take her own life filled Drusilla with unthinkable aversion, especially as she knew it was the Roman way, the way of honour and a high-born way Cornelia had embraced. Marcus had tried to entice her back to Capernaum, though without success. The very thought distressed her, for Capernaum was full of memories, she had pleaded. Marcus did not press her further. Instead, he told her hosts to keep her occupied, to be vigilant, and above all not to let her brood alone.

Although Drusilla was very concerned for Cornelia, and although part of her, the thinking part, was deeply pessimistic, she was still strangely hopeful. It sprang from the benign tranquillity within her. She had an ally in her hope, for James maintained stubbornly that all would be well. Cornelia was one of the blessed.

CHAPTER FORTY-SEVEN

ANTIOCH

Since his return to Antioch Largus had remained in strict seclusion. Secrecy was vital if the advantage of surprise was not to be squandered. Even a rumour would make Gallo cautious and incriminating evidence more difficult to find. What was more, Largus knew his life would be in peril if his presence were betrayed. He knew too much, and Gallo would do anything to silence him, but as long as Gallo felt that he was safe beneath the waves, which was now the general belief, all would be well.

Although Largus lived in a cocoon of security, he was not inactive. On the contrary, his instructions were prolific and mostly passed through Titus to the Tribune's guard. They were his ears and eyes, though they did not know it. To them, the orders were the Tribune's will.

In all this Valerius was kept informed, and Demos too. In fact, the three spent hours together analysing all the moves and counter-moves that lay before them.

'This is the time,' Largus kept repeating. 'The scene is set and all the players are in place, but if Sejanus doesn't grasp the nettle; if he falters now, he will have lost. This is the time. The sea is his, both north and south.'

Valerius nodded. The naval exercises in the north were balanced by manoeuvres linking Alexandria in Egypt with Caesarea.

'Sejanus needs to make the old man panic and board his galley, waiting in constant readiness at Capri, for once the Emperor's on the water he ceases to manipulate the Senate.'

Again Valerius nodded.

'Well, Largus, if Sejanus triumphs we'll be like sitting monkeys waiting for an arrow. Gallo will see to that!'

'Not if I can help it, sir,' Largus reacted forcefully. 'I'll pin Gallo to his past, and when I'm finished Sejanus will disown him – that's a promise, sir!'

'Be careful, my friend!'

'With respect, sir – that's the last thing I intend to be!'

The bitter determination in Largus's voice was like a cutting edge. It surprised the Tribune, but he held his peace. Largus was his own man.

'What's our next move, then?' Valerius asked, changing the subject.

'Caesarea,' Demos interjected. He had been silent for some while.

'The inquiry – is that what you mean? Will Gallo attend this time?'

'I think he will – but the inquiry's not the only reason. You see, sir, if I were the Emperor, and if I slipped past Syracuse in Sicily, I'd keep to the south, to the open sea.'

'Hence Caesarea.'

'Yes, sir – the northern route is too well watched. The Emperor will know this. He knows exactly what's going on!'

Valerius had little doubt that Demos was speaking from experience.

'Will Tiberius flee Capri?' he asked bluntly.

'I think not, sir. This is the time, and fate could fall on any side, but I doubt if the Emperor will lose. He's much too clever, and he has a hidden army at his call.'

Of which you are a member, Valerius almost said, yet he held his tongue.

'So here in Antioch all we need to do is wait – it seems familiar!'

'Yes, sir,' the Tribune's friends replied in chorus.

'Right! When Gallo leaves, we leave.'

Sighing deeply, the Tribune lay back on his couch, and for a moment the burden of affairs lifted from his mind, only to allow the memory of Cornelia and the pain to fill his thought. He had received one reassuring letter from the Centurion but no message whatever from Cornelia. Again, no sanction had arrived either from the Emperor or from Rome, and his father had not mentioned the matter for months. There was little ground for optimism, yet he could not sever the thread of hope. His longing was too sharp. Cornelia was at Ptolemais, the Centurion had written. He would visit her on the way south.

The uncertainties crowding in upon the Tribune were numerous. Indeed, no one worry could claim a single and obsessive attention. Nonetheless, behind the changing pressures of his public life, the constant question of his marriage waited, and when the daily round was done it came to life and would not give him rest. Yet with all this his old illness did not recur, and even though the symptoms shadowed him at times, they failed to gain their crippling hold.

He wondered at his new found resilience, for he thought himself to be the Priest Raphael's worst pupil. He had tried, however, and there had been periods of rest which had happened unexpectedly – like something given. Also given was the moment on the road from Ramah when, after the skirmish, the memory of the Rabbi Jesus had brought a profound sense of liberation. That he would never forget.

It was peaceful now, he thought. Largus and Demos were in conversation, but the sound seemed distant. He felt drowsy.

A sudden noise at the door jerked him into wakefulness. It was Titus. Gallo, he said, had left by sea for Caesarea. Immediately Valerius began to issue orders in his usual quick, precise manner.

'The Senator, my father, can now proceed from Tarsus, and a message should be sent at once to that effect. When he arrives he'll need a guard, for if I know him he'll have the minimum. Demos, you would make the perfect Captain of his escort!'

'Me, sir! I'm no soldier!'

'If you can play the widow you can play the legionary! Titus here will give you two of his best tent parties.'

Titus reacted anxiously, for sixteen men would reduce the guard considerably.

'We'll need replacements, sir.'

'Yes, my friend, but not from the Residency – we'd only get a clutch of spies. We'll try the 'Ironclads' at Laodicea.'

'When are we leaving, sir?' Titus asked.

'First light tomorrow!'

Much as he wanted to, the Tribune could not wait to greet his father, for it would be at least ten days before the message was delivered and his father made the journey, and by that time Gallo would be making trouble in Caesarea.

As the Tribune had estimated, the Senator arrived in Antioch late on the tenth day, and after paying due respect to the Legate he made for the villa of his old friend Demetrianus in the company of the Indian Prince. After the introductions Demetrianus and the Prince's merchant companions were quick to talk of trade, leaving the Senator and his eastern friend alone. This time their conversation was of parting.

The Prince, ever quietly considerate, had delayed his journey south for the sake of the Senator, but now it was time to leave for Egypt, where he was expected, and from where he hoped to return to India.

It was late afternoon, and involuntarily they strolled into the garden. The Prince moved with his usual measured dignity while talking of his friends in Egypt: men of considerable understanding, he maintained, and the Senator was quick to note their names. Continuing, the Prince described the journey he would face to India. It was arduous but fascinating, and the Senator listened intently. The Prince's preference was to journey with the traders, the practised travellers, for they had knowledge of the local customs. A separate ostentatious presence could be dangerous.

They exchanged addresses, hoping the long lines of communication could be bridged, and on the following day the Prince left for Seleucia Pieria, where he planned to join a coastal ship going south. In this Demetrianus had been instrumental.

The Senator had enjoyed the Prince's company for over two months and his sudden absence left a kind of vacuum. Nevertheless, his conversations with Largus, still secluded in his room, and the contemplation of his journey south soon occupied his thinking.

The Tribune Largus was a remarkable young man. He would go far, the Senator was certain, and he would recommend him in the highest places. A sharp mind, needle-sharp, a cool nerve and a look of innocence that belied it all. It was quite a combination.

Largus had been busy, but, more importantly, successful in gathering incriminating evidence against Gallo. Incredibly, the cart that Largus had been forced to surrender was returned to the Villa Maximus, and the old peasant, who was well

318

rewarded for his honesty, was generous with information concerning those who had robbed his village. It was time to act and emerge from his prison-like seclusion.

First, he needed to contact the Legate, and to do this he enlisted the help of the Senator and Demetrianus in the form of a private dinner party – a polite gesture of appreciation on behalf of the Senator. Care was taken that only the Legate and his personal slave would attend.

As the invitation had suggested, the number was at first confined to three, and when the initial formalities were completed Demetrianus suddenly dismissed the servants and turned to face the Legate.

'Sir, one of your young and admiring friends wishes to pay his respects. He awaits my call.'

The Legate was instantly alert amd suspicious, yet his tension eased, for of all men he had least to fear from the renowned Senator and his genial host. He smiled, and at that point Largus entered, bowing with mock gravity.

'Sir, Quintus Sentius Largus and his beard present themselves.'

Immediately the Legate was on his feet.

'Largus, my boy!' he exclaimed.

They embraced, and tears ran unevenly down the Legate's wizened face.

Demetrianus looked on unbelievingly. Never had he seen the Legate display such emotion.

The old administrator's flow of questions was answered frankly by Largus, and the answers left him visibly shocked. The lines on his face were deeply etched, but his mind was very much awake.

'How much is Sejanus behind all this?' he asked.

'The broad naval plan is his, sir, but I'm not sure about the detail.'

'Quintus, piracy is not a detail!'

'No, sir.'

The two men looked hard at each other.

'What shall we do?' the Legate asked.

'Nothing, sir.'

'Nothing! Have I yet to smile at those two snakes – my so-called advisers?'

'Keep them well within arrow-shot. The shafts can fly when we are ready.'

'Largus!'

'Sir.'

'We'll have to be careful. The friends of Sejanus may soon be the friends of an Emperor.'

'Crime is no friend of government and embarrassing allies are soon discarded. Sir, I want your official permission to speak at the inquiry at Caesarea.'

'Against Gallo!'

Largus nodded.

'Gallo is an orator,' the Legate reacted, 'and besides, he's too close to Sejanus. He'll destroy you!'

'I'll risk that, sir.'

The relationship between the suspicious, wizened Legate and his young aide was both unusual and frank, and the smile on the Senator's face reflected this. It alerted the Legate.

'Senator – Demetrianus – the Tribune Largus and I often behave like cooks in the kitchen. I'm afraid we forgot ourselves.'

Later in the evening, after the Legate had left for the Residency, Demetrianus could hardly wait to comment on the Administrator's behaviour.

'Wholly out of character,' he said, 'wholly out of character. The fossil came to life.'

Two days afterwards the Senator left for Capernaum, and with him was a somewhat subdued Junia. Largus had been polite. He had joked with her, but he had only seen her twice, and saying he was busy, as Arria did, was no comfort.

The day following the Senator's departure Largus slipped unobtrusively from the villa. He was bound for Caesarea and accompanying him was a single legionary. The Legate had suggested a senior tent party from the Residency, but Largus had declined the offer. Anonymity was his best disguise.

CHAPTER FORTY-EIGHT

THE TOLERANT FANATIC

As head of the Senator's guard, Demos the Greek wore the uniform of a Roman legionary. He performed his duties with diligence, but at heart he did not feel a soldier. The uniform and the attendant discipline seemed to weigh upon his spirit and he was grateful that his army life was temporary. His enlistment had been ordered by the Tribune as a shield against the knives of Gallo's agents, knowing that the murder of a legionary would provoke a full investigation.

The elder Valerius made few demands, and Demos found himself with ample space to view the pattern of his life. He was tired of his vagrant existence; tired of the taverns and the dockland gossips, the drunkards and the cutthroats. His village near Corinth and the simplicity of its life rose sweet in his mind. Would he ever return? He doubted it, for he could not see himself content with the narrow strip of his father's holding. Nevertheless, he hankered for a change.

He knew his post in the Emperor's service was one of rare privilege. He was fortunate; even so, life in the field was punishing and often tedious. He was getting old, and the edge of his keenness had dulled. Perhaps, with the Tribune's help, he could join the few who organised the eastern agents.

Because of his oath Demos had never revealed his function to the Tribune openly, though it was obvious Valerius had guessed at his secret agency. Almost a year and a half had passed since he had first attached himself to the Tribune's travelling party – his motive to spy upon and test the loyalty of the Emperor's personal Legate. That role had quickly passed to one of service, and now the Valerii had come to dominate his life.

The Senator was not as tall as his son, and his speech and temper were more even; otherwise, their natures were similar.

Demos liked the grey-haired Senator. The Patrician was unassertive in manner, yet, like his son, his most casual word commanded instant obedience. Again like his son, he travelled simply. To him numerous slaves and servants following in his wake betrayed a trivial mind.

As he journeyed, the Senator showed untiring interest in his surroundings, which extended into having long and halting conversations with the local peasants. The habit exasperated his daughter Junia.

'An ox-cart travels twice as fast as us!' she blurted one time in frustration, and Demos smiled. The young Valerius was forceful. Some day she would be a matron, and a power to reckon with.

On one occasion the Senator was much disturbed by what he saw, and when he returned to the wagon his look was dazed. He spoke absently to Demos, the sadness in his voice unmistakable.

'The strong should not prey upon the weak,' he sighed. 'Some say if Rome were absent conditions would be worse. They could be right – at least we've cleared the land of petty war-lords.'

Demos nodded politely, and the Senator made to mount the wagon but stopped short.

'In the Senate I'm laughed at, shouted at or simply ignored. They may not listen, but if nothing else they know what I stand for. I've made sure of that – I must say Sejanus listens. What a strange mixture that man is.'

The Senator pulled himself into the wagon, and Demos walked slowly to the leading cart, his mind full of the Patrician's words. Few thought about the people and their plight and even fewer acted to alleviate their misery, but the man he was escorting did. Demos had learned from the Tribune that the Senator stood for tax reform, for land reform and for the legal rights of slaves. Apparently his friends had labelled him the 'tolerant fanatic'. An amusing contradiction, Demos thought, but a perfect epitaph for the seeker after truth.

322

CHAPTER FORTY-NINE

THE INQUIRY

When the Tribune reached Ptolemais he learned that Cornelia had moved to Berytus with the family of her merchant host. At best this was two days' journey to the north, and the Tribune did not have the time to retrace his steps. Determined rather than angry, he selected his most reliable man after Titus, and along with a well augmented tent party, despatched him to Berytus. The orders were simple – further augment the guard at Berytus and escort Cornelia back to Capernaum.

Immediately, the Tribune continued on his journey south, but Cornelia's move from Ptolemais had unsettled him. Again, the imminent inquiry added to his unease. Nonetheless, the force of duty drove him on, and within two days he reached Caesarea. Gallo had already arrived, but that he had expected.

Far to the north, on the road near Sidon, the Tribune Largus was quickly making his way south.

At Capernaum Drusilla waited, her feelings of elation shadowed by anxiety. She was elated by the news that her father had left Antioch, but the terse note from her brother was worrying. Cornelia was returning to Capernaum by order. She was also anxious for Marcus, knowing that Gallo could turn the inquiry into a legal trap. Nevertheless, a feeling of hope predominated.

Pilate's fastidious administration saw that the inquiry opened exactly on time. All those summoned were present, with the exception of Gallo. He, as usual, was late.

His absence infuriated the Procurator, and he grew progressively agitated as the tedious voice of a scribe droned through the opening formalities. Then, just as the scribe was concluding, Gallo entered the hall and strode defiantly to his place of prominence, his ebullience spilling generously about him.

As if in the theatre, the friend of Sejanus looked easily about him, amusement dancing in his eyes. He could see Valerius sitting stiff and formal, boredom personified, and beside him was Tullus. In love at fifty – what an ass! Gallo's words spun silently in his mind. The cursed Centurion had always thwarted him, but today he would destroy him. Involuntarily he smacked his lips at the thought of his imminent polemic.

Gallo's opening words were chosen to affect a disarming grace. He praised the Procurator and his administration. He acknowledged the painstaking care evident in the preparations and apologised for his unavoidable absence from the first hearing. Then, slowly and deliberately, he began to focus on the subject of the inquiry.

'I first met the Tribune Marius when I arrived in Antioch over a year ago.' Gallo proceeded to paint the picture of a young, budding officer keen to learn and succeed within the legionary service. 'A week or so later,' he continued, 'I met Marius again, and to my considerable surprise he approached me for advice. Now, my honourable Procurator,' Gallo scanned the hall with an apologetic smile, 'if the advice had been about the circus, or a wager, possibly I could have claimed the laurel of an expert, but, sir, this was not the case. Marius required military advice.' Gallo's eyes fed on the amusement present in the hall and his voice dropped to a matter-of-fact level. 'I was at some disadvantage, and my difficulty was compounded by the somewhat unusual nature of the late Tribune's request. He wanted to experience life in the ranks without the protection of privilege.' Gallo became confidential. 'I had heard of this before and my legal experts told me that such eccentricities were not without the law; though I have subsequently learned that there are certain confining prerequisites. Nevertheless, at that time we advised Marius to proceed with his plan. The question was, where should this anonymous Marius be posted? One place was common to all our minds – the garrison at Capernaum. Not only would he experience life in the ranks, but he would learn from the most famous and experienced soldier in the East, Marcus Tullus.' Gallo turned to face the Procurator. 'You may imagine, sir, that all this was treated by us as a casual, if not humorous, affair.'

Pilate nodded unsmilingly, but the aides that flanked him were clearly amused; even the Centurion's face carried the wisp of a smile. There was no humour, however, on the features of the Tribune Valerius. He was furious at Gallo's hypocrisy.

Gallo then began to relate how he had received complaints from Marius concerning the actions and attitudes current at Capernaum.

'I dismissed such complaints, of course.' He looked across at Tullus. 'In fact, I began to think that the mind of Marius was rigid and fanatical, but the complaints continued. Some were petty in the extreme, such as no Latin being spoken at a dinner party. He wrote about streams of unkempt Jewish messengers and of the Centurion's inordinate attachment to local superstitions. He particularly mentioned the near worship of a Rabbi trouble-maker by the noble Tullus and his friends – you will remember this same rebel was executed a few months ago – and Marius was convinced that the brave Centurion Tullus was in close collaboration with the followers of this late and convicted criminal, the Rabbi at Capernaum.'

The gavel of Pilate crashed on the bench before him. He was clearly agitated.

'The Tribune Gallo will remember that the Rabbi Jesus was not condemned by Roman law – it was customary law.'

Gallo smiled widely.

'With the greatest respect, my noble Procurator, you are the agent of Rome, and you gave the word!'

The gavel hammered on the bench again.

'Proceed!'

Pilate's voice was unmistakably bitter. He was still troubled by the events of the Passover week and he knew that Gallo sensed it.

Gallo bowed, his mockery thinly disguised. Again he grew confidential.

'To be honest, I found the Tribune Marius a nuisance, and I did not dream that his rantings against the Centurion Tullus could be founded on fact. So I saw to it that he was removed to Palmyra. It was far away, and I thought the life of a large garrison would restrain him. Somehow my cautionary instruc-

tions went unheeded, and almost immediately the newly uni-
formed Tribune found himself in charge of a troop of soldiers
on their way to Jericho. What may or may not have happened
in the mind of Marius we do not know. However, we do know
that he arrested the Centurion Tullus on the road between the
rebel nest-bed Qumran and Jerusalem.'

Gallo's address was turning at last, the Centurion thought,
but he still entertained a smile. It was all so predictable. He
looked at his friend Valerius. He, however, was tight-lipped
and explosive.

Gallo went on to describe the details of the march through
the wooded hills on the eastern side of the Jordan valley. In
this he used the previous evidence of Titus liberally.

'We have only the words of the soldiers Titus and Tullus.
Marius cannot defend himself.' Gallo effected a lengthy pause.
'We are told by both the survivors of the ambush, the
Legionary Titus and the Centurion Tullus, that Marius would
not listen to their predictions of danger. Indeed, my earlier
description of Marius would tend to support this. Alas,
Marius is not here to speak for himself. He died with his men.'
At that, Gallo hung his head in apparent memorial.

'Gallo, for the sake of the gods,' the Tribune exploded, 'get
on with it! We want the truth, not your verbal theatricals!'

There was a short, sharp rap from the Procurator's gavel,
and the Tribune mouthed an apology.

Gallo acknowledged the Procurator's authority and continued. He sighed deeply.

'The recollection of the fate suffered by Marius and his men
had diverted me. I will endeavour to accommodate the noble
Tribune's need for alacrity,' he said, bowing towards Valerius
with disarming grace. His mockery was blatant.

'This court,' he continued, 'was called to inquire into the
unauthorised arrest of the Centurion Tullus and the subsequent ambush of those who conducted the arrest. So far the
common conclusion, voiced at an earlier hearing and now, has
labelled the late Marius as plainly mad.' Gallo swung round
dramatically, his eyes fixing on Tullus. 'I believe that this conclusion is wrong – tragically wrong!'

Gallo allowed his words a measured time to act.

'The Centurion Tullus is in close contact with the Jews. These Jews are almost exclusively members of a dangerous sect whose leader has just been executed. This leader – this god-man – was hailed by his followers as a king.' Gallo's sarcasm had a gloating intensity. 'The noble Procurator here,' Gallo gestured with energy, 'the noble Procurator ordered 'The King of the Jews' to be scribed on a notice and nailed to the cross of crucifixion as a deterrent to other aspiring royal bloods. This was the leader the noble Tullus revered. Honourable Procurator, I will ask the question we must all ask. Was Marius a fanatic and a fool, or was he a lone voice fighting the deafness of those in authority? – not least the Tribune Gallo.' He slapped his breast in self-deprecation. 'These are the questions to be answered; questions that only the Centurion Tullus can answer!'

Gallo turned to face the Centurion.

'Four years ago the Centurion Tullus travelled to Rome. What was his mission? Whom did he meet in that queen of cities? I put it to this inquiry that the honourable Tullus spent most of his time with the friends of Jewry. Jews are not confined to Jerusalem, for the legions of the faithful are spread throughout the Empire. The obscure god-figure crucified in Jerusalem was not a prophet for the Jewish capital alone but for the whole widespread nation of the Jews. The suffering of their prophet was expected, but not his death. This myth is common knowledge. The faithful expected their divine prophet to step free of his suffering, and with the legions of his God march on barbarian Rome. Indeed, to the followers of the prophet the events of the Passover week were a disaster. The Centurion here,' Gallo added, pointing dramatically at Tullus, 'made a desperate effort to save the prophet Rabbi, but he was stopped by Marius.'

Involuntarily the Tribune Valerius jumped to his feet.

'This is preposterous nonsense!' he blazed.

'The noble Tribune will be given opportunity to speak in due course,' Pilate said quickly.

Gallo just managed to control his amusement as he watched Valerius resume his seat. Then his eyes switched to the Centurion, but Tullus was unmoved. Well, he thought, it was time for the final javelin.

'May I proceed?' Gallo asked the Procurator, bowing politely.

Pilate nodded.

'Noble Procurator, in the town of Capernaum a tall giant of a man, a Jew, roams free among the fishing folk. A month or so ago this man was seen clasping the arm of Tullus, which, of course, was after the Centurion's arrest and subsequent escape. Noble Procurator, who is this tall and powerful Jew, this friend of Tullus? I will tell you!'

The face of Pilate seemed to freeze. The hall grew still.

'This friend of Tullus, this powerful Jew, was none other than the same rebel leader who massacred Marius and his men! At the very least, noble Procurator, why is this outlaw not arrested?'

The sound of shock was audible. Dramatically, Gallo spun towards the Centurion.

'Why, my noble Centurion, why?'

The Centurion turned almost placidly to face his accuser. His gaze did not waver. Instead, the beginnings of a smile played about his face.

Curse you, Tullus, Gallo said to himself. Curse you and your self- righteous friend. He was furious, for Tullus was unbroken.

In a deliberate way the Centurion rose to face Pontius Pilate.

'The honourable Procurator will allow me space to answer?'

'Yes!' Pilate returned sharply.

Tullus stood silently as if collecting his thoughts. All eyes were upon him, and those of the Tribune Valerius were intent and worried, for he had not heard about the meeting between the rebel leader and Tullus in Capernaum. The anxious lines on the Tribune's face were obvious to Gallo as he sat back in his chair. The Chief Centurion was showing a brave face, he thought, but he was trapped. There was no escape.

'I will start with the last question,' the Centurion began.

'And you'll end with it!' Gallo's mumbled words were audible and brought amusement to the faces of his aides.

'Silence!' Pilate snapped.

'Before I begin to answer the Tribune Gallo's last question, I wish to make it clear that the Tribune Valerius had no knowledge of the chance meeting between myself and the rebel leader just mentioned. I also wish to be categorical in stating that in no sense am I a lover of rebellion. Too often the forces of destruction hide within the clothing of reform.'

'Objection!' Gallo interjected. 'This is not a lecture!'

'The Centurion will confine himself to the facts of the matter.'

Tullus bowed in acknowledgement.

'About five years ago I was on patrol in northern Galilee when I came upon a village that had received what some call 'the only answer'. I was appalled and protested immediately – there'll be official records. The village had been decimated – every tenth man! In addition to this insane brutality, their property was destroyed. There was an inquiry, of course, but it dragged on and had little effect.'

'What's the point of all this?' Gallo interjected.

'The point is simple. The rebel leader in question came from that village. He witnessed the butchery and no doubt resolved to avenge his village. He also witnessed the visit of my patrol and the work of reconstruction that I ordered. Now I will return to the recent occurrence.

'After the ambush and my fortunate rescue by a local goatherd another event occurred which, for myself, is relevant to the Tribune Gallo's question.' The Centurion's voice was deep and resonant. The earlier note of tension had dissolved.

Gallo's face was dark and brooding. The cursed Centurion was gaining the sympathy of the inquiry.

'My goatherd benefactor,' Tullus continued, 'decided to transport his invalid soldier to the nearest village. I was still shaky on my feet and prone to a near insatiable desire for sleep, so I found myself lying on a donkey cart on a slow and tedious journey. Then I was awoken by a harsh sound, the sound of men shouting. I opened my eyes, and there before me was a tall, powerful man carrying a goat. I knew a lot in that moment. I knew that the cart was surrounded by rebels. I knew that Jacob – that is, the goat – had been killed by one of the outlaws. I knew that the big, curly-haired man before me was their leader and was protecting the goatherd from the vicious humour of his men, and I also knew that he recognised me. This he confirmed by mouthing my name. Suddenly the rebel leader jerked his head away. The rest you know from the statement given by the honourable Titus.

'So, noble Procurator, when I met the rebel leader in Capernaum I met the man who had saved my life. Our meeting was almost without speech. He told me pointedly how he had changed his profession. Why had he come to Capernaum? Why had he taken the risk of approaching me? I had him watched and I made enquiries. As you know, my contacts in the town are good. I was told he was leading a normal life among the fishing fraternity. Even so, we continued to watch.

'He began to make himself a self-appointed guardian of my servant James and the Master Felix. In fact, my servant believes he was instrumental in warning the Tribune of the planned attack on his guard near Ramah. Why was he doing this? Was it in payment against the damning debts of his past? Then, in reference back to what I have already said, I was told the origin of the ex-rebel was the self-same village that had suffered decimation. I resolved to remain silent. I would not betray his trust. Indeed, if, as a result of this inquiry, charges are pressed against him, I shall appeal to the highest level.'

'Appeal you may,' Gallo shouted, as he jumped to his feet. 'Not only your rebel friend but you yourself will face your due deserts. Crime is crime – it cannot be explained away!'

Gallo was furious. His plans were being thwarted by a mere Centurion, a jumped-up farmer's son.

Pointedly, Tullus turned and faced Gallo squarely.

'Yes, crime is crime, and who knows it better than you? Not many weeks ago I witnessed the death of a friend from wounds suffered during the ambush near Ramah. He was a friend dear to me, dear to the Tribune Valerius and dear to all who knew him. The attack was not carried out by Zealots. No, the attackers were not Jews, but rather criminals gathered from the alleyways of Ptolemais, with gold their promised fee. Who was their paymaster, Gallo? Who, Gallo? It's now my turn to ask the questions!'

Gallo stepped back involuntarily before the sheer power of the Centurion, and for the first time since he could remember he felt the rise of fear. He recovered quickly, though, allowing his energy to spill into laughter.

Pilate forgot to use his gavel, and Valerius watched mesmerised. Marcus Tullus was formidable.

Still laughing and trying desperately to regain the initiative, Gallo pointed dramatically at Tullus.

'You will ask me questions! You, the teller of sentimental tales – you, the friend of superstition – you, the lover of rebels – you will ask me!' Gallo's voice had risen to screaming pitch. Then suddenly he laughed with abandoned mirth.

'You, the once iron soldier of the east, soft on a sea of perfume at Capernaum. You will ask . . .'

'Gallo, by the gods . . .'

The Centurion, blazing with anger, stepped forward, but the hand of Valerius gripped his arm.

'Marcus, he's goading you. Let him be. He'll destroy himself.'

The Centurion bowed his head.

'Thanks – I lost myself. The slander aimed at your sister was too much for me.'

At once Gallo dropped his voice to simulate the sound of reason.

'The leader of a rebel gang is abroad in Capernaum: a man responsible for the death of a Roman officer and his men.' He shook his head gravely. 'No word of yours, no counter charges, however wild and spurious, can erase the crime. Roman justice must be . . .'

Gallo froze, his eyes locked on the hall entrance. The sudden silence was almost eerie.

'Largus!' Gallo mouthed, and fear moved on his face a second time. Again his imprisoned energy burst into laughter.

'Baby Quintus, where have you been – to Neptune's seat and back? Your face is white enough.' Gallo gave his voice a playful lilt, but the jibe fell flat.

'Silence!' Pilate's shouted command and the sound of his gavel were as one. 'This is an inquiry, not a tavern!'

With deliberation, he turned to the newcomer.

'Tribune Largus, the despatch I have been handed authorises

you to speak at the inquiry. You will have an opportunity after the midday recess.' Pilate's voice was businesslike.

'I should like to speak now, sir, while everyone is present.' Largus had no intention of waiting till the afternoon, for in such an interval Gallo could slip the net.

'Tribune, we'll all be present in the afternoon,' Pilate reacted with annoyance.

'Yes, sir. Nevertheless, I should like to speak now – the matter is urgent.'

Largus came from the Legate, and, ever careful, Pilate conferred with his aides. Valerius watched, poised on the edge of his seat. He tried to catch the eye of Largus, but his friend stared straight ahead. 'I'll pin Gallo to his past.' The Tribune remembered the words of Largus well. He should have guessed that this would be his forum.

The gavel rapped lightly on the bench, and Valerius left his world of thought.

'Proceed, Largus, proceed!'

At once the voice of a scribe resonated in the hall.

'The Tribune Quintus Sentius Largus.'

During the exchange between the Procurator and Largus Gallo had remained both sullen and silent, but now, as he jumped to his feet, his timing was wrong.

'I object! I demand the right to complete my statement which I was forced to stop.'

'No one forced you to stop, Tribune. You did so voluntarily,' Pilate replied.

The gavel hammered hard.

'My ruling stands. The Tribune Largus may proceed.'

For a moment Largus remained unmoving, as if he had not heard the Procurator's words. Then slowly he lifted his head. All attention was on him. He was white-faced, the Tribune noticed. Gallo was right – of course! He had shaved his beard.

'Noble Procurator,' Largus began, 'we will all have heard about the tragic loss of the naval galley amongst the islands south of Ephesus. The full complement of men, with the exception of three survivors, is missing and presumed lost. By the grace of the gods I am one of those survivors, and, like most survivors, I have a story to tell. In my case, it is one of treachery.' Largus paused and looked straight at Pilate.

'My noble Procurator, it is generally held that the galley sank without trace, but I guarantee that within a few hours of the tragedy innocent-looking fishing boats had cast their nets close to where the galley sank. It wasn't fish they were after, sir – it was gold!'

The gasps about the hall were audible, and Largus, his head lowered, waited for silence.

'Noble Procurator, the warship was carrying a large consignment of gold. Certainly it ran into a storm, but that did not endanger the quinquereme. No, it wasn't the storm but the skilful seamanship of island pirates. The quinquereme was holed. Who told them of the galley's cargo? For it was well disguised in boxes labelled 'wagon parts'. Only six men knew of the special consignment.'

Largus continued with cool precision to list those who knew about the gold shipment. Then, pointedly, he accused the two professed friends of Caligula of being Gallo's agents.

'They knew about the shipment,' Largus said slowly, articulating each word with care, and with measured deliberation he turned to face the agent of Sejanus. 'The Tribune Gallo did not leave Antioch until a major part of the gold was in his possession. I can assure this inquiry that documented evidence is safely secured.'

For a moment the ice-cold, unrelenting stare of Largus seemed to hold Gallo frozen. Then he erupted in fury.

'I demand that this man be charged with criminal slander. This lie, this devious, demonic invention must be punished! The field of execution awaits you, Largus. That I promise!'

Gallo's voice had reached its screaming point again, but Largus sat unmoved until the hammering of Pilate's gavel brought the hall to silence.

'This inquiry is adjourned for three hours,' the Procurator pronounced.

At once Gallo crashed from the hall in raging anger.

Pilate watched him go before turning to his aide Maximus.

'By all the gods,' he said wearily, 'this is a nest of adders.'

For the Procurator and his aides the three-hour recess passed quickly. All knew that the implications of the morning's hearing went far beyond the boundaries of Caesarea. Rome would be watching, and Capri would ask for every detail. It would be a major challenge, but Pontius Pilate was determined that no one would accuse him of indolence. Every last formality would be observed.

Valerius, the Centurion and Largus were in their appointed places when the Procurator resumed his chair. Gallo was late, but as such behaviour was expected, no one took much notice.

The preliminaries being brief, the inquiry was soon ready to proceed. Still Gallo and his men had not arrived. At once demands were issued ordering him and his friends to take their places, but the guards could not find them in the waiting rooms allocated, and Pilate's anger mounted as word was sent to his hired villa, again without result.

Wholly exasperated, Pilate was about to adjourn proceedings when a despatch was handed to him. It was marked urgent, and he read it instantly. His immediate shock was obvious, and his gavel rapped with strange finality.

'This inquiry,' he announced, 'is postponed indefinitely.'

At once he beckoned the Tribune to approach. His message was stark and dramatic.

'Sejanus has been executed for treason.'

The two men looked at each other for some time, but the Tribune felt no elation. He knew the treason law was brutal.

'Gallo will have heard the news as well,' Valerius said pensively.

'No doubt.'

'And no doubt his chariot is already on the move.'

Pilate nodded.

'The world has changed, Tribune – suddenly what was, is not! It's difficult to comprehend, and seems more dreamlike than a firm reality.' The shock was still present in the Procurator's mind.

After taking his leave, the Tribune relayed the news to the Centurion and Largus, and together they walked from the hall, each man deep in thought. Outside the graceful buildings at the heart of Caesarea surrounded them, but their eyes were unseeing.

'The switch from fame to infamy is swift,' Valerius said pensively.

'Yes – the pent-up hatred of the Senate will be merciless, when even those who praised his cook will be in danger,' Tullus responded. 'The gods have mercy on his family.'

'I second that,' Largus interjected. 'I met his daughter once.'

All three fell silent again, until the Centurion voiced his concern for the situation at Capernaum. The garrison was depleted, and Gallo, full of desperation, would not feel himself restrained by any formal need. Anything could happen, even some last bitter revenge.

Once alerted, Valerius ordered an immediate departure. Largus, however, was to stay behind and gauge the mood of the city in the wake of the momentous news from Rome.

CHAPTER FIFTY

FLIGHT

Gallo's flight from Caesarea was frantic in its haste and, fired with desperation, he pushed his men and horses to the limit. There was no time to waste, for he knew too well that orders would be out for his arrest.

Shocked and angry, he whipped and shouted at his horses. Tiberias was his goal, where he planned to enlist the aid of Herod, who, he felt, would not have heard the bitter news. So, only halting briefly in the dark night hours, he drew up at the Tetrarch's palace as the dawn was breaking.

The Tetrarch was not in residence, the servants said, but Gallo knew he was. To Hades with his camel face! How had he heard so quickly? Furious, he ranted at the wall-eyed guards until they grew belligerent. Then, boiling with frustration, he turned upon his men.

'Why stand idle with your mouths agape? Scour the town! We need supplies – tents, bedding . . . go!'

The hard core of his followers, the so-called road-surveyors, obeyed, but eight men, legionaries from the Residency garrison at Antioch, simply turned about and rode away.

'Less mouths to feed,' he mumbled to his intimates. Nonetheless, it was a stark reminder of his sudden change of fortune.

In the town his men soon found the traders had been ordered not to trade, and Herod's guards were everywhere, it seemed, to punish disobedience.

'The scheming, black-souled fox,' Gallo grated bitterly. 'Would I had the power, I'd grind him to dust. Damn him to Neptune's depths – we've lost two hours!'

'Sir,' whispered the juggler, the one-time slave of Marius, 'why not try Capernaum? For being a Roman in Rome's service, you need only sign for your supplies, as the bill could be charged to Antioch.' The slave shrugged his shoulders in an offhand way, but there was a serpent cunning in his eyes.

'What if they know?'

'They'll not have heard – Tullus and his lanky friend will bring the news themselves, and we're well ahead of them.'

'You're right! – you are a clever one. I like your plan; I like it very much! Jug, you are an artful demon!'

Gallo smiled with satisfaction. The plan was subtle; a last defiant jab at Tullus and his pious friend.

They arrived at Capernaum before midday. Gallo looked dazed, almost stupefied, as he approached the town, but beneath the shell of surface impotence he was watchful and alert, knowing there was a possibility that the garrison might have heard the shattering news from Rome. He doubted it, though, and even if a message had arrived from Rome it would remain unopened until Tullus was present.

For some time Gallo had noticed tent-like structures standing against the houses as they moved closer to the town. Some were plain, others ornate, and all were roofed with palm leaves and greenery. Another mad custom, he concluded; the Jews were always having festivals. Even so, he was curious.

'Jug, what are those flimsy shelters with the plant life of the Jordan on the top?'

'I don't know, sir.'

'Find out!' Gallo called imperiously. He loved the dramatic flourish and with that the whole troop came to a halt, the time-conscious urgency of their purpose forgotten.

Obediently the slave approached one of the lean-to tents, the curious of the party following behind, but while he was asking questions in his halting Aramaic the soldiers, possessed by hunger, picked at the fruit hanging in abundance.

'Leave the fruit alone!' Gallo bellowed, but it was too late.

Desperately he tried to save the situation.

'Jug, give them gold! – apologise! – anything! – just keep their hot blood off the boil.'

The slave had no success, for the townsfolk were enraged. The Roman strangers had defiled their shrine, and gold would not allay the fault.

'Idiots!' Gallo ranted at his men. 'Have you no sense? We want supplies from these people!'

Exasperated, Gallo thumped the side of his chariot, and the horses, startled by the sound, jerked forward. Then he looked behind in time to see an angry group of townsfolk gathering. Hotheads, he muttered to himself, why were they so touchy?

'Jug, what is their stupid festival? Did they tell you?' he asked the slave, who had joined him on the chariot.

'The Feast of the Tabernacles, sir. Something to do with penance and a reminder of their poverty on some long march or other . . .'

'Penance!' Gallo exploded, 'I would have thought the hovels they inhabit were penance enough!'

When he arrived at the garrison entrance, Gallo was at once charming and deferential. He was met by the veteran Atticus, as Cornelius had not yet returned from receiving his promotion. The old soldier was suspicious of the smooth-tongued officer, especially as he knew his reputation. Nevertheless, Atticus could not disregard the orders of the powerful Tribune, but he halved the quantity that was ordered, and that, coupled with his slow, methodical ways, tested Gallo's patience to the limit.

'This senile old fool is going to scratch about until the cursed Centurion comes,' he whispered to the juggler slave standing restless at his side. 'Take two men to the market and buy what food will keep us going for at least two days. We'll join you as soon as this walking corpse allows us!'

Happy to be active, the slave rushed off immediately, leaving Gallo in the courtyard of the garrison fort, where his beguiling tongue was quick to calm the slightest ruffle in proceedings. Repeatedly he apologised for the disturbance of his hurried call, explaining how a pressing duty required his presence at Caesarea Philippi on the morrow – a false trail, of course.

Gallo was pleased with his performance. The audacity of it all appealed to him. Indeed, he almost burst out laughing when he thought of how Valerius would react. Then suddenly he saw the figure of Drusilla framed by the doorway of the main building. Cold as an icicle, he thought, and just as he

338

remembered her in Rome. She disappeared inside the building immediately, but her presence lingered in Gallo's mind like a last, fateful glimpse of the Empire. For a moment the thought of exile held a terrible finality, but he dismissed his introspection rudely.

'To Hades with Rome!' he muttered to himself. 'To Hades with its clever women! Where I'm going the women don't talk back.'

Gallo was himself again.

To Drusilla, the sight of Gallo was a shock. What was his business with Atticus? Why had he come to Capernaum? Where were Marcus and her brother? At once she rang the bell for James, who told her that the Tribune Gallo had called for supplies.

'Atticus asked him about the inquiry,' James continued, 'and was told that it was routine and friendly.'

'Do you believe him, James?'

'No, my lady, he's much too sweet of tongue for me.'

'By all the gods, I've just remembered!' Drusilla burst out anxiously. 'Felix and Sarah are in the town. We must warn them that Gallo's here. He's nothing less than a criminal, and who knows what he might get up to? We must be vigilant! And, James, please let me know when he's left the town.'

James rushed off to warn Felix, leaving Drusilla anxious and disturbed. She dared not think of Marcus. He had to be safe, but her fears were insidious. She closed her eyes tightly. Please, please, not now, not now. Her inner pleading was intense, and she turned to the grace she knew: the light that had come with the Rabbi Jesus.

'I must learn to trust,' she whispered to herself. 'No matter what happens I must learn to trust.'

James slipped through the courtyard past Gallo and his followers, now almost ready to move, and hurried on towards the town centre. He quickly spotted Felix and Sarah close to the market area and was within hailing distance when someone approached his Roman friend. This, of course, was not unusual, as the townsfolk had taken Felix to their hearts.

'It's that juggler slave,' he said aloud, spitting in the dust before him as a measure of his distaste. 'Shifty-eyed, cunning, crawling,' the muttered commentary of James continued until he was close enough to hear the sound of anger in the voice of Felix – an unusual event, to say the least.

'Don't speak to me like that!' the grey-haired Roman barked. The sudden authority in one normally unassertive held the nearby townsfolk watching.

'Who are you, freedman, to tell me when to speak or not?' the slave shot back. Years of bitterness burned in his voice: the bitterness of a slave resentful of service yet forced to serve, a craven, sycophantic service coated with cunning. He hated it. Now before him was Felix, the very symbol of stability and everything he could never be. This was his opportunity, and the desire to strike out, to destroy and to seek revenge was like a frenzy.

'Freedman!' he shouted, leering at Felix. 'Freedman, what would you do if we took your brat away?' It was a hollow threat, but the vindictive hatred that possessed him had its way. Roughly he grabbed at Sarah and began to fondle her, and Felix, trying desperately to intervene, was flung to the ground. At once James leapt to the rescue, while all the while the slave roared with mocking laughter.

The soldiers, two from the garrison and two of Gallo's men, had been talking and were now alerted, but before they could act a powerful, curly-headed man had come to Sarah's aid. It was the ex-rebel leader, and with a seeming lack of effort he flung the juggler slave away from him as if he were a weightless sack.

The slave collapsed in a humiliating heap, and for a moment dust rose about him. He swore hatefully and his adept juggling hand moved quickly. A knife flashed through the air, catching the tall Jew before he had time to move.

The two Capernaum soldiers were instantly at the side of Felix, and Gallo's men stood beside the slave. The situation was ugly, but Gallo was coming, his powerful voice booming in the shocked silence.

'Make way! Make way!'

With nimble swiftness the slave leaped to the side of his master in the chariot. Then the watching townsfolk suddenly erupted, and Gallo, seeing the situation dangerous, lashed with his whip. The horses, stung to action, made a brutal passage through the crowd.

Gallo had no idea what had happened and had no desire to stop and find the cause. Anyway he assumed it was the Jews. They were always squabbling over something. Again his whip lashed out, and yet again, until they were beyond the town's perimeter, and standing at his side the slave was filled with gloating satisfaction.

The wounded Jew, the one-time rebel leader, was carried to a house close to the synagogue. He had no kinsmen, though those who knew him had been called. Felix and Sarah were at his side, and James had gone to seek the aid of Drusilla, as she had her own medical box, had access to the garrison supplies, and had a skill when dealing with the sick.

She responded immediately, and the veteran Atticus, nervous for her safety, sent eight soldiers to accompany her. She spoke fluently in Aramaic to the injured Jew as she dressed his wound, and tears of gratitude welled in the eyes of the erstwhile rebel leader. He knew exactly who she was – the future wife of Marcus Tullus and the sister of the Roman officer who had destroyed his rebel band. It was another sign, but what did his Lord require of him? What was his duty? He closed his eyes and began slowly to repeat the words of Isaiah:

'Let the wicked forsake his way, and the unrighteous man his thoughts: and let him return unto the Lord, and he will have mercy upon him; and to our God, for he will abundantly pardon.'

Pardon he needed, pardon he craved, for his deeds were black and heavy on his soul. He opened his eyes. The Roman lady was still at his side.

'Rest,' she said gently. The sound was soothing, and at that he fell asleep.

The house where the ex-rebel lay was not the only focus of attention. Many had come from the hills to join their kinsfolk for the Feast of the Tabernacles, and amongst them were those not tutored in the docile ways of Capernaum. One, who viewed the Roman presence as a sacrilege, had the natural power to gather men about him, and the young bloods came to him, fired by the insults of the afternoon. They sought revenge, they said, against that devil of a round-faced Roman and his men.

The sun was low when a party of twenty left the town. They did not go by road. Instead, they used their fishing boats, believing it was quicker than the lakeside way. The loud-mouthed Roman, they believed, was bound for Bethsaida-Julias, where, they thought, he would seek accommodation for the night. His last night, their forceful leader said with relish.

Just as the fishing boats were pulling out from the harbour the Tribune and his guard arrived, and with them was the Chief Centurion. Marcus was safe, though Drusilla soon learned that neither he nor her brother could stop. The shadow of Gallo was long.

The Tribune had received Imperial orders to arrest his fleeing enemy, but with Gallo hours ahead instant decisions were necessary. As usual, his orders were delivered in his quick, staccato way.

'Gallo's speed will be reduced by virtue of the baggage carts he acquired here at the garrison. I will head a small vanguard of cavalry and outflank him. Then we will try to pin him down until Titus arrives with the main guard. When this happens we can press for his surrender – as you know, our orders are to take him alive. I think we can take it for granted that his stated destination is an invention.'

'He's hours ahead, sir,' Titus cautioned. 'He could be difficult to find.'

'I doubt it – Gallo's too bombastic to be stealthy. I don't think we need worry you with this adventure,' he added, turning to Tullus.

'There's a complication, sir,' the Centurion began, careful to be formal in the presence of Titus and Atticus. 'A number of the town's youths have vowed to avenge the day's events and have already left to pursue their promise. I've sent a restraining message by one of the fishermen, but the Galileans are headstrong, and if they find Gallo before we do the situation could be difficult, to say the very least, for a Galilean who takes up arms against a Roman, no matter what the cause, is branded rebel.'

'We could speak for them.'

'The authorities would have their names, and memories can be long!'

'Well, join us if you wish, but are you fit enough?'

'I'll do!'

'Where's Felix?'

'I'm told he's with the wounded man.'

'I should like to see this man. He who protects Felix protects me.'

The Tribune had already asked about Cornelia, but as yet there was no word of her approach. He quickly read the letter she had left him. It was about her being a blight on his career. How wrong she was! The Gods be praised that he had ordered her to Capernaum.

CHAPTER FIFTY-ONE

ARRIVAL

Drusilla could not sleep. The joy of seeing Marcus and her brother; the momentous news from Rome; Gallo's visit to the garrison; the injured Jew: there was too much rushing in her mind for sleep. There was also worry, for the mission of Marcus and Lucius was not without danger.

Deciding to visit the wounded man, she arose before dawn and eventually, escorted by eight legionaries, she made her way to the town centre. She found Felix dozing on a couch close to the sickbed of the injured man. He awoke as she approached.

'How has he been?' she whispered.

'Feverish, but he's resting now. His fevered talk was full of remorse – his rebel past, I suppose. When the light strengthens the shadows deepen.'

'Until they're washed away,' Drusilla added, thinking of the Rabbi. 'You go and rest. I'll need to examine the dressings, and Sarah can help me,' she added, looking at the young girl sleeping soundly on a rug and cushions spread upon the floor.

'I think he's going to be all right,' she continued softly after peering closely at the prostrate Jew. 'Do we know his name?'

'Yes – Daniel Ben David, the son of a village elder.'

Drusilla scanned the small, sparsely-furnished room. It was spotlessly clean.

'Does the family not need this room?'

'They're in their tent. It's the 'Tabernacle' feast.'

'Of course. I'd forgotten.'

Drusilla walked with Felix to the door.

'I got the feeling from an unusually diplomatic James that our care and interest could be overdone,' she said shyly. 'In other words, I don't think you need rush back, if you know what I mean.'

Felix nodded wearily.

'James will know,' he said with finality. 'The town is jealous of its custom, and a Roman is a Roman.'

Once outside, Felix breathed deeply. The morning air was like a liquid tonic. He acknowledged the guards waiting on Drusilla, one of whom broke away to escort him to the garrison. About half way to the fort Felix was approached by one of his friends, an old, bent elder called Zechariah.

'The blessings of the morning to you, Master Felix.'

'And to you, Zechariah.'

'It's going to rain,' the old man said. 'It often starts at the Tabernacles.'

Felix looked up. It was clouding over.

'John, the Disciple beloved of his Rabbi, will be here within the next three days,' the elder continued.

'Zechariah, you must let me know immediately he comes,' Felix responded eagerly.

'I will, Master Felix, I will.'

The friends parted and Felix continued on his way.

He was deep in thought as he entered the courtyard, and at first did not notice the wagons and carts parked inside. When he did, he guessed Cornelia had arrived. Then he saw the familiar grey-haired figure of his master descend from the wagon.

For a moment Felix stood watching as if the scene before him were unreal. There was Junia, a young lady now. And Arria, dear Arria – she lived for the Senator.

'Is that your twin brother, Master Felix?' The blunt words of James sounded at his side.

Felix turned, his face animated.

'Please, James, could you go to the town and tell the Lady Drusilla that the Master – I mean her father – has arrived.'

James nodded and hurried off.

'Master,' Felix called.

The Senator swung round.

'Felix!'

They rushed to each other and embraced.

'You're looking well, Master.'

'And you, Felix.'

They looked at each other, their faces full of delight.

'I've so much to tell you,' Felix began hurriedly. 'I've met men of astonishing stature, awesome, Master, in this very town. I've so much to tell you,' he repeated.

'And I too, Felix. I made friends with a Prince from the East. We met at Ephesus. You should have been there. The man's philosophy was remarkable. Yes, Felix, I can see the night lamp flickering.'

Junia edged closer to her father's side, and Felix, seeing her, held out his hands. At once she threw her arms about him.

'Dear Felix,' she whispered into the folds of his tunic.

Felix was deeply moved, and Arria was weeping. Gently the Senator put his arm around her shoulder, and for a moment all three were silent while emotion was contained.

'Where's Drusilla? Where is my son?'

'Drusilla's in the town, Master, tending the sick – I've sent word that you're here. And Master Lucius is pursuing the Tribune Gallo; he has orders to arrest him.'

'Sejanus won't like that!'

'Sejanus has fallen, sir.'

'Fallen – by all the gods! When was this?'

'The news has just arrived.'

'What a fall.' The Senator looked blankly before him. 'I'm glad I'm not in Rome. The knives of hatred will be busy – his family?'

'The worst, Master.'

'By mighty Jupiter! When will we shed our brutal past?' The Senator's look of pain was obvious. Then he saw Drusilla.

'My daughter!'

'Father!'

They embraced each other tightly.

'Father, father,' she murmured, her face buried in his chest.

There were tears in the Senator's eyes. For once, his reserve had failed. She embraced him again.

'Father, I'm so happy, so incredibly happy. Come,' she added quickly, 'you must have something to eat and drink.'

'Before I do, my dear, will you take me to the shrine? I must give thanks for the journey.'

Then he remembered Cornelia. 'Where is my beautiful Cornelia?'

346

'She should be back soon. Lucius has ordered her return.'

'I see – all is not well.'

'Lucius still awaits permission and Cornelia has grown to think her position is hopeless. In fact, I believe she thinks herself a hindrance to him.'

'I thought Tiberius . . .' But the Senator stopped in mid-sentence.

Slowly they moved off towards the altar with Felix and Junia following behind.

'Master Felix.'

It was the voice of Demos, and at once Felix turned towards the sound.

'Demos, you rogue, you're in uniform.'

'Briefly, Felix, briefly!'

'Come, join the Master at the altar. We can talk later.'

CHAPTER FIFTY-TWO

PURSUIT

The instant obedience that Gallo had always enjoyed from his followers was growing less evident. He held the power of patronage no longer, and they knew it. In fact, another four men deserted him at Bethsaida-Julias when they stopped to find a guide.

'Fools,' Gallo growled, 'they don't speak Aramaic and their Greek is almost non-existent. Where can they go? The army? They'd put my horse in prison, never mind my bodyguard!' Gallo looked at each of his men closely. 'There's a community of exiles where we're going. The Latin tongue is spoken. We have gold. All we need to do is wait, and not for long. The lecher of Capri has but a little time to sport himself!'

The stop at Bethsaida-Julias was longer than Gallo had planned, and the finding of a guide had been a slow, frustrating business. Indeed, as at Tiberias and Capernaum, precious time had been wasted. What was more, the light was fading and his men were drowsy.

Darkness came quickly. There was a cloud cover and torches were necessary. Therefore progress was slow, but this did not trouble Gallo over much, for he knew his pursuers would have the same problem. He was troubled at their next stop, however, when they found that a baggage cart was missing.

'The idiot has fallen asleep,' Gallo grated, anxious to discount any suggestion of further desertion. 'We can't turn back to look for him, for it would cost us too much time – anyway, it's not the important baggage,' he concluded, with studied casualness. Nevertheless, Gallo was worried, as mistrust and uncertainty, the enemies of the fugitive, were growing in his mind, and he knew the border of the Empire was distant.

The boat journey of the angry townsfolk was speeded by a favourable wind, and on landing on the northern shore, their leader sent two scouts ahead to Bethsaida-Julias, where they quickly learned that Gallo had journeyed south and not north to Caesarea Philippi as he had indicated loudly at Capernaum. Something had made the Roman change his mind, the leader guessed. He was puzzled, though, for the loud-mouthed Tribune had avoided all contact with officialdom.

On returning to their boats, they found another fisherman waiting, the Centurion's messenger, but the leader of the men from Capernaum was disdainful.

'We're not babies who need a Roman mother,' he said angrily. 'It is our duty to avenge ourselves!'

There were dissenting voices, however, for the word of the Centurion was respected.

'Well, I'm not turning back,' their leader cried, 'but those who have no stomach may!'

The situation was as old as time.

They cast off quickly and sailed south, while to the east, beyond the bulk of the Golan, a storm was raging. The rumble of the thunder was distant and the lightning erratic, but all the time it was drawing closer.

The Chief Centurion's message had explained Gallo's strange behaviour. The bastard Roman was a fugitive. The question was, what would the round-faced bombast do? Or rather, what would his guide suggest? The leader of the Jewish band was in a quandary, though he dared not show it, as any lack of resolution on his part would make his followers turn their boats for Capernaum.

What would he do if he were advising the Roman? Get rid of the stupid chariots and carts and travel light. Then he could cut through the hills and avoid the obvious way, the valley of the Yarmuk. He could be on the way to Petra, though, but the leader of the men from Capernaum did not think so. Then, with sudden resolution, he ordered the men to pull to the shore a few miles south of Bethsaida-Julias.

The chances of finding the Roman were small. Even so, a blind resolution kept the leader going. He and his followers were, of course, on foot. It was dark, but the near-continuous lightning from the storm behind the hills made progress easy.

When they reached the road, they scoured the surface for a sign of newly-made tracks, peering blindly until the lightning gave them sight. It was fruitless, for the hard road surface was unremitting of evidence; as well as that, the softer ground on either side had not been recently disturbed.

'They've turned into the hills somewhere up the road,' he said with brisk authority, and at that began to walk towards Bethsaida-Julias, the men from Capernaum, grumbling and reluctant, following behind.

Not long afterwards they found tracks turning off towards the east.

As the night wore on, Gallo's fears subsided and his old brash confidence returned. No one, especially Valerius, would dream that he was travelling south. Indeed, at Bethsaida-Julias he had instructed the juggler to spread the rumour that he was travelling north – the slave was good at that. All was going well and he was happy with his guide, an astute Greek-speaking man who felt the need to earn his pay.

Alone amongst his followers Gallo enjoyed the storm raging to his left, and when they turned east away from the Sea of Galilee the thunder seemed to enfold them with outstretched arms. Gallo liked its grandeur, especially as there was no rain. The centre of its fury was still to the east.

Gallo had been drinking liberally from his wine-bag as he leaned against his chariot, and his men were quick to follow his example. In fact, the fugitives had abandoned all pretence of army discipline – a fact that Gallo did not mind. They were far from trouble, and tomorrow was another day. The guide thought differently.

'You must press on, sir,' he urged. 'Your enemies will have local guides as well, and we must abandon these chariots and carts – they're useless in the hills. The horses can be used as pack animals, but we must move quickly.'

'They'll never find us here,' Gallo replied grandly. 'My friend,' he added, putting his arm round the guide's shoulder, 'we've been on the road since midday yesterday.'

'You should press on – you're paying me well, sir, and that's my best advice.'

Gallo's now tired and wine-fuddled mind found it difficult to focus, and in the moment of decision he was ruled not by prudence but by habitual reaction. He stopped.

The guide resigned himself to waiting, and as the time slipped by the heart of the storm drew perceptibly closer. The horses were frightened; even so, the men who took turns to mind them were prone to fall asleep. It would only take one crash of thunder overhead to scatter the animals. Troubled by the situation, the guide decided to awaken Gallo.

Gallo was reluctant, but once awake he was quickly filled with a new urgency and soon bullied his men into action. The guide was amazed at his resilience.

Moving further up the valley, they found a convenient gulley where the carts and chariots were abandoned. This accomplished, the guide pointed to the track ahead, and they began to ascend amongst the sparse tree cover. The sky was growing light, for the dawn was close. Then the lightning stopped, and it was suddenly silent, eerily silent.

Gallo lifted his head to the sky.

'Jupiter, my friend, your night torch served us well,' he boomed, his right arm swinging high in an extravagant gesture. Then a blinding flash of lightning, followed by its wake of thunder, rent the air. The horses reared.

'You shouldn't speak so loudly, sir,' he muttered, turning as the one-time slave of Marius gripped his arm.

'There are armed men up ahead. I saw them clearly in that flash of lightning.'

Gallo peered ahead in the thin light of early dawn.

'By the gods, you're right! They're bandits!'

Instinctively Gallo looked back to survey a possible retreat, only to see the unmistakable form of Roman soldiery in the faint, shadowy light; Valerius, no doubt, and that cursed Centurion.

'Hades burn!' he swore. 'I should have known!'

There was only one way of escape. He had to get to the other side of the trickling river, yet the banks were steep. Kicking at his horse's side, he forced the sliding, slipping animal down the steep incline. His men were soon about him on the river bed, but the bank before them was formidable. Swearing with frustration, Gallo jumped from his horse and began to coax the frightened creature up the bank.

A flash of lightning and its thunder were as one, and with it the first heavy drops of rain began to fall.

Gallo and his men were much too frantic in their efforts to hear the crashing, booming noise that was fast approaching them. On and on it came until its roar was deafening. At last Gallo was alerted. He felt a rush of air and then it hit him: a wall of water, tossing him and his trapped companions like helpless playthings in its wake.

The guide, who had not moved from the bank, watched unbelievingly, and above him the men from Capernaum stood shocked. Below, though nearer now, the Tribune and the Centurion looked on with amazement.

'A deluge in the hills releasing itself,' the Centurion said, in answer to the Tribune's questioning stare. 'It's a known hazard in the south.'

It began to rain heavily, torrentially, and water streamed from the helmet and armour of both officers. Then, as if at some divine behest, the rains stopped and the ink-dark clouds began to pull away.

'His ways were violent and larger than life, and his death was just the same – it's strangely lawful,' Tullus said reflectively.

'Marcus, he was a criminal!' Valerius responded bluntly.

The Centurion dismounted.

'I'd better speak to the men from Capernaum,' he said, as he began to walk slowly up the slope towards the Galileans.

'Who is that?' their leader asked sharply.

'Our Centurion.'

'Your Centurion!' The Jewish leader's voice was disdainful, yet he moved to meet the approaching Tullus.

'You're an able leader. We could do with men like you in the army.'

The Centurion's compliment took the stubborn Jew by surprise. He nodded.

'In the sacred writings of your honourable tradition there is much wisdom,' Tullus continued. 'Does it not say in

Deuteronomy: 'To me belongeth vengeance and recompence.'?'

At that the Centurion bowed, swung on his heel and returned to join the Tribune.

For a time the Jew stood without moving. He resented a Roman quoting from sacred scripture, but at the same time he was impressed.

CHAPTER FIFTY-THREE

THE GATHERING

The garrison fort was racing with activity. There were the necessary preparations for the arrival of the Tribune and his guard. As well as that, quarters were required for the soon expected Tribune Largus.

Drusilla had accepted the renewed offer of hospitality by the Ben Josephs, but with the arrival of Junia and Arria the low rambling house was filled to capacity. Again, Cornelia was expected at any time, thus adding to the number. In the circumstances Ben Joseph and his wife retreated to their servants' quarters, but it was an arrangement that could be only temporary.

Escaping from the general bustle, the Senator and Felix, with four legionaries discreetly in attendance, slipped into the town. As usual, the Senator was full of questions, and the fact that Felix seemed to know so many people made him question further.

'I don't know why we brought a guard, for all we've met are smiles! I know you have a winning way, but here you have excelled yourself!'

'We share a common memory, Master.'

'You mean the Rabbi that you followed.'

'Yes – there's much I need to tell you.'

'By what I've seen this morning it would seem so. I liked your friend Zechariah. He's a dignified old gentleman.'

'He's not much older than we are, Master!'

They laughed.

'Who did Zechariah say was coming?'

'A young Rabbi named John. He's young in years but old in wisdom, and of all the people you may meet he is the one you must not miss.'

'With that recommendation I have no option.'

It was well past midday. The sun was warm and pleasant, and after completing a leisurely circuit of the town's centre the Senator and Felix returned to the garrison fort. They had just arrived when word came that the Tribune and his guard were close.

There was a sense of triumph in the air as they entered Capernaum, for news of Gallo's end had preceded them. The Tribune and Tullus rode together in front of the guard, and the children of the town ran amongst the soldiers unrestrained. There were waves and shouts. Their own Centurion had returned, having avenged the wrongs that they had suffered.

In the open ground before the garrison building the Senator waited, with Felix by his side. Close behind was James the Galilean. His feelings were mixed, for he knew that change was in the air.

'It's Father!' was all the Tribune said, as he jumped from his horse and ran to meet the Senator.

They embraced, and Felix, watching the reunion, found it difficult to control his emotion.

'My dear son, you have heaped honour on our ancient house.'

'Father, I've lived a hundred years since I saw you last, but before anything else is said you must meet my friend Marcus Tullus.'

The Centurion stepped forward.

'I am honoured, sir,' he said evenly.

Tullus had the figure of a soldier, powerful and trim, but the Senator discerned an inner substance in the man before him. Yet for all his obvious strength there was a gentleness in his eyes and manner.

'I see a Roman worthy of our ancestors.' The Senator smiled widely. 'My daughter has described you well.'

'Sir, not all my faults, I trust!'

The sound of James smacking his lips was audible. He did not understand the Latin tongue too well, but he sensed his master had behaved with dignity.

'Lucius, you'll need to observe the rites for a safe return. We must not delay you, as your sister Junia is impatient to see her hero brother – though I do believe you have a rival.'

'A rival!' the Tribune reacted with pretended shock.

'Yes – Quintus Largus.'

'Largus! No, never, he's shaved his beard! He's not the man he was.'

They laughed, but suddenly the vision of Cornelia cut across the Tribune's thought, and at that he turned quickly towards his guard.

After the rites had been observed, the veteran Atticus approached with despatches for both Valerius and Tullus.

The reaction of the Tribune was immediate, and his face glowed with energy.

'Tullus!' he cried, gripping the Centurion's arm. 'The Emperor has given his permission: Cornelia and I can marry, and it's you I have to thank. You wrote to Lamia. You are a friend indeed. And I see you're not unknown to the Governor,' he added, with a knowing smile.

'Yes – I've been the Governor's agent for the past three years or so.'

'I'm not at all surprised. Indeed, I seem to be surrounded by agents. There's yourself, and Demos, of course. He's obviously one of the Emperor's sleepless men – and there's the inimitable Largus. He's surely more than an administrator?'

'No! Largus throws his own javelin!'

The Tribune nodded briefly.

'He's in no one's pouch and that's for sure. – Titus!' he called across to his guard captain, 'be generous with the wine this evening.'

'The men will like that, sir!' the old soldier responded.

Valerius laughed lightly before turning to the Centurion.

'I dare not tell the men the cause of my gesture lest they keep the town awake all night! But, Marcus, why has Cornelia not arrived? Berytus is not far distant.'

'Ladies travel slowly, sir,' Tullus answered, even though he shared the Tribune's puzzlement.

As if bidden by some invisible power, both started together for the Ben Josephs' villa, where they found the sisters waiting on the portico.

'Junia, my little sister, you've grown up,' Valerius said, hugging her tightly.

She only said his name, she could not think of anything to add.

'Meet Marcus Tullus, Junia,' her brother prompted

'Sir, I am honoured,' she responded, quickly regaining her composure.

'And I, to meet you, my dear,' Tullus returned. 'Ladies – your brother has good news,' he added, bowing to the Tribune to continue.

'Cornelia and I have received the Emperor's blessing – the news has just arrived.'

Both sisters immediately enveloped their brother with embraces, and after feigning exhaustion he extracted himself.

'We have Marcus to thank. He wrote to the Governor Lamia, who in turn checked with Capri. Apparently a message was sent and was received at Caesarea, but somehow it went astray.'

Junia pulled at her brother's arm.

'Come inside,' she urged, 'we must tell Father, and Arria will be overjoyed.'

'Drusilla,' Tullus said gently, as Junia and the Tribune went inside.

'Yes, Marcus.'

'Wait a little. I, too, received a letter from the Governor,' he continued, handing the roll despatch to her.

Quickly she scanned the contents.

'Marcus, a Prefecture – an island close to Ephesus – we are going to grow grapes!'

Leaving the roll on an adjacent ledge, she slowly put her arms around his waist, leaning against him as if she were nestling on a couch.

'Prefect Tullus, sir.'

'Yes, my lady,' he said softly.

'When can we be married?'

'Soon, my dear Drusilla, soon!'

The next day Largus arrived from Caesarea, to be greeted warmly by the Senator and his family. The Senator liked the young Tribune. Quintus Largus was clever and able, but he subjected his ability to a fine sense of tact. His wit was always

357

ready, though he could be an implacable enemy – Gallo had learned that all right. He was intolerant of the criminal element, yet from his conversation he had convinced the Senator of his pragmatism. Perfect material for an administrator.

Much to the inner amusement of Drusilla and her father, Junia blushed when Largus presented himself: an embarrassment he was quick to dispel.

'I'm sorry I offered my beard as a cushion filler,' he said lightly, patting his shaven face.

'Then, sir, the padding of the Empire has been distinctly bettered.'

They laughed, with the Senator and Drusilla joining in. It was clear to Drusilla that Junia liked her brother's friend, though for his part he did not seem to pay her much attention. Poor Junia, life's lessons could be hard.

When the reception for Largus was drawing to a close, Felix quietly withdrew and headed for the town. News had reached him that the Disciple John had just arrived, and, intent on seeing him, Felix rushed to the area near the synagogue. Above all, he wanted his master to meet the young Jew, for to the mind of Felix nothing was more important.

As he approached the synagogue he was amazed to see the wounded Daniel Ben David sitting propped against a wall close by.

'Daniel, are you wise?' he reacted.

'My body heals quickly, Master Felix, but my mind needs the care of a Rabbi.'

'That, Daniel, is a general requirement!' Felix responded, while sitting down beside the one-time rebel.

Ben David moved awkwardly, careful of his shoulder.

'I'm serious, Master Felix!'

Felix was immediately alert.

'I'm consumed with guilt. There's no rest from it! None!'

Felix listened intently as Ben David began to tell how his doubts and questioning had arisen.

'When I saw Tullus lying stunned amongst the dead at that accursed ambush, something happened to me – inside, Master Felix. I didn't admit it at the time, but something changed.

'Later, as you know, my own men were overwhelmed, and as I was escaping I tripped and knocked myself unconscious. Now this is hard to believe, but nonetheless it's true! When I came to, I found a water-bag lying beside me, with the crest of the Tenth Legion inscribed upon it. I found the event incredible, like an act of God, for I myself had left a wine-bag by the side of the fallen Tullus.'

Ben David shook his head, reflecting his continued amazement. He then described how he had been drawn to Capernaum. The pull was irresistible, he said. In time he met Tullus, and Tullus had not betrayed him.

'The honour of Tullus and those about him, and you, Master Felix – your understanding ways: all are as a mirror in which I see my vicious past in sharp relief. You are Romans. How many like yourselves have I pursued with vengeance in my heart? How many have I . . .?'

Ben David stopped, the look of despair out of place on his manly face. His eyes appealed for help.

'You've tried to make recompense, Daniel,' Felix said quietly.

Ben David nodded.

'It was you who sent word to warn the Tribune of danger on the road to Ptolemais.'

Again Ben David nodded.

'How did you know?'

'We guessed,' Felix answered. 'Daniel,' he continued, 'acts of virtue are commendable. That goes without saying, but the answer to your misery is not in some crude balance of right and wrong.'

Felix looked up in time to see the Disciple John emerge from the synagogue.

'Daniel, do you know the young Rabbi talking by the synagogue entrance?'

'Yes, Master Felix – they tell me his name is John.'

'Well, Daniel, if you want to know the truth about yourself, seek his companny.'

'I'll do that.'

Felix made to rise from his stool, but took his seat again as Ben David continued.

359

'There is a question from the past that will not rest. Who left the water-bag by my side when I lay stunned and helpless? Do you know? If not, it is a question that will always haunt me.'

'An intriguing question,' Felix responded pensively, his eyes watching the Disciple John, for he did not want to miss him. Briefly, he turned to Ben David.

'According to James, it was Titus who pursued you after the ambush in the valley – no one else did, apparently.'

'The veteran Titus, the Captain of the Tribune's guard – amazing. Why?'

'Like James, he sensed that you had seen Tullus in the cart. Titus himself told me so. He also saw that you protected the goatherd. Daniel, Titus rewarded nobility. That is why the water-bag was left – honour dictated it.'

'Now I know the reason why the Great Sea is a Roman lake.'

Felix rose to his feet.

'Remember, Daniel, you're not made of iron! Your shoulder needs some rest.'

Leaving Ben David still propped against the wall, Felix strode towards the Disciple.

'It is a blessing to see you,' John responded warmly.

'You bring the blessing, sir,' Felix returned. He meant it, for in the young man's presence his sense of child-like bliss was tangible.

The Disciple John immediately agreed to a meeting with the Senator, and, elated at the prospect, Felix quickly returned to the garrison building. The time fixed was after midday on the morrow; the place, the Ben Josephs' villa.

CHAPTER FIFTY-FOUR

THE MEETING

In the main reception room of the Ben Josephs' villa the Valerii and their friends were gathered awaiting the Disciple John. The buzz of conversation rose and fell and the sound of laughter was frequent. Only the Tribune was silent, being very conscious of Cornelia's absence.

The gathering was arranged in two informal groupings. One, centred on the Senator, included his daughter Junia, the Tribune Largus, Arria, Felix and Sarah. The other had naturally gravitated around Tullus. Drusilla sat on cushions in front of him, while James, his servant, stood behind and at his side were the Ben Josephs. Two of the Ben Josephs' servants were also in attendance, yet the low-ceilinged room did not seem crowded.

Outside, Demos waited with the Senator's guide, his task to welcome the young Jew and show him inside. He, too, had been invited to join the gathering if he wished.

Although used to the Senator's ways, Demos still found the Valerii strange. Here they were, gathered in the simplest of villas to meet some obscure native teacher. True, he had been told stories of great wonder about the teacher's Master, but they were stories, and who could think them real? Not even a Greek! he thought with some amusement. Yet the Tribune believed them, as did the Chief Centurion, and what did Largus think about it all? Probably, like himself, that holy men were best avoided, for they rarely washed! Even so, Largus was inside and dutifully in place – Demos shook his head – and so in turn would he be.

When the Disciple arrived, Demos, although prepared to be sceptical, was immediately impressed. This was no ordinary man, for despite his youth and unassuming manner there was a strange compelling authority – gentle yet wholly present.

'Welcome, sir,' Demos began. 'The Senator is with his family and friends and has asked me to conduct you to his presence.'

'Thank you,' came the quiet response.

The Senator was drawn to his feet as the Disciple entered, and the men followed his example. Typical Valerian oddity, Demos thought, watching from the edge of the gathering. Senators rose for the Emperor and their peers, but for few others.

With quiet simplicity Ben Joseph introduced the Disciple John to his guests. The scene was one of a happy family, and the young Jew responded with a natural and easy charm. Lime water and sweetmeats were offered, after which the Senator felt it time to speak.

'Sir, I see that you enjoy the blessing of the few, for it is clear you live at peace within yourself.'

'It is my Master's peace you see.'

'May I ask the nature of your Master's peace?'

'My Master's peace is of the Father.'

The Senator's questioning look expected more.

The Disciple smiled.

'Philip, one of our number, once asked the Master to reveal the Father. The Master's response was thus:- 'He that has seen me has seen the Father.'"

The Senator sat bolt upright. So few words had been spoken, yet their implication was staggering. He knew the use of 'Father' symbolised the Creator. He had learned that from Felix. Felix had also repeated the Rabbi's saying 'I and my Father are one.' Then the statement had been a concept of unity, but now, on the lips of the Disciple, the same assertion was alive and undeniable. He was very close to something, something he had always sought.

The Senator sat on the edge of his couch in silence. There was a natural dignity in his bearing, but he wore it lightly. His eyes looked down. He was still, very still indeed. He looked up to join the gaze of the Disciple, and for a moment no thought came to separate the single fullness of their meeting. Nothing was said, and the Senator again looked downwards. The eyes of all were upon him. Then the words of his eastern friend sounded in his mind. 'The Self is one'. The words repeated. Was the oneness he had felt on meeting the Disciple's eyes the same oneness referred to in his friend's tradition? Was it as simple as that?

Excitement waited to agitate his thought, but the Senator had trained his mind well. He remained calm and again looked up at the Disciple. There was still a sense of oneness, but expectation had brought its cloud of thought, the fresh quality had gone; yet he knew that the young Jew was still dwelling in that freshness, that same sense of liberation that, for him, had been so brief. If this was the Disciple, he thought, what must the Master have been like?

The Senator broke the silence.

'Sir, who was your Master?'

'My Master is!' The answer came like a shock to the Senator, but he felt it to be true. Indeed, reason supported it.

'You may have heard of our father Abraham?' the Disciple continued mildly.

'Yes, I have heard of your ancient patriarch.'

'Once my Master was asked if he were greater than Abraham. He answered: 'Your father Abraham rejoiced to see my day: and he saw it and was glad."

The words of John were alive in the mind of the Senator. It was as Felix had maintained. Amazing. No wonder his old friend and servant had pressed so eagerly for a meeting. Felix had used the Rabbi's words 'Before Abraham was, I am' to stress the Teacher's universal nature, and he, the Senator, had agreed and nodded, but only in an intellectual sense. Now it was real.

'An incarnation of the universal – a son of the Father,' he whispered. The Senator had no doubts, and Drusilla, watching her father closely, saw the lines on his face soften.

With deliberation the Senator turned to Felix.

'Good Felix, you told me of this, but I did not comprehend – and you, my noble son – you beheld this mighty Rabbi.'

'Yes, sir.'

'And you, my beloved daughter.'

Drusilla did not answer. She was close to tears.

'And Marcus Tullus, your desire to remain in Capernaum and defer your promotion is well explained.'

The Senator's attention returned to the Disciple.

'Sir, we are honoured, greatly honoured by your presence.'

The Disciple smiled, and the Senator was filled with love, but at the same time questions rose numerous in his mind. The long conversations with his Indian friend had added to his thirst for knowledge.

'Recently, in the city of Ephesus, I had the fortune to meet an Indian prince who told me much of his tradition. He told me of the great ones who had lived in the human form. According to his teaching your Master is of the highest . . . Such men, he said, were born by fiat of will, and not of the flesh . . .'

'The word was made flesh,' the Disciple said simply.

'The word!' the Senator exclaimed. 'My friend's tradition speaks of a perfect word, ever fresh and new, which contains creation and from which all words proceed.' His voice was filled with animation.

Felix was enthralled. The meeting was, as he had hoped, a blessing.

There was a look of infinite tenderness in the face of the young Disciple as he looked at the Senator. When he spoke, every word was compelling.

'In the beginning was the word, and the word was with God, and the word was God.

'The same was in the beginning with God.'

The room was soundless as the Disciple paused. Then he continued.

'All things were made by him; and without him was not anything made that was made.'

'Amazing, beautiful.' Again, the grey-haired Patrician's words were whispered and barely audible.

The Senator sat in silence, his body still. Tullus, too, was still, and Drusilla, aware of this, was careful of disturbing him. Sitting opposite his sister, the Tribune gazed at his father, his respect obvious. It was certainly obvious to the alert and astute mind of Largus.

Largus was very much awake and had missed little of the strange, compelling conversation, and though he did not understand it all by any means he found the general atmosphere remarkable. Even the air seemed clear and clean.

The young Rabbi was special, that was self-evident; and the Senator was a Stoic whose philosophy went well beyond the level of fashionable speculation. In fact, he was a true Stoic, whose very mode of life was his philosophy. Largus liked the Senator and his unusual family and he knew that they liked him, though Junia's fondness made him uneasy. Her eyes followed him everywhere, and even now she was watching him. He did not dislike her. On the contrary: she was witty and attractive, and she was a Valerius, a glittering prize, but Largus was wedded to his independent ways, the darker side of which was isolation, and in the present potent atmosphere this sense of isolation was intense. Up until that moment Largus had never questioned his solitary and independent bent, but now he did.

The Senator's head was still bowed reflectively, and no one disturbed the silence. Then the Roman Patrician lifted his head.

'I have many questions. My only fear is that our time of meeting may be limited.'

'Sir, I will be in Capernaum for some time. You can command.'

Startled, Ben Joseph turned to his wife. He did not need to speak, for to them it was obvious that the Senator was greatly blessed.

At that moment a servant entered hurriedly and handed a message to Demos, who in turn passed it to the Tribune. His face blanched as he read the contents.

'It's Cornelia,' he said in obvious distress. 'My noble host, Father, sir – I must leave immediately,' he added, handing the despatch to Felix as he rushed outside.

'What's the matter, Felix?' the Senator asked evenly.

'Cornelia is at Ramah and too ill to continue.' Felix turned to face the Senator. 'Master, that is where Venio, your son's devoted servant, died.'

'Oh, no!' Drusilla moaned.

Junia was weeping.

The eyes of the Senator and the Disciple met. Nothing was said, but the running emotion was contained.

The Disciple rose, and Ben Joseph immediately escorted his guest to the door, where he turned to face the gathering.

'I am sorry,' he said simply, and no one doubted that he was.

Once the Disciple had left, Largus jumped to his feet.

'Sir, the Tribune needs a companion,' he said, bowing to the Senator.

The hand of Tullus tightened its grip on Drusilla's shoulder.

'Trust,' he said gently.

CHAPTER FIFTY-FIVE

RAMAH

The Tribune decided to use a two-horse chariot with a mounted escort, and from the beginning the pace was frantic. Largus rode with the Tribune, but he let his friend take the reins. It was better that Valerius had something to do.

Aided by a thick cloud cover, darkness fell before they reached Ramah, and being without torches their progress was both slow and prone to accident. However, with the help of local shepherds they continued until the flickering lights of Ramah grew visible. As they approached, a small troop of legionaries, with torches blazing, marched out to meet them. At once Valerius was escorted to the house where Cornelia lay.

The entrance was lit by numerous torches, and on either side legionaries stood on guard. Close by, a Galilean sat hunched against the wall, his homespun clothes wrapped closely about him. It was chill.

'Who is that man?' the Tribune snapped.

'He's with the Jewish healer, sir,' the guard captain answered.

'What healer?' Valerius barked, suddenly stopping in his onward rush.

The guard captain cleared his throat nervously.

'Sir, it's the young Disciple of the Rabbi Jesus – the Disciple John.'

'John!' the Tribune reacted with astonishment.

The Galilean by the wall was on his feet, and the Tribune turned to face him.

'How did you travel here so quickly?'

'We had ponies, sir. We know the hills.'

'What is your name?' The tone of the Tribune's voice was perceptibly softer.

'Ben David.'

'Ben David! – the Master Felix told me you were wounded.' Valerius turned abruptly to the leader of the guard. 'Let this man rest within.'

Largus, standing at the Tribune's side, could see quite plainly that the tension on the Tribune's face had disappeared, and when Valerius turned towards him his look of joy was unmistakable.

'Quintus, Cornelia is safe,' he said quietly.

Ben David, who was waiting for the Tribune to pass inside, heard the words clearly. He did not know the Latin tongue – even so, he knew the sound of certain faith. It was another sign.

Once inside, Valerius was quickly shown to Cornelia's room. Two soldiers stood by the door, which was opened as he approached. He went inside, but Largus did not follow.

Cornelia lay on a large, ornate bed, apparently asleep, her hair loose on the pillow and framing her face. How incredibly beautiful she looked. Quickly his eyes switched their focus to the Disciple John, who was sitting on a stool some distance from the bed, his posture upright. The stillness was tangible.

John rose noiselessly as the Tribune approached and led him quietly from the bedside.

'The fever has gone,' he said softly. 'She is resting now and her sleep is deep, and when she awakes she will be well.' He smiled. 'It's time for me to go.'

'Sir, have you a place of rest for the night?' the Tribune asked, gripping the Disciple's arm tightly.

'I have friends here. There will be room for both Ben David and myself. Thank you for asking.'

'It's the least I can do.'

Again the Tribune gripped the Disciple's arm in silent token of his gratitude.

Valerius closed the door gently as the Disciple left. Then, with equal care, he carried a chair to Cornelia's bedside, where he sat down quietly to wait. In time he began to doze fitfully.

Cornelia awoke as the dawn began to lighten the room. She lay quite still, trying to cognise her surroundings. The bed, the room – it was all strange. Then she remembered being ill. Of course, this had been her sick-bed. As yet unaware of the Tribune's presence, she moved her head to the side. Her heart leapt. Her beloved Lucius was dozing in the chair beside her.

'Lucius, darling Lucius,' she whispered to herself, savouring the joy of unrestrained affection; but the shadow of hopelessness was quick to follow. They could never marry, never. She had been ill and Lucius had come to see her; that was all. Dreams of happiness were pointless and only added to her misery. Still she watched him. Slowly his head lifted. Then his eyes blinked open from their shallow sleep.

'Cornelia.' He mouthed her name noiselessly.

In the same instant, for that was how it seemed, he was kneeling at her bedside, his arms stretched out, his hands holding her head. Gently he kissed her on the mouth and forehead.

'My sweet girl,' he said tenderly.

'Lucius! Lucius!' She kept repeating his name. She could not restrain her feelings. It was impossible.

'Lucius, we're torturing ourselves. We cannot marry. Can I not become your . . .?'

'My beautiful Cornelia. You have not heard. I sent a message but you were too ill . . . My sweet love, the Emperor has given his permission.'

'Lucius!' Her cry of joy echoed in the room. and leaping out of bed, she was suddenly beside him on the floor. They embraced tightly while she wept and called his name wildly.

'Calm, my love, calm.'

'Oh, Lucius, I'm in my nightgown.'

'My dear girl, you're modesty itself. I can only see your nose.'

They laughed happily. He looked at her lovingly. She was radiant, and for a moment he held her at arm's length, savouring her beauty. Her eyes were full of love – love was everywhere.

'Last evening, my dear, when you were very ill, the beloved Disciple of the Rabbi Jesus made you well.'

'The Disciple John,' she whispered, her eyes wide.

'Yes.'

'I can't remember anything.'

She grew pensive.

'Lucius.'

'Yes, Cornelia.'

'Could we ask the Disciple John to bless our marriage?'

He drew her gently to himself.

'Yes, my dear, we could – in fact we will. Now it's time for you to dress and me to make due preparation for our journey to Capernaum.'

After kissing her lightly on the forehead he left the room, walked through the vestibule to the entrance and then out into the morning air. At once the sound of an angry voice drew his attention. The tone was pompous and came from a large, rounded man. The language was Greek.

'You take over my villa,' he protested, his arms gesturing in a grand manner.

'Only a few rooms, sir,' the guard leader responded, remaining calm and polite.

'Only a few rooms! You surround my house with soldiers. All night there is continual disturbance. Neither my wife nor I could sleep, and now I hear that vagrants and fakirs have been inside – the cost of cleaning!' The man threw up his hands in emphasis. 'I will complain at the highest level; that I promise, for I have powerful friends in Antioch!'

'So have I!' the Tribune snapped.

Startled, the owner of the house spun round to see the Tribune and the broad stripe of the Senate. Fear gripped him instantly.

'I'm sorry, noble sir. I did not know that you were here.'

The Tribune said nothing in return. Instead, he turned to Cornelia's guard captain.

'See that this man is adequately recompensed for our intrusion.'

The owner of the house muttered his thanks, bowed extravagantly and quickly disappeared round the corner of his villa, no doubt glad to have escaped an awkward situation.

'You were tolerant, sir,' Largus said. 'I've seen men put in chains for less.'

The Tribune nodded casually.

'We requisitioned his home, and disrupted the quiet enjoyment of his property. His resentment is natural. Anyway, Quintus, it would take a lot to make me angry this morning.' He yawned. 'Tell me, have you discovered the bath-house?'

The morning was beautiful, the air crisp and invigorating. In the open space before the villa Cornelia's wagon was drawn up and waiting. So, too, were the legionaries of her guard and beside them the few cavalrymen holding their horses, and, of course, the Tribune's chariot.

All eyes were on the villa entrance, for at any moment the Tribune and his lady would emerge. Three days earlier the legionaries had watched Cornelia carried into the villa in a semi-conscious state. Now they were told that she had fully recovered. In their minds there was no doubt. The Jewish leader had performed a miracle.

Cheering broke out spontaneously as the door opened and the Tribune and his bride-to-be walked into the sunlight. Largus gasped.

'A prince and princess,' he whispered. He had not seen Cornelia before. She was beautiful, and regal in her bearing. No wonder Valerius had been distraught.

The Tribune raised his hand, and the cheering stopped instantly.

'Last evening the Disciple of the Rabbi Jesus cured my lady. We owe the happiness of this day to him – thank you, men,' he added. Then, with Cornelia by his side, he walked across to where Largus was waiting.

'My dear, meet the Tribune Largus.'

'I am honoured, sir.'

'My lady, I fear the sun will be displeased. He has a rival!'

'Sir, knowing my joy, perhaps he will allow the indiscretion.'

They laughed.

'Sir,' Largus began respectfully, 'may I suggest that I be a messenger of good tidings? I could take the two-horse chariot and some of the cavalry.'

'Take all the cavalry, my friend. We have the guard that came from Ptolemais – it's more than adequate.' Smiling, he looked down at Cornelia. 'We have no thought of rushing.'

The reunion of Cornelia with the Valerii and their friends was joyful, and after all the general round of greetings were over she turned to Drusilla.

'My lady,' she said quietly, and tears were in the eyes of both as they embraced.

'Is it not time to call me Drusilla?' the older woman said.

'I would prefer it as it always was, my lady, for I've lived as if I were your daughter.'

Drusilla smiled. 'Be it so,' she said, her voice full of affection.

CHAPTER FIFTY-SIX

THE PARTING

James had shown a bright face to his master. Indeed, embarrassed by his sadness, he had grown more blunt. With Felix, though, his guard was not so strong, and as they walked from Cornelia's reception Felix saw the obvious signs.

'Is there anything wrong, James?' he asked gently, knowing that the Galilean was sensitive to prying questions.

James said nothing for some time. He wanted to talk, but the old habit of restraint was strong. Then the words burst out.

'The new Centurion is arriving tomorrow – I mean Cornelius. The Master will be leaving.'

'I'm sure Tullus would want you to accompany him.'

'How can I, Master Felix? My people are here. This is my country, and my Greek . . .' James shook his head. 'It would be like going into exile.'

'Yes, I see,' Felix responded quietly. There was little he could say, for the bond between Tullus and his servant was strong.

The next morning James confronted the retiring Centurion directly.

'When are you leaving, Master?'

'Soon, James – are you coming with us?'

The old Galilean servant hesitated.

'My kin are here. This is my country,' he reacted with exaggerated bluntness.

'Ben Joseph would like you in his household. He'd be a gentle master.'

James smacked his lips and shifted awkwardly on his feet.

'You will never want, James. I will see to that.'

James moved his lips to form the words of thanks, but no sound came.

'Things come to pass, Master,' he managed to say, looking uneasily at Tullus.

'But, James, there is that which does not change.'

'It's not easy, Master.'

'No, James.'

James turned and looked at Tullus for what seemed a long time.

'You're a good man, Master,' he said. Then he swung abruptly on his heel and walked away.

ALLISON & BUSBY FICTION

Simon Beckett
Fine Lines
Animals

Philip Callow
The Magnolia
The Painter's Confessions

Scott Campbell
Touched

Rosemary Cohen
Above the Horizon

Hella S. Haasse
Threshold of Fire
The Scarlet City

Catherine Heath
Lady on the Burning Deck
Behaving Badly

Chester Himes
Collected Stories
Cast the First Stone
The End of a Primitive
Pink Toes
Run Man Run

Tom Holland
Attis

R. C. Hutchinson
A Child Possessed
Johanna at Daybreak
Recollection of a Journey

Dan Jacobson
The Evidence of Love

Robert F. Jones
Tie My Bones to Her Back

Francis King
Act of Darkness
A Hand at the Shutter
Ash on an old man's sleeve
The One and Only
The Widow

Ted Lewis
Plender
The Rabbit

Colin MacInnes
Absolute Beginners
City of Spades
Mr Love and Justice
The Colin MacInnes Omnibus

Indira Mahindra
The End Play

Demetria Martinez
Mother Tongue

Susanna Mitchell
The Colour of His Hair

Bill Naughton
Alfie

Matthew Parkhill
And I Loved Them Madly

Alison Prince
The Witching Tree

Linda Proud
A Tabernacle for the Sun

Diana Pullein Thompson
Choosing

Ishmael Reed
Japanese by Spring
Reckless Eyeballing
The Terrible Threes
The Terrible Twos
The Free-Lance Pallbearers
Yellow Back Radio Broke-Down

Françoise Sagan
Engagements of the Heart
Evasion
Incidental Music
The Leash
The Unmade Bed

Budd Schulberg
The Disenchanted
The Harder They Fall
Love, Action, Laughter and
    Other Sad Stories
On the Waterfront
What Makes Sammy Run?

Luis Sepúlveda
The Name of a Bullfighter

Debbie Taylor
The Children Who Sleep
    by the River

B. Traven
Government
The Carreta
March to the Monteriá
Trozas
The Rebellion of the Hanged
General from the Jungle

Etienne Van Heerden
Ancestral Voices
Mad Dog and Other Stories

Tom Wakefield
War Paint